EDWARD HOWER was born in New York City and attended Cornell, Makerere University College in Uganda, and UCLA. He was a secondary school teacher and television entertainer in Kenya. The author completed the writing of THE NEW LIFE HOTEL in London where he lived on a Creative Writing Fellowship from the National Endowment for the Arts, and he has been awarded a Residency Fellowship by the Fine Arts Work Center in Provincetown, Massachusetts. Since 1973, he has lived in Ithaca, New York where he has been the administrator of a girls' reform school and a writing instructor at Ithaca College.

THE NEW LIFE HOTEL

EDWARD HOWER

 A BARD BOOK/PUBLISHED BY AVON BOOKS

THE NEW LIFE HOTEL is an original publication of Avon Books. This work has never before appeared in book form.

Excerpts from this book appeared, in slightly different form, in *The Atlantic Monthly, Transition* (Ghana), *Transatlantic Review, Stillwater,* and *Epoch*.

The author acknowledges with thanks, financial support provided by a National Endowment for the Arts Creative Writing Fellowship.

This is a work of fiction. Any resemblance between actual individuals, peoples, places, or events and those which appear in the novel is purely coincidental.

Permission to reprint the epigraph has been granted from: *Rise and Fall of the City of Mahagonny:* original work entitled *Mahagonny,* copyright 1927 by Universal-Edition A.G., renewed 1955 by Bertolt Brecht. All rights reserved. Translated from *Gesammelte Werke.* Copyright © 1967 by Suhrkamp Verlag.

AVON BOOKS
A division of
The Hearst Corporation
959 Eighth Avenue
New York, New York 10019

First Bard Printing, October, 1980

For Josephine,
and
for Danny and Lana

Oh, show us the way to the next whisky-bar!
Oh, don't ask why; oh, don't ask why!
For we must find the next whisky-bar
For if we don't find the next whisky-bar
I tell you we must die!

—Bertolt Brecht
MAHAGONNY
(translated by Michael Feingold)

PART ONE

1

ADIJA STOOD IN THE MIDDLE OF THE STREET, squinting about like someone just emerged from a dark hole into sunlight.

"Black eyes! Angel-witch of my dreams!" the baggage man shouted to get her attention. He swung down sideways off the top of the bus, thrusting a straw basket toward her. "*Eii*, Miniskirt! Don't you want your things?"

Adija just kept staring. The basket struck the ground, spilling out clothes and shoes into the street. Adija jumped back, her hand at her mouth.

Salome watched from her perch on the curb outside the New Life Hotel. She could see the sunlight was too bright for this girl. Girls like you, she thought, with your cream-lightened faces and long, shaggy wigs, look more at home under dim streetlamps.

The bus growled its gears and lumbered away, trailing a cloud of black fumes. The stranger was left bent over her basket. Her buttocks and naked legs formed a rounded arrow pointing to the sky. The town rogues, lounging like reptiles in patches of sunlight along the pavement, murmured their approval. Salome spat at the nearest one's feet—though certainly she had no sympathy for this girl. One Salome was all this bush town could support.

Adija lugged the basket to the curb and set it down beside Salome. "Hello," she said, out of breath. "Greetings."

Salome nodded once.

"What place is this?"

"Musolu," Salome grunted.

"It's nice."

"It's a dung heap."

"Is it in Bashiri?"

"No. In Marembo."

Adija shifted her weight from one foot to the other. Finally she sat down, and resting her chin mournfully on her knees, looked down the street to the dust clouds the bus had left on the horizon. "I wanted to go to Bashiri," she said, "but they wouldn't let me stay on the bus. Someone stole my ticket."

"Why tell me?" Salome expected a knowing smile, a clever remark, some attempt at camaraderie that Salome's tongue would squash like a crocodile's tail lashing out at a marshbird. She waited, poised, but heard only a long sigh. "Where did you have your ticket, that it got stolen—in your brassiere?" Salome asked.

"In my purse."

Her purse. So, she was a city girl. Salome's eyes hardened. Then she saw that the girl's mane of wavy black hair was her own and not a wig; her color wasn't rubbed-in cream, it was her own too. Salome was confused. What a strange color. When the girl sat up, her cheeks glowed red-brown, as if she were reflecting a blazing sunset; when she bowed her head in shadow, her face went storm-cloud gray and the air felt tense with impending rain. All she did was sit and squint. It drove Salome crazy.

"Well, there are all kinds of people on these country buses. You never know who's a thief or what," Salome said. "How much money did you lose?"

"Five shillings," Adija said, and gave a tiny shudder at the thought of the loss.

"You go on a journey with only five shillings? You must have been in a hurry to get out of town."

"I'm always in that kind of a hurry."

Salome cocked her head at the girl. She too had never lived in a place that she hadn't wanted to leave behind her quickly. "Why don't you walk to the border if you want to get to Bashiri? It's only a mile. You should hurry—they close the border at sundown because of the Swila."

Adija just nodded. "What is swila?"

"Swila aren't a thing, they're a people. They're called Swila because they strike like spitting cobras. You don't know of them?"

"How should I?"

"Because you look like a Northern woman. Are you a Moslem?"

Adija's head drooped between her knees. She looked

weary beyond her years, which could not have been more than twenty, Salome decided. "I'm not!" she said. "I'm taken for a Moslem, a Northerner, for an Indian, an Arab, even for a European. But I'm none of them and I still don't know these Swila."

"The Swila are the rebels who have been fighting against the government," Salome explained. "People say they come across the border and steal vegetables from the farms. They come in the night like witches, and in the morning the vegetables are gone. And cattle too."

"And is it true that they come?"

"Myself, I've never seen one. But I've never seen a witch either." Salome laughed, showing the black gaps between her teeth. "I've seen Swila in my dreams, though. They come into my bar, I give them drinks, then I take their Sten guns and shoot up this town from one end to the other." Salome swiveled her head, aiming her face up and down the street. "T-t-t-t-t!" she went.

Adija's face showed no alarm. She just stared at Salome. Then she laughed.

Her laughter shook Salome considerably. She was used to being considered someone too dangerous and unpredictable to ever laugh at. She glared at the girl, glared hard enough to burn a path beyond her huge black eyes and deep into the pit of her stomach. But the girl's gaze didn't drop. Her eyes shone back at Salome like black mirrors.

All right, if this girl wanted to gape at her, let her. It didn't matter, everybody else did. Didn't she have the most enormous breasts in the village, breasts that jutted out from her chest like bombs wearing a pullover? Yes, Salome's appearance was famous. But what was on the outside of her was all anyone, this girl included, would ever see. Her face, the lid of her soul, was as impenetrable as her body was not. Her broad, angry features were knuckles of a fist that kept people retreating in disarray as she approached. Her soft rolling hips were a whirlpool that simultaneously sucked people in toward her. She was a phenomenon that caused much stumbling in place, much confusion that only she could dispel, and only if she chose to. Why, then, was she the one feeling so confused now?

"Why did you want to go to Bashiri?" she demanded.

Adija smiled vaguely. "Well, I was born there."

"I thought so. You speak Kisemi like someone from the coast."

"Yes, that's right."

"I was born there too, and I don't want to go back."

"It's a good country."

"It's not even a country, girl. It's a colony ruled by settlers. You should know that if you were born there."

"There were no settlers in my village."

So: a village girl in city clothes. Salome knew the type well. She had been one herself. "Well, people are no better across the border than here," she said, then quickly added, "but you'll have to find that out for yourself."

"There's many Europeans in Bashiri. I know that. I was hoping I could be a housegirl for one. I could learn English. Then I could get an important job—a shopgirl, maybe."

Salome gave up glaring at the girl. She poked the dirt out from between her foot and her rubber sandal. "I was eager to learn English once. I learned it, and now—" she yanked off her sandal and banged it hard against the curb, "—now I am here."

Adija squinted at the row of shops across the street. They looked like one long train of boxcars, a train that had crashed and been abandoned, leaving its cars squashed together along the roofs. The roofs sagged out over the sidewalk, dangling pots and lanterns and limp sails of colored cloth. Once the shop doors had been green, but they had long ago been tinted the same red-brown as the haze of dust that hung idly over the town waiting for something to churn it up. Adija wrinkled her nose. "I'm here also," she said finally. "And I'll have to stay here, at least until I have some money."

"There's no jobs for housegirls. What can you do?" Salome watched for a trace of a smile on the girl's face. She still suspected that the girl and she were sisters, women who could always make money as long as there were men nearby. But the girl was frowning. She was thinking.

"There's a school here. On the bus I met a teacher, a tall European. He has long yellow hair that falls to his face." The girl touched her forehead, smiling. "He is very handsome and kind. He doesn't shout and act like a god, the way Europeans do. He told me he's new to the school. I think he'll need someone to cook for him."

"How could you talk to him if you don't know English?"

"Oh . . . he speaks Kisemi. He's the son of a missionary from the coast, near my village. He speaks Kisemi better—" she glanced at Salome, "—than many Africans I've met."

"Then he's one of those crazy Europeans who pretend they're African," Salome said. Really, this frail Swila girl, or whatever she was, was bold. "Why didn't you ask to work for him while you were on the bus?"

"We were having so many things to talk about that I didn't think of it. Besides," she added quickly, "I thought I would be going on to Bashiri."

"Of course. I see." Salome was sure she was inventing this story.

The girl stood up. "I want to leave my basket with you."

"Why? You don't know me. I might steal it. You don't even know my name."

"I'm sorry. My name is Adija. What is yours?"

Salome looked up in amazement. Nothing she said bothered this girl. She sighed. "I am Salome. I own half this bar, this New Life." She pointed behind her with her lips. "The other half is owned by an Indian, but soon I'll buy up his share."

"You're fortunate."

"Yes, it's a treasure, as you can see."

Adija looked at the bar: the dusty Tusker beer sign over the door, the grime-colored walls inside, the tables with their armies of flies buzzing on the encrusted tops. Like most other "hotels" in East Africa, the New Life was merely a place to drink and eat; obviously there were no rooms for customers to sleep in. "Mmm," Adija said, turning back to Salome. "Then I can find you here later?"

"Yes, but there's no work. I'm the only barmaid that's needed."

"All right." Adija reached out to shake hands with Salome. "I'm going to the school now. Thank you for your kindness."

Salome watched her go. Adija walked precariously in her pink city shoes, her ridiculous blue miniskirt swinging gaily against the backs of her legs. Salome shook her head and tried to laugh, but she found herself frowning at Adija's basket. Once Salome had owned a basket like it. Her blind old grandmother had woven it for her to take on her journey out into the world that lay beyond her village. "The basket is fat," she'd told Salome, "big enough for both your clothes and your dreams." After a few days out in the world, it had been empty of both.

2

ADIJA WALKED CIRCLES AROUND THE SCHOOL, looking for a house with a bicycle leaning against it. She knew the European owned a bicycle; she had watched him take it down from the bus, outside the school entrance. He had been trying to look like one who is used to taking down a bicycle from the top of an African bus. But as soon as the baggage man had let go of the bicycle, it had crashed down at the European's feet and bounced on its front wheel, almost knocking him over. Many people on the bus had laughed at the expression on his face, but Adija hadn't laughed.

Adija removed her shoes to keep them clean. She peered out from behind hedges and rows of maize stalks. Children scurried out of the huts to stare at her and her legs. Women stopped hoeing and stiffened their backs and stared in the opposite direction when she passed.

The sky was darkening around her, a thick gray-green color that began to press down on her thin shoulders. She padded along more quickly, squinting desperately at each house. Many had motorcars beside them, but none had bicycles. She couldn't go back to the town, to that woman, Salome, without at least speaking to the European. She'd stolen glances at him all the way from Jinjeh; she'd exchanged smiles and once had almost spoken. He'd seemed like a good European, like the children of the missionaries her mother had worked for at times. She could tell he would be like the Europeans that her teachers had taught her about—the Europeans who brought knowledge and hospitals and Jesus to Africa and asked nothing in return for themselves. Surely such people must exist. And surely this tall yellow-haired teacher must be one, surely he needed a servant, surely. . . .

As the first fat drops of rain fell, Adija grew bolder,

tiptoeing across gardens and pushing her nose against win-
dowpanes. Finally she spotted a bicycle. Her eyesight was
too weak to see whether it was *his* bicycle in the room,
but she was too soaked to waste time wondering. She
pounded on the door.

It opened. She lowered her face quickly, staring at the
mud at her feet. The rain was beating noisily on the roof,
and she could hardly hear the voice speaking to her. But
she heard just enough to know that it was speaking in
English and not Kisemi. Her heart sank.

"Come here," he said. Then, in Kisemi, "*Kuja hapa!*"

Adija bit her lip, frightened. This was a rude way to
talk—a command. Bad Europeans shouted at Africans like
that. But perhaps he had learned the language from bad
Europeans and couldn't help speaking primitively. She took
a cautious step forward. She felt his hand on her arm, very
gently guiding her through the door. How foolish she must
look now, shivering in the middle of the room and dripping
all over this foreigner's floor. All she could do was chatter
her teeth at him.

"*Jambo,*" he said, smiling. He did remember her from
the bus.

"*Sijambo,*" she replied in a small wet voice. There was
nothing to do but to say what she'd been rehearsing. Perhaps, if she spoke loud enough, he would understand. "I
am here because I have no work. I need a job. I want to
work for you," she said in Kisemi.

The man stared at her. It was not a rude stare, but one
like her own at times, a stare of puzzlement. She smiled,
and added the English word "housegirl" to her entreaty.

"Ohhh," he said, and started explaining something in
English. Adija was listening so hard that she forgot she
was dripping wet and shivering. She understood nothing
of what he said, but his tone of voice told her that he did
not want her for a servant. Adija shut her eyes briefly,
then turned to leave.

"No, no, don't go!" he said. "*Hapana kwenda!*"

She turned back. He was pointing at the sky, then at her.
He was hugging himself as if *he* were cold and wet. His
gestures were so funny that she had to smile.

He took a suitcase from the back of the bicycle, banged
the suitcase down onto the table, and opened it. He was

very clumsy, moving as if he thought she might vanish
before he had a chance to show her what was inside.

A towel. He was handing her a towel. She inspected it
and made sounds of approval, then tried to give it back. He
wouldn't take it back. He made motions of drying himself
with it. The idea of drying her hair in front of a strange
man, especially a European, embarrassed her, but she imi-
tated his movements with the towel so as not to appear
rude.

He was burrowing into his suitcase again. Adija waited
to see what he would do next. He brought out a big biscuit
tin with a picture of Queen Elizabeth on it, and from it he
took . . . not biscuits, but another tin, a little one! Adija
gazed in wonderment.

"*Tea!*" he said triumphantly. "*Chai!*"

"*Chai!*" she repeated, covering her mouth to keep her
laughter in. Did he want to know if she knew how to make
tea? No, he didn't want her for a servant. He was making
movements of holding a cup to his lips. He wanted to know
if she wanted to drink some tea with him.

"Yes. *Ndio,*" he answered his own question. He picked
up a chair and took it into the next room. In an instant he
was back, snatching up another chair. He took long strides,
flapping his African rubber sandals against the cement
floor, and narrowly missed banging the chair and himself
against the walls. Adija knew she should flee, but the man's
frantic chair-moving had her transfixed.

"Bread! *Mkate!*" he said, pointing at a loaf he had produced from the tin.

Adija nodded encouragingly, and he smiled, his hair falling over his forehead. He motioned for her to follow him
into the next room.

The next room wasn't a bedroom, as Adija had half-
expected, but a kitchen. A fire was burning in the stove. He
motioned for her to sit down in one of the chairs facing the
open grate.

She grew more uneasy. How could she accept the hospitality of a strange man without making at least a gesture
or two of refusal? He'd think her a cheap town girl who
could be had for a cup of tea. But since a cheap town girl
was what she'd been for some time, and since she had no
place else to go, she sat down in his chair. She'd stay for

however long she was welcome and see what would happen.

But this was too much. He was running water into a kettle and washing it out. No, he couldn't do that, it was too embarrassing. She stood up again. "In Africa, a man does not wash dishes and serve tea to a woman," she said, loud and clear so that he couldn't fail to understand.

He merely stared at her, one hand poked down inside the kettle. She took the kettle from him and told him to sit down. Again he smiled at her. What did he think so amusing? *He* was the amusing one. She turned her back to him and scrubbed out the kettle. It was filthy; mice had been playing in it. It was fortunate that she had taken over the washing, or she would have found herself drinking mouse-shit tea.

He had a little paper sack of sugar, but no milk. Very curious. Only the poorest people drank their tea without milk. A European, a teacher, couldn't be poor. He had no spoons either, so they had to stir their tea with the blade of his folding knife. But the tea was hot, and he was obviously enjoying drinking it with her, and that made it taste almost good.

When he tried out his few words of Kisemi, his face got pink and he looked angry with himself. This poor man. Europeans were so inhospitable to each other. One could not arrive at a journey's end to find food and companionship waiting. One could find only a cold, empty house with no food on the shelves and not even a plate for the food one had brought. And Europeans said Africans were savages!

Still, this European owned more than she did just now. She wondered if he would ask her to repay his hospitality by going to bed with him. If he even had a bed! She decided that if he had one, it would be all right, but if he had none, she would not do it with him on the floor. Unless he forced her. He didn't look like a man who forced women, his smiles were too gentle. Besides, wasn't it true that Europeans didn't force women? No, they didn't force *their* women, that was it.

"I . . . Gordon," he said.

Adija nodded and smiled, lowering her eyes politely.

"Gordon," he repeated, tapping his chest.

That was his name. He wanted her to say it. "Gordi," she said.

"Gordon."

"Gord'n," she said. "Gordon." That was better—he was nodding.

"Adija," she said, tapping her own chest. Her own chest was soaked; her nipples were pushing out the thin wet cloth. She dropped her hand to her lap.

"Ah—DEE—jah," he said carefully. "Adeeja."

"Good! *Nzuri!*" Adija laughed, pulling her blouse away from her wet skin to let the heat from the fire warm her breasts. "Gordon . . . Englond?"

He shook his head. "America."

"*Aah, Mwamerika.*" Adija nodded enthusiastically, as if she knew all about Americans. In fact, she had never met one before. She seemed to remember that England was a province of America, or perhaps it was the other way around. If only she could inquire about his country, and make him feel welcome in hers. Adija shook her head sadly and smiled at him.

Suddenly she started. Someone was banging on the door. Gordon looked annoyed, but he went to answer it. Adija snatched up her shoes, letting the towel fall to the floor, and tiptoed to the kitchen door that led outside.

Voices approached from the next room. She turned the doorknob. Already in her mind she had slipped outside and was scurrying down the mud path behind the house. She twisted the doorknob hard both ways. But it refused to turn! The teacher and his visitor were entering the room. Adija whirled around and pressed her back against the door.

She kept her eyes fixed on a point on the floor. When finally she glanced up, she saw the two of them standing with their backsides to the stove. They were talking in English. The visitor was an African, a schoolboy, by the looks of his soggy green uniform. Now he was looking at her. She turned her head sideways, looking at the door as if she could blast it open with her stare.

"*Jambo,*" the schoolboy said with a lecherous grin in his voice.

He had a long brown face and bulging, insolent eyes, and Adija didn't like the way they were crawling up her bare legs like insects with icy little feet. She turned her face further away.

"The new teacher is more clever than he looks," the schoolboy said in her language. "Already he has a Mini-skirt to beautify his kitchen."

Adija made a disdainful clicking sound.

"Miniskirt is too proud to greet one of her own kind, *eii?*" Now the boy's eyes were fastened like pincers to her nipples.

She covered her chest, pretending to scratch her shoulder. "My own kind is born of woman and not like you, whose father fucked for you in the asshole of a camel!"

The schoolboy's gaze left her and bounced off the ceiling and walls. He opened and closed his mouth several times. Adija didn't wait to hear a reply. Pressing her shoes against her belly and looking as dignified as possible, she padded into the first room.

But the door was locked here too! What did these Euro-peans fear, that they had to lock themselves *into* their houses, as well as locking Africans out? She rapped on the door and waited.

The teacher came up beside her. By pushing a tiny pim-ple at the base of the knob, he was able to turn the knob and open the door. Adija stepped through, leaving a frag-ment of a smile behind her.

Not looking where she was going, she stepped into a puddle. Her foot shot out from beneath her. Had he not caught her arm, she would have fallen on her face in the mud.

"Adija, where . . . ? *Wapi* . . . ?" He looked worried for her.

"I don't know where I'll go, I haven't any money, I—" But he wasn't understanding her language, no matter how clearly she spoke. "Musolu!" she shouted through the barrage of raindrops. "New Life Hotel!"

The teacher held out his towel to her. "*Kwaheri ku-oana,*" he said, smiling.

He was trying to say Goodbye-until-I-see-you-again. "*Kwaheri ya kuonana,*" she said, laughing. She accepted the towel, wrapped it around her shoes, and showed him the bundle she had made. "If you come and see me, I'll give your towel back to you," she said, forgetting to speak clearly. His puzzled look made her smile. "Or perhaps I'll come and see you. And you'll fall in love with me and give me a motorcar and I'll be your wife and then no one can ever abuse me!"

Gordon nodded and smiled again. Adija laughed—not to mock him, but because she felt so strange talking to him like this. "I'll give you many beautiful children too," she added, wriggling her toes in the mud. Then she turned and fled into the rain.

3

GORDON STARED OUT THE DOOR UNTIL THE frail figure of the girl vanished into the torrents of rain. For a while, he was sure he could still hear her footsteps, but the sound was only that of the downpour itself, a pulse in the air like the roar of a river flooding its banks. He was soaked now himself, but he didn't move from his doorstep until he heard scuffling behind him and remembered the schoolboy.

The boy welcomed him to the school, and informed him that he was to be the new housemaster of Tembo House, to which he was invited for an inspection after dinner. As fortune would have it, the boy was a candidate for House Prefect. Gordon nodded patiently while the candidate described his leadership qualities. The boy would have liked to have been asked to stay for a cup of tea, but Gordon, studying the arrangement of cups that Adija had left on the kitchen table, suddenly felt reluctant to disturb the scene. As soon as the rain had subsided to a drizzle, he showed the boy to the door.

Returning to the kitchen, he broke off a piece of bread and chewed it slowly. When he'd first entered this room, the brooding gray-green afternoon light had given it a look of unutterable barrenness. The cement floor, the lichen-colored walls, the enormous black smoke-stain behind the stove—a dungeon. But now the room was warmer. Was it just the fire in the stove that made it so? No. He gazed at the empty cup that had been for the girl, Adija. Though he had planned to look for a broom and some blankets as soon as the rain let up, he lingered where he was. There was peace here. He had been accustomed to the echoing din of a university dormitory, had longed for quiet and privacy, and now he had it, and something more. Still staring at the chipped empty cup on the bare table, he thought: I have seen that girl before, and not just on the bus.

The rain stopped, and the air outside was alive with the conversations of dripping leaves. Slanting sunlight blazed across the school compound from a gash in the clouds. Walking to his window, Gordon remembered waking in his dormitory room in Karela to watch the pale green light of dawn stream across the quadrangle, and with it the scents of green dew and red-brown earth. Flowers had quivered in the mist like flames. Then the sun's rays streaked through the branches of the petaled trees, singeing away the mist, leaving the air so vividly clear that his eyes ached. Invisible birds screamed overhead. Someone across the lawn switched on a radio, and the twang of African guitar music added an itchy rhythm to the morning.

Women passed his room on their way across the campus: nurses returning from the night shift at the hospital, wives of university groundsmen fetching water in silver tins they carried upright on their heads. Beautiful. They glided into view, their skirts swaying at their ankles, their faces shiny and animated. Their smiles were blinding white. As they called out to one another, high-pitched greetings fluttered like ribbons in the air.

Gordon's silent cries of longing had followed the women along the paths, snagged on the cactus spears, burned in the thorn trees' petals. And all day—sitting in lectures, bicycling around the city—the memory of them taunted him in every flash of color and bird's cry and note of women's laughter. It is all *there*, he screamed to himself, pressing his knuckles against his forehead. How long do I have to be shut off from it by my ignorance of their language, their customs, their land?

Did Adija remind him of these women? Yes, almost. Her high fluttering voice was like their greetings. But none of the women was the one she reminded him of. Who, then?

He stepped away from the window, picked up the teacups, and washed them in a hard stream of cold water. He had to clean this house, had to clean himself up and report to the headmaster. He carried his suitcase into the bedroom and dropped it onto the mattress. A cigar-sized cock-

roach thumped onto the floor and scuttled away. The bedroom was as barren as all the dormitory rooms he had lived
in from the age of eleven.

Again he remembered watching the women glide
through the dawn light. Yes, that sensation of trembling on
the threshold of something dazzling was what this Adija
had brought back to him. Why had he let her go? He was
no longer a foreign student, watched over carefully by
university officials. Why hadn't he urged her to stay?

He knew why.

He flung open his suitcase and piled his clothes and
books on the dusty ex–Colonial Office bureau. In a few
minutes he was unpacked, with nothing left to do but pace
through the empty house. He made himself a cup of tea,
and sipping it from the chipped cup, stared out the kitchen
window.

It was on one of his bicycle excursions away from the
university that he had first seen her. He remembered that
much. Now slowly he mentally retraced his movements
through the city of Karela.

He rode past the stucco classroom buildings, the lou-
vered-glass wall of the library with its grassy moat, past the
tennis courts and flowering hedges and the green lawns of
the lecturers' residences. Cutting down a footpath, he
wound his way behind the groundsmen's quarters, where
women cooked over smoking braziers in the dirt yards. The
stench of rotting fruit rinds added heat to the air. At the
bottom of the hill, he emerged into a small marketplace:
sagging wooden kiosks, a poster advertising BIO-GEM
ringworm tablets, pyramids of fruits and vegetables on
blankets. The women sitting beside them pulled in their
legs as he coasted by. A group of men hammering the
remains of a car body into roofing sheets paused to watch
him, and for a moment the air stopped ringing with metallic violence.

Beyond the market was the district post office. He was
there to mail a letter to Irena, a girl he had once loved
desperately and lost and was trying to win back via air
mail, promising her an escape from her troubles in America. Though now he rarely thought of her, he had been
distraught about her then. Had Adija reminded him of her?
Only her long, thick black hair was similar. . . .

Outside the post office, he found a policeman looking

over his bicycle, which he'd left leaning against the wall. The man's face was smoky black; his khaki uniform remained stiff as he paced.

"Illegal to put this here, on pavement." The man glared at him, a blood vessel throbbing in his temple. "Against the law."

"I was only gone a few minutes," Gordon said, approaching the bicycle. He stopped short. The man didn't move from his path. A heavy truncheon swung from his hand.

"Plenty can happen, 'few minutes.'" The man paced slowly around the bicycle, inspecting it. "Why you not having motorcar? All European have motorcar."

"I don't want one."

The policeman's eyes narrowed at Gordon. He flicked his truncheon up into both hands and jabbed the bicycle seat sharply with the end, sending the bicycle clattering to the pavement. Then, turning his back, he walked away. His heavy shoes thudded across a lull in the traffic noise as if in an empty room.

Gordon's hands trembled as he picked up the bicycle. He was almost surprised that it had not been shattered to pieces. He mounted quickly and sped away down the tree-lined road to the commercial district: Karela.

The city of Karela hummed with foreign investment beneath the bright yellow sun. The pace slowed only when the afternoon rains splashed down in sheets, settling the ubiquitous red-brown dust and causing greenery to sprout up almost visibly along even the most congested motorways. Along the ridge of the tallest of the seven hills that made up the city, modern offices, banks, luxury flats, and hotels were growing up almost as fast as the vegetation. To people on foot, these new steel and glass buildings offered no shelter from the sun and rain. It was beneath the trees between the older Government Houses that they waited to take part in the development which, according to the politicians, was transforming the newly independent nation of Marembo. Waiting for jobs, for school places, for decisions concerning their housing, health, and food supplies, these people made up a host of perpetual supplicants, given hope by the dignity of the façades of the solid old edifices that had been designed during colonial times as civic temples, complete with heraldic insignia over the doorways to sanc-

tify the sweaty labyrinths of officialdom within. As the new
buildings went up, few politicians seemed to notice that the
space for waiting between them was shrinking. And few
would have dared predict that these structures along the
ridge might one day cease to preside majestically over the
city, and begin to appear huddled together against the life
that was flooding up from the hungry valleys below.

Gordon, who sometimes waited out a rainstorm against
the wall of a government ministry, was more uneasy about
the foreign investment boom than many of his fellow students at the university. It seemed to be producing a rash of
buildings identical to the ghastly high-rises in Azima, capital of the neighboring country of Bashiri. Or worse, cheap
imitations of the tacky suburban shopping centers that his
father's company in America had built until one of them
collapsed, causing scandals, investigations, and ultimately
bankruptcy. Gordon managed to ignore the new buildings,
finding plenty of areas even along the ridge that seemed
sufficiently African to him. During his first weeks in Karela,
he had discovered quiet old hotel verandahs where he
could sit beneath perfumed bougainvillaea vines, listening
to orchestras of cicadas in the purple twilight. The peace-
fulness of these scenes soon made him restless, however;
they began to remind him of summers on Long Island and
winters in Barbados.

Gordon abandoned the old hotels when the American
students from his teacher-training program invaded them.
Having lived in boarding schools and then alone in New
York during college, he found these students a strange lot.
They had been class officers at big state universities and
New England private colleges; they'd been football players
and cheerleaders; some of them even went to church on
Sundays. They all seemed to have two parents each, who
lived together at home, year round. And now they had
left home for the very first time to come to Africa. But
they'd go back someday, Gordon knew, to the same sorts
of wealthy communities they'd come from. That seemed
especially strange to him, though he supposed it shouldn't
—they were not trying to get away from America in order
to start again in a new country, as he was, but were merely
in Africa to *have an experience*, one they seemed confident
would have continuity with their past lives and future ca-
reers.

But then, some people's lives possessed golden threads of continuity, invisible to their owners but visible to people who had none. The threads spanned their owners' lives like the ropes that lead people up hillsides out of flooded areas. The threaded people didn't have to pull themselves along very often, but if the nights grew too dark and the waters rose too fast around them, they could always grab hold. Those who had no such guidelines frequently stumbled against the threads, got caught by the neck and were flung backward into the mud. Gordon had learned to stay away from people with golden threads.

In Karela, he had widened his field of exploration, pedaling down from the ridge into the maze of narrow streets along the hillside that acted as a buffer between the "European district" and the "African town" below. Small Indian groceries and dry-goods shops gave out odors of spices onto the crowded pavements. African women in traditional many-layered skirts harangued the Indian merchants with high-pitched voices that blended rage with laughter. Hand-carts piled high with coffee sacks rumbled out of alleyways. Screaming children careened down the cobblestones whacking tin hoops. Indian wives in bright blue and gold sarees sailed past the shop-fronts. Every time Gordon got lost on these side streets, he was barraged with unfamiliar clashing sights and smells and sounds, which kept him in a state of perpetual stimulation. Sometimes he rode about all morning and afternoon, becoming so exhausted that he had to push his bicycle back to the dormitory in the evening.

He didn't mind the exhaustion, but his days began to seem aimless and frantic. He had come down off the ridge, but still he had not penetrated the surface of Africa. Perhaps it was the language barrier that was keeping him back. But perhaps he was merely being impatient. He began to pedal more slowly, and found the roads that led down into the valleys and out into the countryside.

What to him was country was still part of the city, but here, it was the precolonial city that he was discovering, the capital of the ancient kingdom of Marembo. Gordon had seen the king several times at university dances. He was a young man, with heavy-lidded eyes and a serene, light brown face. He would arrive at a dance with his enormous sister, give a very drunken speech, and then be driven off in his beautiful old Rolls Royce, often with several female Marembo students clustered around him in the back seat. His kingdom was nearly defunct, its administrative functions having been taken over by the national government, but the people still revered their king, and the old capital continued to survive, though it was becoming overcrowded with rural people lured to the city by the promise of jobs and cash.

Gordon pedaled along the red-brown murram roads lined with coffee and banana trees, and gardens green with cassava and maize. Here the roads were full of people, not vehicles. The people were all African, and unlike the African students, none of them spoke English. Gordon had no idea what they were talking about. He was the strange one here. He rode cautiously at first, dismounting when the roads grew crowded, and waving overenthusiastically when ragged children pointed at him. He came to a large, open market where women spread clothing, plastic jewelry, and piles of vegetables and fruits in rows on the ground—all in a patchwork pattern that stretched to the bank of a foul-smelling river. Walking up and down the rows, he inspected the merchandise as the women shouted prices at him. He bought something on every visit: pineapple wedges, local Crane Bird cigarettes, groundnuts, a shirt, and once or twice a small packet of cannabis, which he smoked along secluded footpaths that looked down on the river.

It was stronger than the marijuana that he was used to in New York, and he didn't much like smoking here. It increased his racial anxiety—a holdover from America that was ordinarily dormant. The Africans in Marembo had never been enslaved, nor made to work on European estates as the Bashirians had; they had fewer reasons than most black people to hate whites. Still, there was some resentment: white was privilege, white had been until recently the colonial policeman in the noisy, dust-spewing Land Rover and the judge who gave a neighbor a disputed piece of land or sent a son to jail. Being alone and being dressed obviously as a student was a help, but Gordon was aware of occasional angry glances coming his way along with smiles and curious stares.

After a while, though, he became a familiar figure in the markets and roadways. He drank home-brewed banana

beer in tarpaulin-shaded outdoor "bars," where he struggled in broken Kisemi and English to answer questions
about the university and America. He began to join the
crowds watching games of checkers along the roadside. He
had no idea how to bet, but he tossed his pennies onto the
ground with the others. People dropped coins into his
hand, or took them away, after each game, and became so
used to seeing him that some of them asked him for loans.
Gordon began to feel that he was participating in the life
around him somewhat, instead of just watching from the
roadside. On these excursions, he felt happy—much hap-
pier than he could remember being ever before.

Gordon washed out his teacup and removed his sweaty
shirt. It blazed with Marembo flags—not a good outfit to
wear to the house of the headmaster, a British colonial
retread whose position would probably be Africanized
soon. But instead of putting on a clean shirt, he found
himself standing before the window again with the old one
squeezed in his hand in a salad of color.

He remembered the women he had passed on the roadways, and how they had lowered their eyes when they saw
him looking their way. Marembo women were brought up
not to look directly into a man's face. Occasionally, though,
a woman standing in a doorway or hanging out her wash
would watch him carefully and when their eyes met, would
smile radiantly. He wanted to stop and talk, but he feared
the awkwardness that would ensue from his not knowing
the language well enough.

Then one day he met a girl pedaling a sewing machine
under the overhanging tin roof of a shop. He had been
fascinated by the speed with which her fingers pushed the
light blue cloth under the needle and down onto her knees
in billowing folds. When she turned to smile at him, her
face glowed gold in the slanting rays of the sun; her black
hair appeared alive with flecks of light. The palm leaves
overhead crackled in the breeze and suddenly hushed. The
rhythm of her legs seemed to be churning up a silent storm
of surf that splashed playfully over her lap. Then she
stopped, removing her hands from the machine, to watch
him. The cloth slid down her knees; her shiny brown legs
were bare beneath the table. Laughing, she gathered the
blue folds into her lap again.

"*Balunji*," she greeted him, and wiped her forehead.

"*Asebyateno.*"

"*Ay-ee-i-i-i-i* ... ." That soft, high tag end of a greeting that women threw out from between white teeth, fastening their smiles as if with light ribbon to whomever they were saluting until the note faded to a ripple of laughter and vanished. Gordon stopped breathing. It was a magical sound, obliterating all others, erasing the shop and the trees and the road so that while it lasted, the girl sat alone in a blur of red-brown and green.

Gordon tried his few words of Marembo, and she replied shyly, musically. But when he attempted some Kisemi phrases, she laughed and shook her head—her own language was all she knew.

Pointing to a chipped Coca-Cola sign on the wall beside the door, she smiled at him again. It was a bone-shaped sign and had once held a thermometer. Coca-Cola: the ultimate *lingua franca.* Gordon wondered, was she inviting him in to buy a drink, or what?

Before he had a chance to figure out a response, an old woman shouted at the girl from the yard of her hut across the road. What sounded like angry words were exchanged. Gordon, watching from the roadside, waved and pushed his bicycle away. His fingers gripped the handlebars as if he were trying to crush them.

Gordon noticed the shirt in his hand and threw it into the corner. He splashed water on his face and let it dry in the breeze from the window. Yes, she had been the one Adija had reminded him of. That smile, that voice. But the girl at the sewing machine had had short hair, African style; her skin had been much darker. But all that didn't matter.

And now, wasn't the memory finished? He'd found what he'd been searching for. But still, he lingered by the window. There was more.

He had met girls who looked almost—but not quite—like her in the dance halls on the outskirts of the city, where he went with the African students from his dormitory. Frequently the only way he could get to sleep at night was by drinking and dancing himself into an exhausted stupor. Like the girl at the sewing machine, the young women in these dance halls wore Western clothes—cheap plastic sandals, short skirts, thin blouses that showed bright brassieres beneath. Occasionally they wore makeup and wigs and clutched at the arms of prosperous-looking men in suits, both Britons and Africans. More often, they sat at tables at the edge of the dance floor, sipping Coca-Cola, dancing with whoever asked them. When the music stopped, they returned to their tables to wait for the next invitation. They weren't prostitutes, Gordon was told, but unemployed women looking for temporary financial assistance, or shop-girls, secretaries, nurses having a night out. He danced with them. Sometimes they seemed embarrassed, anxious to get back to their tables. Sometimes they lingered with him when the music stopped, watching his face. He noticed that as the evening pulsed noisily on, they seemed to gradually disappear. Where did they go?

"With you, brother," his friend Kolo told him. "Here you are like the King of Marembo—any girl in the kingdom is your wife for a night."

"But why?"

"You're obviously a man of very high status. A university student is a big catch for a woman here. And white too—you must be rich." Kolo laughed at Gordon's perplexity, then added to it. "But, of course, you are engaged to the girl back home."

Never in his life had Gordon the experience of looking out across a room full of beautiful women and knowing that he could have any one he wanted. The idea was both tantalizing and frightening. He had not really been engaged to Irena, and now that she had faded from his mind, there was nothing to prevent him from finding out where these girls disappeared to.

One night, Gordon, a long-haired Irishman named Butler, and four African students crowded into someone's Renault and drove to the outskirts of the city. They stopped at a building that looked like a private house but was a "hotel"—a restaurant that served liquor but had no rooms to rent. There were six tables set up on the cement floor, a paraffin lantern, and a radio that played twangy African pop music. A fat Marembo woman brought the students round after round of beer. She also served bowls of crisp brown things that, on close inspection, Gordon discovered to be termites fried in oil. He had seen people opening sacks under lampposts where the flying insects swirled about in clusters like small snowstorms along the night streets. This was where they ended up.

Kolo pushed a bowl of them toward him. "You're welcome to share these with us," he said, smiling sideways.

"Thanks." Gordon took a deep breath. He crunched a few termites between his teeth. At first they tasted like salty cooking oil, then . . . well, termitey. He took a long swig of beer.

The students applauded and laughed. After several bottles of beer, Gordon munched on the insects as if they were peanuts. He also ate two servings of delicious steaming banana mush with rich vegetable gravy.

At midnight when they left the restaurant, the old African city of Karela was alive with the sounds of electric guitars and conga drums. Gordon's group ran into more students and a man who claimed to be a Zulu *mganga*, a "witch-doctor" from South Africa. He had his "receptionist" with him, a lady so fat she had to sit on two people's laps in the back of the Renault. At the Crested Crane Club, Butler did some magic tricks, drawing a considerable crowd and offers of free drinks if he would reveal his secrets. His refusal angered several people who claimed to have already paid for rounds. The Zulu defended Butler, expounding upon the sacred nature of magic, but had to beat a hasty retreat when a member of the audience accused the doctor of once having prescribed some herbs for his piles that had made him break out in spots. "Constipated leopard!" the students shouted out the windows of one of the cars as they screeched into the night.

At the Blue Nile Club, Gordon began to sweat away several gallons of the beer he had drunk. He loved the music and the rhythms of the crowd. The twanging, pounding beat flung him about the dance floor in waves of energy as potent and precarious as surf. He held churning waists of turbaned Congolese women, he inhaled their urgent perfume and soaked in the sweat of their glistening arms and shoulders. He felt the touch of a slim Marembo girl's hand; he locked eyes with her as they danced; he swallowed those burning eyes like live coals and with them all the turmoil swirling around him. The turmoil glowed hot in his belly, burning away a lifetime of noxious uncertainties. He was part of it all now, part of the music and laughter and motion, part of Africa. He was another limb of the great thrashing beast, the crowd; its heartbeat throbbed out to all its parts, mindless, in unison with his own. He wept with happiness from every pore.

But he was greedy. Inflated by new confidence and freedom, he wanted more. He wanted to take the feeling of the dance floor away with him. He wanted to take it out into the warm smoky Karela night and into one of those mud huts that the people, when they finished dancing, went home to. Home to. He wanted a home-to. By day, the huts looked so very inviting: little rectangular thatched-roofed houses, banana trees sprouting in the yards, families sitting around the doorstep, mothers playing with running, naked children, men joking together and greeting everyone who came by—even him—with waves and smiles. He had to have this Africa too. He had to have more.

And, wanting more, he turned what he'd had sour. The mud floor of the hut was cold. The shady coolness beyond the doorstep was only a flesh-chilling draft. The chatter and laughter were silenced in the dark; only the cries of the girl's baby in the next room—cries of the pain of hunger—reminded him of the family scenes he'd viewed from the roadside by day. The girl was hard-boned and rhythmless and undernourished. Without her purple brassiere, her breasts were little pouches of brown skin. Her belly rumbled, empty. Gordon lifted himself over her to keep from hurting her, but afterward, as she lay motionless with her eyes squeezed shut, he was sure that he had crushed her pelvis.

Finally she rose. Squatting over an enamel bowl, she washed herself with a rag. The weak yellow lantern light streaked on her cheeks, and now he could see her eyes as she tried to smile for him. Turning away, he dressed quickly.

He had become another pale foreigner reaching desperately for his wallet to pay his passage back to a world that was familiar and clean and safe.

But even then, as he stumbled away through the darkness, he knew that he could not go back to stay. He would never again be satisfied to watch from the roadside, no matter what he found when he left it.

Gordon stepped back from the window, his eyes unfocused. He walked into the kitchen and suddenly, with a violent backhand motion, flung the tea from his cup into the sink. The jagged pattern of the splash remained on the gray zinc after the tea had streaked down across it toward the drain. He would have thrown the cup itself—had felt his grip on it loosening for a split second—except that in his mind it had become Adija's cup. He set it down carefully in the sink.

Then he put on a clean shirt and went to meet the headmaster.

4

FROM BEHIND, YOU COULD SEE THE BAR WAS only several packing cases nailed together, but the front had been painted with glossy orange and green stripes—the colors of Marembo's flag—and looked very nice, Salome thought. On the opposite wall was a mural of the flag being carried down a city street at the head of a raucous parade. The artist had carefully detailed the leopard-skin vests and plumed headdresses of the marchers, but their faces were all identical, each perhaps a self-portrait of the artist. Several men in the parade carried horns. The words "SAINTS GO MARCHING IN!" blasted out of a tuba. The other horns shouted "UHURU! FREEDOM! UHURU YA MAREMBO!!! ♪♫♩♫♫ ♪♫♪♫♫♪." Like it or not, Salome stared at this mural all afternoon and evening. Sometimes even in the night while she slept, she saw the same man marching toward her, with all his twin brothers lock-stepping behind him.

A year-old calendar and an advertising poster were all that broke the dust-colored monotony of the other walls. Behind Salome, where she did not have to look at it, a girl in a tight satin dress grimaced from the poster. The girl, wearing a pale deathmask of paste, was saying in a balloon that came out of her mouth, "I Use Ambi Cream For a Lovelier, Lighter Complexion!" Customers smiled at the contrast between this slim, composed girl on the wall and dark Salome, with her bursting bodice and her fierce, restless eyes. They often laughed when they spoke of Salome, calling her a madwoman, or worse, but they never did so in voices they thought she could hear. But Salome heard everything.

Salome leaned her elbows on the bar and pretended she was deaf. Now and again she took a sip from a glass of beer, or poured some foam on the counter for the flies to drink. When she grew tired of watching them washing their feet in the bubbles, she tried to smash them with the palm of her hand. She always missed.

After the rains stopped that afternoon, the men who had taken refuge in the New Life went out again. Salome had privacy now to go through Adija's basket. She pulled out each article and laid it on the bar. Blouses, skirts, a dress, underwear, . . . a saree. Was this girl an Indian? No—there at the bottom of the basket was a tin crucifix on a broken chain. Not an Indian. Not a Moslem either, despite her Moslem name and looks. A mystery, this Adija. But none of Salome's affair. She stuffed the clothes back into the basket and went to lug in another case of beer for the evening crowd.

Later, she heard a fight down the street at Ambani's Bar, the place that sold cheap home-brewed liquor. She took out her machete in case any of the brawlers, drunk and bloody, should try to get into the New Life to enlist reinforcements. Then she stood in the doorway, blocking it. Shadows collided in the flickering light on the sidewalk, the wireless screeched, glasses shattered, people grunted and roared. The noise echoed under the roofs of the shops on the other side of the street. Salome was pleased with the diversion.

As the fight subsided, a figure came out of Ambani's and sat motionless on the curb at the edge of a tongue of moth-fluttering lantern light. The figure wasn't recognizable, but it was familiar. Salome edged toward it, not knowing why she was doing so. The face turned. It was that Adija.

"What are you doing here, girl?" Salome asked, dropping the machete to her side.

Adija stood up slowly. "Ah, you've come," she said, smiling.

Salome frowned. This girl acted as if she'd been *expecting* her! Salome wanted to turn around and go back to the New Life, but the light flickering on Adija's face made her skin vibrate, almost shimmer, like the sun on dark water, and Salome couldn't stop staring at her.

"What do you want?" she asked finally.

Adija shook her head. "I was looking for work in that bar, and a man tried to hit the girl standing beside me. She was telling him he was the father of her baby."

"So you got in the way."

"If he'd hit her, she might have lost the baby," Adija said.

"And she'd have been glad. Babies are a nuisance to such women as go to Ambani's."

"No, she wanted it. She said so." Adija turned sideways, and Salome could see that her blouse was torn at the shoulder and her eyes were wet from weeping. "Besides, I didn't get in the way. I *was* in the way."

Who had asked her for an explanation? Not Salome. But Salome didn't move.

"I'm always in the way," Adija said. She stared out across the street into the blank dark faces of the shops. "I even lost his towel."

"What are you talking about, girl?"

"The teacher's towel. He gave it to me to keep my shoes dry."

Salome smiled. "Yes, the one who was going to employ you. He probably couldn't even speak your language, could he?"

Adija turned her head away sharply. The yellow light turned the tiny damp hairs on her neck to live sparks.

"You left your basket with me," Salome went on. "So I was thinking, 'Adija will come back for it, so that I won't have to watch it all the time to see that no one steals it.' But instead, you went someplace else."

"I was ashamed," Adija whispered. She fixed her huge black eyes on Salome, and when she spoke in her faint voice, it was suddenly the loudest sound in the street. "I don't know where I can go tonight. If it were daytime, I might know. I might still want to go to Bashiri. But not tonight." She shook her head like one speaking to herself. A spot of blood on her cheek flashed in the lantern light. "I can't go back to where I was, but I can't go forward either . . ."

Salome saw the thin bones in Adija's shoulder pushed out against her skin, the hollows between them long valleys of shadow. She knew what the girl was talking about, knew so well it hurt to hear it. "Even people with no place," she said, her voice suddenly drained of belligerence, "they can't live in the air like a bird with no feet. They stop someplace, any place."

"I've no reason to stop any place."

"You do. Your reason is: You're too tired and frightened to move. Later, you make up stories to explain why you've stayed, and you forget the true reason."

Adija smiled vaguely, as if she had been sure Salome was going to say something like that. Salome shivered. The silence between her and Adija became agitated, as if silent bees were swarming near her face. She tried to brush the prickly feeling off her cheeks. Her mouth opened, but no sound came out. Aah! this girl was a witch! Casting her into Adija-witch-silence! Insisting that Salome share her lostness. . . .

"Why don't you speak?" Salome stamped her foot. "Speak, girl!"

"I want to stay with you." Adija's voice was very soft. Her eyes were forlorn. She looked as though she would faint if Salome did not reach out to catch her.

"Just for tonight, though," Salome said. "You hear?"

Closing her eyes, Adija nodded.

She had to wait while Salome brought beer to some customers. She didn't move from the corner of the bar where Salome left her. You couldn't tell if she heard all the inquiries about her, or felt the stares of men's eyes. She let her head drop, her thick, dirty hair falling over her shoulders. As she turned her face slowly, she could see the dusty walls around her, and the identical marching men with their flags and slogans. She looked at them as if she had seen them before, every day. As for the men at the tables, she must have seen them too, but in the same dazed way. She was simply waiting. She appeared quite peaceful, like a condemned person viewing the scaffold and the crowd with the eyes but not the mind.

*   *   *

Salome showed Adija to the room beside her own room behind the bar, then hurried back to work. Alone again, Salome felt more herself, and concentrated once more on beer-selling, a skill for which she was famous.

Salome knew that every man has a certain capacity beyond which he does not really need to drink, but will do so recklessly if properly encouraged. Her goal, then, was to lead a man up to this point and push him past it, rendering him unable to leave as long as he still had money in his pocket. As a man ordered more beer, he noticed an increasingly hot glint in her eye. As she leaned over to put down his beer, he caught a glimpse of the top-swells of her breasts jiggling in his face. She parted them with both hands and peered down between them, demanding, "What are you looking for in my cardigan?" Then she laughed and flounced away. She occasionally sat with him for a few minutes, drinking the beer he'd bought her. Each man was led to believe that she would come tumbling into his lap, unable to restrain her passion for him, as soon as he had finished one more beer.

There came a point when a man grew impatient, just on the verge of slamming down his money on the table and storming out. At this point, Salome came careening around the bar toward him, hips rolling, eyes ablaze. "Drink!" she screamed, and slammed down the bottle with all the violence he would like to have unleashed on her. "You needn't pay for this one, since I've been keeping you so long. But if you don't want me, don't drink it!" As he drank it, and the next, which was not free, and the next, Salome kept up her smiles and nudges, but she never let fade that look from her face that told him, "If you try to leave now, I'll kill you."

Very occasionally, she kept her implied sexual promises —if she couldn't get the man too drunk to walk. Back in her room, he insisted that she remove her clothes. She always refused. Someday, perhaps, but not this time. She blew out the lantern. Here, have this . . . And the man had to settle for lifted skirts and a few quick thrusts into the tightness between her thighs. She didn't demand payment, or plead for a "gift" from him, but inevitably a ten- or twenty-shilling note happened to fall out of his trouser pocket in the dark. Her last goodbye left him pissing quarts of beer into the grass outside her room. She could leave and be back at work in the bar in five minutes.

Tonight, though, she found herself abandoning her techniques. Jeremiah wanted her. Jeremiah Kongwe was a member of the Bashiri secret police, the Special Branch. Everyone feared him, even Salome. He was a short man, bulging in the belly and buttocks; his head was shiny brown except above the ears, where patches of hair stuck to his skull like sand on a wet coconut. Salome would have laughed at him, even knowing who he was, except that whenever she saw him, she remembered her past, and an old rage gripped her stomach like a cold, steel hand.

"How are you, Salome?" He greeted her in English.

"Not bad, until a moment ago." Salome set down a beer before him.

Jeremiah flashed her a smile, the smirk of a man teasing a puppy. It covered the offended look in his eyes. Salome's unreasonable hostility bothered him. He would have to threaten her into bed, and though he was used to having women that way, he would have preferred a willing Salome. He'd known Salome a long time. "Don't I even get a smile of welcome to your establishment?" he asked, making a swipe at her thigh.

"Three shillings fifty," she said in Kisemi, stepping back deftly. She hated him to speak English to her. "Right now, in advance."

Jeremiah folded his arms. "Pour it for me, darling."

Scowling, Salome tipped the mouth of the bottle over his glass. She let the beer gush in until the foam rose over the top and poured onto the table.

"You're very sloppy."

"Flattery will get you no place."

"Goddammit!" Jeremiah jerked back from the table. Beer was dripping into his lap. "Get a rag, woman! You play with me, you can find yourself behind bars with no one to play with but yourself!"

Salome looked down at the puddle at his feet. "Some men are able to hold themselves until they reach the latrine," she said.

Throughout the evening, as she served him and then reluctantly took him to her room, she kept a picture in her mind that protected her against what she was feeling. The picture was the same each time Jeremiah visited.

In it she pretended that she was sitting on a green hillside overlooking the village where she had grown up. She could see the rust-colored roofs of the shops and the railway station below, and beyond them, the peak of Mount Bashiri rising in the distance through a shelf of white clouds. She never tired of looking at the mountain, the home of her people's God. Massive and holy, it was something felt as much as seen. It watched over her and her people and blocked out the worlds that lay beyond it.

Her little daughter, Wairimu, sat beside her, plucking stalks of grass from around her toes and tossing them down the hill like tiny arrows. She rested her head against

her mother's knee, and Salome told her stories of the Hare
and the Antelope, and why the Hen and the Hawk cannot
live in peace. She told Wairimu about the adventures of the
ancestors of the Samoyo people: how the men, by attacking the women when they were all pregnant at the same
time, had come to capture from the women the leadership
of the tribe. That such beings had walked these very same
hills and valleys filled Wairimu with wonder. She stopped
her grass-plucking to look up wide-eyed at Salome. Salome
smiled back and was silent with happiness.

"Look at the roofs of the shops," Wairimu said, gazing
down into the valley. "They're burning in the sun!"

And truly, they were beautiful, the poor tin roofs turned
to flaming gold by the magic of a child's noticing.

"And look—the train is starting its engine!"

Salome had to look. Wairimu and the hillside faded.
There, in the darkness of her room behind the New Life,
the picture changed.

One moment, the locomotive was in the valley below
her, squatting there on its track like an armored slug.
Clouds of steam shot out from beneath the thing's belly;
smoke spurted from its smokestack. It cringed there behind
the steam and smoke, visible only in black patches as if
glimpsed through shifting fog. The fog spread out over the
ground in a shadowy puddle.

The next moment, she was in the locomotive. She was
burning. A fire was glowing close to her flesh. Within her
flesh. She was the locomotive. She was grinding, scraping
her pistons. Hissing and clanking. Wallowing in the puddle. Sinking.

Suddenly amid all the din, she could hear nothing, could
feel nothing, nothing at all. She was no longer that snorting
black engine she had seen in the valley. . . .

She was the other engine: the reflection of the locomotive that lay beneath it in the puddle. This engine could
make no sounds, could feel no fire or steam pressure. It
could only thrash in unison with the pumping of the locomotive on top of it. At times she thought she would be
crushed or sliced to pieces. But that was impossible. She
was merely a mirror image, made neither of flesh nor of
hard black steel but of vapor and smoke. And when the
machine above exploded all over her, and then slowed,
then ceased its movement, she was left undented. Soot

settled in her eyes, blotting out the last of her senses, bathing her in soft darkness. She lay still, wishing the darkness would cover her forever.

"Salome—"

"What?" Salome opened her eyes. It was Jeremiah talking. He was sitting on the edge of the bed, leaning against her leg. She moved her leg away. "Leave me alone now," she grunted.

Jeremiah stood up and pulled on his trousers. He gazed down at Salome sprawled on the bed, looking as if she had just fallen from a great height and landed in a heap. He felt bad. Salome was not a woman to be so easily crushed. "You know, an agent like myself, he must do many unpleasant things. But one thing I would never do is to take an old friend back across the border for trial."

Salome made no sound or movement. Jeremiah was one of the few people who remembered that years ago a warrant had been issued for her arrest, on the charge of destruction of property. During Bashiri's war of independence, she had carried food and bullets into the forest to the guerrillas, and when she could get it, military information she overheard in the house of a Colonel Ennis, where she had been made welcome to visit when his wife was not at home. After Colonel Ennis's men had killed Kariuki, the guerrilla leader whom she had been supplying in the forest, Salome had smashed everything in the colonel's house and fled to her village. The people there, however, believed that she had betrayed Kariuki to Colonel Ennis and refused to hide her. She had fled again to the back streets of Azima, the capital of Bashiri, and from there across the border into Marembo. It was not so much a trial she feared, but the judgment of her people. They were mistaken about her, but there was no way she could defend herself.

"If you come back with me now," Jeremiah was saying, "you can't go for trial. There's too much excitement about Uhuru approaching. People are saying, 'Let us live in peace with our former colonial oppressors, and even their henchmen. Let us forget the past.'"

"I'm no henchman. I committed no crime against Africa." Salome rolled onto her back and stared at the ceiling, as if pleading with it. "No crime," she repeated.

"All right. And Ennis has returned to the U.K."

"I don't believe you."

"I know it."

"He doesn't matter. I'm not going back."

"It is a good time. Many Africans are going into business now. You are a clever woman, even somewhat educated. You are successful with this bar. You would have
more opportunities in Bashiri."

"I don't want 'opportunities.' "

Jeremiah stood up, buttoning his shirt. "You think people still believe you were a collaborator, don't you?"

"Collaborator!" Salome sat up suddenly. "How did you
get your job, collaborator?"

"Render unto Caesar . . . as long as Caesar is in power."
He put on his suit jacket, ramming his hands out through
the sleeves. "But I don't work for Caesar any longer. I'm a
nationalist."

"Now that everyone is a nationalist. Now that the Europeans have given you permission to be a nationalist."

"All right, Salome. You're not coming back this time?"

"No."

"You have nothing to fear from me. I only want to
make an honest woman of you."

"Ah, the sewer rat wants to make the dung beetle smell
sweet!"

Jeremiah brushed down the lapels of his jacket. "You
can't stay in this dung-heap town forever," he said. He
reached down to shake her hand in parting, but Salome
rolled away from him, pulling her blanket around her. Her
head spun violently. She felt sickness in her stomach,
churning her toward the edge of the bed. Jeremiah left
without closing the door. She did not see or hear him go;
she knew he was gone by the chill he left behind him.

*　*　*

Salome blew out her lantern and lay back on the bed.
She waited for darkness to settle over her again. But the
room was not dark. A flickering light seeped across the
ceiling from where the partition between the rooms did not
fit. That girl, that Adija, was awake. She had heard everything! Salome felt the same flush on her cheeks as she had
when talking to Adija earlier.

Adija would be full of questions now. Well, Salome
wouldn't answer any. She'd go to sleep. She lay very still.
Every little noise outside was amplified: a door slam-

ming on the other side of town, the crunch of dirt beneath
someone's feet on the street, the swelling buzz of insects.
She had never thought about these noises before. Her room
had never seemed lonely before.

"Why do you keep the lantern burning?" Salome demanded finally.

A rustling noise. "I—I couldn't sleep. I didn't like the
darkness." Adija's voice was faint behind the partition. "It
sounded as if you had a bull in there."

"Hah! A hyena, perhaps. A little bald hyena."

Salome heard muted laughter. Suddenly she was laughing too, although nothing was amusing her that she could
think of. "I think you've heard those sounds before," she
said.

"Sometimes."

"Where did you come from today?"

"Jinjeh."

"You sometimes went to the Flamingo Bar?"

"You know that place?" Adija asked.

"Of course."

Silence.

"I sometimes worked there. I didn't like it—I don't like
those places."

"That's right. You thought you would find better ones in
Bashiri."

"I didn't know what I would find. But I had to leave
Jinjeh," Adija said. "I stole a saree from an Indian woman
I was working for. I didn't want it, I just took it because
she owed me wages." Adija was moving about now. A
scrambling sound, as if she were going through her basket.
"But then I put the saree on and I liked it. Now I want
more sarees. They're beautiful, don't you think?"

"On you, perhaps." The girl was confessing to stealing
because she had overheard Jeremiah talking about a "trial."
She was trying to get close to her. "You who have the
mouth of an African, the nose of a European, the hair of
an Indian, the skin and eyes of a Northerner—you could
wear anything."

"Do you think I am very ugly?"

Salome felt bad. "No, you're not very ugly," she said.

"Sometimes I even think I'm lucky to look like all those
people."

Adija must have been standing up in her room now. Her voice was echoing, sometimes coming from the partition and sometimes seeming to be in Salome's room itself. Salome pulled the blankets tighter around her. She was used to solitude, not a disembodied voice in her room. "Who *are* your people?" Salome asked, finally.

"My father was an Arab—but I'm not a Moslem. My father was killed by thieves. My mother, she was his housegirl. She was African. It was she who unlocked the door to let the thieves in." Adija was breathing fast as she spoke, as if she had been storing up this information for a long time and was afraid she would be smothered before getting the chance to tell it all. "My mother is dead also. She fell off a bridge and drowned. She was a Moslem but she became a Christian. . . ."

Salome couldn't concentrate on what Adija was saying. Every night, she lay very still, and to keep out unwelcome thoughts, pretended hard that her head was the scooped-out shell of a pumpkin. Thoughts assailed her anyway, pictures of the day's details, monotonous and lurid— bottles, insults, coins, laughter, bodies, marching men's faces all sloshing together inside her skull like vomit. Tonight, Jeremiah had brought pictures not only of Musolu but of Bashiri, of war. Adija was showing her Jinjeh and the coast, thieves and drowning. Salome was dizzy and sick.

Adija asked her something, but she didn't hear what it was. Now Adija was moving about again. Salome rolled over on her back. The light on the ceiling flickered like a gecko lizard darting back and forth from the partition. Salome shut her eyes. The light streaks appeared inside out behind her eyelids, splashes of ink-black water constantly falling off the dark horizon, tilting her over with them. "Adija—I'm not used to talking to anyone at night. I got drunk, I need to sleep."

"Look!"

Adija was standing in the open doorway. She held the lantern in front of her. In its light, she was purple. A purple gauze was wrapped over one shoulder, across her bare chest, around her hips, and down to her ankles. It was more a visible breeze than any cloth. It whispered as she moved. The beauty of Adija made Salome gasp.

"I threw away the top. It was too big," Adija said. "Here, let me put this down." She set her lantern down beside Salome's. Orange light splashed across her face. She rose from her kneeling position, the saree rippling and settling around her again. "I've not shown it to anyone," she said. "Do you like it?"

"Yes," Salome said. "But—but why do you show it to me?"

"Because you're my friend. You're the only one who's been kind to me." Adija turned around in a full circle, the purple spreading around her. "Besides, if you've been in the Flamingo Bar, we are sisters," she laughed.

Salome said nothing. She had never had a sister.

"Do I look like an Indian? I don't want to. But sometimes it's better to look like something, instead of just anything at all." Adija stood still. The gauze gathered at her nipples and fell in tiny waterfalls across the smooth flesh of her belly. "Do you know what I mean—it's good to look like something that people can recognize."

"Yes, I understand that."

"So you like my saree?"

"You look—it's very beautiful on you."

Adija's teeth flashed in the light as she smiled. "I thought you would be wanting something to take your mind off things tonight. I hoped so."

"Why?"

"Because I couldn't sleep. I heard you, and I wanted to be with you."

Adija sat on the side of the bed. Salome felt a patch of heat where her knees were touching Adija's thigh. She shut her eyes. Once again, her head began to spin. She sat up suddenly. "What do you want? Are you a witch?"

"Don't say that." Adija's voice was brittle and scratchy.

"Why? Do you believe in them?"

"Me?" Adija turned her face away. "But you, surely you don't. You speak English, you've been to school. You can't be fearing them."

"No." Salome sighed. "Sometimes I just get chilled."

"Didn't you sleep with your sisters for warmth when the nights were cold? And brush their hair, and talk secrets with them?"

"I had no sisters," Salome said. "But I know sisters do that."

"I had none either. I wanted one."

"It's not very cold tonight. I must be trembling because I feel sick."

"Myself, I was trembling before." Adija squinted down into the lantern. "I wanted to cry when I heard you talking with that man."

"Why? You couldn't understand. We talked in English."

"I could understand. The sound of your voice was full of shuddering."

Salome tried to see into the shadows that hid Adija's enormous eyes. She felt their enormity, even though they were invisible. "How could you know that?" she asked.

"I could. I have heard the shuddering before." She shook her head slowly. "I want to stop thinking about it."

"So do I. But I can't."

"Yes. We . . . can."

"No. How?"

Adija leaned sideways, slowly, cautiously, until she was resting against Salome's shoulder. "Please," she whispered. "I want to stay here with you. I want you to be my sister."

Salome's arms went out as if of their own accord. She wrapped them around Adija. Lying back, with Adija upon her, she shut her eyes tight. Again the inside-out black streaks washed across her eyes, tilting, tilting away from her. She lay still for a long time, not daring to move lest she spin out of control. She held Adija close, and did not mind that the girl's tears were warm against her cheek.

The tilting gradually stopped. Salome felt not as if she had taken a weight onto her, but as if one were lifting off her body. Something heavy, much heavier than the frail Adija, was coming unstuck with a faint, pleasant pain. Now there were no pictures in her head, none at all. They were washed away. In their place was space, vast space, wrapping itself softly around her like a warm night sky full of rain.

5

GORDON WATCHED THE RAIN STREAK DOWN his window, half-hoping that the drenched figure of a girl would suddenly appear out of the translucence again. If the schoolboy hadn't been in the house with her on that first day, he might have believed that Adija had only visited him in a blurry dream.

He'd thought of visiting that New Life Hotel she'd mentioned to see if she truly existed, but in the six days he'd been at the school, he'd left the grounds just once, to go shopping by car in the British farming community of Kabale, across the border. Why hadn't he gone into Musolu village? He'd been busy with classes, preparing lessons, attending meetings, being invited to dinner by other masters. And going into the village was apparently not done. The other masters seemed to believe that Musolu was the name of the school alone. If a town of that name existed, it was a scruffy satellite to the school, where only last-minute shopping might be done. All these were good reasons for not going to look for the New Life Hotel. None of them, however, were his reasons. He knew the extent of his loneliness—the memory of the girl in the hut in Karela was still too fresh.

The rain stopped as suddenly as it had started. By the time he had collected his books for the morning classes, the air shone with such clarity that he could smell the greenness of the land around him. He walked along the oval roadway that separated the neatly landscaped masters' residences at one end from the whitewashed classroom buildings at the other. In the middle of the oval was a playing field, which now was strewn with long puddle-mirrors on whose surfaces clouds floated across patches of blue sky into ragged grass. Behind him, the land was lush green and cobwebbed with red-brown footpaths that led toward the mountain, where they rose into the mist that hid the high peak. Minutes ago, the mountain had been gun-metal gray; the sun had appeared on the land's edge to pour fiery red light down the slope like lava. Beyond the classroom buildings, streaks of white mist lay along the plain; the sunlight dissolved them gradually on its way to the other horizon, revealing more bright fields and paths and scattered thatch-roofed huts. The countryside was alive with the cries of birds and children and the lowing of cattle. Dust clouds raised by cattle's hooves hovered above the paths; smoke curled up from the huts. The day was suddenly warm. Gordon, walking into the warmth, understood why the local people believed that they were living in the center of the world.

A small round-faced boy in a green school uniform approached him from one of the cinderblock dormitory buildings. Noticing the master's bare toes in his rubber sandals, he couldn't help but smile. "Goodmorning, sir," he said.

Gordon grinned. "Hello."

"Are you liking this place?"

"Yes, very much," Gordon said. "This is where I want to be. I think it's where I've always wanted to be."

"*Eii!*" The boy stopped. He hadn't expected such an answer. The master's face looked very intense, but somehow not frightening. "Then you heard of this place before you came here?" he asked.

"Musolu? No. But I heard about Africa. Some Marembans where I worked in America told me about this area."

The boy nodded. "Oh. You were teaching in America?"

"I was a waiter in a kind of restaurant—a club for university professors. Most of the waiters were Africans and West Indians."

"How could you be a waiter in a restaurant?" The boy cocked his head. "Here, a waiter does not become a teacher."

"No, I suppose not," Gordon said. There had been times when, buried in some stinking steamy kitchen, he had himself wondered if he would ever become a teacher.

"Parents don't pay school fees in America?" the boy asked.

"Sometimes they do. Mine didn't."

"Here, many boys work during the holidays to pay

school fees. Everyone in their family works to get the money." The boy watched the new master's face. He still couldn't believe that a European master could have carried dirty trays in an eating place and been shouted at by ordinary people sitting at tables. He had never spoken to a teacher about his life outside the classroom before. The other boys in his dormitory had chosen him, on a dare, to go find out about the new master. They had reckoned that he would get his face slapped, literally or figuratively. The boy was determined to astound them with the information he brought back. He pressed on after even hotter items.

"Was Miss Marsten a waiter in America too? Did you know her there?"

"I don't think she was a waiter, but you'll have to ask her," Gordon said, smiling. "I didn't know her until I got to the university in Karela."

The boy held his breath, then let it out. "Do you like her, sir?"

"Pamela? Sure. She's not my girlfriend, if that's what you're asking."

The boy squeezed his fists at his side with delight. He was the first boy in the school to learn the new schoolmistress's Christian name. Already his mind was working to find an amusing rhyme for "Pamela" that would become the name by which all the boys would call her among themselves.

"I think Mr. Wickham-Marshall likes her," he said, feeling a little dizzy with success.

"That could be." Gordon laughed. "You're quite a gossip, aren't you?"

"Me? No, sir!"

"Just curious, then."

"Yes, I am ever curious."

"You're in my third-period class, but I've forgotten your name."

"Pius Otieno, sir. Form 2C."

"Right. Are you pious too?"

"Pardon?" The boy looked away. "You mean, am I a Christian? All the boys are Christian. It is the rule."

"I see. Do you prefer to be called 'Pius' or 'Otieno'?"

"Myself?" No master had ever asked him what he preferred to be called. "I am called Otieno by my family. And my friends too. Yes, I prefer that."

"Okay, Otieno." Gordon smiled, seeing the boy square his shoulders. "While we're on the subject of names—I'm not crazy about being called 'sir.' "

"Why is that, s—mister?"

"When I was a student in boarding schools, we had to call the masters 'sir.' It meant that they were supposed to be some kind of nobility, and we were the dirty *lumpen-proletariat*—low class. We had to ask permission every time we wanted to take a piss, and then be grateful if they said yes."

Otieno laughed out loud. "It is the same here, sir. I mean, mister."

"I'm sorry to hear that."

"Really, it is very hard not to say that word, though. We are all used to it."

Gordon sighed. " 'Mister' isn't much better, is it?"

"I don't think so."

" 'Mister Lockery' isn't bad. If you can remember that, okay. If you can't, I guess it isn't all that important."

"Mister Lockery" still sounded strange. Gordon had never held a job in which he supervised others before. For seventeen years, school and work, he had taken instructions from others and connived to avoid being victimized by their rules. Suddenly, in a matter of days after leaving the university, *he* was the one people were supposed to obey. The other masters acted as if they had been giving orders all their lives; Gordon wondered if he could ever get used to it. In each of his six classes, thirty-five students all stopped talking in unison when he entered the room. Fifty boys in the dormitory he'd been made housemaster of awoke when he told them to. Some of these "boys"— though they'd listed their ages as fifteen, the maximum age permitted for entering secondary-school students—were not boys at all. They were older than he was, he'd been informed, with wives and children at home, some of them. Yet they called him "sir." He couldn't help feeling a little like a fake.

No—he wasn't going to be distracted by the hierarchical colonial trappings of the job: the titles and the formality. He was a teacher. He had important work to do—he was training the future leaders of a new nation. He was *doing* something for the first time in his life, instead of waiting around for something worthwhile to do. And he was well prepared to do it. Gordon had never experienced confidence before—he'd never had anything to feel confident about. Now he did.

"Are *you* a Christian, sir?" Otieno asked him, as they passed between two classroom buildings.

"Well, no," Gordon said. I will play the game, he thought, but I will not lie.

"Sure? What are you, then?"

"I'm an ex-Christian. Sort of a pagan."

"No!" Otieno stared at him. "How is that possible?"

"Wait until you've sat through four years of chapel services. Then we'll see if you can still ask me that question."

Otieno smiled. "I think I will not have to wait so long."

"Oh? I see." Gordon nodded. "Pius the pagan."

Otieno laughed nervously. "But you, sir—you are European. From America."

"America's the land of pagans."

"No, sir. I think you are joking me."

"Why?"

"We saw a film of America, and the people were praying. It was before the planting season. They were praying for rain to fall." The boy gazed earnestly at Gordon.

"Maybe I'm the only pagan," Gordon said, trying to be more serious.

Otieno's mischievous smile returned. "Now we are two, here at the school."

"Right," Gordon said. "What film did you see?"

"Its name was *Farming the American Way*. It was about tractors. The Information Service of the United States lent it to the school."

Gordon had seen such films during his teaching observation in Karela. They were supposed to be handy for periods in which the teacher had no work prepared. "I'll bet it was terrible," he said.

Otieno turned his face away to hide his grin. "It was somewhat boring," he said. Then he looked back at Gordon. "I think the boys here will like having you at the school, sir. You are very strange."

Gordon laughed. He was about to ask Otieno what on earth he meant, but the boy ran off toward some students sitting on the steps of a dormitory.

Before morning assembly, he stopped in the staff room to see if there were any messages for him in the wooden cubby hole that was his mailbox. There were none, he was glad to see. Perhaps he would get a free evening.

The staff room was dark, despite the sun, and smelled of disinfectant. On the long wooden table where teachers corrected papers during break were stacks of exercise books and quizzes. Gordon looked at some.

List three reasons why Thomas More was a great man.

and

David Copperfield's father was imprisoned because he owed money. TRUE_____ FALSE_____

and

What climatic conditions make Monmouthshire an ideal region for the cultivation of roses?

and other such questions assessing knowledge that no future leader of an emerging African nation could afford to be without. No revised post-Independence syllabi had reached this bush school yet, that was certain. His own subject, history, was still little more than colonial history. Gordon looked through some English notebooks, since he would soon have to start teaching an English class. The essays had titles like "The Importance of Education," "How New Inventions Improve Our Lives," "The Most Difficult Commandment To Follow," and "Common Mistakes Using Gerunds." Gerunds? No, that was just a grammar lesson. Gordon reckoned he had better remember what a gerund was; it would not do to make a "common mistake." He flipped through another notebook. The ever popular "Life in My Village." But this one looked interesting. He read the essay.

WITCHCRAFT IN MY VILLAGE

A woman in my village was accused of bewitching one of her husband's other wives. This was because this woman was behaving in a very strange way, all the people said, even wearing strange clothes and immitating foreign customs. Lual the witch doctor was summened by the family to suck the devilment from the woman's stomach with his cows horn. During the ceremonny, the air inside the hut was as stagnant as water at the bottom of a pond. All was still to the gaze and silent to the ear. Finally the doctor was finished his sayings and his sucking on the horn. The witch woman began to scream because some women were holding her down and she was fearing very much. The people said the witch was screaming in her. But when Lual stood up, she stopped her noise. Then she merely cried and embraced the other wives. Great astonishment fell on the people of my village to hear that Lual had removed the devils from the poor pathetic woman, who afterwards never behaved in a strange way any more, and even soon became with child.

Many of the powers of witch doctors are diclining nowadays because many people are giving up their primitive customs and begin to realize the wonderful works of the Living God.

THE END

The teacher, Miss Stuart, had generously sprinkled the page with X's and arcane grammatical squiggles calculated to exorcise any creative devils from the boy's writing. She had written "WHAT NONSENSE!" beside the first paragraph, and marked the essay with a large red "D." The hypocritical last paragraph about the Living God was probably all that had saved the paper from a failing grade.

Gordon would have written "EXCELLENT" across the top of the essay and given it an "A." But, then, he wasn't offended by the idea of witchcraft. Some of his fellow university students had spoken of it—albeit with some nervous humor at times—as a force to be reckoned with in Africa, a belief system capable of causing real harm, physical and emotional, to people who thought themselves bewitched or who were themselves accused of witchcraft.

Miss Stuart's obvious horror at the contents of the boy's paper was, come to think of it, a more respectful attitude than that of some of the masters, who liked to tell amusing stories about the various "superstitions" of their

houseboys and other "natives." Gordon, who'd read about
witchcraft beliefs in anthropology courses, did not con-
tribute to these discussions. He considered the talk racist,
and faintly dangerous as well. Who, after all, is without
demons in some form? To laugh at the forces of anxiety,
terror, and madness, no matter how a culture expressed
them, was to declare oneself invulnerable to them—a dec-
laration, Gordon felt, that constituted a gilt-edged invitation to disaster.

Right now, this dark staff room, with its musty smell of
pedagogy, seemed inhabited by the spirits of severe old
missionaries prodding the air with red marking pens. Feeling restless and claustrophobic, Gordon walked out into
the sunlight toward the morning assembly.

* * *

The assembly grove was partially ringed with tall shaggy-
barked gum trees, and offered a long view of the plain that
sloped down from the school. Into the grove marched a
noisy crocodile of future leaders, bearing benches borrowed from the dining hall. Toward the end of the procession, chairs rode high on boys' heads. The chairs were for
the masters; the benches, arranged in three neat semicircles
facing the chairs, were for the boys.

When the masters entered, the boys grew silent and took
their seats. A prefect in a green blazer solemnly handed out
hymnals. Miss Stuart walked into the center of the grove,
and unfolded what looked like a large battered suitcase,
transforming it into a small pump organ. Everyone waited:
three rows of Africans, brown and green, facing a row of
Europeans, pale pink and mostly khaki. The land around
the grove was busy with the sounds of cocks crowing and
cattle mooing and people chopping wood, but here all was
orderly and still. The scene reminded Gordon of a print out
of the archaic history text he had been issued—a party of
English explorers and porters waiting in a bamboo courtyard for an audience with a tribal king. Only here, the king
was not African, the king was—here he was, striding into
the grove with his wife waddling behind—the headmaster.

Mr. Griffin, HM, was a large soft-looking man who
always wore a felt hat outdoors and, perhaps as a result,
was paler than one would have expected a career colonial
education officer to be. His wife was as round as he was,

but very much redder in the face. Her legs were so fat she
had difficulty walking; she spent most of her time in a
sitting position in the English country garden behind her
house. At the first staff meeting Gordon and Pamela had
attended, she had served the tea; so conscientious was she
at filling cups, whether they needed it or not, that the table
was a puddle of milky brown liquid before the meeting had
even gotten under way. The headmaster had welcomed the
two new teachers. He hoped everyone would make them
feel at home. The school had a long tradition of excellence
to uphold. Since Independence, of course, the tradition was
in danger of being eroded. Standards were declining. It was
all due to the ruling that the school could no longer recruit
teachers directly from the mission headquarters in London,
but had to accept whomever the government supplied. The
government was in the habit of supplying inexperienced
young teachers from the university in Karela. A neighboring school had got some Americans last year, and they
hadn't worked out at all. Hadn't a clue about local conditions, traditions, and standards of excellence. However, we
must work with what we have, he said somberly. A warm
welcome.

At assembly this morning, Mr. Griffin seemed quite
cheerful. Positioning himself in the shade, he removed his
hat and led the school in a short prayer. After the "Amens,"
he stroked his mustache and wished everyone a good
morning. "I believe we have some announcements." He
clasped his hands behind his back, a belly-out at-ease
position. "Miss Stuart?"

Miss Stuart, a woman with a drawn, no-nonsense face
and sensible walking shoes to match, stood up behind the
organ. She had been assigned to share her house with
Pamela, who was learning Kisemi from her as well as a
rigorously scheduled household routine. The two women
had invited Gordon and Clive Wickham-Marshall to dinner. Though Gordon had been grateful for the nourishing
food—sausages, mashed potatoes, and veg.—he couldn't
help feeling that Miss Stuart was watching him and Pamela
for a sign that some sort of depravity was going on between them. (Mr. Wickham-Marshall had prudently kept
his eyes lowered whenever he spoke to Pamela.) Now as
Miss Stuart addressed the assembly, her voice rang with

the authority that only piety, Gordon supposed, could bring to such people.

"I wish to remind the staff that the chamber music group will meet in the chapel Tuesday at eight o'clock sharp. Thank you." Miss Stuart sat down again.

More announcements followed, each master standing, saying his piece, and sitting down again. House football matches. Literature Club meeting (boys). Conservation Society meeting (staff). Rehearsal of Handel's *Messiah* (staff). Religious Discussion Evening topic: A Christian Education in a Corrupt Society (staff and boys).

This was going to be a busy week, Gordon thought. We're all like a big family, he had been told; we like to do things together, it's so necessary out here in the bush. The idea of "family" held no sanctity whatsoever for Gordon, but he supposed he could see their point. If he wanted to get along with them, he would have to participate in some activity too, though he couldn't imagine which one.

Some announcements from the headmaster: School blazers should not be left in the dining hall during football games. Any boy caught chasing a ball into a master's garden—particularly Mr. James's tomatoes, which were severely trampled yesterday—will find himself on the weekend clean-up squad.

The headmaster stepped forward. "I think that concludes —oh, yes, Mr. Longo."

Mr. Longo was the only African on the staff, a tall, vigorous-looking man who was both science and sports master. He didn't pop up like a puppet when called upon. He stood up slowly, and smiled. "I was listening to the wireless this morning, and I heard news that will interest you Bashiri students. Bashiri Party candidates were victorious in the two bi-elections in Lugogo South and the Rewa Hills districts yesterday."

The boys erupted into cheers and hissing, laughter and groaning.

Mr. Griffin turned sharply toward them, his forehead rippling. Silence.

"Mr. Longo, I believe we agreed to confine our announcements at assembly to the affairs of the school," he said.

"We did agree to that, *Bwana* Griffin," Mr. Longo replied. The sunlight winking on his shiny brown forehead gave him a mischievous look. "But I haven't come to the main part of my announcement."

Mr. Griffin clasped his hands tightly behind him. This was his school, but it was on Mr. Longo's continent. "Well, then, do proceed, *Bwana* Longo."

"Thank you." Mr. Longo bowed. "The Musolu Bashiri Student Association will hold its monthly meeting tonight in the dining hall. We will debate the issues raised in the recent elections. All Bashiri—and other—students are urged to attend. Plus, of course—" Mr. Longo smiled at the headmaster and the row of masters, "—all friends of *Uhuru ya Bashiri.*"

Gordon nodded. He had decided what activity to attend.

It was time for hymns and prayers. Mr. Longo's act was a hard one to follow, but Miss Stuart was up for the challenge. She peered chin-up over the organ until all traces of fidgeting ceased. Suddenly those knees that had been clamped so forbiddingly together began pumping frantically, as if she were riding a velocipede being pursued by bears. "Number 124!" she shouted, and a hundred hands fumbled through hymnals. The organ wheezed and hummed. The melody, minus some broken sharps and flats, fluted consumptively into the air.

Cracking boy sopranos and rumbling basses obliterated the melody and flushed a small flock of birds out of a nearby gum tree. But soon Miss Stuart's quavery mezzo was the loudest voice of all. She dragged the congregation along for three more hymns. The boys clutched their books and clenched their faces. There was not one in the lot who didn't look as if he fervently hoped the organ would explode from overpedaling.

"Thank you for helping to make a joyful noise unto the Lord," Miss Stuart said, finally resting the organ. "I'm sure Jesus has heard us, and that He will speak to us and bring us a message, if we can open our hearts to Him as we have our mouths." Her eyelids were half-closed, trembling. She had been brought up a Quaker, and favored silent prayers. "During the period of silence, if anyone hears a message from On High, or simply feels moved, I hope he will feel free to share that experience with us."

Silence in the grove. Many of the masters and some of the boys were sitting forward in their seats, eyes closed.

With all this tranquility about, Gordon reckoned that he ought to feel tranquil too. But it was hard. Long silences made him nervous, as if an enormous wave were hanging over him, about to break. The rare moments of serenity he had known had occurred in the midst of noisy crowds, like those in the dance halls of Karela. His total involvement with the sounds and human commotion around him freed him from his crippling awareness of himself, of his aloneness—he was not alone in these settings, he was part of something. Perhaps he had come to Africa to become part of something, something lasting, with such an overwhelmingly alien life of its own that it absorbed him, changed him, and freed him to become—what? He didn't know yet. But he would. All around him, lives were being transformed; everyone was caught up with the idealism of freedom, democracy, self-determination—words which in America could not be uttered without embarrassment or cynicism, but which in Africa seemed new. There was a role for him to play here.

Where? In this grove? No, this scene was a vestigial colonial tableau, the last of the past. He was on the edge of something but not quite there yet. Eventually the headmaster would be replaced, the mission-recruited teachers would be gone, and only those few whites committed to living in an independent African nation would remain. He would be one of them.

But now, he was fidgety. The silence was interminable. Surely he could learn to find some serenity in it, like the others. Shutting his eyes, he pictured Irena's crumbling summer house, the warm, soft lawn in the faintly buzzing heat of the afternoon. And Irena, lying beside the pool, sipping iced ouzo, reading poetry, her dark eyes glowing. Irena, turning onto her belly, pointing her red toenails to the sky, staring vacantly into the pool. The pool: a great empty pit in the lawn, cement cracks zigzagging along the bottom, oily-stemmed weeds and bramble bushes sprouting from the cracks. The elephant trap, he and Irena called it. She read from his notebook:

> I dream of wild animals thrashing
> In the tar of night.
> Their tangled screams sink in the darkness.
> What will become of us?

Irena read her own melancholy poems, the verses bouncing sonorously off the six-foot markers. Grinning, she lay on her back, and shut her eyes slowly.

He watched her: an old fantasy. Her lips partially opened, drawing in long streams of air and fluttering them out again to set the leaves overhead in whispering motion. Her hair was damp and cool in his fingers. He slid a strand of it down her chest, tucked it beneath her halter and held her breast in his hand. She pressed his hand, then moved it to her belly, pushing it gently down past her navel, and left it under the top of her jeans as she unsnapped them for him. Down into the soft damp fur that pushed up against his hand . . . he felt the lips opening against his fingers, he touched the warmth and moistness of her and watched her roll against his hand, squeezing it, turning her head so that her breath flowed hot against his groin. . . .

Gordon blinked hard and crossed his legs, glancing around. No one was looking at him. The boys shifted positions in their chairs; the masters sighed. Miss Stuart's legs remained poised but motionless at the pedals of the organ. Her eyes were still closed in prayer. Or had she died sitting there?

Gordon folded his hands over his full lap. So much for idealism, poetry, serenity. He shut his eyes and concentrated on the antierotic image of Miss Stuart. She was pumping her knees again. Her legs moved slowly at first, then faster and faster until they were a blur. The organ propelled her slowly from the ground in a crescendo of chords; she floated above the treetops toward the heavens. The clouds parted; angels in oxfords and starched white wings glided on golden sunbeams to lift her into the midst of their orchestra. The other masters were pulled up behind her, their chairs falling away as they rose. The headmaster floated up like a blimp. His wife paddled happily beside him in the blue air. The lot of them disappeared behind fluffy white gates. Cheers broke through the grove; schoolboys ran about on the grass, kicking footballs into tomato patches. Gordon wandered smiling in their midst. . . .

The girl with the enormous eyes, Adija, was wandering with him. Her footsteps were light on the grass, her voice rang with laughter. There was no awkwardness between them now, no painful hesitancy. Their gestures—"Come in out of the rain," "Let me serve you tea"—were more eloquent than thousands of pages of words. Those primitive motions of his became ideas that she grasped like treasures. Adija . . . standing in the rain on his doorstep, shy and frail and blindingly beautiful . . . not turning away to run slap slap through the mud, but bursting through the translucent curtain of rain into his arms. In the warmth of his kitchen fire, he peeled off her wet clothes, dried her gently with the towel she'd brought back to him, kissed her cool brown skin as he stroked the cloth over her. You make me happy, she said in the movements of her body. Her nipples rose against his lips, her arms encircled his neck. On the bed with her, he pulled up the blanket and buried the two of them beneath the soft silence of cotton. As the storm crashed down on the house, hammering on the tin roof and streaming past the windows, they lay safe and dry and warm, holding each other . . .

Serenity.

The schoolboys on their benches were looking nervously about. Gordon sat up straight, blinking. In the shaggy branches of the gum trees a breeze was stirring, causing the leaves to rustle with a sound remarkably like that of falling rain. Three birds soared across the bright blue sky, wings flapping slowly. They were cranes, the national birds of Marembo. As they flew closer, some of the masters looked up, smiling at the grace of their flight. Messengers from Heaven, perhaps, bearing glad tidings for the faithful.

The boys looked up too. As one of the birds glided over, they ducked down, covering their heads with their hands. Stifled laughter rippled along the rows.

The masters did not cover their heads, though they looked as if they wanted to. Several cast worried glances at the headmaster, hoping to see him take appropriate action. The bird approached again.

This species, Gordon remembered, was for all its beautiful plumage, a very ornery bird. It liked nothing better than to—

Yes, there—to leave its message: a greenish white glob splattered on the organ.

The headmaster rose from his chair. "I believe we have trespassed into the territory of another of God's creatures," he said. "And we are not being forgiven our trespasses."

The grove rang with laughter. Even Miss Stuart was smiling grimly. The HM beamed at her: Good sport, Miss Stuart; close call, what?

Everyone ran for cover.

6

WHEN SALOME OPENED HER EYES, THE SUN-
light was already glowing fiery orange in the cracks around
her window. The thin square of wood was the door of a furnace, the furnace was the whole outdoors, and it made her
room hotter than a chamber of Hell. And emptier. The
weird daytime semi-darkness intensified the emptiness.

Salome rapped on the partition between her room and
Adija's, as she had done every morning this week. Each
time she had been sure she would hear nothing but a
vacant echo of her fists against wood, but each morning
she had heard Adija's bed creak, the sounds of her blankets
being pushed aside, and the voice of Adija, yawning, chattering, laughing.

Today, no sound came from the other side of the partition. Salome stared at the rough boards, then pressed her
face down into her mattress, her eyes burning.

Before Adija, she had awakened alone and empty—that
was life. But her emptiness now was a silence shrieking to
be filled. She was no longer content to be alone.

Salome stared at the ceiling. A gecko lizard clung there,
upside down and motionless. Salome moved, and the lizard
vanished into the room behind the top of the partition. She
felt sick with sorrow. Like that lizard that scurried along
walls and ceilings, Adija was frail and soft. For all the
gracefulness of her walk, she had nowhere to go. She was
scurrying about nervously from place to place, pricked by
fright as the gecko was by shadows jumping up behind it.
But unlike that creature, she could not change her color
to blend in with things around her, no matter how hard she
tried. Adija blended with nothing, she rhymed with no one.
Salome wanted to weep for Adija, but there had been no
moisture in her since the death of her child years ago.

Dressed, she stumbled out into the sunlight, and immediately felt foolish. The street and the shops were all still there, and so probably was Adija. Salome had merely overslept—her brains had been broiling in that hot little room of hers.

And there, around the corner from her room, was Adija, sitting on the curb outside the New Life. Salome rubbed her eyes. She approached Adija slowly, cautiously. How pale the girl looked in the morning sunlight, especially in that purple saree. Didn't she know how mad she looked, her bare feet stretching into the street, right in the middle of the village—and dressed in a purple saree?

"What are you doing out here?" Salome demanded groggily.

Adija looked up and smiled. "Just sitting. Waiting."

"For what—your European, the one who was going to give you a job last week?"

"No." Adija glanced down. "He can't have a young African girl for a housegirl. The other teachers would think bad things about him. That's why he couldn't hire me. I'm not really so stupid that I'm ignorant of that."

Salome nodded. "So? . . ."

"I was thinking about what you were telling me last night."

"I don't remember what I said. I was drunk," Salome said quickly.

"I know." Adija laughed. "You were asleep when I got up and went to my room."

That's why I was cooking in my own pot of sorrow this morning, Salome thought, but she kept silent.

"I was thinking I could stay here with you. I could work in the bar." Adija gazed at Salome, her eyes too huge and bright for a hangover morning. "This place is not so bad—if you still want me to stay. Do you?"

Silence sizzled in the street like Salome's headache. "Let me think about it," she mumbled.

Salome tried hard to think. But the matter was not for thinking. Her brain was charred. The decision had already been made elsewhere. "Come on," she told Adija, and took her across the street to the shop of Patel, the New Life's co-owner.

"Listen to me, you speckled old miser," she said to Patel

in her loud voice. She called him speckled because his brown cheeks were mottled with age. "This girl is the daughter of an Indian merchant. In his youth, he told her mother stories of his wealth, and then he abandoned the poor creature."

Patel shrank back behind the counter.

"She could be your own daughter!" Salome insisted.

"No, no! You must not talk in this way!" Patel shook his finger at Salome, glancing about nervously. His wife was somewhere nearby. "I never do those things in my youth. Always I am honorable man!"

"Forgive me, Uncle." Salome's voice was subdued, but her eyes still glinted mischievously. "I only wanted you to take pity on her and give her a job. I know you are honorable."

Patel glanced at Adija in her saree, shook his head, then busied himself arranging spools of thread along the counter. "Is impossible. Impossible," he muttered.

Salome pretended not to hear. "You're so honorable, you make me want to be honorable too."

"What?"

"Yes, when the taxman comes this year, I will be honorable, and I'll tell him that I don't own all the New Life, only part of it."

Patel looked up from his spools of thread, his forehead wrinkled.

" 'Who owns the other half?' the taxman will ask me," Salome continued. " 'Why, *Bwana* Patel, the old gentleman who has the shop across the street,' I will say. 'He is a modest man, Mr. Patel—he doesn't want anyone to know how rich he is.' "

Patel leaned over the counter, his face close to Salome's. "Keep quiet your nonsense, woman!" Then he straightened into a dignified pose. "Taxman you speak of, he will want to know why your taxes, you don't pay," he said, smiling smugly.

"Oh, no. You don't understand. The taxman, my friend Cyrus Kaplanget, he pays tax to me!"

"For what, he does that?"

"For this." Salome smoothed her skirt down over the V of her lower abdomen. "Kaplanget keeps an account in my bank," she said. Adija hid her face against Salome's shoulder to keep from laughing. "His money is the same color as mine, you see. He doesn't have to go to Exchange Control to get permission to change it into rupees."

Patel's eyes throbbed. The mention of Exchange Control sent a cold sweat creeping up the back of his neck. What the tax people would do to him was nothing compared to what Exchange Control would do if it discovered how much money he had been sending out of the country illegally. Uhuru for Marembo, what a curse! It had forced him to do business with a black woman who practically showed her private parts in public.

"This girl wants twenty shillings advance, and forty a week to start," Salome said.

"Thieves," Patel moaned. "I am beset by thieves."

"You won't regret it, Uncle. Everyone in Musolu will come to the New Life to see the new barmaid. We'll be rich."

Patel heaved his rounded shoulders. It was true, he had to admit. Of course, Salome would skim off most of the profits herself. But then she would be able to buy him out sooner. Why hadn't she pointed that out to him at the beginning? No, she just enjoyed tormenting a poor old man.

"Yes, yes, all right." He smiled with great effort, showing his teeth. They were stained and uneven like the fragments of old china people cemented on the tops of walls to keep robbers out. "I am happy for you; you have found a sister, someone to talk with while you working so hard." Patel looked paternally at Adija, who had stopped hiding her face behind Salome's shoulder. "You will be more happy in your work, Salome."

"And you as well, I think."

Patel frowned, puzzled. "Why?"

"Because you can gaze at her and dream of your honorable youth."

"Get out! Leave me!" Patel yanked his tin money box from beneath the counter and pulled out a twenty-shilling note. "Here, girl. May the gods protect you from this fanged hippopotamus!" Patel turned and hurried away.

"You made him angry," Adija said.

"Nonsense. I'm the only entertainment he has in this bush town." Salome handed Adija a key. "Open the bar—

the back door—and you'll find a pot, charcoals, some coffee. Make us some coffee—I'm sick of tea every morning." She took Adija's hand and squeezed it into a fist around the twenty-shilling note. "And don't lose this today."

Salome watched Adija cross the street. Then she ducked behind the counter and stepped into the back of the shop. She perched herself before Patel on his high stool. "I have something here that you will like," she said, and reached down into her bodice.

"If I want melons, I can buy at market."

"Buy them with this." Salome removed a thick wad of bills, and dropped it into Patel's hands.

Patel counted the bills off the top, his chubby fingers caressing them as he laid them down one by one on his desk. He and Salome then went over the books of the New Life, figuring profits and expenses into two ledgers, the one Patel kept in his desk and the one he kept hidden beneath the floorboards of his parlor.

Today she gave Patel all of her share of the cash. Between them they had enough for a new Mercedes Benz. The shillings would be exchanged for American dollars by a cousin of Patel's, who would buy the car at almost half price. The Mercedes would then be driven into the Congo and be sold at a huge profit. The Congolese francs, though worthless outside the country, bought a great many black market diamonds in Katanga Province. Patel's cousin would fly back from Katanga to Azima with the diamonds and sell them to a British jeweler for pounds sterling, some of which would be airmailed inside an *Africa's Wildlife* magazine to another Patel cousin in Bombay, and some of which would be converted back into African shillings and returned to Salome. Salome kept the shillings in a hollowed-out rafter above her head. She had been part owner of three Mercedes Benzes in the past two years, though she could not have passed a driving test if the examiner had been her own brother.

Her business concluded, Salome crossed the street to the New Life. Adija had bought a pineapple and a cardboard container of milk for the coffee.

"How much did you pay for that milk?" Salome demanded.

"Seventy cents."

"I get milk for twenty cents a quart, not seventy cents for one of those paper things."

"Oh. Where do you get it?"

"A man who keeps cattle brings it to me. Why do you pay to have them send it to factories to have the taste taken out of it? That milk is for Europeans and African politicians who are afraid of catching African diseases."

"I only got it for you," Adija said. "I don't use it in coffee."

Salome knocked open one of the shutters with the handle of her machete. "Yes, you coast people drink your coffee black as mud."

"Are you angry?"

"No, no. I bought a motorcar this morning. I'm always nervous when I buy a motorcar."

"Truly. You have one?"

"I'm only joking." Salome tossed the machete onto the bar. "You mustn't believe everything I say."

* * *

There was a lot of work to be done in the bar. The meat and chapathis had to be fried, the eggs boiled, the tea made, the beer transferred from the cases to the shelves, the mugs washed, the floor swept. But Salome couldn't remember a morning that had gone by so fast since she had arrived in Musolu. She started scrubbing down the tables; by the time she had finished, Adija had swept the floor and started the fire without even being asked to. The bar was ready to open an hour early.

Adija sat at one of the tables, drinking beer and tucking her hair up under her orange plastic comb. She didn't look up when the first customers came in. The two men sat at their table watching her until she rose to serve them.

"Two beers?" she asked, smiling down vaguely at them. "Yes."

"Pilsner or Tusker or Guinness?"

"Two Tusker."

"Some lunch?"

The men shook their heads. "Who are you?" one asked.

"I am Adija. I work here now."

"Hello, Adija."

"Hello. You don't want chapathis?"

"No. Are you Indian or Moslem?"

"I am from the Coast. I am African." Adija's smile grew vaguer. Her eyes darted around the room. "Two Tusker, then," she said and returned quickly to the bar, her bare feet padding against the cement.

Soon Adija was carrying trays of chapathis and beer to all corners of the room, scurrying here and there with her saree streaming out behind her like the plumage of a bright tropical bird. Her vague smile remained nailed tight to her face. Her eyes did not meet those of her customers for longer than the flicker of a giggle, when their greetings amused her for some reason. Often she served one kind of beer when another had been asked for, but the men were too busy watching her to notice. Her pure coastal Kisemi discouraged them from trying to communicate their hunger for more than food and drink to her. They spoke rough fragmentary Kisemi, and felt unsure of themselves. They were rural people: farmers, hawkers, helpers at the dispensary, road workers, assorted local bus passengers; the sight of an African-looking girl with long wavy hair and a saree was sufficient to stun them into quizzical silence.

Not everyone, however, was silent. "I feel a fresh, cool breeze in this stagnant hole," said Simon Waga, in English. Waga was the nurse in charge of the local dispensary. He wrote poetry and applications to foreign medical schools in his spare time. "What enchanted breeze has carried you to this unwholesome place?" he asked Adija.

"I don't speak English," she said in Kisemi, tapping her fingers on her tray.

Waga translated his question, tugging at his goatee in discomfort. His poetic language sounded awkward in Kisemi.

"Ah." Adija nodded. "Well, I didn't come on a breeze. I came on the Jinjeh bus."

"Jinjeh Adija," Waga said, smiling. His homophone of "ginger" was lost to everyone but himself, but he laughed anyway. At first it was a sad laugh—this girl was too ignorant to appreciate him—but it ended on a happy note, for he saw that she was pleased by his unusual greeting. "A Guinness," he told her. Though Tusker was all he could usually afford, he was in a mood to celebrate something.

Martin Elima, the Chief of Police for the district, came

in at midday. Dark and burly, his muscles rippled visibly beneath his gray uniform shirt and short trousers, as he strode to his favorite table by the window. The other men greeted him, and no one laughed when he opened his mouth to show two long protruding front teeth. The teeth were like the cowcatcher of a powerful locomotive—something you didn't get in the way of. "I see Swila Number 101 has arrived," he said, addressing Adija and gathering some laughter from nearby tables. He called himself Swila Number 1, and gave numbers to whomever he happened to be drinking with. "101" was the number he gave to people he was meeting for the first time. He didn't usually give women numbers at all, but Adija was an exception because of her appearance.

"The only Swila in this town are the bandits on your police force," Salome said, stepping beside Adija. She kept her voice cheerful, but she was uneasy. People not in on Elima's tired joke might really think Adija was a Northerner and a rebel spy.

"Until last week, I didn't know what a Swila was," Adija said.

"Welcome to the Swila," Elima said. "We are all Swila here. Your friend Salome is the biggest of the lot."

Salome swelled out her chest. Elima roared with laughter. Salome pretended to smile, and disappeared.

Adija turned to go fetch him a plate, but Salome had already done so. When Elima wanted lunch, he got it free —one of the courtesies Patel and Salome extended him in return for his staying out of their affairs. "He likes you," Salome said.

Adija wrinkled her nose.

"You can refuse him, but don't insult him," Salome warned. "He's dangerous."

Though the New Life was crowded at lunch time, it emptied quickly afterwards. Salome had to preside over an empty room all afternoon. She stood in the doorway staring out into the street.

When Adija asked her what the people of this region were like, Salome merely shrugged. "They are just peasants, village people," she said. "They're like the people of my home village in Bashiri. Just raising crops and families and growing old and dying."

"Still, their lives are not bad," Adija said.

"Not bad," Salome said. She watched a man walking up the street. He wore a ragged shirt and short trousers that had been repaired many times. His feet were red-brown from walking in the dirt. "I might have married a man like that. It was my mother's wish."

"Why didn't you?"

"I was in school. Then the war came . . ." Salome's voice faded.

"Then you went to the city, I think. Afterward, you couldn't go back to the country again."

"Something like that," Salome said. "You know, Ambani, who owns that bar you were fighting in, he can go to anyone's farm and eat with the people. He knows them, and speaks their language. Myself, I know three languages —Samoyo, Kisemi, and English. Yet the only place I can go with them is to the city—where no one will feed you or speak to you, unless he's trying to take something from you."

"That man, Jeremiah. He speaks your language. Is he Samoyo?"

"Half. Part of his family is Rukiva. They live near here, just across the border. He is always wanting me to come with him to visit them. He wants to impress them that he has an educated woman."

"But you won't go with him?"

Salome sighed. "Someday I will, probably. Just to get out of this town."

Adija nodded. "My village looked different from this one," she said. "The earth wasn't red, it was sandy. There were palm trees, and the ocean. I used to play by the ocean. It was lovely sometimes."

"I was in Mirini," Salome said. "It's hot there."

"I didn't live in Mirini. Just nearby," Adija said. "When my mother took me to Mirini, I was very frightened. All the people, and the motorcars, and the men at the docks rolling big black drums down the ramps from the ships. The drums made a sound like thunder. I wanted to go home. But when I was home, I got bored with my village. I used to think: In Mirini, it will be better. People won't call me a slave girl because my mother was housegirl to an Arab. I won't be called a savage because I'm not a Moslem. So when my mother died, I went to live in Mirini. I was still frightened of the place. But I stayed." Adija laughed. "I stayed until I left."

"I wonder how long you'll stay here," Salome said, glancing at her.

"I don't know. How can one know that?"

Salome drank her beer in silence. There was no answer to that question. She gazed outside and tried to let the familiar emptiness seep into her like mildew. A dog lay sprawled in the street, motionless, as if crushed by the heat. No breeze stirred the dust or flapped the clothes hanging still in the shop doorways. Four old motorcars, round-topped Peugeots and Fiats, lay pointing into the curb like pigs asleep at a trough. Today, Salome could not lose herself in the town's monotony; it troubled her as never before. Adija wouldn't take long to grow restless in this town.

Salome suddenly stepped out of the doorway and crossed the street. In a few minutes, she returned with a large cardboard box.

"What have you got?" Adija asked.

"Just something to amuse you. Look." Salome pointed to the picture on the box.

"A wireless! Is there really a wireless inside?"

"Open it and see."

"Oh!" Adija tugged open the flaps on the top of the box.

"Take it out."

"Oh, no. I might break it. It's too expensive."

Salome pulled the wireless out. It was a red Japanese transistor with a big dial and many buttons and knobs on the front. "This is to keep you from getting too bored here," she said.

Adija touched one of the knobs cautiously. "It's very beautiful."

"You can learn to play it. It has stations in Cairo, Peking, London, Addis Ababa—anywhere you want to listen to."

"My god!" Adija whispered, one of the few English expressions she knew. She felt the smoothness of the plastic, and ran her fingers along the copper grill of the speaker. "You just decided to buy it? Just now?"

Salome smiled. "I didn't buy it. I made Patel give it to us for the bar. To bring in more customers. But really, we can play it whenever we like."

"Show me how it works!"

The wireless filled the New Life with its singing and talking and squealing. Adija couldn't keep it on one station for more than a minute, even if she liked the music there. There were so many different things to hear. She kept the bands gliding up and down the dial all afternoon.

Toward evening, Salome wandered back from the doorway and said, "I think I saw your European. He was sitting on the hood of a car, waiting for some teachers."

Adija raced to the door. There he was, getting into a car with some men in short khaki trousers. They must have been shopping. She'd missed him! If only she hadn't been playing with that wireless, she might have gone and greeted him in the shop! She could have pretended to buy something. Still, she could wave now. She started to raise her hand, but dropped it. He was talking in English to the men in the car. They were laughing together, and the Gordon teacher wasn't looking out into the street. The engine started, and the car rolled away. Adija returned to her table and flopped into her chair. She wanted to kick the wireless across the room.

"Was that his car?" Salome asked.

"No, it must belong to another teacher. He doesn't have a car. He has a bicycle."

"A bicycle." Salome shook her head. "Pardon me if I laugh."

Adija turned away. What if she had gone to greet him in the shop—what would she have done then? Well, she could have invited him into the New Life for a beer. But he probably didn't drink. A Fanta, then. No, he couldn't have come in, with those other missionary teachers with him. Adija knew what missionaries thought of places like the New Life and the women who worked in them.

Adija fiddled with the dials of the wireless again. It had so many different languages on it, but none of them were hers. She recognized an English-language station; the words were as incomprehensible as those of the languages she couldn't identify. If only she knew English! She was about to switch off the stupid box when she found a

Kisemi station. She stared at the dial, concentrating on the words of the song to distract herself.. The song was called "My Lovely Elizabeth"; in her last job, she had used the name Elizabeth and imagined that several boys in Jinjeh were thinking of her when they heard the lyrics:

> I am deeply worried at heart
> For the one I love so well
> She has gone from me
> Now I scarcely know what to do
> I just hang my head and cry
> For my lovely E-liz-a-beth.

But those boys were just town louts, and this Gordon was a teacher, and a kind man—he would never beat her, like they would have done.

But why did he ride a bicycle, as if he were a town-lout?

Maybe because he didn't want to behave like a big-man. He was one of those Christians the missionaries had told her about, who lay aside their worldly possessions and live a life of serving others. She didn't know why anyone would want to do that, but it was supposed to be a very good thing to do. Yes, she should admire him for having only a tinny, bumpy, cheap old bicycle. Her mind wandered with the music.

Perhaps he could only afford a bicycle because he had to send money to his wife and children in his country. Or perhaps he had a girlfriend who made him buy expensive clothes. Adija would never do that to him. But what did it matter? He was never going to buy her things. She'd throw them back in his face if he tried! She didn't need a European to buy her the things she wanted. Look, she'd been in this town only a week and already she had a big new wireless that must have cost hundreds—thousands!— of shillings. There were plenty of Africans nowadays with as much money as Europeans. Look at Salome. And she was just a woman! Adija forced a smile at the wireless. She didn't need that European.

What did she need? She must need something, because she was constantly feeling a terrible lack this past week. Lack. It was an awful sensation that didn't seem to have anything to do with things she might want, but was just . . .

lack, a feeling that descended upon her like a thick, hot blanket, stinging her eyes and catching dryly in her throat and making the inside of her skin smart so much she couldn't sit still. Adija turned up the music. She rested her head on her arm, with her ear next to the speaker. Electric guitar notes twanged into her like bullets, almost obliterating her longing.

7

"RISE AND SHINE! LET'S GO! EVERYBODY UP!"
The housemaster's voice resounded beneath the roof and bounced back with an absurd tinny ring. Gordon paced up and down between the row of beds in the dormitory as if trying to escape the sound. He was aware of sullen glances shooting up at him from the pillows as he passed. These were not just schoolboys who came packaged in uniforms, arranged themselves into rows, and turned out homework assignments; they were people who looked scruffy and swollen-eyed and nappy-haired at six-thirty in the morning and did not enjoy having a loud foreigner see them that way.

Hearing the lack of enthusiasm in their housemaster's voice, the students rolled over for a few extra minutes of sleep. That morning, Tembo House was late to breakfast. Gordon's boys had to run from the dining hall, still chewing their porridge, to take their seats at assembly. The headmaster waited, frowning. He drummed his fingers on the cover of his Bible until everyone was still.

"Is Tembo House a house of *wanafunzi*," he asked, "or of *washenzi*?"

Silence. The boys of Tembo House stared down at the ground and shuffled their feet. Some looked about to weep, others ready to kill.

"What's he saying?" Gordon whispered to Clive Wickham-Marshall.

"*Wanafunzi* is 'students,' *washenzi* means 'savages,' 'uncivilized ones'—there's nothing they hate being called more. He really shouldn't use that word."

"From where I stand," Mr. Griffin continued, "I count five boys who don't seem to be sure what they are, *wanafunzi* or *washenzi*. The top parts of them are in uniform. The bottom parts—the feet, to be exact—are not." The headmaster drummed his Bible, deliberating. "Very well. We'll not waste any more time on it now. Will the Tembo House prefect please take down the names of all barefoot boys and give the list to Mr. Lockery following assembly."

During the morning break, Gordon was summoned to the headmaster's office. "There's no doubt in my mind that they're trying to take advantage of your not being familiar with the routine," Mr. Griffin said, furrowing his brow behind his spectacles. "They'll have to learn that when they test you out, they have to pay the consequences."

"I'd forgotten that the boy who wakes them up—that he was away from the school," Gordon said. He stood stiffly in front of the headmaster's desk. "I should have appointed someone to wake them up in his place. I wasn't there early enough myself."

"Nonetheless, they were late, and sloppy." The headmaster narrowed his eyes at Gordon. "Discipline must follow."

"I realize that. I'm going to meet with them tonight."

"The punishment is automatic in cases like this. Those boys, the ones on your list, will be working in the school garden Saturday morning. We've some tomatoes that want weeding." Mr. Griffin pulled some papers toward him across the desk—a gesture of dismissal.

Gordon didn't move. "You appointed me housemaster. It seems to me I should be in charge of discipline."

"I told you, the punishment's automatic. You be the one to assign them to the garden."

Gordon paced to the window and stared out at the boys walking toward the classroom buildings. He heard the sound of Mr. Griffin's pen scratching against paper, and suddenly felt himself trembling. He turned and stared at the headmaster until he looked up from his papers.

"I'm not going to assign them to the garden," Gordon said.

"What?" Mr. Griffin glared at Gordon over the tops of his spectacles. "You don't like the way we run things at this school, do you?"

"That's not what I said."

"Well, like it or not, these rules were here long before you were. And I'm still in charge."

Gordon noticed that the headmaster's cheeks were suddenly splotchy red. "If you order me to assign the boys to

work in the garden," he said, "then I'm going to work there
with them."

"Good heavens!" Mr. Griffin's pen seemed to squirt out
of his fingers. He gathered it in and buried it beneath both
hands on his blotter. "We cannot have masters down on
their hands and knees in the dirt along with the boys—
especially those on punishment. You're mad."

"The hell I am."

"I didn't mean that literally." The headmaster cleared his
throat. "You'll have to learn to control your language
around here."

"I'm sorry." Gordon sat down in the chair opposite Mr.
Griffin. He could see the headmaster had been thrown off
by the apology. "I propose to hold a house meeting tonight, and discuss what we can do to make sure this
doesn't happen again," Gordon said, thinking fast. "I'll be
sending the boys to bed fifteen minutes early tonight. I'll
let them know that if they're late for assembly tomorrow,
they'll be in bed an hour early tomorrow. If that doesn't
work—then I'll see about something more drastic."

The headmaster looked dubious, but he was listening.
All the bluster seemed to have gone out of him.

"I appreciate what you say about discipline," Gordon
continued, "and I intend that Tembo House has as much
of it as necessary. But I'm not going to be unfair to those
kids, especially not right at the beginning of my term as
housemaster. Can you appreciate that?"

"Mn." The headmaster pushed his spectacles higher up
on his nose. "Mn," he said again. "And how much discipline do you believe is necessary, Mr. Lockery?"

"I'll have to find that out."

"You have a lot of things to find out." The headmaster
uncovered his pen and drummed it. "And what are we to
do in the meantime—let the boys run around the place
looking like ragamuffins?"

"No. I don't intend to let that happen."

"We'll see. You go ahead and have your 'house meeting.'
You're new here. You have to learn things for yourself."

"Yes."

"But I'm telling you, I don't want to hear any more
Bolshy ideas about masters working in the school garden. I
don't intend to let that happen, I can assure you."

"It's not my favorite way of spending Saturday mornings," Gordon said, and tried to smile, but it was much too late. Mr. Griffin turned his face away from the smile as if it were a mouthful of saliva. Gordon stood up. "I have a class," he said.

The headmaster shuffled his papers.

Gordon fumed all day. He felt that if he complained to the other teachers he saw in the staff room, they would stare at him uneasily, as if he were taking off his clothes in public. After his last class, he found his way to Mr. Longo's house. It looked identical to Gordon's, with gray cinderblock walls, linoleum floors, and government-issued green couch and armchair in the sitting room. Mr. Longo had tacked a Bashiri flag and some party posters to the wall and laid a bright yellow sisal mat on the floor, which made the house a little more cheerful-looking than Gordon's.

"Do you want some beer?" Mr. Longo asked him, when he'd sat down. Gordon had been the only master to show up at the Bashiri Student Association debate, and Mr. Longo was glad to see him today. "Or have you become an Englishman and prefer tea?"

"No, beer would be great. Thanks very much," Gordon said.

"If my wife were here, she'd think us both uncivilized," Mr. Longo said from the kitchen, taking two bottles of Tusker from the paraffin refrigerator. "But you look like a man who could use a drink."

"I am," Gordon said. When he told him about his confrontation with the headmaster, Longo (as Gordon was invited to call him) nodded eagerly throughout. Encouraged, Gordon continued to unburden himself. Why, simply because he hadn't been willing to parade around the dormitory like a drill sergeant inspecting each boy, should his kids have been humiliated like that in assembly? What was so damn important about wearing shoes, anyway? The boys went barefoot the first fourteen or so years of their lives. They went barefoot playing football in the afternoons at school, didn't they? And what was this *wanafunzi-washenzi* shit? It sounded like the boys were being systematically conditioned to disassociate themselves from the very people who had brought them up and who were now breaking their necks to earn their school fees for them back on the farm. No wonder the university students in

Karela had behaved like aristocrats—snapping their fingers at waiters, ordering taxi drivers to pick up girls for them along the roadside. In a country that was almost entirely agricultural, its future leaders were being trained to feel that agricultural work—the school punishment garden—was a shameful activity, that getting one's hands dirty was degrading. This was nation-building? Who ate the goddamn tomatoes, anyway? Gordon had never seen them in the dining hall. Maize, yes; beans, yes; but no tomatoes. And why didn't some of the other masters speak up?

Gordon took a long slug of beer and sat back, shaking his head.

"Griffin handpicked his teachers," Longo said. "He found people who are afraid to stand up to him. We must be a little patient, unfortunately. Griffin's recruits will start to go soon, after he does."

"I can imagine how he recruited them," Gordon said.

"How?"

"Well, he had them line up outside his office and he told them, 'We want to make sure you all have normal body temperatures, and since I have to be absolutely precise about it, I want you all to lower your trousers, gentlemen, and bend over. I will be coming round with a thermometer.' And those who were gullible and passive enough to take it, they got hired."

Longo laughed, holding his glass tight to keep from spilling his beer. "If you were recruiting, you'd select the ones who refused?"

"It's not my kind of test," Gordon said. "I just made it up."

Longo was still laughing. "You're very hard on these poor English."

"I was just angry." Gordon smiled into his glass. "I feel better now."

Longo watched him. He was not used to this sort of teacher. He was delighted to meet one, but a little uneasy as well. "You were clever, threatening to work in the garden with your boys."

"Clever?"

"Well, you wouldn't actually have done that, would you?"

"Of course I would have."

"Oh." Longo nodded slowly. Now he knew why he'd been uneasy.

"Wouldn't you?" Gordon asked, and immediately wished he hadn't, seeing the look on Longo's face.

"I understand that in China the teachers and students work in the fields together sometimes." Longo gave him a politician's smile. "Does that happen in America too?"

"Not that I know of." Gordon shrugged. "It doesn't matter. No one's going to work in the garden this Saturday, me or them."

"Good." Longo stood up and went to the refrigerator again. He returned with two more bottles, looking cheerful. "The best we can do here is teach our classes and run our houses. Ignore the colonialists. Their day is past. But we have to keep them around a little longer until we have our own people trained."

"I understand," Gordon said. "I'm too damn impatient."

"Let's drink to impatience," Longo said, filling his glass. Gordon lifted his glass, and drained it.

＊　＊　＊

On his way to his evening meeting in the dormitory, Gordon heard music coming from Miss Stuart's house, and passed by to look in the window. The room inside was silvery bright with the glare of pressure lanterns; the faces of the singers, arranged in a tight group, were intensely bleached, as if caught in the perpetual flash of a photographic strobe. Behind the house, jagged silhouettes of banana trees waved slowly in the breeze against a dark purple sky.

From where he stood, Gordon could see Clive Wickham-Marshall, who had especially invited him to attend, standing beside Pamela; both were holding sheet music out before their mouths and enunciating the words with enthusiastic lip movements. They glanced at each other frequently, suppressing smiles. Mr. and Mrs. Griffin stood behind them, with no smiles to suppress; their eyebrows rose in unison every time they hit a high note. Everyone's brow was beaded in perspiration. "Ah-le-lu-lyah! Ah-le-lu-lyah!" they all sang, and the house seemed to reverberate with joyful noise and high spirits. Gordon walked by slowly feeling a little envious, and simultaneously glad that he had a house meeting to attend.

The boys were in a boisterous mood, as if the unpleasantness at the morning assembly had never happened. They liked Gordon's suggestions about electing officers to be responsible for running the dormitory, and took a long time nominating candidates, establishing duties, and setting up rules. When the meeting finally ended, the boys invited Gordon to stay a while.

"Sit here, sir," one boy said, making room for him on a bed where several boys were sitting. "We want to ask you a question."

"Okay."

"Do you know Greek history?"

"A little." Gordon grinned. "Why?"

"We saw a film here last month. The mobile film unit brought it," the boy said.

"It was called *Helen of Troy*," another boy chimed in, and everyone wanted to talk at once.

"The Greek soldiers were carrying women on trays!"

"Those women were wearing very little clothes!" Much laughter.

"There were men fighting with spears, sir, like Africans."

"But they were having feathers in their hats."

"Helmets, not hats, useless boy!"

"They were fighting a war about a woman named Helen."

"Why were they killing each other because of a woman? Women are not so important as that."

"I would put a spear through you if I could have one like that woman in the film!"

"You are too puny to even lift a spear."

"Really, sir, was that woman a witch? There was one man in the film who was ever looking bewitched."

Gordon nodded. "I never thought of it like that, but perhaps—"

"It was a very interesting film." Someone pushed the boy who had asked about witchcraft off the end of the bed. There was much laughter as he landed on the floor, his feet flying up.

"Can you teach us Greek history in class, sir?"

"No, just make the van bring us more films about Helen!"

"I'll see what I can do," Gordon said.

The discussion continued, in horny-hilarious boarding-school fashion, until the ten o'clock drum boomed out from the next-door house. Everyone heard it, and conversations died down. A few students went to their beds and lay down, but most stayed where they were, watching the housemaster's face. He did not look pleased.

"Listen, we established at the beginning of the meeting that you guys were to go to bed fifteen minutes early," he said, standing up. "I've enjoyed talking to you, but you had the clock facing you, and you should have broken up earlier."

Silence.

"Okay, I won't make a big deal out of it tonight. But let's get to bed now."

"Sir, can we be excused from assembly tomorrow?" a boy asked.

"What?"

The boy covered a grin with his hand. "We don't like all that praying. Do you like it, sir?"

"I think a certain gossip has been at work among you." Gordon looked around for Pius the Pagan, but didn't spot him. "Anyway, the answer is no, you cannot be excused from assembly."

"But why?"

"You cannot be excused from assembly. Forget it." Gordon stepped out into the aisle to address everyone. "This morning, several of you got into trouble—and got the house in trouble—for not wearing shoes. All of you got the headmaster angry for being late to assembly. Now you want to know if you can be excused . . ." Gordon paused. What to say next? "You chose to come to this school, and when you did, you knew that you had to do what the school told you to do, if you wanted an education. Whether you like the rules or not—that's not the question. What's important is—"

What the hell was he saying?

What's important is that you don't give me a hard time and make me look bad, was what he was saying. And he was sure everybody knew it. And what *he* knew now was that the boys would never respect him if he didn't enforce a set of rules they didn't like. It was crazy, but it was true.

"It is time for you to go to bed, right now!" he said finally. "You agreed to the rules, and you're damn well going to follow them. You understand?"

The boys glanced at each other. "We understand, sir," one said.

"That's good." Gordon smiled.

"May I go make a short call now, sir?" the boy asked.

"What?"

"Urinate, sir. May I?"

"May I go wash my face?"

"I need to get my laundry."

Gordon wiped his forehead. "You were supposed to do all that before."

"But, sir, my bladder, it is bursting."

"All right, go on."

"Thank you, sir."

Gordon shook his head. "Thank you, hell. You're all getting up a half-hour early tomorrow morning. And then another minute earlier for every minute you stay up tonight. Get moving!"

The boys ran to the latrine and back, laughing and snapping towels, but they were all quiet in their beds in less than five minutes.

"Good night," Gordon said in a loud voice. "I'll expect your officers to get you up at quarter to six. Any questions?"

Silence.

"I like you all too much to let you get in big trouble at this school and mess up your education," Gordon said. "Or mine," he added, and blew out all but one of the lanterns hanging from the rafter.

He stood in the aisle with the last of the light in his hand now. Looking out over the rows of silhouetted mounds on the beds, he listened to the rustle of bedclothes and coughs and throat-clearings amid the stillness. Soon even those noises subsided. All that could be heard were the insect sounds of night. Although he couldn't see them, he knew that forty pairs of eyes were still focused on him. They were watching and waiting for him—the self-appointed light source—to go away.

I have become a schoolmaster, Gordon thought. He blew out the lantern. Total darkness descended instantly. The stillness in the room was absolute and unnatural. He had just decreed darkness for everyone in the place; he had not thought to get himself out first and had been caught by his own decree.

Outside the dormitory it was as dark as it had been inside—darker, for he was alone. He looked for matches to light his lantern, but he had none. Turning the corner of the building, he saw Miss Stuart's house shining silver white, the only light on the compound. Gordon walked slowly toward it. But he stopped outside the window again beside a tree where the glow from the house started to become dim on the grass.

The rehearsal of Handel's *Messiah* had broken up. Miss Stuart had served everyone cake and milk-tea, and now was collecting the plates. People were smiling and wiping crumbs from their lips and yawning happily. The gurgle of conversation flowed out into the night, but by the time it reached Gordon, it was unintelligible.

Gordon was hungry. He could go in and have some cake with them. But what would happen to the smiles then? The headmaster would watch him, frowning, and they would all pick up his gloom. Gordon could try to ignore him, try to make conversation with someone—whom, he couldn't imagine, except perhaps Pamela, who would have to stop enjoying Clive's undivided attention. She would be polite about it. They would all be polite. He would be too. And no one would be fooled.

Gordon stayed where he was.

He'd often stood out on a street watching the glow from some window, listening to the music and the people talking inside, wishing he'd been invited. And now that he was invited . . . somehow he was too late. It wasn't only that he didn't *want* to become more of a schoolmaster than he already was, but that he *could* not. He'd missed the opportunity to join these people. By spoiling his welcome by arguing with the headmaster this morning. By offering to work in the school garden. But earlier than that too. When he'd decided not to take Pamela out and had gone drinking at the Karela dance halls instead, and ended up in that hut. Earlier. When he'd decided to leave America and go to Africa. When he'd left his parents' home. Earlier than that even. When? He didn't know, and it didn't matter.

Now the masters were leaving the house, carrying their lanterns. They moved through the darkness in small clus-

ters, each in its own swinging bell of light. The lights
moved along the oval roadway and split into smaller bells,
one moving into a house and lighting it up from inside the
window, others continuing on. Soon all the houses along
the oval glowed silver white. Then, one by one, the houses
disappeared into the darkness.

Gordon heard footsteps approaching. He stood very still,
squinting, seeing nothing but night. A figure appeared several feet from him and moved on: Pamela—he could tell
by her brisk determined walk. She must have walked Clive
home. Well, good for her, good for them, Gordon thought,
listening to her footsteps grow fainter. But he felt sad.
Pamela was a pleasant girl, honest, sweet smile, big soft-
looking breasts . . . but you had to be a member of the
Hallelujah Chorus to get at them. Gordon tried to laugh.
The silence of the night drowned him out.

Gordon headed back toward his house. The air was
warm yet uncomfortably invigorating for a night with
nothing better to offer than correcting papers and staring at
cinderblock walls. Overhead, the stars popped out at him, a
vast hilarious party illuminating the silhouette of the
mountain. Arriving at his house, he switched his radio on,
lit his lantern, opened his windows.

At sunset, he'd been able to see the fires and wisps of
smoke curling up from the huts down on the plain. He had
heard human sounds on the breeze: the chopping of firewood, the rustling of maize stalks as children ran home
along a nearby path. Now the only sounds were the
sounds of night: insects crackling and dogs howling and
the ululations of owls. He felt like the last human being
alive on earth. Rain clattered on his roof, then stopped
quickly, leaving silence. The darkness crept into the house
up to the fringe of the cone of yellow light from his lantern. He watched his shadow out of the corner of his eye,
distorted and flickering, the only shadow on the wall.

He stepped outside . . . and pitch-black moistness swallowed him. All the incredible fertility of the earth blasted
him with its odor. The smell was sweetness at its orgiastic
extreme—the scents of a thousand grasses and flowers
blended to a chaotic overripe aroma that he gulped in
eagerly. His feet slipped in the mud. With every step, he
touched a bush that soaked him in rainwater and made
him shiver uncontrollably, happily. His eyes could not

grow used to the massive darkness of a continent of night, but they could not stop straining to try.

There was no moon now. No stars. The darkness had swallowed them too. He was drowning in the stomach of darkness. Had drowned. Was swimming back to the surface. Breathing in the night's scent and feeling its moisture pricking his skin, he groped for his bicycle along the wall of his house. He knew of a place where there were lights swallowed them too. He was drowning in the stomach of darkness. He had never truly doubted the place's existence; a schoolmaster named Mr. Lockery had merely locked it out of his mind for a time.

He found his bicycle and pulled it sharply toward him. He couldn't see yet, but he knew the direction of the town and the New Life Hotel as if he had been there many times before.

PART TWO

8

SALOME APPEARED THAT EVENING IN HER fuzzy Afro-American wig and a green mini that flared out in pleats just below the curve of her buttocks. Her yellow blouse was so tight it had to be fastened with a big eye-shaped plastic pin. Several men said they had never seen her looking so smart, but they didn't say it to her. One man did ask if he might admire her pin more closely; when he leaned forward, she twisted her shoulders and boxed him in the ear with her breasts. Salome had been in a rare mood since the new girl had come.

Adija was sitting with a young man in a shiny black suit. He was buying her Guinness. At first, she found it bitter, like spoiled palm wine, but when she mixed it with Tusker, it wasn't too bad. Soon there were so many bottles on the table that it was difficult to find room for elbows.

The name of the man who was drinking most of the beer was Muchomo, Julian Muchomo. He was a salesman for the Pfaff Sewing Machine Company. A very very big German international multinational corporation. Muchomo was a pioneer. He was helping the nations of Marembo and Bashiri to go forward. He was providing the people with better lives. That was what Uhuru was for, wasn't it?

Yes, said Adija, filling his glass.

Women could make new clothes for their children. Soon there would be no more ragged children. They would all be dressed in bright clean clothes. Well-sewn, not coming apart at the seams. Every day, Muchomo visited them, bringing them good news like the early missionaries with his attaché case full of bright smiling pamphlets. When they saw his putt-putt scooter coming, they all ran to greet him wanting to hear about the wonderful sewing machine.

You must be proud to have such an important job, said Adija, filling his glass.

Muchomo admitted that he was. Really, he was a pioneer. The Pfaff Company was going to buy him a car next year, a German car, so that he could visit people in even more remote areas. These were his people. He spoke their language and knew their customs, and they trusted him. They were good people, salts of the earth. He was helping them to go forward. He was bringing them progress. He *was* progress. Would Adija like to see one of his pamphlets?

Oh, yes, said Adija, filling his glass.

He had sold more sewing machines than any other salesman. Except two in Azima. But then it was easier to sell things in the city. There you didn't have to go tramping through soggy fields and shitty cow pastures to collect payments. You didn't have to get into quarrels with lazy people who refused to keep up their payments. You didn't have to carry a repair kit with you because these ignorant people never understood how to take care of their machines. Oil them regularly, he'd told them, over and over. He gave them tins of oil. But did they use it? No. Aah!— they must drink it! Next year, next year, going to work in Azima. Work in nice air-condition office. With a secretary answer phone. No more these fucking cow pastures for Muchomo. Muchomo going to be city man. Big man.

Nice, said Adija, filling his glass.

When Muchomo went Azima, Adija come visit. He take her ride in his Mercedes. Take her dancing New Stanley Hotel. She like that?

Oh, yes, said Adija.

Good. Is bargain, yes?

Adija smiled and sipped her beer.

Good. Now—let's go, woman.

What?

Go. You have a room, don't you? I want you.

Don't squeeze my arm, darling. I just have to go use the latrine. You wait for me, all right?

Good. Hurry up.

While he waited, Muchomo started finishing the mostly full bottles he had bought for Adija. They were all over the table, hardly touched. No use wasting good beer. As long as one could still lift one's arm, ha ha.

After some time, a friend of Muchomo's appeared, looking for him. He and Adija and Salome picked Muchomo up from his chair and helped him to the curb. There he vomited a stream of rust-colored liquid into the street. Afterward he was limp as a fish and difficult to stuff into his friend's small car. Adija waved goodbye from the curb as the ancient battered car chugged away. Muchomo's forehead was resting against the bottom of the window, so he couldn't see her waving.

Gradually all the customers went home, leaving Adija and Salome alone in the big empty room. Yellow lantern light lay on the concrete floor like spilled egg. A fat sausage-fly dive-bombed the lantern, caromed blindly off the walls with loud, soggy thwacks, and fell into the dregs of someone's beer, where it floated in slow circles. Adija went behind the bar to wash some glasses. Closing time, Salome said to herself.

But then a customer walked in.

To Salome, Gordon's walk across the empty room was that of a nervous policeman shouldering his way through a mob. She'd seen Europeans entering African places before. When a European sat, his buttocks didn't slump down happy to have found a resting place; no, he sat slowly, as if he weren't sure the chair's seat would hold his weight. Though he moved his head about casually as if looking for old friends to greet, his eyes darted here and there as if in readiness for a spear flying at him out of nowhere. Europeans could be amusing sometimes.

Salome stood by his table, waiting silently.

"*Jambo.*" Gordon glanced a smile off her forehead. "Uh, *pombe.*"

"What kind of beer you want?"

"Oh, you speak English. I'll have, I don't know— Tusker."

"You want cold or warm?" Salome asked, smiling.

Salome's amazing bosom hovered inches above Gordon's face. The eye-shaped pin that kept it all from tumbling out seemed to be watching Gordon carefully.

"Well . . . cold, please," he said.

"We got no cold. Only warm."

Gordon glanced up at her. "I see. Okay, bring me *two* cold ones then."

"What?" Salome screwed up her face. "What wrong with you? You want Tusker, *eii?*"

"*Ndio.*" Gordon nodded.

Salome could understand English, but not this foreign kind of English. The man hardly opened his mouth at all when he spoke; this somehow enabled the words to come out twice as fast as normal but at the same time without much distinction between consonant and vowel sounds— he talked like a Sten gun shooting watery porridge. Whatever he had said, Salome didn't much like his tone of voice either. "Your pale-faced friend is here," she said to Adija, who was bringing a tray of glasses in from the washbucket outside. "But don't go too close to him. He's mad."

"Why do you say that?"

"He's jabbering nonsense." Salome yanked the top off a Tusker with an angry pop. "Look at him—I just mocked him, and he's still got a smile on his face."

Adija looked. "That's because he's seen me," she laughed. It wasn't quite true; Gordon hadn't seen her at first. Now he looked up and waved to her, smiling.

Adija started to lift her hand; then, grinning, she turned away. She started arranging the glasses on the shelf behind the bar. Not watching what she was doing, she jammed one against the other, cracking them both. Suddenly she was angry with herself. *She* should be serving him! "Salome—"

Salome had already gone to his table. "Three fifty," she said, putting the bottle and glass down before him.

Gordon frowned. He counted out two shillings and seventy-five cents and set it down in a little pile on Salome's tray. "I know how much Tusker costs," he said.

Salome knocked over the pile with her finger and counted it. "Seventy-five cents more," she said, glaring at him.

"No. No more." Gordon had been overcharged for months in Karela before he had discovered that many barmaids charged two prices, one for ordinary Africans and one for élites and Europeans—Europeans who were too ignorant or timid to question the prices. He was damned if he was going to start paying *mzungu*—(European)—prices here. "Nonsense," he said, looking up into Salome's uncomprehending face. "Three and a half is nonsense and you know it."

"*Eii, mzungu,* you listen to me—" Salome snatched the bottle from his table, making bits of foam fly like feathers. "You come in here, you think you can—" She cleared her throat and looked away. Then she wiped the bottle on her skirt and put it back down. "We closing very soon," she said, and walked quietly back to the bar.

It was not like Salome to miss the opportunity to make a row when one presented itself—she enjoyed pounding on tables and shouting at people—but before she had had a chance to start, Elima, the Police Chief, had walked in and taken a seat near the teacher. She was not on good terms with Elima today. The night before, he had asked her how much Adija charged, and Salome had told him "One million shillings, and over my dead body."

"I see. I will wait until the time is ripe," he had said. "Anyway, my taste is for women with more flesh on them . . ."

Tonight he gave Salome's thigh a squeeze again. "*Eii,* Salome. What's the new teacher doing in this sinful place?"

"He come down the hill to look at the Africans. Somebody told him there was a game reserve down here."

"Someone was right—it's a hippo reserve!" He tried to get both hands around Salome's thighs but she slipped away to the bar. She set her machete down on the counter and watched.

Adija brought a bottle of Tusker and a glass out in front of the bar. Swaying in place, she looked as if she were searching for a seat in a crowded room. If only Gordon would beckon her to his table. Adija's eyes swelled to droplets of dark liquid that would fall and splatter if the faintest quiver of disappointment should pass across her face.

But there, Gordon had seen her eyes. He was waving to her. She approached him, smiling, and sat down on the edge of a chair. Then, seeing Elima approaching, she scurried back to the bar.

Elima sat down in her place. "Hello, my friend."

Gordon made an effort to smile. He had been anticipating Adija; he had found her. And now here was this cop. "Hello," he said, reaching out to shake hands.

"You are the new teacher at Musolu School."

"Yes, I came last week."

"I know. In a small town, news travels fast. It is my job to know all the news. I am Chief of Police here. My name is Martin Elima."

"I'm glad to mēet you," Gordon said. "Gordon Lockery."

Elima nodded and took a long drink of beer. Gordon drummed his fingers on the table.

"I am not often here at night. My office is in Mbure," Elima said eventually, "but there was a motorcar crash nearby to this place. Very bad."

"What happened?"

"Man in a small van, he hit a child. Child was running in the road. The man got out of the van to see what happen, the people attack him. He is at dispensary now, that man. Also the child, but the child will live, I think."

"The man—the driver—he won't live?"

Elima spread his hands wide and laughed. "I don't know. Waga, the nurse, he doesn't know. Man hurt very bad," he said. "Let me warn you—if you hit someone in the road, don't stop to see what happen. Never. Just drive to next police station and tell them there. Then police can come back with you. If you stop, people will kill you."

"I've heard of that," Gordon said. "Why do they do that?"

"They don't like motorcars drive fast, make dust on roads, and they not even having bicycle to ride. It is their custom, I think," Elima said. "I tell you because you are European. Maybe you don't know the way African behave."

"Well, thank you." In fact, Gordon had been told of this custom before.

"Is all right. Even man in the van, he was African, not *mzungu*. Perhaps he new to driving, perhaps he from city. He just look around, see only empty road, bushes, no people. But when he get out, they are all there—many, many people, very sudden . . ."

Adija slipped back to the table, bringing her own chair.

"Ah. Swila Number 101," Elima said.

Adija stiffened. She leaned back so that Gordon blocked her sight of Elima.

"Another custom I tell you, *Bwana* Lockery, perhaps

you don't know—about women who work in place of this kind." Elima leaned forward to glance at Adija. He thought she had made the decision to refuse him, not Salome; he was insulted that this girl, just arrived here a few days ago, thought herself good enough to turn down the Police Chief. "You let them sit with you, then they expect you buy them drink."

"That's okay—"

"You buy them beer, they expect you to go to their room. Now you know this custom, you can make choice." Elima leaned forward; his wave to Adija was playful, but what he said to her in Kisemi was: "Go away, stupid woman! Can't you see that two men are talking?"

"This girl brought her own beer over here," Gordon explained. He smiled his vague faraway smile; this helpful bucktoothed cop was making him uncomfortable. Gordon saw as much depth and kindness in his eyes as in his brass buttons. "Anyway, I already know her. She's all right," Gordon said.

"Aah, you know her already." Elima eyed him murderously. "You move fast. Most people in this town don't move so fast."

"She was at my school." Gordon lit a cigarette, then, thinking again, held out the packet to Elima. "She was looking for a job as a housegirl."

"I see." He took a cigarette and lit it from Gordon's match. What was a schoolteacher doing smoking cheap, filterless Crane Bird cigarettes? "I was only joking with you, you know," he said, and stubbed out the cigarette.

"Oh."

"So now she has job here. She moves fast too. But you know, she is expensive. One million shillings."

Gordon nodded absently, giving Elima no encouragement to elaborate.

Elima laughed. "That old man Griffin, he send you back to England straightway, he learn you hire housegirl like this one. You lucky you didn't hire her."

"Griffin wouldn't have liked it, no. Do you know him?"

"Griffin? Yes, yes. He very famous in Marembo. He is old-school colonialist. *Kali sana*—very strict. But working very hard for educating Africans. Those old Englishmen, they do many good things for Marembo. But now is time for a change. We have *Uhuru* now." Elima poured another glass of beer and drank half of it. "Myself, I be glad when he retire this year. For me, just personally, he is a son-of-a-bitch."

Adija knew only a few English words. "Million shillings" she understood, and hearing that had made her furious. Now Elima was saying more insulting things about her. She had no way of knowing how the teacher was taking them—he kept his face so tense all the time. "Bitch" was another word she knew. When she heard Elima say it, leaning close to Gordon to talk confidentially, she was sure Elima was talking about her. Then the teacher smiled, hearing "bitch"! That was too much!

"Why do you insult me to the European?" she demanded in Kisemi. "Now you make him agree with you. You bastard—you'll never get your filthy hands on me!" Adija picked up her glass to leave.

"No—stay!" Gordon reached out and touched her wrist. She hesitated, off balance, then sat down hard again in the chair. She wiped her eyes and scowled hard at the floor, as if getting ready to spring.

Gordon started to pour Adija's beer, but she covered the top of her glass. At the bar, Salome reached for her machete; she knew Europeans could turn as mean as police chiefs when they were refused. But this one had no temper. He put his hand on top of Adija's and very gently lifted it from the glass. He didn't do it the way men often forced girls to drink, to get them drunk. There was no mocking expression on his face. Nor did he have to pull Adija's hand very hard.

She squinted at her beer glass as he filled it. Then she picked it up and drained it. "You see, policeman—" She belched loudly. "You can tell him nonsense about me, but he won't believe you. He's not ashamed to drink with me. That's because he is good, and you're—" Adija's courage stopped there. She snatched the bottle up and poured herself another glass.

Elima rose to his feet. "I have to leave you now," he said stiffly to Gordon. The rage in his eyes was magnified by a glaze of alcohol. "I wish you luck in your teaching. Pass my greetings to *Bwana* Griffin."

"I will." Gordon rose too, offering his hand. Elima

shook it briefly. "Maybe I'll see you here again," Gordon
added, trying to appear friendly.

"Yes, I think we will meet again sometime." Elima
backed off, scowling, then turned and walked out the door.

Salome watched him cross the street, then bolted the
door. "You want more beer, *mzungu?* We closing soon,"
she called to Gordon.

"My name's not *mzungu*."

"*Eii?*"

"It's Gordon." He offered his hand. I *am* going to make
friends in this town, he thought.

Adija grinned.

Salome paused and thought a moment. Then she shook
his hand. "*Jambo*, Gordon," she said. "I am Salome."

"Pleased to meet you."

Salome shifted her weight from one foot to the other.
"Good," she said. "I am pleased to meet you also."

Gordon returned her stare. "We are both pleased to
meet each other."

"I can't understand you English. You talk too fast."

"Sorry," Gordon said. "Can I have another beer before
you close?"

"All right. Tusker?"

"Yes, please. A warm one, not cold." Gordon looked for
a trace of a smile on Salome's face; he found none. "Bring
one for yourself too."

"Bring us two Tuskers," Salome said in Kisemi to Adija.
"I want to talk with your friend."

Adija looked hurt. "Why do you want to talk with him?"

"To warn him about Elima."

Adija nodded and left the table.

"Listen, *mzu*—Gordon," Salome said, switching back to
English. "I going to talk with you about this Adija, *eii?*"

"All right."

"I know European like you—missionary—"

"I'm not a missionary!" Gordon said.

"All right, you teacher at missionary school. You come
to Africa to help Africans. That very good, wonderful. But
sometime, European want to help African, he don't. He
just hurt us. He try to get into African life. Now you, you
got much education, *eii?*"

"Mmm."

"Much education, much money. Adija, she is simple girl, just village girl without no home now. No education, no money. Village girl like Adija, she can think European like you can help her. Maybe you think that too. But listen, after you help her, you just go back to England, and—"

"America."

"America. That why you talk so strange, I think." She took a sip of Adija's beer. "You go back to America, marry Engla—America girl. You have you life. But Adija, she have to stay here after you go. You understand what I tell you?" The third eye in the valley of Salome's chest glared at him.

"I understand," Gordon said. "But I'm not going back to America. And I'm not getting married."

"Is it? How you know that? You just young. How many years you got—twenty?"

"Twenty-two."

"So how you know what you going to do?"

"Well, I know what I'm not going to do." Gordon saw Adija approaching. "And listen, Salome, I didn't come to Africa to help Africans. I came for my own reasons. I'm not going to try to help Adija or anyone else. I just came in here tonight to get a drink and talk to people."

"Why you can't talk to people at you school?"

"I get tired of talking to them. I like to meet new people, all right?"

Salome looked away.

"*Jambo*, Gordon," Adija filled his glass, then Salome's, then her own. She sat down, smiling at both of them. "I'm glad you came here," she said to Gordon in Kisemi. "I was wanting to return your hospitality."

Gordon nodded.

"He doesn't understand you," Salome said.

"I know, but it's better to talk than to sit here in silence."

Gordon's eyes darted from Salome to Adija to Salome. "What's she saying?"

"I'm no teacher. Why ask me?" Salome said.

"Because you speak both languages."

Salome saw Adija's eyes pleading with her to translate.

"All right. Adija said—" She stopped. Hadn't she just refused to be a translator? Had Adija's eyes cast a spell on her? It wasn't amusing. She took a Crane Bird out of Gordon's packet on the table and lit it with one of his matches. Pff—what cheap cigarettes! "All right. Adija said it is better to talk Kisemi to you—even she know you don't understand it—than to talk nothing," Salome said. "Don't ask me why she say that. I tell you before, she is silly village girl."

"It's true, about talking," Gordon said. "If she talks to me, I'll learn the language." He turned to Adija, smiling, "*Ndio.* Yes."

"*Ndio. Nzuri.*"

"*Nzuri.* Good."

"You see," Adija said brightly to Salome. "He likes to speak Kisemi."

"Such an interesting conversation. I can't wait to hear more of it."

"I'll teach him." Adija turned to Gordon and touched his chest. "*Wewe ni mwalimu—*" she pointed diagonally up in the air, "*—katika shuleni.*"

Gordon knew *mwalimu*, and figured out the rest from the direction she was pointing. "I am a teacher at the school," he said.

Salome sighed and drank her beer.

Adija touched her lips, thinking. She tapped the table. "*Ni mesa.*"

"Table."

"*Pombe.*"

"Beer. I know that one."

"He already knew beer," Salome said. She reached across the table and touched the top of Adija's head. "*Kitchwa nazi.* Coconut head. Crazy."

Adija jerked her head away, laughing. "*Naende kajitombe!*"

"Shall I translate that?"

Adija clapped her hand over her mouth. "No!"

"Adija told me that I should go fuck with myself," Salome translated.

"I didn't know you could say that in Kisemi."

Adija leaned forward, both hands held tight over her mouth. She felt Gordon watching her, grinning. Her hair shone like a million tiny wires on fire. "You're evil, Salome. What did he say?" she asked, raising her face.

"You call me evil, then you ask me to help you. You *are* mad!"

"No—tell me!"

"He said you are an ugly, rude, vile person for saying such a thing to your good friend Salome."

"He didn't! You're talking shit!"

Salome turned to Gordon. "Now she says—"

Adija flicked her glass out toward Salome, but only a few bits of foam flew out. Salome laughed. Adija leaned forward, trying to look seriously at Gordon, to show she was above this sort of talk, really. He was grinning so hard, though, she had to cover her face again. "You're making him think bad things about me," she accused Salome.

"You're the one saying the bad things."

Adija partially uncovered her face, peering up at Gordon from between her fingers. "If he didn't enjoy it, he would have gone home," she said.

It was true, Adija decided. The teacher was smiling very happily. The tense look that had been on his face was gone. His eyes were looking kindly at her. "*Macho yango ni kibulu,*" she said, suddenly noticing that his eyes were blue, and pointing to them. When he repeated what she'd said, she clapped her hands and touched him on the shoulder to congratulate him.

His hair was yellow, his nose was long; he had two ears, two eyes, one nose, one mouth. Adija was a woman, Gordon was a man. Adija was a small woman, Gordon was a big man . . .

Salome watched the two of them and drank her beer and smoked one cigarette after another. Now and then, she helped Adija say things in English—not because she wanted to help her learn English, but because it was the only way she could stay in the conversation. She found herself laughing at Adija's antics.

A change came over Adija. That look of a starved restless fawn was gone. Her movements were no longer cautious. She no longer touched things as if she feared they might lash out at her like snakes. Now she touched the table, the cigarette packet, even Gordon's arm, as if she were their master, or at least their equal. Though she was giggling like a schoolgirl, Adija seemed to be growing up before Salome's eyes.

It made Salome smile to see the change, but she was uneasy inside too. The girl didn't just point to her blue skirt, she leaned back from the table and lifted it up an inch or two, giving Gordon a look at her long pretty legs. Did she mean to? Certainly. She was showing off for him. The little bitch. She was offering laughs and smiles and gestures to him like a woman serving up an endless variety of sweet-tasting dishes.

As long as Salome kept joining in the banter, Adija and Gordon were amusing to watch. But there were moments when she found herself sitting alone. Adija and the teacher were far away, specks in the distance. Sometimes she felt it was she who was fading away, like a lantern running out of paraffin. She drank more beer and made an effort to laugh again. It was good to laugh. She hadn't laughed about anything for a very long time.

She had been drinking all day, and reached the point where she knew that one more bottle would make her say terrible things to Adija. "Adija," she interrupted, "lock the door when he leaves." She stood up, her chair tipping backward with a crash. "Fucker!" she swore at it, and leaned over carefully to set it upright again. Her plastic pin broke, and she had to stand up quickly. "Don't forget his money. For the beer," she said, holding her blouse together. The pin dangled between her breasts at a baleful angle.

"Are you drunk?" Adija asked.

"I am never drunk, girl. I only let people think so," Salome said, and walked unsteadily out the back door.

Gordon put his money on the table. He and Adija slowly drank their beer. When he finally stood up, Adija did too. They walked together out onto the pavement. Adija watched his face as he stood staring out into the night as if searching for something. Then he sat down on the curb and smiled up at her in such a way that she knew it was all right to sit beside him.

Cautiously, she rested her head against his chest. "I'm cold," she said in Kisemi. "Put your arm around me."

Miraculously, he understood her. Adija shut her eyes, almost afraid to breathe lest he disappear.

His fingers were moving in her hair. She felt uncomfortable at first, because men always wanted to touch her
strange wavy hair. But his fingers weren't exploring its
texture, they were just stroking. They seemed content to
just do that. She reached up and touched his hair too. It
felt soft and silky. She felt like shivering and giggling at the
same time. Eventually, though, her body relaxed, and she
let all her weight sink against him. She had never touched
a European before. Or smelled one so close. He had a
bitter smell to him, but it wasn't bad. She would grow used
to it. She took his hand and put it down inside her blouse.
His hand was cold, but it stroked her gently, the way one
might stroke a baby bird.

The street was empty, with only the silhouette of the
shop roofs and the bulge of the mountain showing against
the black sky. Adija began to feel contented. She didn't feel
any further need to teach him Kisemi, or to learn English,
in order to be interesting to him. There was no need to do
anything now to reach him. She was as close to him as she
needed to be.

From the room behind the bar, Salome's wireless suddenly blared out twanging dance-hall music. Adija glanced
behind her into the pale light spilling out the bar door
along the concrete. She noticed that Gordon was looking
behind him too. Was he thinking of dance halls like the
ones in Marini and Jinjeh and of the way men treated the
girls in them—as she was? It was possible. This man was
not like the men she had known in those places. And
somehow she knew that if she invited him to her room
now, he would come, but afterward she would never
see him again. She gave his wrist a careful squeeze; her
breast felt his fingers leaving. His hand had become warm
inside her blouse. Suddenly the night seemed cold again.

"*Kwaheri kuonana*," she said, and remembered the day
she had said that to him on his doorstep. Yes, she had seen
him again, as she'd said she would.

Gordon stood up. "*Kwaheri kuonana*."

The way he kissed her before he left—with his tongue
inside her mouth! Was this European a savage?—made her
want to claw at her face with both hands, as if a tiny
animal had been loosed into her and was sliding into the

depths of her belly. She managed to stay on the curb waving to him until he was out of sight. Then she turned and ran inside, crying out in a faint high-pitched voice that she had never heard before.

9

SALOME'S ROOM WAS THICK WITH DARKNESS. The air smelled stagnant. Salome was breathing hard, as if asleep. Adija tiptoed to her bed and sat down cautiously on the edge. She had so much to try to say.

Suddenly Salome's arm fell across her lap. Adija gasped. The arm tugged at her, pulling her down. Adija whimpered softly but she had no strength to resist. She was frightened —Salome seemed angry, the way she was tugging at her. Salome's arms and legs were all over her, heavy and thrashing like a great octopus released out of the darkness.

Later, Adija sat on the edge of the bed and wept silently. She didn't know why. Was she still frightened? But she was safe now. She could survive—she had survived among strong, hard women because she knew the secrets of making them happy. But there was such violence in Salome! It was as if Salome had wanted to please her and punish her for something at the same time.

Adija didn't know what to do or say; she sat and wept. Finally her eyes focused on the wall. Dresses and cardigans and blouses and skirts hung on nails all over it, like headless people. They blurred and flickered in the weak lantern light.

"You have so many clothes," she said finally, avoiding Salome's stare.

"A mechanic has the tools of his trade, and I have mine," Salome said. "What's the matter, Adija?"

"Nothing."

"Would you like to hear the wireless?"

"Yes."

Both the Karela and the Azima stations were broadcasting news programs. Cabinet ministers of all kinds doing this and doing that, the King of Marembo arguing this and that with the ministers. Whenever anyone talked on the

wireless, it was always ministers and politics. Adija didn't
know why Salome liked to hear the talking—what was
politics to a woman? Finally, Salome changed the station
and found some Kisemi music. Adija smiled faintly, hearing the music. She stared about Salome's room; the packing crate Salome used for a table, her collection of soaps
and towels and enamel plates and metal spoons. Salome
had many things, but in the yellow lantern glow, the room
looked sad. "You have only the things you need," Adija
said finally. "You have much money, yet you don't buy
nice things."

"Perhaps someday I'll find something to spend it on,"
Salome said. She lay back and stared at the beam above
her bed where the strongbox was. Soon she would have
to get another one, it was getting so full. "I am pregnant
with money and one day I will calve," she said. "Printer's
ink will stream down the insides of my legs and a soggy
wad of paper will fall to the earth between my feet like a
big stone."

Adija stared at her.

"One day I will return to my country a rich, rich
woman. Money is what they understand there. Then no
one can—" She shook her head hard, scattering the
thought like water. She noticed Adija's strange eyes upon
her. "Are you all right?" she asked suddenly.

"I don't know. Are you?"

Salome rolled over and pushed her cheek into the mattress. "I don't know. I just know I feel something, and that
is better than feeling . . . nothing."

"Are you sure?"

"Yes."

"It's confusing me, this town." Adija wiped her nose.
"There are so many bad people—Elima, that sewing machine man, all of them—and yet they want me. And when
I meet one good man—I don't know what to do with
him."

Salome made a disdainful clicking sound.

"It's true, I don't. I was never so confused until I came
here. I think this town is bad, even though you're here. But
even you confuse me sometimes."

Salome glared sideways. "You know, that policeman
would have dragged you off yesterday if I hadn't stopped
him, and you would never have met this 'good' man of

yours. Perhaps I should have let Elima have you. Then you'd begin to know what 'bad' is."

Adija stared hard at Salome. This woman had so much power. She got everything she asked for—from Patel, even from the Police Chief. She was afraid of nothing. And now this woman was her friend. "Thank you for helping me in this bad place," she whispered to Salome.

Salome shook her head. It made her uneasy to hear Adija call it a bad place. Adija seemed innocent enough to believe that there might be better places for her to go to. She might go off looking for one. "You don't know what 'bad' is," she said, returning Adija's gaze. "You're always saying this or that is bad, but you don't know."

She looked down and saw that Adija was listening to her. This girl would listen to her!

Bad. Bad, she told Adija, is when you hear angry strangers' voices and the crackle of flames outside the walls of your hut, and you know that the voices and flames are after you. And you taste the wind of machete blades swinging blindly out in the night. You smell the burning of straw roofs and damp clothing, you smell the flesh of your family burning. You inhale the stink that you cannot breathe, but you cannot move from the spot where you are hiding. You cannot move but you cannot stay; at any moment the roof will fall on your head in an explosion of sparks and smoke.

Bad is when you are somehow out of the hut and you hear the buzzing of airplanes like giant murmuring wasps approaching from across the hills. So you run screaming into the forest, with the tree branches crashing and pieces of sharp metal whistling all about, knocking down your neighbors as they too run screaming. You can't stop to help them, because the shrieks of falling bombs have entered your body like a swarm of wasps under your clothing. You must run and run and be knocked down and gouge your face into the earth and scramble up and run and run deeper and deeper into the forest where you can be safe from the flying death.

And Bad is when you find yourself alive afterward, and alone.

And Salome told Adija about the war, how she had spied among the Europeans and home guards for the guerrillas, and carried information, along with bullets and food,

up into the camps in the mountains. She told her about the
long treks through the forests, and how the cuts in her feet
had stung from the sharp rocks on the trails. When finally
she arrived at a camp, a warm fire was blazing under the
rock ledge. The stone by the fire was warm and soothing to
her sore back. Kariuki, as leader, slept in the place nearest
the fire. He also had his choice of food bearers. His choice
was always Salome, who in those days used her African
name, Wairimu.

Kariuki was tall and strong as a Poken warrior. His
beard and wild eyes and plaited hair gave him the appearance of a madman. But he was not mad. He barked his
commands, and attacked the firewood with his machete as
if in rage, but the rage was just to frighten his men into
remaining loyal. At night, when she lay beside him on the
warm rock, he was merely a tired, sad man. His soldiers
were starving. Rain and forest dampness were rotting away
their morale. Already three had died of pneumonia, five
had deserted. His battalion was too weak to make any
more raids. There was nothing to do but stay in the deep-
est, wettest part of the forest and wait for reinforcements.
But where were the reinforcements to come from? The
British lines around the forests were tight. He had had no
new recruits in four months. What was happening outside?
Had the people been intimidated? Why had they not all
risen up together and murdered their oppressors in their
beds, burned their farms, blown up their jails, and called
the guerrillas out of the forests to lead victory marches
against the white armies? Tears welled up in Kariuki's hard
black eyes, as he asked Why? *Why?*

The tears were there because he knew why the people in
the villages and farms had not risen up in arms. The few
leaders who had not escaped to the forests were in detention. The people were numbed by terror and confusion. At
any time of the day or night, a knock on the door might
mean a father, a brother, even a whole family snatched
away to be beaten and tortured and locked in great pens
like animals. What was most terrifying was that the man
who beat on the door of the hut with his rifle might not be
a European but an African—a neighbor, someone whom a
few years ago you had helped with the birthing of a cow,
or who had lent you a son to help with your maize harvest.

"The enemy is our own people," Kariuki said, staring

into the coals. He glanced up, his eyes reflecting their glow. "Even you, Salome Wairimu. We know they let you through the lines so that you can go back and report on us."

Salome Wairimu trembled. Suddenly she feared for her life. Kariuki's long rifle, which she admired so much, the barrel glinting silver in the moonlight—it could turn on her. "I tell them lies about where your camp is," she said. "I tell them you have Sten guns and bombs. I say that your men are many and strong."

"I think you do."

"It is the truth. That is why they haven't come after you here."

Kariuki shook his head slowly. "No. Even if they knew where we were, they would not come to fight us. We are harmless to them here. Why should they let us show our strength in battle? Much easier for them to let us die off, or quarrel and kill each other while we squat here forever in idleness."

Salome Wairimu ran her hand across the muscles of his back, rubbed them until the knots were gone and the skin shone smooth in the pale red light of the coals. "Your courage is known to everyone," she told him. "You are a legend in the villages."

Kariuki rolled onto his back and stared up through the branches into the night. The blackness of the night was reflected in his eyes. She rubbed his shoulders and chest and thighs and watched his face to see his gaze slowly return to her. The sky was the inside of a vast dark skull, his own, and it was a great distance to travel from the depths of his torment back to the fireside where Salome Wairimu waited. Finally, the darkness left his eyes. They focused slowly, warmly, on her. Then he flung her from him and pinned her on her back beneath him. He became a warrior again, attacking her in a slow, mounting rage. She cried out for mercy, she wept in joy and terror.

Too soon, the terror was over. It slammed her back down on the rock and left her lying there beside a man whose gaze was once again lost beyond the treetops, whose body was still aching with restlessness.

On that last visit to him, she had watched him roll back over on his side and smile at her. It was not his usual

ironic smile, but an almost tender expression. She waited
for him to speak, wide-eyed as a child.

"When you go back, Wairimu, you must tell them something. Say we are going to Muraa village in the north."

"Why?"

He glanced away. "Just to upset them. To make them
take their troops there for nothing."

"Ah, you want to divert them."

"You are a clever woman, Wairimu."

"Where will you go, truly?"

Kariuki lay on his back again, staring into the sky.

"You don't want to tell me where? You don't trust me?"

"I trust you. I trust you to do what I tell you," he
said.

Salome Wairimu nodded. She felt very happy and strong.
She knew that a man did not ask a woman to obey him
unquestioningly unless he considered her his wife. "Where
can I visit you next, though?"

"If you obey me, you will hear where I am." He would
say nothing more, and she asked him no more questions.

The next morning, she awoke full of happiness. When
she opened her eyes, she saw that the sunlight was already
streaking palely across the forest floor. She sat up quickly,
ashamed to have slept so late. The rock beneath her was
cold. The skin and bark shelters had vanished. The ashes
from last night's fire had been swept away into the underbrush. The clearing was green and still and empty, as if no
human had ever visited it.

She did as Kariuki had ordered.

And he kept his promise to her. After the suicidal raid at
Muraa village, she did hear where he was. He was with his
ancestors.

No one knew that he had planned to die. No-One, whose
name had once been Wairimu. Whose name was now only
Salome. Salome the traitor, as she was known in the village where she had been born, where she could no longer
live.

There is only one place for people who cannot live in
their villages, whether they leave because their people
scorn them, or because they have seen the world and want
more of it than the village can offer, Salome told Adija.
That place is the city. It is a bad place, and it is the only

place. It was the place where I had Kariuki's baby, the daughter I hoped would live to be called Wairimu.

"She didn't live?" Adija asked.

Salome shook her head. I don't think you know what bad is, Adija, she told her. You don't know what it is like when you are walking and stumbling in the streets of the white man's city late at night with no company but the ache of emptiness in your belly. There is no hope of food or a warm place to lie down; there are only rows and rows of locked shops and office buildings; there are only the closed slats of cardboard-and-tin shacks, and heaps of stinking garbage lying in the gutter that you walk along. You sift through the garbage with your toes, hoping to find a piece of sodden bread or a bone with some rotten meat on it. And when you find something like that, you put it in your mouth and you chew it and you swallow it. But you know that nothing you find to eat can put enough milk in your breasts to feed your baby, your baby who is ill because there is no milk in your breasts to feed her. There is no one to help you, there are only old men in the dark doorways, drunk and sick and squatting to shit in the street like dogs. You see an old man snoring in the mud beside the foul city river, and you know that in the morning the people will crowd around the river bank to watch him floating on his belly. You know this will happen unless you can move him away from the bank. But as you are trying to tug him further from the poisonous water, you feel his trousers peeling like a coating of rotten flesh, and you feel his skin beneath the cloth also peeling away under your fingers. And so you must leave him where he is lying, and hope that perhaps he will wake before he rolls into the water. You must leave him and you must not think of him, because your fingers have already touched death hatching in the damp soft flesh of his body.

You think it is bad here, Adija. But I know there are worse things than boredom and shivering in the chill of a quiet night. I tell you, it is good to be shivering, because you know there is feeling in your body. There is no feeling when you are watching your baby lying in your lap waiting with its eyes open for death. Your own child—staring, motionless, too weak to whine, too weak even to reach out for your dry breasts. You try to hold her gently, so that you will not jar the little heart and stop its beating. Yet you know that at some moment—the next minute, the next day, it doesn't matter—the heart will stop. Nothing you do can make it keep beating. When it has stopped, you hear nothing. Your body is as cold and lifeless as the one in your arms. You have no more weight than the tiny bundle you carry in your arms as you stumble toward the river. You hear the splash of the dark river on which no stars shine, and it is the only sound in the silent night. The feeling of the cold water against the skin of your legs is the only feeling you have. It is all there is to tell you what you have just done. You walk away with your arms already remembering, already aching for the tiny weight and the warmth of the daughter you had, the child who is now rolling away, slowly, over and over, bumping head and tiny knees against the death-slimed bottom of the river.

You do not look at that river that takes everything and gives back nothing, not even the reflection of the moon. And you dare not look at the moon to guide you, for the moon is the single eye of a madman and that eye has seen what you have done. It is rolling on through the vapors, on and on, and yet never moving in its stare; and the vast dark sky above the clouds is a frozen, mocking, one-eyed corpse. Despite yourself, you look up and exchange glances with the moon. And then you know that there is no difference between what you have done and what you may do, between yourself and the silence of the night around you.

That is what feeling nothing is, Adija. That is what Bad is. That is why I do not think that this place, or any piece of ground with shops or huts or crops on it, is bad. Bad is not a place. Bad is knowing and remembering. I think there are things you know and remember too, though you try not to. No place can rid you of your knowing or let you forget. No place, except . . .

Adija stared at Salome's face. "Where?"

"When you are with someone . . ." Salome shut her eyes.

Adija did not understand all that Salome had said, except in the feeling she had, the feeling of Salome lying cold and heavy against her chest. Adija shivered with the chill of the woman, as if she could become frozen by just touching her.

She could not move from beneath the great weight of
Salome, she could only hold it close and hope that warmth
would come. And warmth did come. Adija felt it first in
the tears that slid down Salome's cheeks. Amazed, she lay
quietly and comforted her sister, Salome.

10

THE CHILDREN RAN AWAY, SHRIEKING. THEY dashed into the huts to alert their mothers, then ran outside again, heedless of their mothers' warnings. Some crouched behind granaries, their faces pressed into the small thatched roofs. Others climbed up the pole fences of the cattle pen. There, concealed behind fans of banana leaves, they could watch the strangers from a safe distance. Their whispering blended with the buzz of flies and the slow shifting sound the leaves made in the breeze.

The tall white man stopped in an open space in the center of the compound. His parade of green-uniformed schoolboys halted behind him. The children were suddenly as still as huts and granaries and fenceposts.

Gordon wiped the sweat from his eyes. Open doorways of huts stared back at him, dark rectangles of shadows. He noted signs of life in the compound—a maize cob lying abandoned on a stone mortar, a dress hanging in a window, still dripping from a recent washing. Footprints were everywhere, and the scent of dust seemed freshly raised by scurrying feet. But there was no one in sight.

"What should we do now?" His voice sounded loud in the silence.

Peter Wanjala, the Rukiva boy that Gordon had chosen as the group's interpreter, glanced around uncomfortably. He wished he had never heard of oral history field trips. He caught sight of a shirtless boy chasing a cow across a field, and wished he could be fleeing into the underbrush with him. "We can just wait, sir. Someone will come," he said.

"I think we should go away," Pius Otieno said.

The two Marembo boys crowded close behind Otieno. Ordinarily, they had no use for this small, cheeky Luo, but he had just expressed their feelings exactly. They were not happy about being chosen for this field trip, either.

Throughout history, their kings, the monarchs of the great Marembo empire, had made serfs of placid tribes like these Rukiva who lived near the school. What could possibly be interesting about learning the history of serfs? The boys watched their teacher's face for some flicker of uncertainty, a gap between his resolve and his present predicament into which they might drive a wedge.

"No, we won't go away just yet," Gordon said. He wiped his face again and looked around hopefully. "Someone'll come soon." He glanced at Wanjala, but Wanjala looked away.

"Perhaps we could try another farm," Otieno insisted.

"No, this is the one we want. Elija is the biggest man around here. We get his support, we'll get all the people's support." Gordon had done an undergraduate minor in anthropology; he knew that to get information about people, you always went to the headman first. "Then we'll be able to go on lots more field trips," he added.

"It is very hot in the sun." Mwanga, a Marembo, touched the top of his head. "These people are very rude, not to come out and greet us."

"I'm the one who's got to worry about sunburn, not you," Gordon laughed. "Go sit in the shade if you're hot."

But no one moved. Without the teacher the boys had no reason for being here. They didn't want to be separated from him, even by a few paces.

"You're looking nervous, sir," Otieno said. "Why do you want to stay?"

Gordon shrugged. "I'm always nervous. It's my nature." His eyes followed the wavy lines that the conical thatched rooftops made against the sky. They were a soft yellow brown, and the sky was bright blue behind them. "No, I'll tell you what it is, Otieno," he said. "I love new situations. Places that are utterly foreign to me. I get excited when I'm about to learn something I knew absolutely nothing about before." He smiled. "Can you understand that?"

Otieno grinned and shook his head. He liked Mr. Lockery because he would talk about himself as if he were not a "sir," as if his students were not students but people. "I don't understand," Otieno said.

"Excuse me, sir." Mwanga was holding the top of his head again. "It is very hot here."

"Yeah, okay, Mwanga. We'll go find some shade." Gordon led the four boys to a shady spot under an overhanging roof. He took out his packet of Crane Birds. "Go ahead. We're off school grounds," he said, offering the packet around. Everyone took a cigarette but Wanjala, the Rukiva. He didn't want his own people to see him with a cigarette. They would think him pretentious, smoking like a European or a town rogue. He was embarrassed enough, waiting here like a beggar, uninvited and unannounced, and keeping company with a gang of arrogant royalists.

The two Marembo students began to speak their language in low voices. "Henry Morton Stanley, the great explorer, was kind to his native bearers," Mwanga said, sounding like the history textbook. "He won the Africans' devotion by giving out cigarettes."

"And showed his humility by lighting them for the Africans with his own match," Ssanango added.

"Yes. He made a fire with a tiny stick. A wondrous invention from across the great waters. The natives thought him to be a god." Mwanga took a long drag on his cigarette and wrinkled his nose. He was used to filter tips. "But his true colors were shown when all the natives died, poisoned from his Cheap Bird cigarettes."

Ssanango was holding his cigarette like a fountain pen. He made a face too, though he didn't know one brand of cigarettes from another. He had some catching up to do. "I think his barmaid friend's mattress must be covered with tobacco crumbs every morning, after he has pedaled his bicycle away," he said.

Mwanga grinned. "She has to sweep them out of her cunt with a broom." He bit his knuckles to keep from laughing.

Gordon frowned at them and the two boys kept silent. He didn't, of course, know their language.

Wanjala tensed. He heard footsteps approaching. "What do you want me to say, Mr. Lockery?"

"You remember—what we talked about in class."

"I remember some things you were saying. But I am forgetting too much."

"All right. You introduce us first. Then you say we're interested in finding out about the way things used to be here. The way things were before Europeans and other tribes came, before there were shops and motorcars and schools. We want to talk to the old people, so that we can learn from them."

Wanjala opened his mouth. He wanted more prepping. But it was too late.

A woman hobbled out into the courtyard, her eyes lowered to avoid the stares of the strangers. Her breasts dangled visibly beneath her faded dress as she came forward. She was not old; her hobbling was caused by a club foot. The toes of one foot were pointing backward. Wanjala's heart sank. That a mere woman should have been sent to greet the visitors was a bad enough sign. But this woman—he knew of her—was a cripple; she was Elija's only barren wife, the outcast among the other wives. "*Jambo*," he greeted her, as politely as he could manage.

The woman shook his hand, her eyes still lowered. "*Jambo*."

Wanjala repeated what the teacher had told him, almost an exact translation. Then he added some words of praise for Elija, the head of the homestead, and offered apologies for disturbing him.

The woman said that Elija was not at home. She glanced behind her. Muffled voices were coming from the hut she had just left. She repeated what she had said in a quavering voice.

"The woman says that Elija is not present, sir," Wanjala said.

"Ask her if there's someone else we could talk to."

Wanjala took a deep breath. He continued his greeting, praising Elija's livestock and the abundance of his fields. As he spoke, he glanced at the hut where the muffled voices were growing louder. The woman balanced herself on her one good foot by holding her hands out from her sides. She kept upsetting her balance by trying to cover the worn-through places in her dress where dusty brown skin showed through. Wanjala glanced at her and at the hut, and decided not to ask the teacher's question.

"The woman says there is no one else here to talk to," he reported.

"I didn't hear her say anything, Wanjala."

The commotion in the hut burst outside. A man appeared in the doorway, thrashing his arms. A woman scrambled out in front of him. She tried to push him back inside, but he flung her from him. She fell against the wall of the hut with a wail. The children who had been tugging at the man's trousers scattered.

The man lurched forward, waving a heavy, twisted walking stick in the air. His shirt was buttoned awry, showing his stomach, but he did not look foolish. His hair was white and his eyes glowed with red veins. His stride, though unsteady, was the stride of a man used to having people jump out of his way. He came to a halt in front of Wanjala and waved his stick in the air. What, he demanded, were these strangers doing on his land?

Wanjala stumbled backward. The walking stick had passed dangerously close to his face, and the man's breath was a powerful stench. Wanjala started to explain why they were here, but the man cut him off, roaring. When he finally closed his mouth, he planted the stick firmly at his feet. The stick said: You approach no closer than this.

"What's the matter, Wanjala?" Gordon asked.

"He is very drunken, sir." Wanjala took another step backward. "He is saying many nonsenses."

"Is he Elija, himself?"

"Yes, he is," Wanjala said. "We should go, sir."

Gordon wanted to step back too, but he didn't. "What's he saying, Wanjala?"

"He says I have cost him the bride-wealth for his daughter. But it was not me, sir. I swear it by the Holy Ghost!"

"What are you talking about?"

"He has mistaken me for another Rukiva boy. This boy is in Form 4. He made one of Elija's daughters to be with child. Now Elija cannot get bride-wealth for her. It will be difficult to find any good husband for her, he is saying. He wants a fine to be paid for his daughter's child. He will kill the boy who is responsible, if he does not get it." Wanjala wiped his face with both hands. "Elija is angry, sir," he added.

The old man lifted his stick and shouted several rapid sentences. His voice was as deep as a man twice his size and weight.

"He is also angry because there are Marembo boys here. He does not like Marembos."

Mwanga and Ssanango had been grinning at each other, but their faces suddenly became very sober.

The old man leaned forward, reached out his hand, and

clutched Wanjala's shoulder as if the boy were a mere
rabbit. A woman wailed. Children gasped, a mass intake of
breath from all sides. They were suddenly visible: totem
poles of small brown faces peering around the corners of
huts. Wanjala shut his eyes tight. He expected a blow from
the stick at any second. But Elija only shook him hard by
his shirt and pointed the stick at the teacher. He roared
and belched, roared and waved his stick in the direction of
the school. The bristly beard beneath the corners of his
mouth was shiny with saliva. He gripped Wanjala's shoulder tighter.

"He says the school is responsible," Wanjala whimpered.
His eyes were clamped shut. "He says teachers should be in
their classrooms teaching. They should not be roving about
the countryside to bother the honest farmers." This, in
fact, was a loose translation. Elija's diatribe had been
about teachers who let their schoolboys run wild, destroy-
ing the morals of the local girls, and failing to show proper
respect for their elders.

Gordon clenched his fists to keep his hands from trembling. "Tell him we're sorry we've bothered him. Tell him
also—Wanjala listen—" Wanjala tried to twist his face
away. "Tell him I'm going to speak to the headmaster of
the school. The headmaster will make the boy pay the fine
for the daughter's baby."

"But the headmaster does not know which boy it
is."

"No, but you do."

"I can't tell."

"All right, but then Elija's going to think it's you."

"It's not, sir!"

"How do I know it's not? Elija's pointed at you."

"It is only because I am from the school."

Gordon said nothing.

"If I tell you, he will hear. He will send his sons to beat
the boy."

"Well, what's his Christian name?"

"Robert."

"Whose class is he in first period?"

"Miss Stuart's." Wanjala opened his eyes. "Make him let
me go, sir!"

"Tell him I know who the boy is. I'll tell the headmaster,
and Elija will get his fine."

Wanjala's voice cracked as he spoke. But Elija's grip on him remained firm. Elija wiped his mouth and spoke in a low voice, his jaw protruding.

"He will not let me go unless I tell him the boy's name now," Wanjala said.

Gordon glared at the old man. For a moment, their eyes were locked. "He will never know the boy's name or get his fine," Gordon said slowly, "unless he lets you go right now. And unless he agrees to talk with us."

Wanjala spoke. Elija turned back toward the teacher. His jaw was still thrust out stubbornly, but there was a trace of a sly smile in his eyes. Gordon smiled back briefly, then waited.

Elija shoved Wanjala away from him.

Another gasping sound came from all sides. The huts themselves seemed to have been holding their breath and swelling, but now were settling back to normal size. A woman wailed; it was a happy-sounding wail this time. The crippled woman stopped shielding her eyes from Elija—the explosion was over.

A woman in a phosphorescent yellow dress ran up to Elija. He grunted and tried to step away, but she moved closer to him. She smiled and touched his cheek. Her voice was high and soothing. As she moved, her yellow dress billowed out about her ankles, reflecting the sunlight's glare with a brilliance that was surprising among these earth-colored huts. The old man continued to protest to the woman, but now and then he smiled too, as if the sun itself had rolled into his courtyard to bathe him in its rays.

The woman held Elija's arm and spoke to Gordon in Rukiva.

"She is apologizing for the behavior of her husband," Wanjala said. "He was celebrating the birth of a son when we came. He was drinking much beer."

Gordon nodded. He smiled at the woman and at Elija. "Are you all right, Wanjala?"

"No, sir. It is giving me much anguish." Wanjala rubbed his shoulder, a neutral spot of pain between his resentment toward his teacher and his anger at Elija for shaming him before his teacher. "My people, they are not like Elija. They are not drunkards," Wanjala said, his voice cracking again. "It is very unfair I have to show him to you."

"I'm sorry you were embarrassed," Gordon said.

Wanjala rubbed his shoulder harder. "It is very unfair."

The woman in yellow touched his shoulder. He jerked away. She spoke softly to him, and though her face looked worried, her voice was edged in laughter. She beckoned with her hand for him to go into one of the huts, but he turned his face away.

"Was she inviting us to stay?" Gordon asked.

"No."

"All right, we'll leave. But if you're lying about what she said, you'll be insulting her and her family," Gordon said. "And you'll be in trouble with me too."

Wanjala cleared his throat. "She said we can stay if we want. Elija told her that. But he only wants to show us his daughter, the one who is with child."

"All right."

"I thought you would not be wanting to stay, sir."

Gordon looked at Elija. Elija's eyes still burned, not with alcohol or hatred, but with the fierceness of an old man determined to hold and protect all he had until the day he dropped dead. Wrinkles deepened around his eyes, spreading all the way to his jaw. The man's face might have been carved in dark volcanic rock.

"Hell, yes—I want to stay," Gordon said.

The students sighed. Gordon decided not to hear them. Mwanga spoke up. "Sir, I can't feel happy to stay in this place. These people are uncivilized."

Gordon turned around. "Mwanga, you've been a pain in the ass all afternoon. At this point, I don't care if you're feeling happy or not."

"But, sir—"

"Listen, Mwanga. One day you're going to be working in government. You'll be making decisions affecting the lives of people like these. You can't know what they need if you've spent your last ten years cloistered in boarding schools, soaking up 'civilization.' What the hell do you think you're being educated for—so you can quote Shakespeare in your love letters and ride around in a Mercedes impressing your friends?"

Mwanga glanced at the ground, then turned his face away and glared at the treetops. He did quote Shakespeare in his love letters. When he daydreamed, which was often, it was of riding around in a Mercedes impressing his friends. But what was wrong with that? Every student had similar plans. There was no point in spending all these dreary years in school if you didn't get a Mercedes at the end. Or at least a Ford Zephyr. When he graduated from university, he certainly wasn't going to ride around on a bicycle like a peasant or a crazy foreigner. He wanted to say something clever about bicycles and Mercedes, but he couldn't think of anything.

The woman in the sun-colored dress spoke to Wanjala.

"Elija says we can come inside and take some beer," Wanjala said.

"May we drink beer?" Otieno asked. "We are off school grounds."

Gordon pretended to think for a moment. "We'd be insulting them if we refused. Right, Wanjala?"

"It is so, sir," Wanjala said gravely, hiding a smile behind his hand.

"Let's have some beer, then."

The reception hut was cool and dark inside. It smelled of earth and cattle dung and of the dry thatch of the roof. Women set wooden chairs along the walls for the guests. A Victorian wicker armchair was brought in for Elija, but he did not appear for some time. The women moved silently, their bare feet padding across the mud floor. They were young women, and it was impossible to tell whether they were Elija's wives or daughters or even granddaughters.

One of them opened the wooden windows, letting in dusty beams of sunlight. A chicken fluttered noisily up onto a sill and perched there, clucking softly. It was a good sign, Gordon decided, that the chicken felt at ease enough to join the guests. The unruffled clucking sound calmed him. He began to sketch the interior of the hut, and instructed the boys to do likewise.

The only furniture besides the chairs was a heavy Pfaff sewing machine console. It stood on curved ornate legs of black iron, guarding the door importantly. A lantern hung from one of the rafters. There were plates and cups and enamel pots on top of the walls, in the space below the roof. The walls were of red-brown mud, with vertical poles visible at intervals. On the walls were framed photographs. A family cluster. A shy bride in white who stood slightly off balance holding a heavy Bible. Two schoolboys in uniform, one solemn and stiff, one smiling painfully at the camera.

Gordon instructed each boy to write down nine questions to ask Elija. The questions were to be in three categories: life in the days of Elija's father and grandfather, life in Elija's younger days, and Elija's life during the last five years. "Use your imagination," Gordon said. "Ask good questions."

The students had rarely been asked to use their imaginations for a school assignment. They were puzzled and disturbed. Gordon showed them the questions he was writing in his notebook. Gradually they began working silently, looking about and tapping their pencils against their lips in concentration. Writing their own questions was harder than writing answers to someone else's questions, but it was more interesting.

Elija appeared in the doorway. He sat down slowly in his wicker chair. He looked around at the students and frowned. Wanjala explained that they were writing questions to ask him about his life. So well respected was Elija that the school had sent the teacher and his students to collect his biography. Elija had never held a press conference before; he was torn between being suspicious and being flattered.

"*Sigara!*" he said, pointing at the pocket of the teacher's shirt. Gordon took out his Crane Birds and shook a cigarette part way out of the packet. Then, thinking again, he took out several cigarettes and held them out to Elija with both hands cupped, African fashion.

Elija stared at him. Then he roared with laughter.

The boys laughed too. Elija had seen a cigarette packet before. He knew that to take a cigarette you merely extracted it from the opening in the top.

Gordon felt his face reddening. He was so ignorant— what the hell was he doing here, really? His fingers shook as he lit Elija's cigarette. Elija did not stop chuckling until the end of the cigarette went up in flame. He blew it out, then he sat back and watched Gordon return to his seat as if he expected him to do a handstand for an encore.

"You have good intentions, sir," Otieno said.

Gordon laughed. "I know. Sad, isn't it?"

"No, sir. It is good."

"Thank you, Otieno." Gordon composed his face. The chicken on the windowsill clucked cheerfully. "Oh, shut up," he said to it.

Wanjala smiled. It was Rukiva tradition, he explained, to
bring a gift to the family of a newborn child. Elija's wife
had just given birth to a son. She would be bringing it in
shortly. Gordon took twenty shillings from his wallet. He
told Wanjala to give it to the mother as a gift from everyone, with the compliments of the headmaster as well.
Money was not the usual sort of gift, but judging from the
look on Elija's face, it was a very acceptable gift.

The woman in the bright yellow dress appeared. She
held a tiny brown baby in her arms. Elija beckoned her
inside. She smiled shyly, glancing at her husband and then
down at the ground, at the feet of the strangers. Wanjala
presented the twenty-shilling note to Elija. Elija tucked it
into the woman's hand. When Wanjala stood up to take a
closer look at the baby, Gordon did too. The baby stared
hard at Gordon, the expression on its face poised between
amusement and terror.

Gordon retrieved his notebook from the chair and tore
out a page. Several barefoot children gathered outside the
door to watch him fold the paper. They giggled when they
saw the paper become a hat. Everyone laughed to see the
baby with a hat on. Even Elija was smiling.

The baby squinted up at its mother, then burst into
tears. She hugged it tight to her breast, laughing, the same
look on her face she had used earlier to calm her husband.
Elija raised his arm, and the look faded. The woman
stepped backward out the door, her eyes lowered, her smile
private: a proper African wife once more.

On instructions from Gordon, Wanjala complimented
Elija on his new son. Elija nodded solemnly.

The son was good. It was so.

It was good to have children. Children were the real
wealth of a man.

But if a girl had a child and she had no man to marry
her, it was not good. Elija shook his head. No, such a girl
could not bring many cattle for a bride-wealth. Would a
young man of a good family pay many cattle for the privilege of marrying a girl who was already spoiled? No. Only
a young man of a poor family would ask for her. He would
perhaps give only one thin cow. What was a father to give
his own sons, then, that they might go and seek brides
from good families? He would have but one thin cow to
give his sons. Good families would not welcome his sons.

They would say: Look, this young man has but one thin cow.

Elija shook his head. He tapped the floor with his walking stick.

If Elija could not marry his sons into good families, people would say that Elija's family is not a good family. Did Elija want people to say that? No, he did not! Elija beat the floor with his walking stick.

If Elija could not even force his daughter's abductor to pay the proper fine, people would say that Elija has become weak! Was Elija a weak man? No, he was not! Elija pounded the floor with his walking stick.

Elija sat back in his chair, finished. Dark veins throbbed on his temples.

The chicken flapped its wings and dropped out of sight behind the windowsill. A feather fluttered slowly to the floor. The hut was very still.

"I think this is not a good time to ask him questions about his grandfather's life," Wanjala whispered.

Gordon swallowed hard. "You could be right."

Elija turned his head and shouted at the door. There was a flurry of footsteps behind the walls of the hut. Children who had been eavesdropping fled in all directions. "He wants to show you his pregnant daughter," Wanjala said.

But when the girl entered, Elija ignored Gordon. He clutched the girl by the wrist and pointed his walking stick in Wanjala's face. He shouted at the girl.

Except for her full breasts, the girl looked no older than twelve. Her arm tensed across the little bulge in her belly, her fingers clutching at the faded material of her dress. No, she said, and turned her face away to hide her tears. No, he is not the one.

Wanjala sat back in his chair, still trembling. "I told you!" he whispered. "He should have asked her before he tried to strangle me."

"He wouldn't have gotten any information out of you, that way," Gordon said.

Elija glared at Gordon. He wanted the real father's name. He wanted Gordon to write the name on a piece of paper and give him the paper. Gordon lit a cigarette and puffed it slowly, stalling for time to think. "Tell him," he said, locking eyes with Elija, "that I cannot give the boy's name."

Elija did not wait for a translation from Wanjala. He pointed at the teacher's notebook, making writing motions with his finger.

Gordon wrote in his best legal English that he pledged to help Elija receive compensation for the loss of bride-wealth caused by his daughter's pregnancy.

When Elija demanded that Wanjala read him the letter in Rukiva, however, Wanjala added the boy's name, for good measure—his two Christian names and his three Rukiva names. He promised, as he pretended to read the paper, that Mr. Lockery, himself, would deliver the boy to Elija within the week. Wanjala had no faith in the teacher's good intentions. Nor did he trust Elija not to send his sons after him one night, if the real father were not produced. The beating he would receive from this boy was nothing compared to the rage of Elija and his sons.

Elija mouthed the name of his daughter's seducer several times, committing it to memory. He had no faith in the teacher's promise either. The paper was just to show the headmaster, when he visited the school later in the week. With the paper and the boy's name, he was satisfied. He saw the wisdom of his young wife—she had been right to calm his rage earlier. Of course, his rage had been wise too. He had twenty shillings, a paper, and a name that had been authenticated by a European teacher. It was good. He had done well. Elija smiled.

He shouted out the door again. It was time to celebrate with some beer. Beer! he shouted. My visitors have seen my new son, and now the visiting ritual can be resumed. Beer! Elija has been victorious! he shouted at the women. Elija, who has never been to school—Elija, who cannot use a pencil or read from a book—Elija has defeated the teacher, the man who has studied in the universities of Europe! Let no man say that Elija is weak! Bring beer! Let no teacher, no schoolboys, say that Elija does not know hospitality! Bring beer! Let this herd of educated billy goats hear the story of Elija Lukivya Waga, son of Waga Walumbe Chemai! Bring beer!

"Beer is coming," Wanjala translated. He took no consolation from the boys' smiles. He glanced uneasily at the teacher, but Gordon was grinning at Elija, and took no notice of him. "Elija is saying that he has defeated you," Wanjala said.

"Let him think so."

Wanjala stared at Gordon's face. The teacher did not look as if he had been defeated. Wanjala looked at the ground, shame-faced. "I told him the boy's name," he confessed.

"I know you did. I heard you."

"I was fearing him very much."

"I know. I was too."

The women brought in beer in glass mugs. They served Elija first, then the guests. The beer was thick and a little bitter.

"Do you like African beer, sir?" Pius Otieno asked.

"Of course," Gordon said. "Did you ever meet a man who didn't like beer?"

"You see?" Wanjala said, turning to Mwanga and Ssanango, "Royalists are not the only ones who can make good beer."

Elija sat back in his chair and stretched his arms along the armrests. Tell your friends to get their pencils out, he said to Wanjala. Elija is ready for the first question.

11

THE HEADMASTER STARED GLOOMILY OUT THE window at the graying skies. He had hoped to plant some zinnias before the afternoon rain set in. This bright young American was such a bloody nuisance. "I want to talk to you about that, um, oral history field trip you took last week. You should have cleared it with me beforehand."

The hell I should have, Gordon thought. You would have said no, and it would never have happened. He stared out the window, smoking, his palm full of cigarette ashes.

"By going to Elija's farm, you made him think that he had an ally in the school. You increased the political importance of his family and clan a hundredfold. I don't suppose you realized that, did you?"

"No, I didn't." Gordon walked to the window and dropped his cigarette ashes out. "Do you know Elija?" he asked, curious.

"Indeed I do. The man led a rag-tag delegation to the District Office in Mbure to complain about us here last month. He demanded that we admit more boys of the Rukiva tribe to the school. What he meant was, more of his own sons." The rain crashed down against the roof, a sudden downpour. Mr. Griffin gave up all hope for his zinnias. "But now Elija feels we are on his side. His brother was in yesterday asking me to give testimony at the *baraza* about one of his sons."

"What about?"

"You've no doubt seen the men sitting around outside the Regional Government Officer's office on the way to the village. The native court is holding a *baraza*—that's a palaver, a trial—about all the troubles hereabouts. Elija's uncle wanted me to swear that his son—his son's Lukivya, a student here—hasn't been involved."

"Was he involved?" Gordon asked.

"I haven't the foggiest notion. What the boys do on their holidays is their concern." Mr. Griffin polished his spectacles on a handkerchief. "But I'm certainly not going to testify to anything. To testify is to take sides. That's my point. I'm not going to have the school involved in any tribal or family feuds—we're a government school now, and we must stay above politics. Besides, if Elija's enemies thought we were with him, we could be in for some serious trouble. There have been a dozen huts burned down already."

Like to get some boys to sit in on this *baraza*, Gordon thought. A little modern history won't hurt them at all, after all this Dr. Livingston-I-presume horseshit. "What's the feuding about?" he asked.

"Cattle rustling. Just like your Wild West." Mr. Griffin leaned further back in his chair. Why did this young man have to smoke such foul-smelling cigarettes? "But there's a lot of politics in it too. Disillusionment with Uhuru, and all that. It could lead to an awful row if it spills across the border into Bashiri. You know the people over there are trying to secede. If they get stirred up and vote in the opposition party, it could lead to civil war."

"Are the Swila involved in this feuding?"

Mr. Griffin's brows shot down into a scowl. "Now where the devil did you hear that nonsense?"

The New Life. But Gordon knew better than to say that. "I just heard they were around here."

"Yes, well, you can just forget that particular rumor. If it gets around, next thing you know the government will make this a restricted province. D'you know what that would mean?"

"Everyone would have to have passes to get in and out of the area."

"Passes? That's nothing." The headmaster tapped his pen hard against his desk top. "You've seen bands of men roving about with spears lately? The watchfires in the night? Well, if the government starts thinking they're Swila, we'll have the bloody Marembo army camping out on our doorstep. With those blokes about, everybody will be grabbing up spears. I'd be inclined to get one myself." Mr. Griffin cleared his throat. "Let's not hear any more about the Swila, thank you very much."

"Yes, all right."

Mr. Griffin rose. "In future, please conduct your, um, research on the school grounds, Mr. Lockery. If you wish to wander about the countryside on your own time, that's your lookout. But you may not take any schoolboys off the compound. Is that clear?"

Very clear, Gordon thought, walking back to his house in the rain. Don't Get Involved—the Headmaster's Creed. Keep students secluded from the life around them. Read them *She Stoops to Conquer* and *Great Christian Martyrs,* line them up and make them recite, teach them to copy verbatim notes off the blackboard—but do not, at all costs, allow them to get involved with their own people and affairs. No wonder they wrote essays like the ones that were waiting on his table to correct.

He slammed the door shut and slumped down at his table. Picking up a notebook, he read:

> I will be a big man in every way, with a wife. She will work my shamba. I will read Shakespear and have many servants. I will buy a radiogram. I will always be using long trousers and not these shorts because then I shall be a very tall man who can't use a pair of shorts. I will drive a Mercedes to my office. . . .

The title of all the essays was "Myself as I Shall Be in Ten Years." It had been assigned by a teacher whose composition class Gordon had taken over. He picked up another notebook:

> I will be generous to those who have not been so fortunate than me. I will visit many places in Bashiri and give my salary to help poor people. I will be talking to them to learn their problems. . . .

That was refreshing. He read on:

> By this time, I will be gathering much fame. The poor people will have confidence in me. The most important step in my political career will have been achieved. My fame and my money will cause people to vote for me. . . .

He lit a cigarette and opened another notebook:

> I hope to keep up with the high standard of living
> the imperalists have introduced both mentally and
> physically with the help of God. . . .

And there you have it in a nutshell, he thought.

The history he was teaching was still imperialist history, a year after the country's Independence. Great English Explorers and Early Arab Empires on the Coast. The students were bored with it all, but were nervous when he told them he thought their textbook was of dubious value. How could a book be good or bad? A book contained right answers—since it was a book, the printed word, it was truth. On a test, you either wrote what the book said, or you wrote something different and got points off. It was simple. Learn the book, pass the examination, get a good job with government, drive a motorcar, take beautiful women to the cinema—become an important man who has everyone's respect. But fail to learn the book, then you were finished: You became a half-educated peasant, scratching away at the dry earth just to keep your family from starving. The education process was a matter of life or death—hadn't teachers been telling them this since their first day in primary school? And now this new American teacher was confusing them.

He had written the Education Ministry several times, and finally the new Africanized syllabus and new textbooks, in which Africans played key roles, were going to be sent. The headmaster, of course, was furious, but the boys would eventually appreciate the change.

They did not, however, as yet appreciate Gordon's abandonment of the imperialist teaching method in use throughout the school: writing notes on the board for the boys to copy. Gordon made the boys write their own notes from outlines he provided. He realized it was hard work, he told them, but they could not learn anything by rote memorization—except to parrot the words of foreigners and people in authority. The boys struggled with their new task and grumbled continuously. Gordon stifled his impatience.

It will take time, he thought, looking over the schoolboys' papers. But, then, I have plenty of time.

He went into his bedroom and dried his hair with a towel. He was still dripping from the rain. The house was chilly. The next time the women came around selling firewood, he would have to buy some. He lay on his mattress and pulled the blanket over him. One of these days, he'd have to get some sheets.

The house was dreary when it rained. Dreary when the sun was out too. Dreary also at night, for that matter. After six weeks, he still had no pictures to cover the cinderblock walls, no curtains on the windows, no furniture except the government-issued stuff that had come with the house. The only trace of human habitation was his mess: books and papers all over the table and floor in the sitting room, dirty clothes under his bed, dishes providing an insect-sanctuary in the sink. The house looked no different from his dormitory rooms at college and all the boarding schools. A rat's nest.

Yet this was his new home. He meant to *stay* here.

If he was going to survive here, he would have to make his house as different from the rest of the school as he could. He tried to think of ways he could make the house his own. The idea was frightening. All his adult life he'd carried his home around with him like a turtle. He'd had nothing to keep him anywhere, owned nothing he would be sorry to lose. But he had to make a home somewhere, didn't he? He had to surround himself with something . . .

He thought of the houses his father's company had built: the roar of bulldozers, uprooted trees crashing to the ground, strangers grunting and cursing and hurrying away at sunset, leaving tangles of machinery behind them. And of his own house: his father bickering with the contractor about the delays, his mother screaming at the moving men. Then all the personal touches that make a house a home: the tables you could not set glasses down on, the floors you could not run your toy cars across, the couches you could not rest your feet on. His father had been proud of the house. Look, he might have said, it is bigger than my neighbors'. It is mine.

Gordon thought of Elija's farm: The clusters of neat huts with their roofs of woven straw, the little granaries full of maize, the pens where the cattle blended their lowing with the creaking of wood as they scratched their necks against the poles. That was a home. Everything in it was made with the hands of men and women of a family. The red-brown earth had not been obliterated and replaced, it had merely been reshaped. The home kept the color and smell of the earth around it. Even its shapes were not so different from those of nature: anthills, beehives, acacia trees, the hills and mountains themselves.

That was a home, Gordon thought. A man could value that. His people had made it. He could say: Look, this is what I and my family have done. Even my tiny daughters combed the grass. Even my young sons pushed handfuls of mud into the cracks in the walls. It is done. It is ours. It is us.

Gordon stared at his cinderblock walls. Nothing in this house was him. He felt as hollow as the house. I have come all the way to Africa to escape this hollowness, he thought, and now I am suffocating in it again.

He had been thinking of getting some pictures and curtains. But he knew they wouldn't relieve the feeling. Strangers had built this house, strangers had lived in it before him. A stranger still lived in it. He needed someone else to share it with him.

He paced the room. He switched on the school's battery-powered tape recorder. A voice spoke to him. His own voice. It spoke Kisemi adjectives. The colors: green . . . brown . . . purple . . . black . . . There were no colors in the room but gray—walls, hands, sky . . . He opened his Kisemi grammar and his mind began to work in sync with the tape recorder, determinedly filling in the silences.

He carried the Kisemi book everywhere. He studied it while he ate, he mouthed sentences between classes. Everything he saw he turned into Kisemi. That is a tree, a green tree, a big green tree with branches. That is a girl, a lovely girl, a slim lovely girl with eyes . . . He had even begun to dream in Kisemi. While he studied, he did not hear the rain pounding on the roof, he did not see the gray walls around him. The room filled up with colors and chattering and laughter. He spoke to Adija of trees and flowers and houses. Adija lives in the house . . . with trees in the yard . . . with flowers on the roof . . . She replied to his sentences, laughing, waving her hands, tossing her hair.

When the rain stopped, he rode his bicycle across the compound toward Musolu. The sun had come out again, glowing red now; ripples of gold and purple clouds fanned out across the sky. Gordon gazed up as he pedaled, his tire tracks crisscrossing behind him in the mud. Two boys came toward him, dribbling a football across the soggy grass. "Good evening, sir," one greeted him. "Do you take your evening meal in the town?"

"No. Why?"

"No reason." The boy kicked the ball to the other boy, who let it go by him. "We see you pedaling into town sometimes, that's all." He ran after the ball. "Good evening, sir," he called behind him.

He watched the boys running across the field. They were curious about him. That was normal. Still, there was no use letting everyone know he went to the New Life every night. It wouldn't do to set himself up to be accused, in some future staff meeting, of trying to unravel the school's moral fiber. Gordon pedaled on across the compound.

When the boys reached Tembo House, they reported that they had just seen Mr. Lockery headed for the New Life again. The boys exchanged knowing smiles.

Rumors about Mr. Lockery had started the day after he had met Elima, the Police Chief, at the New Life. Elima had complained about the new teacher to his driver, Jonathan Waudo. The teacher would rather talk with some cheap barmaid, he'd grumbled, than me—I hope he catches himself a good dose of syphilis. Jonathan Waudo mentioned the incident to his wife, and his wife mentioned it to nearly all the women she met in the market. One woman who heard the story was the wife of Seth Chemai, the school night watchman. Chemai stopped in every Thursday midnight at the school toolshed, where the Rukiva Student Association held its meetings. Since tribal societies were outlawed at the school, the Rukiva boys gave Chemai all the stolen coffee he wanted, as insurance against being chased out of the toolshed. He sold them tins of home-brewed beer his relatives made and regaled them with gossip from the village.

Stories about Mr. Lockery proliferated about the school like ants in sugar. It was said by some that he was an agent of the CIA and Adija was a Swila spy; the two were secretly supplying guns to the Swila rebels in a last-ditch attempt to postpone Bashiri's Independence. (This was the year that James Bond books were slipped between the covers of *Silas Marner* and *Intermediate Algebra*.) Others said that Adija was a Jewish witch who had ensnared Mr. Lockery in a spell; together they wandered about the countryside by night, robbing graves and eating the flesh of the dead and incidentally setting huts on fire. (This version the prefects told to wide-eyed underformers by flickering candlelight.) Only the most gullible students really believed that Mr. Lockery and Adija were spies or witches, or even lovers—it was difficult to imagine schoolmasters doing sex with anyone. But no one publicly doubted the truth of the stories. To scoff at juicy rumors about staff was to side with the enemy and risk the censure of one's allies. It was just a question of time now before the rumors reached the staff themselves and, eventually, the headmaster.

12

MANY MORE CARS AND BICYCLES THAN USUAL lined the street outside the New Life Hotel. Inside, the air squeaked and crackled with the blare of the wireless. Two new pressure lanterns swung from the rafters, their silver glare making the figures below vibrate as if the air were charged with lightning. Patel had supplied paper Bashiri flags, which now hung gaily from a wire above the bar. Their blue and yellow stripes clashed with the Marembo orange and green motif of the barroom, but nobody cared. It was the night of Bashiri's Independence. Though few Bashirians were present, everyone was in a mood to celebrate, and the bar was jammed.

What did these people know of the suffering that had won Bashiri its Independence? Salome complained to herself. The bloodshed, the families broken apart, the concentration camps—they knew nothing of it. Except for Elima —he had been a soldier in the army fighting against the Bashiri guerrillas—the bastard. What right did he have to celebrate? Or Jeremiah, for that matter—he and hundreds of other collaborators with the British were going to reap the fruits of Independence, with their government jobs and positions in foreign companies, their London suits and Mercedes motorcars.

She had talked of this when her friend Maina had last come through Musolu. He was a famous Samoyo traditional singer who had fought in the war, and was going to be allowed to sing on the wireless as part of the Independence celebrations in Azima. One of his songs was going to surprise people, he'd told Salome; she was especially eager to hear it tonight because she had supplied some of the words herself. On the back of the bar was a big alarm clock, to remind her when to turn on the wireless. At midnight, the Union Jack would be lowered at the football

stadium in Azima and the new Bashiri flag would rise up
the flagpole amid the cheers of the crowd. Despite her
misgivings, Salome was eager to hear those cheers.

In fact, she had been the one to steal the pressure lanterns from Patel's store and to hang the paper flags. On a
borrowed sewing machine, she made a new dress of silky
blue and yellow material that fastened over one shoulder,
leaving the other one glistening black. She wore nothing
beneath the dress; her breasts rolled about and her thighs
hissed beneath the cloth as she moved. She had slit the
cloth up one leg, and clamped her fuzzy Afro-American
wig on top of her own short hair.

Simon Waga, the nurse, had been wanting to write an
Uhuru poem for days. When he saw Salome, he had his
inspiration. He scribbled on his note pad, oblivious to the
din around him, and handed her the result as she came
sweeping by.

> Face of bristling black sun
> Dazzling above two radiant globes
> Broken loose from their orbit
> And dancing like rainbowed elephants
> Mad with joy for celebrating Uhuru—
> Uhuru ya Salome! Uhuru ya Bashiri!

Waga stroked his goatee as he watched Salome read the
poem. She stood frowning, one hand holding the beer tray
with the poem on it, the other resting on her hip. Then she
tossed it on the table, laughing, and left a bottle of beer.

Gordon, who had pushed his way slowly through the
crowd, sat down across from Waga and picked up the
paper. "Another poem?" he asked.

Waga nodded. "Read it." He looked away, smiling. As
the teacher read the paper, Waga had trouble keeping his
eyes off his face. "What do you think?" he asked.

Gordon grinned. "It's terrific. Did you have any luck
with it?"

"A free beer." Waga shrugged.

"Don't knock it. That's more than I ever got for any of
my poems."

"I started one about your friend Adija. I'll show you
sometime."

"Okay . . ." Gordon was looking around for her. The

rumble of conversation and music came at him out of the vibrating light in cacophonous waves; he couldn't see her in the crowd or hear her voice anywhere. When Salome came by again, he asked her where she was.

"Washing glasses, I think. We're too busy for Kisemi lessons tonight."

"I can see that."

"Maybe she's entertaining a visitor in her room." Salome smiled. But then she looked worried. Gordon had half-risen in his chair and spotted Adija at the same time she had. Martin Elima the police chief was holding Adija's arm across the bar and grinning at her; she was trying to pull away, her face contorted.

"You stay out of it," Salome snapped at Gordon, and made a move toward the bar. Just then Adija freed herself and Elima turned away, laughing, his buck teeth glinting in the bright light. "She's all right," Salome said to Gordon. "But I think this isn't a good night for Europeans to be here."

"There's only one," Gordon said, watching Adija step out from behind the bar with a tray of beer bottles. He couldn't catch her eye; people were shouting at her for beer from all over the room, and she was having trouble telling where the voices were coming from.

"You should go home," Salome said.

"I *am* home." Gordon frowned, trying to watch Adija. He didn't like the idea that a wall of men constantly blocked his view of her. Nor did he like the way some of them grabbed at her when she served them. Some of them were new tonight, come across the border from Bashiri to celebrate in the only town of any size for miles around. Some of them were drunk already, leaning back in their chairs and shouting raucously to each other. People who knew of Salome's reputation for fiercely keeping the peace would not have behaved that way.

Salome shook her head and banged a bottle down in front of Gordon. "Keep him drinking quietly," she said to Waga. "Maybe you can explain the facts of life in Africa to him."

"It's true, there's only one of him," Waga told her, but she had already turned away, hoping to avoid being no-ticed by the man pushing his way across the room. As if she could have avoided notice, dressed as she was.

"*Eii*, Salome!" Jeremiah rushed forward to shake her hand. "I bring you greetings from Azima. Uhuru ya Bashiri!"

"Uhuru ya Bashiri," Salome mumbled. "Why didn't you stay in Azima?"

"I had to come see you on this special night." Jeremiah chuckled and sat down. "You've got a big mob here, don't you? Come, put that beer down and join us."

Salome didn't want to sit with him, but he pulled her arm until she fell into a chair. Jeremiah was much stronger than he appeared. "You look good, Salome. A real Samoyo big mama!" He rolled his head in imitation of her rolling walk, and flashed his white teeth. "Salome Wairimu and I are sister and brother of the same tribe," he explained to Gordon and Waga.

"Don't make me vomit," Salome said in her language.

"Introduce your friends, Salome."

"Waga and Gordon," she said under her breath.

"I am Jeremiah Kongwe." He released Salome's arm and reached across the table to shake hands. "I come to this village often to visit my family. They live nearby."

"Goat shit," Salome said in Samoyo. "You've come to spy on the *baraza*."

Jeremiah laughed. "Salome thinks I have come to arrest her," he explained. "But I am not that brave." The lantern light glinted on his bald brown head whichever way he turned—it reminded Salome of a searchlight on a detention-camp tower. "I could not harm my sister, anyway—we were born in the same village, Salome and I."

"If your family lives near here," Waga asked in Rukiva, "how is it that your 'sister' is Samoyo?"

"My father was Samoyo, my mother Rukiva," Jeremiah replied in the same language, then switched back to English. "I think you are the nurse in charge of the dispensary here."

"Yes, I am." Waga was pleased that the man was aware of his importance in the town, but disturbed that a stranger had information about him. The rumors that this Jeremiah was a Special Branch man must be true. Perhaps he was covering the *baraza* to discover if any Bashiri Swila were involved in the hut burnings. Waga shut his mouth and looked away.

"I think you are the Anglo-American Overseas Project teacher at the school here," Jeremiah said to Gordon.

"Right." Gordon took a gulp of beer, eyeing Jeremiah over the top of his glass. "How'd you know?"

"We have teachers from your project in Bashiri. It's my job to know about all the foreigners who come into the country." Jeremiah gave Salome's thigh a squeeze.

"You're from the police?" Gordon asked.

"The government." Jeremiah smiled. "In Bashiri, we have been having our own government for a year now. We have been giving the settlers time to escape before we declared official Independence, you see. Anyway, how are you enjoying these parts, Mr. Lockery?"

"Very much."

"The countryside is very beautiful—do you find it?"

"Yes." Gordon glanced at Salome, who was slipping away, and wished he could too.

"When the season for the boys' circumcision dances comes, you should come to see them. Not many tribal ceremonies are still going on these days. I know you Europeans like to watch them." Jeremiah stood up, holding his glass. "Excuse me, now. I see my friend Swila Number 1, the Police Chief, and I must go greet him before he becomes too drunk to recognize me."

Adija stood in the back doorway, resting, watching Jeremiah move across the room toward Elima's table. She would have to push past him in order to get to Gordon's table, and pass directly by Elima. He would reach out for her, and this time she might not be able to shake loose. She would have to stay away from Gordon a while longer. Anyway, Salome had warned her not to favor any particular man tonight, including Gordon; if one man appeared to be making headway with her, she would become more desirable in the eyes of other men, and there was sure to be trouble as a result. With the barroom packed wall to wall with customers, a private fight would explode into a public brawl in minutes, Salome had said. But Adija wasn't so sure these men wanted to fight over her—they seemed more intent on drinking and arguing about politics.

Some men were saying that the Western provinces should secede because the new Bashiri government was already favoring the rich city people and the tribes in the east; others said, no, the new government would help all its citizens. Salome had explained it to her so that Adija could agree with anyone who might—for a joke, of course—ask her opinion. Adija didn't like politics. They were keeping her from sitting down quietly with Gordon.

But he too was talking politics, or at least he was listening to Waga talking about it and waving his hands about the way he did when he was explaining Important Matters. Adija took a drink from her glass, not hearing the shouts for service from the men around her. Perhaps it would not be a bad idea to have some men fighting over her—then Gordon would show more interest in her. She smiled, then frowned. No, that wasn't fair—she'd been the one to put off his interest; he hadn't forced himself on her because he was a kind man. Why was she discouraging him? Perhaps because she was afraid of Salome. Perhaps, too, because she wanted those quiet evenings with the three of them talking Kisemi together to go on forever. She had the two people she liked most close to her—what more could she want?

But looking around her now at the mob of men, with Gordon in the midst of them, sweating and glancing around, she knew that he was not comfortable here any-more and that those quiet evenings would not continue as they had. And when his glance found her, and she smiled back at him, she could see that he was watching her like a man who wanted more than talk.

But soon he would go back to his school. He was only visiting here. He always had a safe place to go back to. While all she had was the New Life Hotel. Which was better than what she'd had before coming here, but still, she realized, not safe. She had to admit, staring into the noisy room, that she was scared here. The bright light and smoke hurt her eyes, preventing her from even seeing Gordon sometimes. Under ordinary circumstances, she had to be up close to see him—or anything at all—clearly. Tonight he was just a bleached-out face-shaped space in the shadow-and-glare sea of dark figures around her. She wanted more of him than that. She wanted to be able to tell him that she was frightened here, and to have him take her away to a safe place with him, some place clean and quiet—like his school, or a real hotel in the city, or out into the countryside where there were big green spaces to walk around in.

A glass suddenly shattered against the back wall. Adija moved behind the bar as two men stood up, shouting at each other. They lurched across a table at each other, their eyes red-rimmed, beads of sweat standing out on their foreheads. The procession of men in the Marembo mural behind them flickered in the lantern light; now their grins seemed to be those of an army advancing toward a battle. Salome swept by, her machete blade glinting at her side. Elima was at the scene too, but no one was paying him much attention. Salome shouted at the two men, and held the machete across her chest like a mirror for the men to see themselves in, Adija thought, and see how foolish they looked as they bellowed drunkenly. They also must have noticed how sharp the blade was, and how strong was the arm that wielded it. One of them sat down hard, the other one pushed his way out of the room, knocking over several bottles and trodding on toes. A slow ripple of resentment followed him toward the door, then gradually subsided as Salome called for more beer and louder music. Adija loaded her tray with bottles and turned up the wireless.

After everyone was served, Adija returned to stand beside the bar. The room had emptied somewhat—friends of the man who had left were trying to quiet him on the pavement outside. Adija felt Gordon's eyes on her again, and took a long drink of beer, feeling a little better. He was admiring her new dress. It was of the same silky material as Salome's but was a dark peach-colored mini. In this light, it was hard to tell where the dress ended and her thighs began. When she stood motionless staring out from her perch beside the bar, the material hung straight down from her shoulders to her thighs. But when she moved, the dress came to life, rippling and shimmering and flowing about her like a banner in a soft breeze. With Gordon's eyes upon her, her hands began fluttering, imitating the language of the cloth. But when he returned to his conversation with Waga, they hung limp at her sides. She was trapped there beside the bar. Motionless, she stared out over Gordon's head, out over the heads of all the drinkers, straight into the lamp hanging on the opposite wall. The glare made her eyes water; it obliterated everything from her sight. The wireless music washed the noise from her ears, and as long as the song lasted, she no longer heard the murmuring of Gordon's English among the other languages vibrating throughout the room.

*　*　*

Waga pounded on the table with his empty beer bottle until Adija finally appeared with her tray. "Girl, I've been calling for you for half an hour!" he said, laughing. "What do you see when you stare like that with your big eyes— palm trees and beaches on the coast?"

"No." Adija put more beer down on the table. "Never."

"*Jambo*, Adija," Gordon said, smiling up at her.

"*Sijambo*." Adija poured beer into his glass, eyes lowered.

"*Habari za usiku*." Gordon continued the greeting.

"*Njema. Na wewe?*"

"*Nzuri, tu.*"

Adija laughed, suddenly feeling happy. They were learning to speak together very well. She understood most of what he said, and he understood perhaps half of what she said. With hand signals and facial expressions, they enjoyed their conversations more, probably, than if Gordon had been fluent in Adija's language.

"Is that your Uhuru dress?" Gordon asked in Kisemi.

Adija mentally untangled the faulty grammar in his question. "Yes. Is it nice?"

"I like it. You're very beautiful in it."

"Thank you." Adija lowered her eyes again.

"Do you want to sit down with us?"

She did and she didn't. She wanted to talk with Gordon, but she didn't want to give Waga the chance to tease her about the "medical checkup" he had given her a few weeks ago. Gordon's Kisemi was good enough now that he might understand. "There's too many people just now. Perhaps I can come back later."

"You're very rude, Adija," Waga spoke up, his eyes grinning mischievously. "The teacher has paid you a compliment and asked you to join him. Maybe you don't like him."

"I do, but—"

"You do like him, but you won't sit with him. Very

strange behavior." Waga shook his head solemnly. "I will have to give you a psychiatric checkup next time."

"Shut your mouth, you—"

Gordon frowned at Waga. "It's okay. She can come back later."

"You see? He's changed his mind," Waga told Adija. "He's insulted."

"Waga, if you don't mind, goddammit!" Gordon said.

"It's all right," Waga said in English. "I'm just joking with her."

Adija swayed back and forth in place, trying to understand Waga's English. Then she glanced away, not wanting to be sucked into his mockery. Still, she wanted desperately to know what he was saying about her, because Gordon was hearing it.

"It's all right, Adija." Gordon touched her hand. "If you're too busy, you can come back later. I'll wait for you."

Adija sat down stiffly. She turned her back to Waga. "This man is telling lies," she said to Gordon, pouting. "He is always writing in his stupid book, with all his English words—" She twisted her face around toward Waga. He had taken out his notebook and was pretending to take down everything she said. "That's all he's good for," she added.

Waga grunted. "She's difficult to write about, your friend."

"You're writing about her?"

"My poem. Do you want to see it?"

"Sure. I'll take a look at it later," Gordon said, glancing at Adija.

"I think my writing is too sloppy. I'll have to read it to you—"

Adija reached out to snatch the notebook, but Waga was too quick for her. She turned around in her chair again, her back to him. She was glad she didn't know English, she decided—she wouldn't have to hear his insults. At the same time, she ached to know it with the hunger of a starving person, and listened hard to try to catch a familiar word.

"Read it another time," Gordon said, "when it's not so noisy in here."

"The noise doesn't bother me." Waga sat back, his note-book on his lap, his brow furrowed with concentration. "Perhaps as I read, I can find an ending for it," he insisted, and began reading.

> Jinjeh-scented Adija
> Mystery-flavored Adija
> A charming schoolgirl, a heart of
>   —money
> A hard-buttocked whore, a heart of
>   —laughter
> A victim waif, a heart of
>   —treachery
>
> No one knows her
> Though anyone may have her
> Or thinks so
> Even men who have entered her secret cave
> Have come out aware only of their ignorance
> A twinkle in the penis, but an ache in the heart
> Returned not from the womb, but a vacant room
> Sticky with shadows
>
> Child, harlot, witch
> Unlike others and therefore
> A threat to everyone
> Yet delightful
> Your mystery distresses me
> Though the whisperings of the villagers do not . . .

"That's as far as I've got," Waga said, putting down the notebook.

"It's far enough." Gordon eyed the notebook, then Waga's face.

"Lies!" Adija snatched the book from the table. "Let me see what lies he's written!" She squinted at the page, as if by looking at it hard enough, she might find it decipher-able.

"It's just words on paper," Gordon said. "It doesn't mean anything about you."

"You think I don't know anything?" She flung the note-book down. "I know some English words. I know 'witch.'"

He is saying I am a bad woman and a witch, but I'm not so bad he can't—" Adija clamped her mouth shut, turning sharply away.

"Just because he writes . . ." Gordon struggled with his Kisemi, "doesn't make you bad."

"You think I don't know how people are calling me things? Swila, witch, evil eye? You think I don't see how women pull their children away from me for fear I'll look at them? I can't see very well, but I can always see that!" Adija whirled around, tears flying from her face. "Now he writes it down on paper! He writes it!"

"No one will see it—"

"It is *written!* In *English!* He wants to make it all true about me, like a book! And I can't—I can't—" She hugged herself tight, shivering. "You—Waga—you are worse than a witch! You cunt of a nurse! You who suck out the asshole of a hyena—"

"Shut up, woman—" Waga gripped the edge of the table.

"You who bite off the cock of a dead crocodile and feed it to your sick mother—" Adija stood up, her chair scraping loudly against the floor, and knocked Waga's glass into his lap with a swipe of her hand.

Waga leaped to his feet. "You're lucky that was empty! Now you mind your tongue, you ignorant bitch, or I'll push that glass down your throat!"

Gordon lunged forward and grabbed Waga's shoulders. "Sit down," he said through his teeth. Waga sat down, still glaring at Adija. Gordon turned and grabbed the bottle Adija was reaching for. "Adija, no!"

She pulled her hand back from the bottle, and wiped her eyes. "I thought you were my friend, Gordon."

"I am."

"You like the things he writes."

"I didn't say that."

She wiped her nose with the back of her hand. "If you're my friend, tear up what he wrote."

"Christ, Adija—" Gordon glanced around. The place had become much quieter suddenly. Men were watching him. Some looked annoyed, others were grinning in expectation of some action. Gordon felt the heat and closeness in the room. The light caught the beads of sweat shining on everyone's forehead. Everyone's black forehead. Gordon cleared his throat and swallowed hard. "You want me to get into a fight—is that it, Adija?"

"No fight. Just tear it up—finished."

"Not 'finished.' You can't—" He made ripping movements with his hands. "—destroy something of someone's without a fight. Especially his own writing. I don't want to fight Waga. He's not my enemy."

"He is!"

"He's not. But he will be if I destroy his poem. Listen, Adija—oh shit . . ."

She turned sharply from him and fled across the room, the back of her hand pressed against her face in a gesture of betrayal and grief. Gordon watched her go, unable to fully believe her theatrics, but unable to remain unaffected by them either.

"That girl is too superstitious," Waga said. "A clear case of paranoia. I read about a case like her in my medical course. She will cause trouble here if she doesn't change her ways."

"Shut up, Waga." Gordon sat down hard. His heart would not stop pounding. He felt wretched.

"Verging on catatonia," Waga continued calmly. He pointed toward Adija, standing motionless beside the bar.

"You should stick to poetry, Waga," Gordon said. "You're a poet, I'll give you that."

Waga smiled sadly. "For me, writing poetry is too often a substitute for action. What else can I do in this bush town but write? But, for you, it's the other way around."

Gordon drained his glass. "What?"

"Action is a substitute for poetry with you. You see it all around you, you feel it—poetic beautiful things, like this Adija. And you think you have to do something about them or you will be missing out." He nodded to himself. "You can't just coexist with beauty—that's painful for you. You have to somehow be part of it."

Gordon glared at him. "How much do you charge for your psychiatric opinions, Waga?"

"Free, my friend. I'm cheap compared to what that girl will cost you."

"You think so, do you?"

Waga closed his notebook and pushed it into his back

pocket. "I don't blame you for being angry with me. I'll apologize to her. Do you want another beer?"

"Yeah," Gordon said, staring into his empty glass. "Why the hell not? *Uhuru ya Bashiri.*"

He watched Adija gazing out over the room, her hair glistening, its anarchic outline ablaze. The silvery lantern light was reflected in her eyes. They apparently saw nothing, yet they glared through all the smoke and noise directly at Gordon, accusing him: You always want more! Entreating him: Have it!

*   *   *

"Quiet! Quiet!" Salome stood on a chair and shouted until the men looked up from their drinks in silence. "I know this man on the wireless. Listen to him!" She had tuned in the special Uhuru Night program from Azima. "He is a street singer, a singer of traditional Bashiri songs."

"You heard him while you were walking the streets?" Elima shouted.

"Listen!" Salome silenced the laughter. "There are Bashirians among you. This is the night of our Uhuru. *Uhuru ya Bashiri!*"

"*Uhuru ya kuma!* Free cunt!" someone called and was told to shut up, amid the laughter.

"Those who are not Bashirians should remember that Bashirians celebrated the Uhuru of Marembo with dignity!" Salome shouted. The noise subsided. Several Bashirians called for quiet, and finally the wireless could be heard.

"His name is Maina. He is a famous singer in Bashiri. Listen to his songs!" Salome said, and stepped down from her chair.

Maina sang a Samoyo song about Wathiri Njama, the hero of the freedom fighters who was feared by British troops everywhere. Wathiri ambushed a lorry and killed all the soldiers inside; Wathiri captured a government store and fed the poor villagers from it; Wathiri was hunted down in the forest like an animal. . . .

As she listened, Salome felt a pain growing in the pit of her stomach that pushed open the cracks in her hardness. When Maina sang of the forest, the knot in her stomach turned cold and cracked and shivers rippled through her.

When he sang of the villages, she remembered not ordinary villages, but rows of whitewashed huts squatting in the midst of mud and barbed wire. She recalled the faces

of the villagers—hungry faces, tense faces . . . mothers
shrieking at their children for playing too loudly, neighbors
and old friends bickering. And the rumors that left the acid
taste of fear in your mouth—rumors of victory, rumors
of defeat, rumors of friends who had disappeared in the
night. . . .

And when Maina sang of death, she remembered Kariuki in the forest.

When she tried to wash that remembrance away with a
long gulp of beer, she remembered her daughter Wairimu
asleep in the gray moonlit river.

When she tried to wash that remembrance away, she
remembered Salome Wairimu hiding by the roadside as the
soldiers' lorries passed; fleeing the city, fleeing the people in
the villages who had raised her, fleeing with the accusations of her people ringing in her head like a blacksmith's
hammer.

And when she tried to wash that remembrance away,
she had to think of Salome of Musolu who had risen from
the dead upon a dung heap, and who now ruled the dung
heap, who piled the dung up around her and watched it
harden in the blaze of the sun as she slowly vanished
within it. . . .

Salome listened; she pressed the knuckles of her fists
hard against her cheeks to hold the hard, dry walls together
against the spreading cracks.

The song ended. There was some applause. None was
louder than Salome's. Conversation resumed. Several men
shouted for more beer.

Adija started to move toward the beer shelf, but Salome
stopped her with a look. "Let them wait!"

Maina sang a new song, a song, he announced, that he
had written for Uhuru:

> Where are the heroes of the revolution?
> They are all around you.
>
> Are they riding in motorcars through the streets of
>   the city?
> Can you see them gazing from rooftop restaurants?
> Can you find them trying on London suits?
> And gathering people to ask for votes?
> No. But they are all around you.

They are on the street corners.
There, the fellow with a stump for a leg,
Blown off by a mortar,
He takes a five-cent piece in his cup
From a woman in high-heeled shoes.
See the man wandering his village in tatters,
Shouting to comrades who have died—
His face is covered with dust.
His mind is covered with ants.
The gun that he fought for your freedom with
Is covered with rust on some old battlefield,
Now a game preserve,
Conquered by the cameras of tourists
En route to Johannesburg.

And the landless plant maize on the roundabouts.
"NO WORK" cries the sign on the factory gate,
Yet the men wait, fingers curled around the bars.
The women wait all day on the grass of the hospital,
Or all night on bar stools, painted eyes
Reflecting the flashes of passing Mercedes.
The mouths of those who wait are silent
But they curse in their sleep—
The sound flies with the howls of vagrants from
    the jail,
Rattles with the dustbins being rifled for food,
Rumbles with the empty stomachs in the backstreets
    of the city.

The guard at the Hilton sleeps in his riot helmet,
Standing at ease.
His police dog twitches on the marble doorstep.

Outside the boutique, the night watchman leans
    on his spear,
Drops a charcoal into his brazier, and waits.
He hears the howls, the rattles, the rumbles.
He is an old warrior, and he is afraid.

Where are the heroes of the revolution?
They are all around you
As you sleep.

Salome stared down into her glass as the man sang the words again in Kisemi. She had heard the wails, the rattles, the rumbles, and sometimes she could hear them still. She had made those sounds herself. Her grip tightened on the glass. She would never make those sounds again. Never!

Adija listened, but her attention wandered. Revolution was a faraway word to her. No soldiers had ever come to her village during the war. The coconuts had continued to ripen and fall from the palm trees; the blue ocean had continued to lick the beaches. The sun beat down, and the children chased each other in the sandy streets, and in the evenings people drank palm wine in front of their houses and complained about the weather. True, the schoolmistresses had spoken of the troubles in the north. Savage men were hanging cats, drinking menstrual blood as their initiation into the terrorist bands. They were slaughtering families in the night. They were cutting babies out of pregnant women's bellies. But the British soldiers were chasing them far into the forests, and soon the terrorists would all be dead. Let us thank Our Blessed Savior for the British soldiers.

The schoolmistresses' tales were nonsense, of course, but they filled the pupils' hearts with horror. Much better to think of other things. A girl in the class had a new green dress; her aunt was a seamstress and got all the pretty cloth she wanted. A neighbor's dog had killed a chicken, and the headman was going to fine the neighbor for not paying for it. Adija's father was drunk again and her mother had a gash in her forehead from the beating he had given her. If Adija came home late from school, her mother would beat her too. Adija remembered the years of the war—boredom and beatings. She wished the song would finish soon. The man's voice was grating, and his guitar wasn't even electric. The last verse began.

Adija felt a hand on her shoulder, not just resting there, but holding her in a grip that rooted her to the floor. She turned to see a mouthful of cowcatcher teeth grinning at her. Elima. His eyes were red-rimmed and narrowed; his look sliced into her face. "Tonight we celebrate together," he said, spraying saliva. "Out the back door—move!"

"No—" Adija shuddered and tried to pull away, but the pain in her shoulder paralyzed her. She looked around frantically.

Gordon stood up.

"Don't tangle with that man," Waga whispered loudly, grabbing his arm. "Don't do it!"

Gordon stepped toward Adija, hardly feeling Waga's efforts to pull him back.

The song ended. The room was silent for a moment, seeming to suck its breath in. Then metallic sounds and grunts came from the wireless. Suddenly a military band blasted the Bashiri National Anthem out of the wireless: trumpets, fifes, and an explosion of drums.

A cry arose from one of the tables. Men were on their feet, waving their fists and shouting.

"That singer should be arrested!"

"No, he sang the truth!"

"Traitor!"

Glasses shattered as they hit the floor. Someone pushed a table over. A bottle spun into the air, spraying a pinwheel of foam, and crashed against the wall.

Salome leaped onto her chair, the machete held high, but this time no one noticed her. She glared around her, still shouting. Suddenly she lost her voice. She saw Elima pulling Adija toward the back door and jumped down to the floor again.

"Let go of her!" she screamed at Elima.

He had been shouting about executing the singer, but now he whirled toward Salome. When he saw Gordon move in beside her, he picked up a bottle and pointed it like a gun toward the machete in her hand. "Get away, bitch!" he growled. He was holding Adija by her long hair; whichever way she tried to move, she stumbled after him like a rag doll. She caught her footing and seeing the bottle in Elima's hand, tried to lunge between him and Salome.

"Damn you!" Elima flung Adija backward. She spun into a table, collapsed over it and skidded to the floor amid the crashing of glasses.

Two men stepped forward quickly and grabbed Salome's wrist. She toppled backward, crying out in rage; the machete clattered to the floor. Elima scrambled after it.

Gordon dove to the floor, rolling in front of Elima, and came to his feet again holding the machete. A hush fell over the room. Gordon staggered back, raising the panga in front of him. His heart was banging in his chest; he felt himself trembling all over. All he could think to do was hold tight to the machete and glare at Elima.

Elima got slowly to his feet and brushed off his shirt. "Listen, *mzungu*, you are carrying a weapon in a bar. That is violation of the law of this country!"

Gordon stepped toward Adija, panting.

"You will surrender it to me, just now! I am ordering you as Chief of Police for this district!"

There were some hisses and some applause from around the room. Then silence again.

"Give it to him, man!" Waga whispered, leaning close to Gordon.

"You don't give me that weapon, I arrest you and make you deported!" Elima was screaming now. His face was shiny with sweat, his eyes bulging.

Gordon glanced down. Adija was still lying crumbled on the floor, her face streaked with dirt and blood and tangled strands of hair. He reached his free hand toward her, groping until he felt the soft cloth of her blouse. She took hold of his hand, and slowly he pulled her to her feet. "Get behind me," he said to her, his voice nearly cracking. When she moved behind him, still holding tight to his hand, he began to back toward the door. The wireless blasted out another thumping military tune, but he didn't hear it; a buzzing sensation swept over him, impelling him toward the pavement outside.

At the door, he let go of the machete. It clanked to the floor. He kicked it toward Salome and then turned and stepped out the door behind Adija.

Down the pavement, his trembling began again but his faintness was gone. If Adija had not been leaning against him, he would have broken into a run. The sudden quiet and openness of the street felt like the eye of a hurricane. Beyond the rooftops of the town, the mountain rose up into a chaos of stars, a mammoth wave impending out of the night.

A wail reverberated down the street. He turned, expecting to see a mob of men stampeding. But only Salome was there, half-silhouette, half-aflame with the silver glare of the lantern from the doorway. Jeremiah had hold of her now, pinning her arm behind her as she roared and thrashed. The pavement was empty again; Jeremiah's voice dominated the noise inside, calming Salome, calming

Elima. It was a speech-making voice, condemning those who let personal matters interfere with the celebration of the historic event of Uhuru. The street grew hushed. Gordon stood on the edge of the pavement, pressing Adija's face against his chest to shield her from the glare of the doorway.

Someone turned the wireless up again. A flood of cheering broke loose from the great crowd in Azima, where the Bashiri flag was rising above the stadium in a crossfire of blinding spotlight beams. Drums pounded, horns blasted, bells clanked, and above it all hung the eerie piercing ululations with which Samoyo women always greeted great events.

"Ei-i-i-i-i-i . . ."

"UHURU YA BASHIRI!" roared the crowd. *"UHURU YA AFRIKA!"*

"Ei-i-i-i-i-i-i-i-i-i-i-i-i-i-i . . ." The high-pitched trilling of the women swelled and took flight like a flock of joyous birds spraying into the sky.

Salome, in the doorway of the New Life Hotel, shut her eyes tight. Her head tilted back. From deep in her throat the sound began, softly at first, like a whimper, then clearing and leveling off into a piercing double-noted wail. The sound reverberated back from the wireless, from her land, erasing all the sounds around her. All was obliterated— memories of war, thoughts of Musolu exile and Adija— and Salome cracked wide open, possessed by the song flying out her throat. The cheering from the wireless subsided, but Salome, tears streaming down her face, kept up her trilling like some solitary mad bird bursting to celebrate the sunrise in the midst of night.

Even after her voice was silent, the air continued to vibrate with freedom, Africa's Uhuru and—Gordon suddenly felt it—his own. He jumped off the pavement into the road beside Adija, delighting in the crunch of the earth beneath his feet. He was aware of himself not as a dim figure on the periphery of life but as one who had chosen to join the race of men, whatever the consequences. He had felt the pain of hurting Adija with his hesitancy until it had become intolerable and forced him to act, and now he had a knowledge of his own frailty and power. His and Adija's, for she was with him, finally. It seemed to him that she had taught him about frailty and power. The two forces, no longer dissonant, gave an almost audible momentum to his walk that was dangerously exhilarating. The night bristled with the cries of insects and stars and vegetable fragrances, but its incredible darkness, which had once tormented him to flight, now opened up before him and Adija as a vast shelter, space in which they might explore the strange harmony of their union.

PART THREE

13

ADIJA SAT ON THE EDGE OF GORDON'S BED,
staring dazed into the darkness. She felt as if her eyes
were bleeding.

She started as Gordon struck a match. A room with four
walls was there, flickering dimly. She squinted at the lantern. The globe was sooty; the light looked like the fire
from a blackened, smoldering log. She was glad the light
was weak; her eyes hurt. "My eyes hurt," she said softly.

Gordon went away. He was back with a cloth. The cloth
was cool and wet. He pressed it gently against her eyes. It
made her shiver but it felt nice. He took her hand and, one
by one, wrapped her fingers around the cloth so that she
could hold it against her eyes herself.

Darkness covered her, promising comfort. Then it
turned cold, like cold water. Not water, blood. The blood
flowed from the lantern and flooded under her eyelids.
No—it was her own blood. The harder she pressed her
eyes closed, the more they bled. She saw Elima leaning
over her, his forehead knotted in rage . . . he was pressing
a glittering fragment of glass slowly down into her eye . . .

She screamed, clawing the cloth from her face. Elima
was gone, but her eyes were still wet. Gordon blocked the
light. He was stroking her hair and saying things to her in
a nice voice. She clutched his hand and held it tight against
her cheek.

"My eyes are bleeding."

"No, you're just crying, Adija."

"They're so big, they bleed very much—" Spasms of
trembling shook her body. They left her quickly. She held
onto Gordon with both hands. "Do my eyes frighten you?"

"No."

She shivered. "I think I'm cold," she mumbled.

Gordon was pulling her up into a sitting position. The blanket was gone, she was sitting naked before him. How naked she was—and filthy, and scratched, and sweaty. "I'm no good for you tonight," she said, hanging her head. She felt him putting a shirt on her. One of his shirts. It was blue, and smelled like fresh soap—clean, very clean and nice. She felt his fingers moving down her chest, buttoning the shirt. It fell to her knees. How strange she must look! But she stopped shivering. Gordon wrapped two blankets around her, then he picked her up and laid her down on the bed.

He was lying beside her now, stroking her hair and the back of her neck. Wherever his hands moved, warmth entered her. Her eyes bled freely, but she made no effort to clamp them shut. As the dampness soaked into the cloth around her cheeks, she took long luxurious breaths; her mouth opened like a beached fish that has just rolled into a tongue of warm salty water and can now breathe all it wants for as long as the tide remains in.

Gordon awoke aching from clinging all night to the edge of the mattress. He wasn't used to sharing a bed with anyone. Standing, he took a long look at Adija. She lay sprawled on her belly, her legs tangled in the blanket, her hair matted in damp ringlets around her face. Quiet snores fluttered her lips. She smelled pungent, a strange heady smell to him, like a pot of heavily spiced food left out in the sun. He wanted to fling himself into that smell, lap it up, and become sticky with it. Yet he stood frozen still beside her bed, rubbing his eyes, listening to her breaths.

The trembling sensation of standing in the eye of a hurricane was still with him. He walked to the window on tiptoe, half-expecting to see Elima's dusty Peugeot parked outside, a gang of uniformed police waiting with truncheons held at-ready in tensed black hands. But the road before his house was empty. The morning was gloriously clear, empty of any storms. The sun's rays beamed down the slope of the mountain, dissolving patches of white mist to reveal bright green fields and conical huts.

There was a lot to do in this house to make it cheerful for Adija. He needed medicine for her cuts, and decent food to feed her. He needed curtains—the windows were all bare, anyone could peer in at her asleep. And the cin-

derblock walls, bare and gray and ugly. There was so much
he suddenly needed. She would need clothes, and a
bath. . . .

Before he left, he set a fire in the kitchen stove to heat
the tank over it that piped water to the tub. He had been
using cold water until now, but that would change. So
much was going to change.

Gordon returned from Musolu with his bicycle laden
with packages. He had eggs and bread and milk and fruit
and as many kinds of tinned food as his basket could
carry. A fat package containing two dozen Tanzania *kente*-
cloths rode on the handlebars beneath his chin. Adija was
still sprawled asleep on his bed. He went to work, covering
the window in the bedroom with a red and yellow cloth
showing palm trees and women cutting cane. The material
was a soft cotton batik, translucent as stained glass. Moving quickly from room to room, Gordon covered windows
and walls with huge yellow leaves, purple sunsets, green
maize fields, fishermen's nets, mountain landscapes, maps
of Africa, gazelles and seabirds and Kisemi slogans.

When he was finished, the house was transformed—no
longer a squat stone fortress designed for foreign civil servants, but a home, part of Africa now. The space within
the rooms was a continuous spray of reflected color and
shapes. Outside in the sunlight, the patterns were echoed in
brown waving grass and green maize stalks. The voices of
cane cutters and hut builders and cattle tenders drifted
through the house with the warm morning breeze.

Gordon heard a car approach, then fade away. It was
only one of the teachers, taking the wife and kiddies to the
game parks. Good. He had the school compound almost
entirely to himself. He and Adija could wander about as
they pleased. He took down two cloths, wrapped one
around his waist and hitched it up so that it hung to his
ankles. This was the way coastal men dressed in their
homes. Adija could wear the other cloth, tucked under her
arms and across her chest. When she got tired of one cloth,
she could exchange it for another and another. She'd like
that. They would wear nothing but these light soft cloths
all day.

Adija woke and wandered through the house. She found
Gordon in the kitchen, standing by the window, drinking

tea. He turned and smiled at her. "How are you feeling?" he asked her.

"Not very bad." She rubbed her eyes gingerly. "I'm well, I think."

He walked up close to her and hugged her. Her hair was soft against his chest. "You look much better. You look wonderful."

Adija looked down, smiling. "I haven't been here for a long time. Your home was different then."

"I remember. It was raining and you were wet."

"You gave me a towel. I never returned it." Adija bit her lip. "The house was very gloomy that day. Now it is beautiful."

"You like it?"

"Oh, yes. I thought I was still dreaming, after I woke up. The cloths, they were like my dreams. Each room has many dreams on the walls. Then I found you here and I thought, 'Yes, I'm dreaming.'" She laughed. "Look, everything is turned round, like a dream. You're dressed as an African, me as a European. You have a dress, and I have a shirt."

"It's not a dress," Gordon said.

"I know. The men in my village wore cloths like that. But I never saw a European with one."

"Now you have."

"Yes."

"You don't care for it?"

"Oh, no!" Adija stepped back and looked at it, then averted her eyes. "It looks very smart."

Gordon cleared his throat. "Thank you," he said, grinning.

"You are welcome."

"Here, sit down." Gordon fetched her a chair and a cup of tea.

"What's amusing you?" Adija asked.

"Nothing." Gordon wiped his mouth, but the smile returned involuntarily. "I'm just happy you're here."

"Myself, I'm happy too."

There seemed to be nothing to say then. They sat and drank their tea in silence, glancing up at each other occasionally and staring out the window together. Neither of them wanted to mention the events of the night before. To do so would have admitted dark shadows to the room—presences of Salome, Elima, jealousy, violence—presences that would have clashed with the environment of bright, colorful cloths that Gordon had just draped over the past. But Gordon and Adija were somewhat adrift in their new setting. Being alone together in this place of quiet and sunlight was like being in someone's dreams, as Adija had said. It was difficult to trust the idea that it was their own dreams they were inside.

"You still haven't learned African customs," Adija said finally.

Gordon grinned. "What, serving you tea, instead of letting you serve me?"

Adija nodded.

"I'll learn. You can teach me."

Adija wanted to laugh. He was the teacher! But he was right. "Yes, I can teach you to make African tea, with milk and sugar boiled in it." She turned her face away, embarrassed. "Today seems all turned round," she said.

"I know. Maybe because we're not working."

"Yes!" How did he know what she was thinking? "There's no time in this day." Adija looked out the window. "But where are your students? Don't you have to teach them?"

"They went home on holiday this morning. They won't be back for four weeks."

"Good. I was afraid you'd have to go. But I have no holiday." Adija pressed her hand over her mouth, furrowing her brows. "I should be serving lunch."

"The New Life's closed. Patel told me. Salome's got a hangover. She got into a fight with somebody about politics after we left, and drank herself under a table."

"Did she get hurt?"

"No, but Patel says she's like a mad dog today. She snarls at anyone who comes near her." Gordon laughed. "What's wrong with her, anyway?"

Adija looked away. "She'd snarl at me too. But I ought to go to her."

"Is she angry because you came here with me last night?"

Adija frowned hard into the table top. She made no reply.

"She watches over you, doesn't she?" Gordon asked.

"Yes. We are friends." Adija glanced quickly around the room. "She is good, though, even if she can't like Europeans." Suddenly Adija smiled. She stood up and went to touch one of the cloths on the wall. "I could go back tomorrow, when the bar opens again."

"Yes, that's good. You can stay here today."

Adija stole a look at Gordon. She liked the funny lopsided way he smiled that told her that it was all right for her too to feel awkward. She liked the gentle way he said things. This Gordon was good. She liked him to be a man who made decisions for her—without shouting or bullying or cajoling. He just told her that he wanted her to stay, and it was somehow instantly what she wanted too. She hugged herself tightly, and doing so, felt the grime and streaks of dried blood on her arm. "I need to wash. Do you have a place for washing?" she asked. She didn't have to ask. Already that morning she had admired the beautiful bathtub that he owned.

She stood frowning down at it. Her face was turned away from Gordon; she didn't want him to see she was frightened of climbing down into the thing, and also of the hot water that would fill it. She had heard about bathtubs from her mother, who had been a houseservant for some Europeans once, but she had only seen them herself in magazine photographs. There was a color picture of a sparkling modern bathroom on the wall of her room, beside all the pictures of motorcars and cabinet ministers' wives and musicians drinking Coca-Cola and film stars smoking Players cigarettes—but the tub in the picture was not nearly as high and cavernous as Gordon's.

"I've seen these tubs many times," she said finally, "but I've forgotten how you keep the water from burning you."

Gordon explained how to regulate the hot water. He turned on both taps, and immediately Adija wished he hadn't. She didn't like the idea of climbing down into moving water. Suppose she should slip in the water? Suppose the legs of the tub broke and it tipped over with her and the water inside? She hastened to unbutton her shirt before the water rose any higher, her concern about the water obliterating any awareness of her nakedness.

"I'll leave you then. Here's your soap—"

"No!" She grabbed Gordon's arm. "You must help me to get inside it! I could fall!"

"Okay," Gordon said.

Adija held his arm tight, leaning most of her weight against him as she lifted one leg cautiously over the side. "I want to do it properly. I don't want to break it."

"You can't break it, Adija. It's very strong."

"Good." Adija pulled her other leg in after her and slowly loosened her grip on Gordon's arm. "Should I sit at the end where the water is coming out of the tap?" she asked.

"No, the other end."

"But how can I keep the water from burning me if it gets too hot?"

"You just lean over and turn the tap."

"Oh." Adija squinted dubiously at the taps. "Yes, I see . . ."

"I'll do it for you."

"Good!" Adija smiled. Once seated, she leaned back slowly, watching the water ripple around her feet. "It feels nice," she said, wiggling her toes. "We had running water in my village, but it wasn't hot. It came from a pump. Everyone went there to buy water every day. It cost five cents for ten gallons. We had to carry it home in tins . . ." Adija looked up at Gordon. He seemed uncomfortable in his *kente*-cloth, trying to sit sideways on the edge of the tub. Her mouth clamped tight over a laugh. She knew what was the matter. "I see that you like me," she said finally.

"What?"

She pointed at his lap. "Your cloth is too tight. Your penis is standing."

"Oh." Gordon shook his head, grinning. "Yes. Well, it does that."

"I'm glad."

"Me too."

"You don't think I'm too thin?" Adija asked.

"Oh, no."

She touched her breast. "These are too small. They're always pointing down. I have only nineteen years and I haven't had any babies, but they can't sit up properly."

"They're nice, Adija. Really."

"I saw a picture of a European woman once and she had no blouse. Her nipples were pointing up in the air." Adija lifted her breasts high. "Is it true that they do that?"

"Sometimes. But I like you." Gordon watched the water swirling between her legs, making the black hairs wave like sea anemones, and he knew that she was smiling now because he was looking at her. "You're very beautiful, Adija."

Adija leaned back and shut her eyes, her face glowing, and motionless, like one who has a beautiful butterfly perched on her forehead that might fly away forever should she make any sudden movement.

When she had finished her bath and dried herself, some of her cuts were bleeding. Gordon showed her the medicine he had bought.

"Does it sting?" she asked.

"I expect so."

Adija squinted at the tiny brown bottle, so tiny, but such power inside. She had never used European medicine except aspirins and worming tablets. "Perhaps it will make my cuts heal," she said, "but you must help me with it."

Gordon carefully dabbed at the cuts with the glass stick in the stopper. The liquid turned her skin a deep red-brown and stung savagely. She sucked air in quickly through her teeth. But the stinging didn't last. It was nice, in a way. She watched him dabbing at her shoulder with the little stick and the sensation was not ordinary pain at all; it made her shiver, but the shivers were more like pleasure feelings, as if he were doing something magical to her that would somehow heal much more than mere cuts. The way he touched her reminded her of a European she had once seen painting a picture of a palm tree with a little brush. The tree was just ordinary, but in the picture it looked extraordinarily beautiful. Gordon was making her look beautiful too. She didn't know how—soon she would have red-brown spots all over her, like a hyena! But she knew what she felt. This painting was like a kind of ritual. It paralleled last night's sequence of events—the pain followed by the happiness of waking up in his room with the sunlight streaming through the beautiful cloth. It seemed you had to feel something painful before you could feel beautiful.

Now that he was finished with the medicine, he would

surely want her. Adija felt strange. She always tensed herself for a man, minimizing any feelings she might have.
But now she was doing the opposite—she was relaxing. All
her muscles were limp and tingling, and the feeling was
terrifying. "I don't want—I—" She ran her fingers over her
body, being careful not to touch the spots where the powerful medicine had colored her skin. Her bravado was gone
now; she was hugging herself again. "I need my clothes,"
she said suddenly.

"I got you something in town." Gordon picked up a
cloth and unfolded it. "Your people wear these, don't they
—the women too?"

Adija's eyes widened. The cloth was purple and maroon;
a scimitar-sailed dhow sailed across it through symmetrical
whitecaps and flying fish. "It's beautiful!" Adija pulled it
over her chest, under her arms, and rolled it tight across
her back. She turned sideways, gazing at herself over her
shoulder in the mirror on the door. She was no longer his
painted picture; she was someone she could recognize
again. Yet changed too—by the cloth's newness and the
fact of Gordon's having bought it for her. Changed just
enough, she decided. The cloth flattened her chest and
accentuated the shape of her belly and hips. I am not so
thin after all, she thought. Let me stay with him, and I will
grow as beautiful as he says I am.

"But I can't wear this to visit a school," she told him,
after they had eaten some of his new provisions. "I should
have a blouse and skirt, and shoes. I have no shoes, even."

"Nonsense. I always wear whatever I please. Who
cares?" Gordon said.

"I don't want your friends to think I'm primitive."
Mshenzi was the word she used for "primitive"; it made
Gordon frown. But he had started to frown when she'd
mentioned his friends. "They are your friends aren't they—
the teachers?" she asked.

"Not particularly. Even if they were, they couldn't make
me ashamed of you. You're not ashamed of yourself, are
you?"

A difficult question. Often she was ashamed—when she
thought about shame, which was as infrequently as possible. But today she was with him. Wasn't he a European
and a teacher, and also a good man? He had said she was

beautiful, and not just to coax her into his bed. He hadn't even asked her yet. He was treating her well, just as he would a woman of his own tribe. "Of course, I'm not ashamed," she told him, laughing.

Gordon's classroom was locked, so he took Adija to the office where all the school keys hung in rows on a board. How he could tell which key was his was a mystery she didn't even try to fathom. She walked around the table, running her fingers along its shiny top, peering at the stacks of notebooks, picking up textbooks carefully, as if weighing them in her hands. Every envelope and rubber stamp and red pen held fascination for her; she had to touch each one, and cautiously, as if each was a ritual object of a priesthood whose inner sanctum she had no real business penetrating.

"This is the place where all the teachers come to talk about which students pass and which ones are bad and have to fail," she said finally.

"They talk about all sorts of things. I just sit in the corner and grade papers."

"But do you decide which students have to leave while you're in this room?"

"I've never heard of a boy failing so that he has to leave school, if that's what you mean. Nobody gets admitted to secondary school who can't pass the courses."

"Oh." Adija leaned gingerly against the table. "My school wasn't like that. It was only a primary school."

"Did you fail?"

Adija nodded. "It didn't matter. My mother had no money to send me, anyway."

"It sounds as if it mattered to you at the time," Gordon said.

"No, I hated school. The students made fun of me because of my looks. They called me a heathen, because my mother gave up being a Moslem when my father got killed. She tried to send me to a mission school, but it was no good either."

"You're a Christian now?"

"Oh, of course!" Adija tiptoed around the table quickly, looking for something to point out that would change the subject. Suppose he asked her about Christianity? She'd be finished then. "Those little boxes on the wall—what are they? They look like wasps' nests."

"Those are for mail. And messages and things." Gordon showed her his pigeonhole. It had a paper in it. Adija pulled it out and handed it to him. "What does it say?" she asked, pointing to the name on the envelope.

"Mr. Lockery. That's my last name."

"Lock . . ." Adija laughed. "Gordon is easier to say."

Gordon was reading the note, frowning. Adija wiped the smile from her face to watch him read. Reading was serious business.

Mr. Lockery:

> I am preparing your probationary report to the Ministry of Education, and would like to discuss it with you, preferably before the end of the holidays.

O.B.F. Griffin, HM

"Shit!" Gordon crumpled the note and threw it into the wastebasket.

"Is it bad news from America? Will you have to go back?"

"No, no. Just a note from the headmaster. He doesn't like me." Gordon was in no hurry to discuss the report. In fact, he planned to forget it.

Adija was still curious but refrained from asking more. The private affairs of the school, especially notes from a headmaster, were too important to be discussed with an outsider, especially a woman.

Adija wanted to know what was behind the office door, so Gordon unlocked it and showed her the school library. She'd never seen so many books in her life. And magazines too—everywhere. Adija picked up a copy of *Drum*. "Oh, I know this one! I have pictures from it on my wall. Miss Bantu South Africa, she is very beautiful, don't you think?"

Gordon smiled. "I didn't see that issue, I guess."

"Oh," Adija said, disappointed. "Did you see Gary Player's caddie's wardrobe? You should wear clothes like that man, not rubber-tire sandals—" Adija slapped her hand over her mouth. "I mean, it doesn't matter. I know you don't like to wear big-man clothes, you're different . . . I'm sorry."

"You can criticize my clothes if you want." Gordon laughed and pulled Adija affectionately by the back of her neck. "It isn't going to make me dress like Gary Player's caddie, though."

"No, I know. I just like the pictures. I put them on my wall—" Adija suddenly dropped the magazine and stepped behind Gordon. "Someone's here," she whispered.

Seth Chemai, the watchman, approached down a row of tables. "Excuse me, sir. I didn't know any of the masters were still here," he said in Kisemi, smiling as if he were embarrassed to find Gordon and Adija. Gordon felt embarrassed suddenly, then enraged at himself for his embarrassment. The man stood facing him, saying nothing, just staring, his bow and arrows tucked under his arm. His earlobes swung back and forth; once they had held ivory plugs. Now he wore town garb: khaki shorts and shirt. He looked as if he was waiting for Gordon to explain something.

Gordon had to say something, but he was goddamned if he had anything to explain. "Hello, Chemai. This is *Bi* Adija," he said. "*Bwana* Chemai."

"Oh, very pleased!" Chemai switched to English. He pumped Adija's hand, grinning. "I am admiring *Bi* Adija very much. I see her in village sometime, I think. She is wife for you?"

Gordon shook his head. In Africa, the English word "wife" could be translated as anything from "wife" to "mistress." The idea of both "wife"—marriage—and "mistress"—ownership of a woman—made Gordon very uncomfortable. "She is my friend," he said finally, aware that that word wasn't much better; it was usually just a euphemism for "mistress." "I was looking for magazines," Gordon said, looking around. "Adija collects them."

"There are the Chinese ones," Chemai said, pointing to a stack on the floor.

"You can take them for your walls," Gordon told Adija. "Take these *Life*'s too."

"Oh, no. You'll be in trouble taking them."

"The headmaster just starts his fire with them. Take them." Gordon edged Adija toward the magazines and the door. "They've got plenty of pictures in them."

"Yes, many pictures." Chemai, having been introduced

socially, wanted to socialize. "But that Chinese magazine, it has too much American aggressors in it. Too much killing. Vietnam. You go to Vietnam, *Bwana* Lockery?"

"No, never. I'm here, and I'm going to stay here."

"Better teach people than kill peasants, bomb villages, I think." Chemai watched Gordon closely, grinning. "You are looking very smart today," he said, eyeing Gordon's *kente*-cloth. "I believe your costume, it is called 'going native.'"

Gordon's hand in the middle of Adija's back hastened her way to the door.

Adija was excited to be in Gordon's classroom. So many days, she had paused in mopping the floor of the New Life and wondered where he was at that moment. Now she was here. "May I sit down?" she asked. Her head was spinning. She'd seen the staff office and the library and now this classroom, with all its charts and pictures of famous people on the walls; she had accumulated a pile of gifts; she had been mistaken for a teacher's wife—and all in one afternoon. She sat down at a desk in the front row, clutching her stack of magazines against her chest.

"This is where you work every day?" she asked, looking around slowly.

"Yes." The room looked barren without the buzzing students. He almost missed them. This was the one place on the compound where he enjoyed himself. "I walk around the aisles like this—" Gordon paced up a row of desks, his head tilted sideways, his arms folded across his chest. He did a parody of himself reading over students' shoulders as he moved along. Now and then he paused, tapped a desk top, pointed out a mistake in an invisible notebook. Suddenly he whirled around, waving his finger at the corner of the room. "Ndova! I told you not to copy from Otieno's notebook. Get back to your seat!"

Adija laughed. "You're very strict. But you're smiling all the time. I think the students like you very much."

"Most of them, I think. I like them, and they can see that."

Adija set her magazines down carefully on her desk. "Teach some more," she demanded.

Gordon grinned. He went behind the teacher's table and found a piece of chalk. "ADIJA NI NZURI," he wrote in big letters on the board. "All right, class—who can read that?" He pointed at Adija in the front row. "Yes? *Bi.* Adija?"

"Oh!" Adija hid her face in her hands. She was frightened. Gordon was too realistic in his act. She felt as if she were nine years old again.

"What's the matter? Adija?"

"Nothing." Adija took a deep breath. The blackboard was a faraway blur. She scratched her forehead in concentration. "May I come to the board, sir?"

"Of course. But please, don't call me 'sir.'"

"All right." Adija walked up to the blackboard and stood with her face several inches from the words Gordon had written. "Adija . . ." She paused, scowling with concentration and fear. Suppose he had written something like Waga's poem? Her scowl faded. ". . . *ni nzuri!*" She turned and stared at Gordon. "You wrote my name. You wrote about me—that I am good." She looked at the board again, admiring the way he had dignified her with the written word. "Is it true?" she asked.

"Is what?"

"Do you think Adija is good?"

"Yes, of course." Gordon smiled at her.

Adija snatched up a piece of chalk. She wanted to write something nice about Gordon, but suddenly she couldn't remember any letters. Her fingers ached from squeezing the chalk so hard. She dropped it back on the tray and wiped her hands on her cloth. To make herself feel less helpless, she read Gordon's words again out loud.

"You are good too," she said. She returned to her seat and slowly raised her face to him.

"Thank you." Gordon had seen her fear and frustration. He came out from behind his table and sat at the desk beside her. "I don't want to be teacher anymore. Not with you."

"Why?"

"It makes us different."

"But we are different." Adija noted the worried look on Gordon's face; perhaps she shouldn't have said that. "It's all right, isn't it?"

"Yes."

"I know I'm ignorant." Adija turned her face away. "You don't like to think how ignorant I am."

"I don't like to think how ignorant *I* am."

"You're not."

"I am, though." Gordon moved his hand slowly along Adija's arm. "I'm ignorant of you. I'm ignorant of Africa. Every day I find out how ignorant I am."

What was he talking about? Him, a teacher, ignorant? What could he be ignorant of? She puzzled it over, then hazarded a guess. "You say 'ignorant of me'—you mean you are ignorant of fucking?"

The Anglo-Saxon ending to the lilting Kisemi sentence made Gordon sit up straight. "Uh, yes—that's part of it, I guess." Damn, this girl was perceptive.

"I am ignorant of it too," Adija said. She looked up and saw that Gordon did not look as if he agreed with what she said. No, of course not. She knew about "it"—the woman in Mirini who had taught her had assured her she was learning all the ways there were, African, Arab, European. But she hadn't meant it that way. "I am ignorant of your ways," she tried.

"My way is no different than anyone else's way," Gordon managed to laugh.

"Not 'your way.' I am ignorant of being with someone like you—someone I like."

"Oh. I understand."

"Sure?"

"Yes." Gordon nodded, taking her hand. "Yes."

"Gordon?" she asked suddenly. "If I were a student in your class, could you teach me English so that I wouldn't fail?"

Gordon frowned. "I suppose so."

"What if the other teachers and the headmaster wanted me to fail? Would you fail me too?"

"No. Not if—if your papers and everything were good."

"And if my papers and everything were not good?"

Gordon felt himself sweating. "I don't know. Why are you asking?"

Adija's face went blank. "You're annoyed with me."

"No."

"My questions are foolish?"

"I think they are," Gordon said. "Yes."

"Because you're not my teacher."

"That's right."

"I see." She looked at him cautiously.

"Good." Gordon smiled. He parted his hands in the air before his face, the African gesture that signified that a matter is closed, finished, *kabisa*.

Adija laughed and repeated his gesture. A European using African gestures was amusing, like a lizard trying to hop like a toad.

"I think you find me very exotic," he said, grinning.

"Oh, no!" Adija said—he had used the word "strange" for "exotic."

"Yes, you do."

"Well, a little."

"Okay," Gordon laughed.

"I'm glad about your strangeness, though. It makes us not so different." Adija glanced away. "Will you show me the building with the thatch roof?" she asked.

The building Adija wanted to see was the old Friends' Meeting House, a cavernous structure with leaning mud walls and two small windows. The headmaster had declared it off limits, fearing that it might collapse. No one had spoken of tearing it down, though. It was a reminder to the missionaries of the faith of their fathers or something, Gordon explained.

At first, Adija felt as if she were in a sacred place again —this one full of spirits of Old Europeans. But she had no need to fear them, she realized, since Gordon was with her. Without an edge of fear to her feelings, the excitement of being in a new place faded. This was just an empty building. They had all been empty buildings today, except Gordon's house. They were places Gordon worked in, but they were just buildings.

She watched him move about in the shadowy light, scuffing the soles of his bare feet against the floor. It was hard to recognize him as a special being with the title "teacher." Teachers didn't wear *kente*-cloths and make funny gestures and get their feet filthy walking barefoot. What Gordon was she still couldn't say, but she was becoming less uneasy about not being able to classify him. After all, she could not say what she was either, could she?

Rainclouds approached, mountains of heavy gray clay blotting out the sunlight. Watching them, Adija stood close to Gordon in the pale light from the window. The building darkened around them. Mice scrambled about in the thatch overhead, squeaking in anticipation of the downpour. The air suddenly smelled fresh and pungent.

The first drops of rain smacked the window frame. Thunder cracked, and a white gash of lightning flashed along the horizon. The rain flung itself down, hissing and steaming against the warm grass. Water streamed off the overhanging roof. The earth below turned to mud then to a splashing brown moat.

Adija stepped back against Gordon. His arms went around her shoulders. She was shivering. "Are you cold?" he asked.

"No."

"Frightened?"

"A little."

They stood for a long time, staring into the rain. Then without planning, they found themselves racing through the downpour toward the house, splashing through puddles, slipping and skidding on the grass.

Gordon slammed the kitchen door behind them. Dripping, he threw more wood into the stove. Soon the flames were crackling up through the burners. The room grew hot. Adija reheated the tea. She stood beside Gordon, watching the flames in the stove and adding to the puddle on the floor.

"I'm steaming," she laughed, unsticking the warm soaked cloth from her belly.

Gordon stepped behind her and unwound the cloth. She raised her arms, and it fell from her. She turned and unwrapped Gordon's cloth.

She was about to hang it over the chair to dry, but Gordon was holding her too tightly to move. She forgot the cloth, and the teapot on the stove, and even the strangeness of the sight of so much pale flesh. Gordon's grip tightened; her toes rose from the floor. Laughing, she clamped her legs around his thighs. He kissed her with his tongue, and though she was new to kissing that way, she was not afraid any longer. Her fear of his strangeness had come and gone.

He carried her into his room, she clinging to him with her arms and legs like someone climbing a coconut palm. They retreated from the clatter of raindrops beneath the blankets.

Gordon had never been with a woman in bed without hearing thoughts grinding secretly behind her eyes, without feeling her watching and evaluating his movements. Always he had been in a hurry to get it over with. Rage overcame him. Thrust by thrust, he silenced those eyes and bludgeoned the accusations behind them into oblivion.

But now he was in no rush. When he caught glimpses of Adija watching him, he saw in her face a drunken happiness like his own. He saw a sweetness in her look that he wanted to hold in his mouth and swallow again and again; he kissed her eyes and each time they opened with more sweetness in them than before.

At first, she opened her legs wide for him and waited. Then she understood that he wanted to touch and kiss her everywhere. Suddenly, she wanted all of him as well. She had never known the enjoyment of touching a man this way—*that* had been her ignorance, and suddenly it was gone. He had not taught her anything, she had just learned with him. There were so many things to do beside that one thing a man did with a woman. There was warmth to feel. There was the salty taste of skin. There was the texture of fingers and knees and testicles to feel against the tongue. There were little laughs inside the chest and gurgles inside the belly to listen to with her face pressed against his cool skin.

She shut her eyes and let her body wriggle with his movements as it would. She had no thoughts of protecting herself or of making sure to give pleasure. There was nothing she had to do to make Gordon like her. She had only to be there with him. And as she learned that, he did, too. The discovery made him reckless. He could do no wrong to her; he could do anything and it would make her happy. Hearing his urgent voice mingling with his breathing, Adija held her tighter as if to both restrain and encourage him.

Suddenly she heard her own voice fleeing her body, along with all her breath and strength. For a moment, she was helpless and terrified. Sobs rushed up through her like shafts of heat, yet there was no terror in them. She was swept along as they flooded out of her. She would have been willing to surge and flow with them forever, even as they receded and finally left her washed up on the bed, gasping and giddy, with the cool soft strands of Gordon's hair tickling her face like the wings of a night full of butterflies.

14

ON THE SECOND NIGHT OF ADIJA'S ABSENCE,
the night of screams still echoed in Salome's head, the
fighting about the heroes of the revolution still played itself over and over every time Salome closed her eyes. She
lay on her mattress, staring at the gecko lizards darting
about on the ceiling, and didn't sleep until the dawn light
paled the undersides of the tin roof through the cracks in
the wall. Then she dreamed. She dreamed of wandering
through a country that was like the place where many
freedom fighters had been buried near her village, a place
of dirt and thorn bushes and the bones of strayed goats.
This time, all the people of her village were buried there.
She passed mound after mound, each marked by some
utensil or weapon belonging to the owner. She recognized
the things and realized she knew all the buried people, but
she could not remember any of their names. The sun
burned hot upon her; her eyes swam with the heat. She
came to a grave without a marker, and walked around it,
again and again. She couldn't leave until she found the
marker. Finally she saw something: a tiny lizard scurrying across the mound where the stomach would be. There,
another one running up a leg. She could make out the outline of the bones beneath the earth now. The body was
crawling with tiny lizards. They darted back and forth,
they poked their heads in and out, they flicked their tiny
tongues out. Suddenly she realized: *They were the
marker*—

She sat up, her mouth wide open, as if she had just
screamed. Had she? She looked around, blinking, as if she
might find the scream fallen to the floor.

Adija appeared that afternoon. She was wearing an
orange skirt made out of a *kente*-cloth and new purple

shoes and blouse. Salome found her busy sweeping out the bar. She didn't ask Adija where she had gotten the new outfit. She knew.

"You're back," she said finally.

"Yes." Adija looked up from her broom. She saw only the side of Salome's face; it was enough to send chills through her.

"I thought you would have flown to America by now." Salome lifted a case of beer onto the bar. "I hired a new barmaid."

"No!"

"No? Why not?"

Adija's eyes darted around the room. "Where is she?"

"I sent her to Mbure, to buy some sarees and pretty clothes."

"I don't believe you."

Salome didn't respond until she had made herself a brandy and Coca-Cola. "I just wanted to see your face when I told you," she said.

"Oh." Adija looked down. "Salome, don't be angry. I want to be your friend still."

"Do you?"

"Yes!" Adija went to Salome and leaned her head against her shoulder. Slowly she looked up into Salome's face. "Don't send me away. I can be your sister and his friend too. There's no reason I can't."

Salome's arm went around her shoulder, as if of its own accord. Why couldn't Adija be her friend and the teacher's too?

Salome knew there was a reason why not. But she had no idea what it was. Adija had presented her with a solution—just carry on being sisters. Did Salome have a better solution? She had none. She could not even articulate the problem that needed a solution. Her mind fought with her to accept Adija's answer. After all, hasn't Adija had men before? Haven't I? They haven't made any difference to us, have they?

Salome shut her eyes and held Adija close. "You didn't come back—not even to tell me if you were all right or not! You might have been hurt, and I wouldn't have known."

Adija held on to Salome's forearm. It was a strong black

arm, heavy and familiar and smooth. She rested her cheek against the arm. She was worn out from exhilaration. "I should have sent a messenger from the school," she said.

At the mention of the word "school," Salome's arm fell back to her side. "It doesn't matter. You're back." She rubbed her eyes. "You left me with a mess to clean up, you know."

"I know. I'm very bad. I'm sorry." Adija picked up her broom again and began sweeping eagerly. "How much beer change did you make on Uhuru night?" she asked, her voice trying to sound light.

"I don't know—twenty-five shillings, perhaps." Salome made extra cash by bringing less than the right change to men who were too drunk to count their money. In fact, on Uhuru night, she had not made much change; her mind had not been on money. But she too wanted to pretend that that night had been no different from other nights. "Finish the sweeping, Adija. I'll clean the pots. We have to cook tonight."

"Cook?"

"Yes. Ambani won't be serving anything for a while."

Ambani's bar had been closed down by the police; two men had stabbed each other there on Uhuru night. So Salome had decided to serve supper in order to attract some of the people who used to eat at Ambani's. Chapathis, rice, and charcoaled meat would be available, but no tea. If the men were thirsty, as they would be from the salty beef, they would have to buy beer. It was a good plan. The extra work would keep her mind off things. It would also keep Adija busy around the place.

Not as many customers came that night, though, as Salome had expected. Nearly everyone in town had spent his pay on Uhuru night. Salome was too tired to bother cajoling the men into drinking. She sat at a table near the bar, sipping brandy and Coca-Cola and chewing at the edges of a chapathi. Adija was wolfing down her third plate of rice and meat—two days of marmalade sandwiches, tinned chicken, and tea had left a hollow place in her stomach.

"Good evening, ladies." It was Jeremiah, standing over the table and smiling his thick-lipped smile. "I have returned, like Lazarus from the grave."

Salome glanced up and tore off a piece of chapathi with her side teeth. "You want a beer, I suppose."

"Of course."

Adija stood up. "I'll get it, Salome."

Salome nodded and chewed her chapathi. "What are you doing here so often?" she asked Jeremiah.

"I told you, I'm on holiday." Jeremiah sat down. "But I'm used to city ways, so my restlessness brings me to your doorstep."

Salome kept her eyes on her plate.

When Adija saw Gordon lope in through the door, she flashed him a smile that, had it been a sound, might have shattered the lantern globes. She had been worried that he would be angry with her for returning to work, but he didn't look angry. He was smiling—a different smile than before, Adija decided. Before his smile had been to cover up uneasiness; now he just looked pleased to see her. She beckoned to him from behind the bar.

"I'm sitting there, having my supper. Wait for me," she whispered.

She filled a plate for him, picking out extra meat from the brazier. At her table, Salome was ignoring Gordon. Ordinarily she ignored Jeremiah and talked to anyone else in sight. Adija paused uneasily, then swooped down on the table to pass out her trayful of beer and food.

"At any rate, Elima is not pressing charges," Jeremiah was saying to Gordon. "You were almost in a great deal of trouble."

"I know." Gordon put down his fork slowly, feeling a slight tremor in his hands. "It could have been awful."

"Yes. Elima will still be looking for reasons to cause you trouble, though. You should stay out of his path."

"I will." Gordon sat back, feeling like a man who has just been pulled into a doorway while angry mobs swarm past, and now fears having his throat cut by his rescuer. He had no idea why he felt this way toward Jeremiah and was inclined to chalk it up to residual paranoia. "Thank you," he said, looking at Jeremiah for the first time, and receiving neither assurance nor discouragement from his bland smile. "I don't know what's going on, but thanks."

"Don't mention it. We don't want international quarrels here. We need foreign teachers to come and help us."

"You want to keep things calm here," Salome said in Samoyo, "so you can carry on with your spying."

Jeremiah smiled at Gordon, ignoring her. "I remember I invited you to come to my farm for the initiation dancing—you and your friends—" Jeremiah glanced around at Adija and Salome. "It will be interesting for you."

"Yes," Salome said to Gordon. "You can see bare-breasted African maidens. Just like on the postcards."

"I'll see if I can get away from school," Gordon said to Jeremiah. This African habit of ignoring a woman was not as offensive to him as it had been. "Thanks."

"And you, Salome?"

"I told you, I won't go back to Bashiri with you," Salome said in Samoyo.

"*Aah*, stupid woman. Do you imagine that I couldn't have brought you across the border any time I wished. I could have you in Azima jail by dawn. But what for? There is no one to press charges against you."

Salome looked away. No one, she thought, except the Samoyo people. "You want to bring us along to impress your family."

"To make a good appearance, yes. All my relations are eager for me to find a wife—you know how the old people are, in the bush."

I wish I still did, she thought. But she said, "I don't want to go."

"All right. I'll take the teacher and Adija. I am sure he can watch out for her well enough without your help." Jeremiah smiled sideways at Salome. "I was going to introduce her as your friend, but now I will just say she is the teacher's wife."

Salome glared at Jeremiah and took a long drink from her glass. "No," she said.

"I know you'll consider it," Jeremiah said, switching back to Kisemi to include Adija and Gordon.

Salome stood up and took her plate to the bar. She did not return to the table until Jeremiah had left. Used dishes and mugs accumulated; Salome was too groggy with brandy to bother with them. After a time, she could no longer bear to watch Gordon and Adija talking, with her alone and out of earshot behind the bar. She joined them.

Quietly drinking the sweet liquid from her glass, she

listened to their talk. They had an evil fascination for her, like a spell.

Adija looked more radiant than Salome had ever seen her. Her great almond eyes flashed; her mouth was an opalescent snake; her gesturing hands were like birds fluttering. When Adija leaned close to Gordon, her voice went tiny and Salome couldn't hear. Rage swelled within her. The rage was drowned in Adija's laughter. Salome had no more mind to think with. Her feelings, left rudderless, swooped and dove against the walls of her empty brain like the sausage-flies that buzzed in blind trajectories about the room, crashing into everything.

Adija nodded eagerly as Gordon spoke. She was just nodding at his enthusiasm for revealing himself, Salome was sure. He was drunk and eager to explain, to be understood—as if by giving Adija an understanding of him, he was giving her something urgently important. Why couldn't he just give her his cock and his money and be done with it? Because that wouldn't satisfy him—he would never be satisfied that way. And Adija, would that have satisfied her? No. Once she had a taste of his urgent words, she too had to have more.

Salome had never really seen Gordon before. She had a mental image of him—white, tall, awkward—that dropped over him like a cloak whenever he came into her line of vision. Now she watched him like a hawk. His lips moved rapidly, trying to unscramble thoughts that came to him faster than he could put them into words. His face was naked, his flesh delicate and rubbery, like the pale skin that forms on top of spoiled milk; you just poke it with your finger, and it comes up sticky and clinging.

Something else was there too. Those watery eyes were capable of burning. Not with anger, but with fierce sorrow, laughter, desire. His awkward hand gestures were sometimes those of a man defending himself against invisible flying objects, but at other times they were hands flailing to form a shape in the air and make that shape real and solid and powerful—something that Adija's nearsighted eyes could see clearly. He spoke as a man who is just learning to raise his voice to demand what he wants. His very vulnerability, so blatantly exposed, was being transformed into power by the urgency with which he displayed it.

Adija was not blind to this power he was showing her.
Nor was Salome . . .

*   *   *

Sometimes, during the nights, Adija was busy with her
razor blade and magazines; in the mornings her walls were
filled with pictures. Snowy Chinese landscapes, cowboys
riding into the sunset, slant-eyed peasant women carrying
rifles, Africa's Number One Private Eye In Action Photos,
Kim Il Sung opening a tractor factory, rockets and bubble-
headed men in spacesuits, an electric frying pan, film stars
kissing under a tree. After a few days, Adija's walls were
completely plastered with smiles and grins, songs and
cheers. Even the refrigerators and televisions and motorcars seemed to be gazing down on her bed in a shiny orgy
of glee.

And Adija herself was giddy all the time. She darted
about like someone poised to dive headfirst into a bed of
flowers. Her mouth twitched as she spoke, about to dis-
gorge a cornucopia of giggles. She never seemed to stay
still for longer than an instant. To meet her gaze was to
be suddenly seized, flung, drowned, and yanked back into
place, grinning idiotically into the hole in the air her image
had left.

There was no way of controlling Adija. She offered no
explanation for her movements. If Salome tried to maneu-
ver her into staying late at the New Life, she would find
Adija missing for days. Salome would stretch herself wearily on her bed at night, and would wake to feel Adija's thin
warm body coiling itself around her. Adija would chatter
and giggle and plait Salome's hair, and suddenly be gone
again. She might be anywhere—scrubbing the floor of the
bar, fingering bright sheets of cloth hanging in the shop
doorways, sitting in a patch of sunlight on the sidewalk
and staring off into space. Or she might be walking up the
hill toward the school, her skirt swinging, her oiled hair
catching sparks of sunlight, her face scanning the horizon
as if it were a shop counter displaying all the precious
jewels of the earth.

Gordon could not predict her comings and goings either.
If he planned to take her to Mbure for a new saree, he
might find himself waiting for the bus alone. If he agreed
to teach her songs on his new guitar—which he'd bought

at her request—he might find himself singing to the cloths on the walls. Like Salome, Gordon knew how to keep busy. He copied the words of Congolese pop songs from the wireless and learned African chord progressions. He put down sisal mats and varnished the woodwork and planted a garden of maize, yams, tomatoes, and bananas. He read cartons of books on African history and literature that arrived at the school from Karela. And often, on returning from some errand, he would smell meat sizzling on the stove in his kitchen; he would find Adija, wrapped in pineapples or dhows or the Mountains of the Moon, scurrying about the room, cutting vegetables and buttering slices of bread. Or, half asleep in his bath, he would open his eyes to find her sitting opposite him, soaping her shoulders and laughing to see the water sloshing over the sides. No longer did she tremble in the bed beside him or thrash about in her sleep. She settled under the blankets as if the bed were the nest where she had been hatched. Gordon awoke in the mornings to find her legs and arms draped over him, her hair spread across his chest in tangled waves. Her body melted in with his movements and she was as weightless as the streaks of sunlight that carpeted the room.

In the New Life, Adija stuck close to Salome and Gordon. While working, her eyes did not meet those of the men she served. When they reached for her departing buttocks, they felt only cloth slipping through their fingers. Clutching Adija's hand around the neck of a bottle did not produce a pretty smile from her, only a look that made a man feel like a public masturbator. The game of trapping "Swila Number 101" was no longer amusing. Fewer men asked to go to her room. Those who did were usually refused, politely and without explanation.

Some days, Adija could not contain her restlessness; she sought to release it in drinking or by taking long walks through the countryside. Once she begged Salome to go with her, but Salome refused. Only foreigners would "go for a walk," she said. You go home from the fields, you visit a neighbor or gather maize for dinner, but you do not just walk about with no destination. Only mad people—or witches—wandered outside of their farms with no purpose, no one to visit, no useful work to do. The people in the countryside were already whispering about the strange pale brown barmaid with the enormous eyes, Salome said; was Adija trying to convince them she was a witch? Adija shuddered: No! But an hour or a day later she would leave without a word. Watching her go, Salome worried for her, but she could not condemn her. She herself ached to return to the farms and fields and paths that lay just out of reach beyond the edge of the town.

Gordon did not worry about what the local people thought of him. He had always been oblivious to strangers' reactions to him, and remained so here. He was as eager as Adija to explore the countryside. Sometimes they would start walking as the sun rose, and find themselves at nightfall looking for a route back, with no recollection of the passage of time or space. Once Gordon started down a path, the country sucked him up and carried him along. There were no destinations, just paths, endless lines pressed into the earth's surface by generations of bare feet.

Standing on a rise, he watched the paths roaming—everywhere and back again, a network of red-brown veins flowing with invisible logic over the green land. Gordon and Adija walked along them, yielding to them, mindlessly absorbing the life around them.

Adija touched his arm. Look: a homestead.

The daytime empty farm: Children-trampled grass yard worn away around darkened doorways of huts. Doorframes sagging but holding up mud walls and thick thatch and, it seemed, that bulging white cloud as well. Beside the huts—miniature huts. Look: storage bins leaning on air, their mouths tilted upward, waiting for meals of maize.

How cool the shadows looked inside the huts, shadows as deep as springs. How warm they must have been too, under the cold moon, warm with the smoke of glowing coals and the warmth of gathering families. And there: One dark hut to cloak the visit to a wife on a smooth cane mat that creaked in the cattle-lowing night and chuckled dryly when the impudent morning sun came crouching like a mouse yellow-eyed in a wall's chink, as two figures rose to blink at the dawn.

Look: Those roots. Where was the gatherer of plants now? Backbone to the sky, face clenched over gray old fingertips, she had dismembered this clot of hairy roots, combed it clean of nourishment, and left it to roll into this

pothole. She'd gone. Her roots would dry and blow away
and rot over there in that thicket where the green buds
sprouted.

Gordon pointed—look: The path had walls, tattered-
leafed banana-tree walls shot through with stripes of sunlight. He and Adija passed along the paths under the sun
into the valley, into lakes of brittle grasses singed beige
everywhere. Except there, and there, and there: Bright
sisal cactus bouquets—green-sculpted flames, glinting
blades that pointed and twisted and leaped

(and sink deeper into me, Adija, than I could have
thought possible)

and writhed against their confining roots in the earth.

Banked now by the mountain, the land began to echo.
Disembodied voices at first: Bass male shouts, field grunts,
the tramp of feet and gasp of whip and dispassionate moo
of protest. Then: men plowing, the ox plodding ahead. A
man straining, steering the plow downward, shoulder muscles shining black. The partner guiding the ox, whip swinging, dust puffing from the lumbering animal flank.

More voices coming: Women-laughter clinking in the
air. There: The women's heads and shoulders appearing
over the rise. Women following men and oxen, shouting,
chattering, spitting cane juice, scolding children. Hoes
bouncing on shoulders, babies on backs. Babies peering
brightly over the tops of swaying cloth cocoons.

A gang of boys chased a single boy with clanking cowbells around his waist. The gang whipped him on with
play whips. Laughing, insulting, encouraging, they tested
the initiate, soon to lose his foreskin, chasing him on toward manhood across the field, into a clump of trees. The
adults and animals followed, vanishing.

Whoop-haaagh! Moooo . . .

Gone.

But the sounds lingered. Poundings on the air. Faraway
and nearby. A flail cracking. A stone pestle in a mortar
grinding. A woman's axe smashing a log to pieces. Birds
crying spiraling notes. Insects buzzing. A hammer pounding, pounding.

The sun beat hot. Beat like a drum, rolling around the
horizon like trembling thunder. The sun exploded slowly,
sliced by the mountain's slope, and bled red along the

paths. The sky's eye shut behind the mountain but still filled the paths with blood, filled the exposed veins of the earth with its light, its warmth . . .

The land began to chill with shadows. The sky's red streaked with purple; above the horizon a purple bruise expanded. And now the paths flowed with molten gold . . .

Golden threads, Gordon thought. I am surrounded by them. They connect the people of this countryside, but they don't entangle me as I make my way through it—they guide me. Yes, they connect me to these people, to this land. I have a golden thread of my own . . . and my life has continuity now. He stared at Adija, her dark face reflecting the last light of the sunset. Suddenly he embraced her from behind so that she cried out in delight and hugged his arms that wrapped around her chest.

You have connected me—he wanted to cry out to her, but knew his words would only puzzle her.

"I'm happy!" He spoke breathlessly into her hair. And then, before he could stop his words: "But what have I connected *you* to?"

She turned and gazed up at him, her eyes wide in amusement or puzzlement. He had probably used an incomprehensible jumble of Kisemi words. Never mind. She was hugging him close now. He closed his eyes and smelled the scents of her hair and the grass and the new coolness of the evening.

Only when the mountain cast its heavy shadow over the land did they realize that they were lost. Gordon didn't mind, but Adija was frightened. She was weak from eating nothing all day but bits of sugar cane. She stumbled as she walked, and rising to her feet with Gordon's help, saw the stars swirling above her. She held his hand tightly now. He had been given directions by an old man who had pointed up the hillside—"School. Musolu. Yes, yes." They headed that way.

A child gave her a maize cob; she picked the charcoaled kernels out with her fingernails and shared them with Gordon. Her legs grew rubbery. Had Gordon shown any signs of fear or exhaustion, she might have collapsed.

They rested on top of a hill. Gordon pointed out the school, its metal roofs reflecting silver blue in the moonlight. Adija laughed, happy to see how close the school was.

As they spoke, the cool wind shifted and brought sounds of screaming from the land to the north of the school. The noises were sporadic and faint, but they were clearly sounds of panic. At times, the wind brought vibrations of running cattle's hooves. Then the scent of smoke. Gordon and Adija saw the smoke, pale and thick, rising behind a hill several miles away.

They saw no flames, but from the hills surrounding the smoke, tiny silver sparks began to appear in the darkness. The sparks moved down the slopes toward the smoke. Gordon recognized them—spears reflecting the moonlight. Spears or machetes, or perhaps rifle barrels.

"Let's go." He pulled Adija along more quickly.

"Are they Swila?" she asked.

"No."

Adija gripped his arm. "But the men in the bar, they say that the Swila—"

"Those are just rumors. It's just a cattle raid, or rival families fighting over grazing rights or something." Gordon kept the two of them going at a fast pace all the way to the school.

Pausing outside the door to his house, they listened, facing in the direction of the smoke they'd seen earlier. All was calm now. The air smelled only of moisture; the only sounds were the buzzing of insects in the underbrush.

"You see, we're all right." Gordon opened the door for Adija.

"It's good to have a house like this," she said.

"Why?"

She lit the lantern and looked up at the solid plaster ceiling. Strips of corrugated metal were visible along the edges.

"Because if someone set fire to this house, it wouldn't burn."

Gordon nodded, but the idea wasn't real to him. The idea of someone wanting to burn down this somnolent boarding school was ludicrous.

"There's wood in the stove," he said, noticing how chilled she looked. "We can warm up some rice and tea."

Adija splashed paraffin onto the wood and tossed a match in. The stove roared into flame, then subsided, so that the fire was visible only through the open door.

"It can burn inside the stove, inside the house. It can't

get out." Hugging her arms happily across her chest, she gazed into the warmth of Gordon's house.

*   *   *

Some nights, Adija couldn't sleep for worrying. She sat up in her room, staring at her pictures on the wall, and made up stories about the people in them to calm herself. "If you stick people to the wall with pins," she told Salome, "they can't move about or shout at you or behave badly. They just have to keep smiling."

Salome rolled over in Adija's bed, avoiding the light. "You ought to have a picture of your *mzungu*, to remember him by when he leaves."

"He's not going to leave."

"He hasn't been here for three days," Salome said.

"He's very busy at the school. The headmaster makes him work very hard."

Salome laughed. "That headmaster probably found out he has an African woman, and won't let him out of the school."

"No." Adija shook her head hard, flapping her hair against her cheeks. Salome's words bothered her. She knew enough about Europeans to know that if one of them turned against his color, the rest all turned on him. "Listen —I'll tell you a story," she said suddenly, changing the subject.

"What story?"

Adija jumped up from the bed and went to the wall. "About my pictures—look!"

Salome looked. Adija's crazy collection. Elvis leered, Satchmo flashed his teeth. A fridge gaped, a television stared. Queen Elizabeth smiled at a procession of schoolchildren waving their Union Jacks. The country's cabinet ministers stood beside their new houses and motorcars and wives, all smiling.

"You see the picture of the king?" Adija asked.

Salome nodded. The King of Marembo was sitting on his throne beneath a crown that looked too heavy for his delicate brown face. Now Adija was pointing to a picture of Rita Tushingham.

"And the girl in the school uniform?" she asked, her voice eager now.

"It's not a school uniform. It's a servant's uniform."

"It's a school uniform," Adija said. "Do you want to hear the story, or don't you?"

"Go ahead. You won't let me sleep anyway."

"Miriamu was a poor schoolgirl," Adija began. She waved her hands about in the manner of the Arab fishermen who lived in her home village . . .

The other schoolgirls mocked Miriamu because she was poor. The men in her town called her a slut, because her father was an Arab trader. Her mother beat her very much. But Miriamu was always happy.

One day all the schoolgirls went to the palace of the king to shout their praises and wave their flags at him. The king had a beautiful big palace. It had four rondavals at the corners, with roofs of woven palm leaves, and high white walls between the rondavals. It was finer than the finest mosque in the city. The king stood on the wall and looked down at the schoolgirls. He was very bored with these parades of schoolchildren. He was not feeling happy that day, because he had not been out of the palace in a long time. But when he saw Miriamu, he smiled. He said: "Here is the most beautiful girl in my kingdom. She is the one I am going to marry."

He sent his ministers to discover who the beautiful girl was.

"Her name is Miriamu," said the Minister for Commerce.

"But she is too ignorant. She is thin and her skin is a strange, pale color," said the Minister for Home Affairs.

"She is not good enough to marry a king. You must marry a girl of a royal caste," said the Minister for Information, Tourism, and Wildlife.

"I am king," said the king.

"If you marry her," said all the ministers together, "we will plot a coup to overthrow you."

"Really, I think she is good enough," said the king.

The ministers all whispered together. "If you wish to marry her, we will have to see if she is worthy to live among us at the palace."

"All right," said the king. "But mind you don't harm her."

"No, no, we won't," said the ministers.

They sent a messenger to fetch Miriamu. "You see that mountain," said the Minister for Education. "There is a cross at the top of it. You just have to bring it to us. The kings wants it badly, but he can't leave the palace. When you bring it back, then you can marry him."

"All right," said Miriamu.

But Miriamu was very unhappy. The mountain was very high, higher even than Kilimanjaro, and its top was covered with snow. She walked along the beach, kicking the coconuts at her feet. She looked up at the mountain and wept. She knew that the ministers wanted to kill her with their test. They didn't want the king to have any women, because they thought he would neglect his duties if he had any. But Miriamu did not want to disappoint the king, so she started up the mountain.

The first night she thought she would freeze to death. She had on only her school uniform. Already there was much snow on the ground. But then she saw a hut. It had white walls like the palace, and a tile roof like her school.

The door of the hut opened. There stood a fierce-looking man. His eyes were flashing on and off, like the signboards of the city. They flashed blue and brown, blue and brown. His hair flashed too, as if there were lightning in it. It flashed yellow and black and red, and sometimes it vanished altogether and the man's skull flashed out at her in different colors. The man had a great bulge in the front of his trousers. It looked like a sack full of snakes. The bulge moved in and out as his eyes flashed. He was a witch, and Miriamu was fearing him very much.

"*Karibu*, Miriamu. Come in out of the snow," said the witch, smiling.

Miriamu was trembling, but she stepped inside. The witch gave her some beer. As he drank, he boasted of all the things he owned and all the things he knew. Miriamu decided to flatter him. What else could she do?

"Your Bata shoes are very smart," she said. "And that suit you're wearing—you must have ordered it all the way from England. I'm sure you are very clever, from watching that handsome television. What a beautiful fridge you have —look how it shines!"

The witch was very pleased with Miriamu's flattery. He continued boasting about all the places he had visited and all the things he knew. Miriamu listened carefully, for she thought he might tell her the secret of how to get to the top of the mountain.

But soon he passed out from drinking too much beer. Miriamu was disappointed. She decided to continue her journey. But when she tried the door, she found that it was locked. All the doors and windows were locked. She could not get out. The house was dark and dirty. She watched the television for a while, and listened carefully to all the programs. But when the national anthem was played and the station shut down for the night, Miriamu had still not learned any useful secrets.

She was hungry. So she went to the fridge and opened it. Then she jumped back. For a *jinni* flew out of the fridge. It was tall and looked like a jellyfish, trailing a cloak of icicles.

"I am the *Jinni* of the Fridge," said the *jinni*. "Ask me a wish, and I shall grant it."

Miriamu was frightened. She began to weep. She told the *jinni* her sad story.

The *jinni* took pity on her, and said: "All right, here is what you must do. When my master wakes, you must give him more beer. Then you must open up his trousers. There you will find a sack of many-colored snakes. You will be fearing them very much, but they will not harm you. Take this tablet, and the snakes will not harm you."

And the *jinni* gave Miriamu an aspirin.

"Take hold of the snakes and push them into all the holes of your body until the snakes are tired and go to sleep. Then my master will be sleepy as well. Tell him he is very wise. But say that there is one thing you are sure he doesn't know. And that is: how to drive a Land Rover.

"He will say: 'Yes, I know even that!' But you must keep doubting him, until he tells you all the things necessary for driving a Land Rover. Give him more beer then. He will go to sleep.

"Now, on his watch chain you will find a silver key and a golden key. The silver key is for unlocking the door of his hut, and the golden key is for starting the Land Rover. The Land Rover is in the yard. You can drive it to the top of the mountain and down again. Here is some petrol for you."

And the *jinni* waved his hand. All the bottles of beer in the fridge turned into tins of petrol.

"Good luck," said the *jinni*. "Now please close the fridge, before I melt like ice cream."

Miriamu did all that she was bidden. The witch finally went to sleep. Miriamu unlocked the door with the silver key and started up the Land Rover with the golden key. Then she drove the Land Rover to the top of the mountain. The road was very winding, but Miriamu didn't get stuck in any ditch, because she knew all the things necessary for driving a Land Rover.

The cross was high on the highest peak of the mountain. She drove backward up to the peak. When the back of the Land Rover hit the rock where the cross stood, the cross fell into the back of the Land Rover. The cross was of gold, and heavier than the heaviest stone. But the Land Rover was very strong. It carried Miriamu and the cross all the way to the bottom of the mountain.

The ministers were surprised to see Miriamu driving along the beach toward the palace. They thought she had died on the mountain. Also, they had never seen a woman driving a Land Rover before. The king was pleased with the cross. He put it in his garden among the palm trees and flowering bushes. The king had many motorcars—Ford Zephyrs and Wolseleys and even Mercedes. But he didn't have any Land Rover. So he was overjoyed when Miriamu gave it to him.

"The story's not over," Adija said, sitting up in bed. "Where are you going?"

"I'm cold." Salome went to the charcoal brazier where she had warmed her maize-meal supper. She blew on the coals, but got only a faceful of ashes for her trouble; the coals had gone out. The lantern too was dimming, and there was no more paraffin. Salome took down the army greatcoat she wore when it rained. She spread it over her on the bed. When she offered to share it with Adija, Adija shook her head.

"You're the one who's usually shivering," Salome said.

"As long as I'm awake, the room's warm enough with the lantern lit." Adija took two cigarettes from her pack, lit them, and handed one to Salome. "I'm going to go on with the story," she said.

The king was very pleased with Miriamu and her gifts. "You see, the girl is clever," he said to his ministers. "She is worthy to be my bride. Summon all the chiefs in my kingdom for my wedding!"

"Just a minute," said the Minister for Defense. "*Bado kidogo*, if you please."

The king waited.

The ministers all whispered together. Then the Minister for Education said to the king: "All right, she has brought gifts for you. But what of us? If she doesn't bring gifts for us, we will plot a coup to overthrow you."

"My army is strong," said the king. "I'll take my chances. Let the drummers drum from all the hilltops for my wedding!"

"No, no!" pleaded Miriamu to the king. "They will kill you if we are married now. Let me first get some gifts for them."

"All right," said the king. "But hurry up. I have not had any women for many years, and I am lonely."

Miriamu asked the ministers: "Do you want some lovely Bata shoes and English suits and televisions and fridges? I know where I can get some for you."

The ministers all whispered together again. Then they all shook their heads. "What we want are some pearls from the ocean. Just go to the ocean and fetch some for us," said the Minister for Foreign Affairs.

"But I can't swim," said Miriamu.

"You don't have to swim," said the Minister for Transportation. "Just go down to the Nyara Beach Hotel and hire a boat to take you to the reef. On the reef you will find a hole."

"It isn't a very deep hole," said the Minister for Finance, chuckling.

"You can reach in and gather up the pearls," said the Minister for Education. Really, that Minister for Education was the wickedest of the lot. "We will be waiting for you on the verandah."

So Miriamu drove down to the Nyara Beach Hotel in the Land Rover and hired an outrigger canoe. The boatman poled her out to the reef. The ministers waved to her from the verandah. They were laughing as they waved.

Miriamu was weeping with fear, for the water was crashing against the reef. But finally she found the hole. It was a deep, dark hole, not a shallow one, as the ministers had told her. She was cursing those ministers very much. She knelt down and reached her hand into the hole though, for she could see the pearls shining up at her out of the water.

As soon as her hand touched the water, something grabbed her. She was pulled down, down into the hole. Seaweeds slid across her face. She thought surely she would drown. But then she got pulled into a cave. There was air in the cave. The air smelled foul and it was dim, but Miriamu could breathe it. She looked around to see what had pulled her down into the water.

It was an octopus that had pulled her down into the water. It must be a witch, thought Miriamu, because it is as strange-looking, in its way, as the man on the mountain. It was black as the underbelly of a cooking pot. Its eyes were full of flames, like the flames that leap out of the end of a rifle. Its arms were very long and strong. At the end of each arm was a weapon. The octopus had knives and spears and machetes and rifles and pistols and Sten guns and even bombs. It waved the weapons all at once at Miriamu and its eyes glowed red.

Miriamu was fearing this witch very much. But now she was more clever than before. She told it: "Look how powerful your weapons are! I think that pistol can shoot very straight. That Sten gun, I think it must make a fearsome noise. Can you slice off a man's head with that machete? I think so!"

Miriamu was gasping for breath as she spoke, for the octopus was wrapping its arms around her tight. She thought that she would be crushed in the arms of the octopus. But it was pleased that Miriamu was admiring its weapons. It gave Miriamu a small knife to look at.

Now Miriamu remembered what she had learned on the mountain. When the octopus let go of the knife, Miriamu pushed the end of its arm into her vagina. She put another arm into her anus, and another into her mouth, and soon weapons were falling all over the floor of the cave. Miriamu was feeling very happy, for the octopus was holding her gently now.

When the last of its arms went limp, the octopus opened its mouth. Inside its mouth was a basket full of shining pearls. Miriamu reached in and took out the basket. She looked down into the basket to admire the pearls. When she looked up, the octopus was gone. In its place was a beautiful woman.

The woman was lying asleep on the floor of the cave. Miriamu rushed to her and woke her. The woman sat up, rubbing her eyes. She was very happy to greet Miriamu.

"*Salaama,*" said the beautiful woman. "Why have you come to this reef?"

Miriamu told her the story of the king and the ministers and the pearls.

"Listen," said the woman, "those ministers are just going to trick you. I know them. They are the ones who bewitched me into the shape of an octopus, many years ago. I will return with you. We will bring my weapons and kill them."

"All right," said Miriamu. "But what if the boatman refuses to carry us?"

"Don't worry. I will give him some pearls," said the woman.

So Miriamu and the woman went back to shore with a boat full of weapons. The ministers were still sitting on the verandah. They were drinking brandy and laughing. But when they saw the boat, they stopped laughing.

As soon as the boat touched the beach, the woman attacked the verandah. The ministers tried to run away, but they were too fat to run fast. The woman threw a bomb, and half the ministers were blown up. They lay bleeding all over the verandah.

Then the woman shot all the rest of the ministers with the Sten gun. They were lying on the floor of the verandah. Their organs were splattered on the walls. They were moaning and cursing and clutching their fat bellies. They all bled to death.

The manager of the Nyara Beach Hotel was very unhappy. "What am I going to do with all these dead bodies on my verandah?" he asked.

"Here, take some pearls," said the woman. And the manager was quiet.

Miriamu and the woman drove to the palace in the Land Rover. The people came out into the streets to see them. They were cheering and waving their flags at them. They were happy that the wicked ministers had been killed. Even the palm trees were happy on that day. They were waving their leaves over Miriamu and the woman as the Land Rover drove through the streets of the city.

The king was overjoyed to see Miriamu. He embraced her.

"This is my friend," said Miriamu, and she showed the woman to the king. "She killed all the ministers."

"My ministers are dead?" shouted the king. "*Eii!* This is the best news in many years!" And he greeted the woman in a very friendly way.

"Well, I will be going back to my cave now," said the woman.

"No, no! You must stay!" said the king. "You can come to my wedding. Afterward, you can live in the palace with us. I will make you brigadier of my army."

"All right," said the woman.

The king summoned all the chiefs in the kingdom. He ordered his drummers to drum from all the hilltops for his wedding. He caused the palace to be decorated with flowers of many colors. The sun shone bright on the day of the wedding. As the king and Miriamu walked together into the chapel, the palm trees lifted their leaves toward Heaven.

After the wedding ceremony, the king and his bride had a big party. All the king's friends were there. Queen Elizabeth was there. Elvis Presley was there, and Shashi Kapoor and Pearl Bailey and Miriam Makeba and Pélé and Satchmo and Cliff Richard and the Shadows, and all the famous film stars. Miriamu and the king and the woman sat at the biggest table. They were not drinking beer, they were drinking palm wine and Bee Hive Brandy and Gilbey's Gin. They were not eating maize-meal porridge, they were eating roasted goat and sheep and prawn curry and coconuts and paw-paw and fish cooked in palm wine. They got very drunk and fat.

Miriamu and the king and the woman stood on the wall of the palace. The people cheered and waved their flags at them. Even the schoolgirls who used to mock Miriamu were cheering. Even the men who used to abuse Miriamu were cheering. Even Miriamu's mother, who used to beat her, was cheering. But now they were cheering only because they were fearing Miriamu.

"Shall I tell the army to chase them away?" the woman asked Miriamu.

"All right," said Miriamu. "Tell the army to chase them into the ocean."

The army chased them into the ocean and they all drowned.

Then Miriamu and the king and the woman ate and drank some more. Even the king got drunk. Even Miriamu got fat. Everyone was very happy on that day.

"And that," Adija said, "is the story of Miriamu and the king."

"And the woman," Salome said.

"Yes." Adija rolled over on her back. Her breasts were flat on her chest, her nipples cold and hard in the chill air. "Was the story good?"

Salome laughed. "I think so. Are you sure you made it up?"

"Of course! You've never heard it before, have you?"

"Yes and no," Salome said. "I have and I haven't."

"Look!" Adija pointed up at the ceiling. A tiny lizard was running upside down along the corrugated tin. It scurried back and forth, then disappeared under the edge of the roof. "It was gray in that shadow," Adija said. "This afternoon, it was orange."

"I don't like lizards. My people say they crawl into your head while you're sleeping and eat your brain."

"I don't believe in witchcraft," Adija said. "I like them."

"You would." Salome shivered. "You're a witch yourself, you know. You've crawled into my brain and now I'm stuck with you."

Adija giggled. She pressed her cheek against Salome's broad shoulder and closed her eyes.

Salome let the lantern burn down. As the globe became sooty, the light shrank down the walls, flickering. Still, it seemed to provide some warmth in the room. Light and shadow flickered on Adija's pictures, making the faces indistinguishable: a wall of glossy squares. Adija pushed closer to Salome beneath the blanket to absorb more of her warmth. Her mouth opened, and soon she was snoring softly.

A car engine roared in the street. Headlight beams shot through the window, flashed along the walls, then vanished. The smell of dust billowed through the room. Salome reached under the bed. She found the handle of her machete and gripped it tight. She lay very still. Shadows flickered down the wall, as if trying to lap up what little warmth there was left in the room.

15

Business at the New Life picked up following the night of the big cattle raid. The Regional Government Officer and his entourage of clerks and secretaries came to eat and drink every evening before returning to headquarters at Mbure. The ranks of the spectators swelled on the lawn outside the government office. People came from miles around to see the men carrying briefcases and frowns in and out of the building.

The squat cement-block office became too small to accommodate the *baraza*. Spectators crowded the windows, cutting off the air supply within. When a delegation of Poken warriors decided to come, with their dung-hardened hair and attendant swarms of flies, the Regional Government Officer ordered the proceedings to continue in the open air. The lawn was trampled by bare feet and polished smooth by concentric circles of buttocks. Government officials stopped wearing their suits, having hopelessly mussed them sitting on the ground alongside elders and spectators. Only their neckties and their inability to speak the local dialects marked them as important people.

Gordon and Adija often passed the *baraza* on their way between the school and town. Sometimes they sat and watched, though they could not understand any of the languages being shouted back and forth. At one point, they saw a scuffle break out in the crowd. A *mganga* had set up shop beneath an acacia tree, selling roots and herbs. One side in the debate insisted that he was selling charms to confuse and weaken its argument. An impromptu youth wing attempted to remove the *mganga*, but was met with a rain of vegetables from the *mganga*'s supporters. At the end of a heated shouting match, the Regional Government Officer ruled that the man must go: the paraphernalia of witchcraft had no place in, or near, a modern court of law, where clear, objective decisions were the means by which issues would be settled. The next morning, six blankets covered with roots and herbs could be seen on the periphery of the crowd.

Gordon remembered a proverb Waga had told him: In times of trouble, witches flourish.

Eventually he came to understand what the *baraza* was all about. As part of a land development scheme across the border in Bashiri, Moroko tribesmen were being given parcels of land formerly owned by British farmers, in return for their support for the government. The Rukiva people, however, claimed that the land had been theirs before the Europeans had taken it, and should be restored to them. This "development" scheme was one more instance of the government shortchanging them in favor of its own representatives, who were now being installed as "chiefs" and living in as arrogant a manner as the former colonial masters. While many Rukiva were putting their energy into the secessionist movement, others were said to be trying to regain their land by force, setting fire to the new Moroko homesteads and raiding their cattle. Even the Rukiva who lived on the Marembo side of the border near Musolu were involved, engaging in stock theft, it was said, and rekindling old familial and tribal feuds.

To complicate matters further, the Poken people of the north began to take advantage of the confusion by raiding cattle from both sides. As the size of the Poken herds increased, Moslem ranchers from the far north were seen in the area, presumably to buy up surplus Poken cattle. The presence of Moslems gave each faction justification for crying Swila when accused of stock theft. A Moslem shopkeeper in a neighboring village had been beaten up, accused of being a Swila agent. The villagers in Musolu continued to whisper about Adija, whose Moslem name and unusual appearance had always aroused suspicion. She had taken to wearing a large silver cross around her neck, but had little confidence in its ability to act as a prophylactic against rumor.

The raid that had so suddenly expanded the *baraza* had resulted in the first death directly attributable to violence. The body of a small child, charred beyond recognition, was displayed. Nothing but the collapse of a fiery thatch roof could have produced such a gruesome corpse.

Women wailed and tore at their clothes as the lump of

flesh was unwrapped by a grim-faced Rukiva elder. The mother rolled on the ground in hysterics. Cries of rage went up. The body was trampled by the pushing, stumbling mob. Two aged watchmen paced back and forth between the gathering factions, wielding bows and arrows. When a van with five armed Marembo police officers arrived from Mbure, people sat down and lowered their voices. The police carried pistols in shiny leather holsters and blew their whistles at anyone who looked violent.

It was the R.G.O.'s task to determine who the genuinely aggrieved parties were. Six hut burnings, eight cattle raids, two sheep raids, and the one human death were before him on the agenda. In the month that the baraza had been in session, he had succeeded in settling three cases.

The R.G.O. looked impressive, pacing about in his khaki trousers, flowered sport shirt, and wide-brimmed felt hat. His qualifications for the post were high: He had completed almost two years of an English literature course at the university in Karela, and had once traveled to Stockholm, Sweden, for a three-week seminar in Cotton Marketing. Unfortunately, he was of the Marembo tribe, and knew little about the languages and customs of the Rukiva, Moroko, or Poken peoples. Thus he required three interpreters—one from each of the three aggrieved tribes. Everything that was spoken reached him three times, in three completely different versions. It was an eminently fair system, but a slow one.

The interpreters became good friends. Each night they drank together at the New Life. They frequently bought rounds of drinks for everyone present. None of them would have been able to afford a beer at the New Life before the baraza; now, Salome noted, they would be able to retire on the accumulated gifts of cattle, sheep, and cash they received from the various aggrieved parties. The customers did not hold the men's new riches against them. For one thing, each took gifts impartially from all sides in the disputes. For another, none of the customers were peasants who were likely to be hurt by decisions reached at the baraza. And for another, civilized men do not turn down free drinks.

Rumors flew about the bar but seemed to do no damage. Spirits remained high. The bar took on the atmosphere of a lawyers' pub, where factional differences dissipated in favor of convivial chatter and heavy drinking. The most persistent rumors were: that the Rukiva and other allied antigovernment tribes were plotting civil war against Bashiri; that the Bashiri government would send in troops to quiet the antigovernment dissidents, giving the rumored presence of Swila in the area as justification; that the Marembo government would send in troops to patrol its side of the border to keep out refugees and watch the movements of the Bashiri army. Opinions were divided as to whether or not the presence of soldiers would further progress in the Musolu area.

Salome, if asked, refused to give any opinion about the rumors. She was not asked often, of course. She was a mere woman, and women do not understand anything as complex as politics.

She sat at the tables with the officials, smiling at their jokes, her eyes roving the room sleepily. The R.G.O. discovered someone who had not heard the story of the five Swedish girls who had visited his Stockholm hotel room in a single night; Salome was able to excuse herself unnoticed. She quietly nuzzled up to a mournful young man in a frayed sportshirt and khaki trousers who happened to be mopping his brow with a handkerchief that bore the seal of the Marembo army. He had gotten leave from his job in the capital to attend his mother's funeral. His mother, he said, had been a wonderful woman. At times like these, Salome said, bringing him a free brandy, one must try to think of the living, and of the simple everyday things that kept one going—one's job, for instance. The young man was a secretary to a colonel, but all he did was type letters. Salome said that not many people realized how important a secretary's job was; she, being a simple country girl, would find it fascinating to hear about the letters he typed and the conversations he overheard. Sipping a new brandy, he told her about some of the letters he typed and the conversations he overheard, protesting that they were not of sufficient interest to distract one from grief. By the time he had convinced her, she had learned a great deal about troop movements. Military supplies were being routed to the Musolu area, meaning that troops would be sent here. She decided that it would soon be time to import more girls to work at the New Life, and perhaps even a snooker table to attract the arriving crowds of soldiers.

16

GORDON FOUND THE *BARAZA* INTERESTING, and was in the midst of incorporating it into a unit on contemporary history when an event occurred that made him fling his lesson plans against the wall in a helpless rage— his probationary report from his headmaster arrived, and it was awful. He needed to get away from the school immediately. He had borrowed Simon Waga's car once for a shopping trip to Mbure with Adija and Salome, but this time he wanted to stay away for an entire weekend alone with Adija, so the two of them took the bus. It was a miserable journey. Gordon got soaked in the rain pedaling down to Musolu from the school, and then got covered with feathers on the bus—someone's chicken broke loose and thrashed all over the passengers until it was recaptured. Ordinarily he would have been amused by the incident, but not today.

He sat pressed against the dirty window, glowering at the child staring at him from its mother's shoulder in the seat in front of him. The child's eyes were clouded over with thin runny pus; flies buzzed constantly around the eyes, yet the child did not brush them away or even blink. Gordon waved his hands close to the child's face in exasperation, but the little buzzing bastards returned immediately to continue their lunch. He felt as if he hadn't seen flies and diseased children since he'd left the city, but of course he had—he just hadn't thought about them. He'd been living in a fool's paradise.

"If you had a motorcar, we could go to Mbure comfortably," Adija suggested. She'd been noticing his uneasiness, and wanted to cheer him up. "We could take many nice holidays."

"It's not the bus, Adija . . ." His voice trailed off. He was too upset to try to explain. The headmaster's report had kept him awake all last night; he felt groggy, like a boxer who has stepped in front of a ferocious punch. Fool's paradise, he repeated to himself for the hundredth time.

Adija was delighted with the civil servant's resthouse in Mbure. The room was bright and clean, with a sink and running water right at the foot of the bed. The bathroom was even nicer than Gordon's bathroom in Musolu; it had green tiles on the wall and a tub with a shiny plastic curtain around it. Flowering bushes bloomed outside the room, red and orange and yellow and purple. Their sweet scents blew in the window with the hot afternoon breeze.

Mbure was down off the mountain, and very warm. Gordon's shirt was soaked again, this time from sweat. It was a good time to take Adija to the film he'd promised her. The cinemas boasted "Air-Cooled Comfort Inside," which meant fans. A Doris Day comedy and an Indian film were playing at the two houses. Gordon was in no mood to explain America to Adija via a Doris Day movie, and chose the Indian film. He sat far down in his seat, chain-smoking and glaring up at the screen between the heads of two little girls standing on the seat ahead of him.

The film began as a comedy, then became a tragedy, then a musical; it switched moods so often that Gordon couldn't tell what the hell it was. This whole afternoon was going to be a trip through cloud-cuckoo land. Adija couldn't understand the Gujerati dialogue any better than he could, so at least they were equally ignorant. The film seemed to be about two brothers, one of whom grew up to become a bandit, the other a Police Chief. It also featured many graceful almond-eyed beauties who were constantly descending staircases in glittering sarees, spreading their arms wide, fluttering their eyelashes, and moving their lips in sync to lilting Indian melodies that sounded to Gordon like the warbling of baby pigs. Adija groaned with pleasure whenever these women came on the screen.

Now the plot again: A flashback, presumably, to a scene between father and bandit son, the former offering sonorous pompous advice, the latter scowling sullenly . . .

"—utter lack of respect for established authority," Gordon recalled from the report. He tried to lock his mind into the film, but it was like trying to grip jelly with pliers. He watched the smoke rise over the heads of the audience into the cone of light blinking out of the projection booth.

The bandit brother was captured, taken to prison; a shadow on the wall of a man raising a long stick, bringing it down; screams . . .

"—fails to understand the importance of classroom discipline." Meaning I won't send my kids off to the headmaster's office so that he can cane their smooth black behinds.

The bandit brother was escaping, running through dark subterranean channels, up one tunnel and down the next, a maze that seemed to lead nowhere . . .

"—refuses to go through established channels in revising the syllabus." The expatriate bureaucracy in the capital still hadn't produced a new Africanized syllabus—was he supposed to keep to the one written during the reign of Victoria?

Flash to the Police Chief's happy family; fat smiling children, fat contented wife in jeweled saree, fat proud Police Chief in gold-braid uniform, the lot of them gathered around the harmonium singing—what?—"Happy Birthday to You" in English . . .

"—does not understand interstaff relations and does not support staff activities." Meaning: prefers drinking in the New Life Hotel to singing second tenor of Handel's *Messiah*.

The bandit brother at large; giving a handful of rupees to a charming nymphet of a street urchin. There, the girl was giving her thanks, along with everyone else in the neighborhood. No starving hordes in this India—the peasants and slum dwellers were a clean, cheerful lot, who loved nothing better than to dance through the cobblestone streets and—literally—over the rooftops . . .

"—implanting dangerous ideas into impressionable young minds." Yes, one should not think about real peasants, but about contented natives in textbooks; one should not try to give the students a sense of who they were yesterday and today, but should force them to memorize dates of foreign explorations. Give them a sense of who they were, and they might begin to ask who the established authority was . . . Gordon glared determinedly at the screen.

The Police Chief was too busy decoding secret messages to do any dancing and singing over rooftops, but he did get his man. Then tragedy: At the scaffold, he discovered that his arch foe was his very own once-beloved brother. The entire cast assembled to weep musically. The theater audience became hushed. Even Adija, who had been shoveling popcorn into her mouth throughout the picture, sat frozen on the edge of her seat.

A horseman galloped on screen, carrying a pardon from the maharajah. The cast broke into jubilant song. Peasant couples embraced deliriously. Brother embraced brother. Their women, draped in radiant new sarees for the occasion, arrived to join in the embracing. The maharajah himself showed up on an elephant; the Police Chief was awarded a medal, and the former bandit drove off in a Jaguar, garlanded with flowers. The theater lights blinked on, and a ragged African boy limped up and down the aisle shouting, "Peanuts! Buy you nice peanuts here!"

Fool's paradise, Gordon thought again. Who will send an elephant to rescue me?

There was not a dry eye in the house, except Gordon's. Adija's face was streaked with tears and flakes of popcorn. She begged to see the film through again. Gordon went to sleep during the second showing.

Afterward, Adija danced out of the theater, spinning around and around along the pavement as if she were swirling a shimmering rainbow-hued saree. Motorists stopped to honk and call out to her. She laughed and waved and clutched Gordon's arm to show the town of Mbure that he alone was the cause of all her happiness.

Mbure had once been a gathering place for European sisal planters, and still contained an old British-style hotel, complete with faded cricket photos in the bar, a fan that creaked round and round on the ceiling, and cold beer. Gordon was the only European on the verandah; the rest of the customers were African and Asian businessmen in dark suits, and men who appeared to be military officers in partial uniform. They looked with disdain at Gordon's rubber sandals and jeans, but he didn't notice. Adija ordered a sweet coffee liqueur and an English-style curry, the kind that came with tiny bowls of coconut and banana and mango. Gordon found the curry too mild, but didn't say so because Adija was enjoying it so much.

After a while, she noticed Gordon staring distractedly into his rice, and began to eat more slowly. Finally she put her spoon down.

"I think you're unhappy today," she said.

"I'm all right. I didn't sleep well last night."

"Why?" Adija tried to smile. "Missing me?"

"Yes." He *had* felt her absence last night. When she was not around, he missed her more than was good for him.

"But that's not all," Adija said.

"You're right." Gordon took a deep breath. At least she had enjoyed all her curry. "They may be asking me to leave Musolu," he said.

"No!" Adija pressed her knuckles against her mouth. "No, Gordon!"

"The headmaster might be requesting a transfer for me. He hinted at it when I saw him yesterday. He gave me a bad report."

"But why?"

"I'm not sure exactly. But it's certain that he doesn't like the way I teach."

Adija lowered her eyes. She didn't speak for a long time. "It's because of me," she said finally.

"No, it isn't. Nobody knows—and anyway, they couldn't transfer me because of something like that."

"They know. They know everything."

"That's nonsense."

"The schoolboys tell them. Two boys from your school were in the town last week, and they called me *Memsahib* Lockery. They ran away laughing."

"The little shits!"

"Yes, little shits."

"The way I work for those kids, the chances I take just to teach them." Gordon wiped his brow with his napkin. "Oh, hell—schoolboys are like that. You can't pen up a bunch of kids in a boarding school and expect them not to gossip about their keepers. I was a schoolboy once."

Adija gazed around helplessly. Her eyes blurred over with tears. Everything had been so lovely today—that clean bright resthouse, and the cinema, and this beautiful hotel. She was having the glimpse she'd been wanting of what life with Gordon might be like; so far it had been all she'd hoped for. Sitting on this verandah, she had said to herself just a few minutes ago: this is the kind of place I want to be, this is the kind of man I want to be with—a man who cares enough about me to take me to a nice place, just to eat and talk and enjoy each other.

Now it was all spoiled. Gordon would leave. She would remain behind in Musolu with the flies in the bar and the men with their greedy eyes and rough hands. And Gordon —he had been happy here too. That was spoiled as well. They would send him somewhere else, probably back to his own country, and he would be lonely again as he'd been before. "I'm sorry, Gordon. I'm sorry you're unhappy." She rubbed her eyes with her napkin. "I must have bewitched you," she said, and choked. It was not very amusing.

"Adija, you're wrong. It's not because of you." Gordon leaned over to lift her chin, but she kept her face averted. "Do you hear me?"

She stared hopelessly past the verandah railing. The blurred figure of a pig—no, a yellow dog—walked slowly into the street and lay down in a heap beside the gutter. From a house nearby came the wail of a baby, loud and piercing and rhythmic; suddenly it stopped, leaving silence like a hole torn in the air. Adija stared at Gordon.

/ "Let's get out of here." He rose from his chair.

She took a last look at the remaining scraps of her curry, and allowed Gordon to help her up out of her chair. "Where are we going?" she asked, holding tight to his arm.

"Just for a walk."

"It's not a good time of day to walk here," she said, glancing at the sinking sun. "We should stay indoors."

"I like this time of day." Gordon signaled a waiter. "Listen, Adija, don't start worrying yet."

"No?" She realized that she had been worrying for a long time already—ever since meeting Gordon.

"We'll work something out. Something will happen."

"What?"

"I don't know. Something."

Adija nodded and managed a smile.

They walked in silence, listening to the buzz of insects from the greenery beside the pavement. The sunlight blazed red on the stucco walls of buildings; wooden fences cast long grate-shaped shadows into the street. Under a tree in the town square, men sat on the ground talking quietly, listening to a transistor radio, watching the passers-by with somnolent stares. Gordon and Adija walked up a lane toward the market, where flowering bushes exhaled a sweet purple mist into the air. Gordon bought some cigarettes; Adija slurped a pineapple wedge. Watching her, he smiled. Having spoken of his troubles, he was feeling a little better. The thought struck him that moving to a place less isolated and more tropical, like Mbure, might not be a bad idea at all. He could ask Adija to come with him. Leaving Musolu would be a good move for her too—she would get out of the clutches of Salome. They walked on toward the edge of town.

"*Bwana! Memsahib!*"

Gordon looked around. Some men were calling him from behind a wire fence across a litter-strewn yard. The fence was attached to a one-story stone building with rusted wire netting over the windows: the town jail. The smell of urine overpowered that of the municipal flowers beside the front door.

"*Bwana*, you help me with a cigarette, *eii?*" a man in the yard called to Gordon. He pushed his face into the fence, his fingers squirming out through the wire.

Gordon stepped across the rubble and weeds outside the fence and handed a cigarette to the man. "*Jambo*," he said. "They don't let you have cigarettes?"

"We can have them, but we have to have money to pay the guards for them," the man said, nodding his thanks. He wore khaki shorts and an undershirt that had rotted away over his stomach.

Gordon lit his cigarette, then lit one for himself. He noticed a swollen purple bruise covering the man's cheek. Other men in shredded clothes watched him from the doorway. An African jail was no place to be.

"Here," Gordon said, pushing the rest of the cigarette packet between the wires.

"Your woman, she's very nice." The man grinned past Gordon at Adija. "*Jambo, bibi!*" he called.

Adija stepped back from the edge of the pavement as if the man's voice were dirty water spreading toward her. She raised her hand and managed a brief smile.

"She's afraid of us," the man said, laughing. The other men laughed too, and waved. "Thanks for the cigarettes, man."

Gordon nodded, and returned to the sidewalk.

"Why do you talk to those men?" Adija asked when they were further along the road. "They're bad."

"How do you know?"

"Because they're in jail."

"Do you think they're as bad as the police who run the jail?"

"No," Adija said. "That's true."

"I was in jail once. Twice, in fact," Gordon said.

"You?" Adija laughed. When she saw that Gordon was not smiling, she turned her face away and didn't look at him again until she had made a frown. "Why?"

"I was in demonstrations against the government. In America."

"Why did you do that?"

"Well, once because of a war we almost started with Cuba and Russia, and once because I didn't like the way the government was treating black people."

"And the police arrested you—even you are white?"

"Yes. I didn't stay in jail very long, though."

Adija shook her head, still incredulous. It was hard to imagine Gordon behind a wire fence begging cigarettes. She wondered if he would be put back in jail by his government if he were sent back to America. But this was no time to ask him. "Myself, I can't like police," she said finally.

They passed through a shaggy little park, their feet crunching on the gravel path. Children kicked a football around on the grass, occasionally bouncing it against a tall stone obelisk that commemorated in worn letters the Soldiers of the British Empire who had given their lives in the Tanganyika Campaign, 1914–1918. Adija picked lichens from the stone as Gordon read the inscription to her. She had never heard about that war, and was glad to know that it had happened a very long time ago, too long ago for enemy soldiers to still be hiding in the forests preparing to come back. She didn't like soldiers any better than police.

Gordon stood on the base of the obelisk, looking out over the slope beyond the edge of the park. The insect buzzing grew louder, backed by a whining sound so high it was hardly noticeable. Gordon smelled water. Something

flickered red between the black-silhouetted tree branches:
the last of the sunset on the lake.

"Let's go over that way," he said, jumping down.

Adija made no reply. She did not look enthusiastic about
Gordon's idea.

Along the dirt path to the lake, children came out of
shacks to stare at them. They stood with their bellies
swollen out, watching silently. Some of them had pussed-
over eyes like the child on the bus. Gordon walked faster.
When he heard the water lapping peacefully against the
shore of the lake, he began to relax again. A big bird,
perhaps a flamingo, rose from the reeds and flapped into
the red sky. Gordon put his arm around Adija's waist and
held her close. "I like this place," he said. "We'll have to
come here again."

"Yes," she mumbled, glancing around.

"What's the matter?"

She didn't have to answer. Suddenly, a high whining
sound surrounded them. Gordon slapped his cheek, his
leg, his arm. Adija was slapping herself all over too. He
yanked her hand and they began running back up the
path. "This way!" Gordon cried, starting to cut across a
patch of underbrush and rocks.

"No!" Adija tugged him back. "Snakes—you can step on
them!"

He heeded her this time. Together they fled across the
park and back onto the pavements of the town. A few
mosquitoes lingered with them all the way back to the
hotel. Under the light from the verandah, they found mosquitoes embedding themselves in their arms and ankles;
each one they swatted turned to a splatter of blood. Adija
began to cry silently. The men in the suits and uniforms
watched her from their tables.

Gordon went into the bar and bought three bottles of
cold beer for himself and the rest of the bottle of coffee
liqueur for Adija. They walked slowly back to their room.
As they stepped through the door, a blast of heat rushed at
them. Adija ran through it into the bathroom and vomited
into the gleaming white toilet. Gordon knelt beside her and
handed her pieces of tissue paper. Leaning sideways
against the wall, Adija clenched her teeth and shut her
eyes. This was the third time in three days she had been

sick, and her breasts were beginning to hurt. Did it mean?
She couldn't bear to think about it, not after what Gordon
had told her. She let him help her to her feet.

When she saw her reflection in the mirror over the wash
basin, she let out a cry. "My hair, it's sticky—don't look at
me!" She pushed her head beneath the tap. "Gordon, I'm
sorry!" she groaned, lifting her dripping face.

Gordon handed her a towel and helped her dry herself.
Streaks of water stained her light blue blouse like dark oil.
She pulled it off and flung it into a chair. Her image swam
before her in the mirror, blotchy-cheeked and swollen-eyed.
She covered her face, fingertips digging into her scalp.
The room tilted. She sat down hard on the side of the bed,
tearing the mosquito netting out of its frame overhead. She
leaped up, staring at it.

"Now I've spoiled that—that cloth too."

"It'll be all right. I can fix it."

"Gordon, you should stay away from me! I spoil things!"
She stared at him, her big eyes shining wet. Seeing that he
was moving toward her, not away, she started to shrink
back. Then she lunged for him and pressed her face against
his chest.

Gordon pushed the mosquito netting aside and lay her
back on the bed. "I won't go away from you," he said, his
voice catching in his throat.

"I don't want you to, but—"

Gordon's weight upon her stopped her words. She
yanked up her skirt and wrapped her legs tight around him.
Someone's breasts were tingling and someone's thighs were
thrusting against him; she heard someone's high voice crying out and felt waves of pleasure rushing past her. But
when he rolled away and she smoothed down her skirt, she
found it difficult to believe that all these things had happened to her, for her mind had not stopped racing for a
moment and every panting breath sounded to her like a
moan of abandonment.

As the night grew longer and quieter, the air became
hotter under the repaired mosquito netting. Gordon leaned
back against the wall, careful not to disturb the net, and
drank beer. The high whine of mosquitoes surrounded
their cocoon of gauze, diving in at them and fading into
the shadows around the walls of the room. Gordon sat
cross-legged; Adija sat facing him, her legs outstretched,

with her toes resting against his knees. She knew he was
thinking hard about important things, and said nothing to
bother him. She scratched her legs, her arms, her neck,
then rested, then scratched again, trying to do it quietly.

Gordon was on his last bottle of beer; Adija had drunk
half the bottle of liqueur. Overhead, the lightbulb throbbed
slowly in rhythm with the faraway hum of a generator.
They sat silent, naked; they lay down together, but not
touching now because of the heat. They sweated and interrupted their scratching to wipe away the sweat. Now and
then they stroked each other for reassurance and smiled
faintly.

"Tomorrow I'll get some medicine for our bites," Gordon said.

"Will you get the kind you used before?"

"No, a different kind."

"Is it better?"

"It's . . . different."

Adija closed her eyes. "It will make us feel better," she
said, unable to believe it.

"It'll give you pink spots instead of · dark red ones,"
Gordon said, smiling.

"Oh . . . good."

"Like a leopard."

"A hyena."

"Hyenas don't have pink spots."

"Neither do leopards. But I've never seen one. Maybe
they do." Adija opened her eyes. "Do they?"

"No."

"Oh." Adija sighed and shut her eyes. The light glowed
through her lids.

"I was just talking."

"Yes, it's good to talk." Adija rolled over on her stomach. "Can you make that light go out? It hurts my eyes."

"Sure." Gordon sat up and slipped through the opening
in the mosquito net. He padded quickly to the wall and
flipped the switch, then hurried back to grope under the
net again. "I think I let one in," he said, slapping his ear.

"Yes. It brought its family with it too." Adija swatted
the sheet. "But there are holes in the cloth. There were
some mosquitoes before."

"I didn't notice them."

"Maybe they only came to me."

"No, I think I just didn't notice them." Gordon slammed his hand against the wall, shaking the net.

Squinting at him through the dim light still made her eyes hurt. She pressed the heels of her hands against them. Her face was sticky. Blood, she thought, and chased the thought out of her mind. Just because I'm drinking too much, I'm not going to start thinking crazy things, she said to herself. Nonetheless, she wiped her fingertips along her cheeks and put them in her mouth. Blood, she thought again, despite the taste of sweat, and she wanted to slap her face hard for thinking it.

"Do you want to sleep?" Gordon asked her.

"No."

"Me neither." Gordon lifted the bottle to his mouth and finished the beer. His eyes were growing accustomed to the dim light from the window. He stared at Adija's damp legs and arms; her face, turned toward her lap, was hidden in shadow. He lit a cigarette, and in the flare of the match, saw that her eyes were wide open, despite her collapsed position.

"Adija, would you like to go to live in the city?"

"Mbure?"

"No, a real city. I was thinking of Karela. I was at the university there, you know. I could probably get a teaching job in Karela if I asked for a transfer."

Adija looked up slowly. "I've never been to Karela."

"It's nice there. We wouldn't live right in the city, but at one of the schools, on the compound."

"They wouldn't let us live there unless I was your wife." The words were out before she had a chance to think. She hiccupped, and clamped her hand over her mouth.

"Yeah, I know." Gordon sighed.

Adija squinted at him. She couldn't see his face, just the red glow around his mouth when he puffed on his cigarette. "Can I have one?"

"Of course. When did you start smoking?" Gordon handed her the packet and propped an empty beer bottle between them for an ashtray.

"I smoke sometimes." She held the cigarette between her thumb and forefinger and put it to her lips. "But you know, African women are not supposed to smoke, at least young women. So I don't do it if anyone can see me."

"But from me you have no secrets." Gordon smiled.

I hope not, Adija thought, and pressed her fingers gingerly against her belly. They came off wet and did not dry; the air inside this tent was hot and stale. Some European inventions weren't so marvelous after all. This cloth tent was worse than a jail—at least the breeze could get in through the wire there.

"I don't know, Adija," Gordon said.

"Don't know what?"

"If I want to be married."

"Oh."

"I was almost married before. It would have been a disaster. I came here . . . not to have any more disasters in my life." Gordon scratched a mosquito bite on his neck until he felt it bleed, and dropped his hand. "I'm used to being alone. I was pretty happy that way—well, not happy, but at least if I screwed things up, I was the only one who got hurt, and I could start again. But now I know you . . ."

"And you're more unhappy."

"No!"

Adija shrank back into the mosquito netting, but her voice kept going. "Didn't you say that?"

"No. I'm sorry. I'm trying to explain." He pushed his cigarette down into the top of the bottle. It fizzled out in the bottom, smelly. "It's hard to explain. And maybe whatever I'm trying to say isn't true any longer."

"Maybe you have to think some more."

Gordon nodded. "I'll be staying in Musolu a while yet. We'll see what happens, all right?"

"Myself, I have to think too."

"We'll have time to think," Gordon said, and wondered why his words sounded so hollow. "We'll talk about it again, all right?"

Adija watched his face turn toward her, but she could make out no features on it in the dim light. The heat of the evening seemed focused under this cone of netting she was in. She wanted to tear it apart with her fingertips, but instead she smoothed the damp hair away from Gordon's forehead. "All right," she said, and curled up gingerly beside him.

❊　❊　❊

They slept late on Sunday morning and missed the only bus out of Mbure. Gordon led Adija out onto the main road, hoping to catch a lift. Sunday was a bad day for hitchhiking; the road was deserted. Raindrops began bouncing in the dust around them; they tried to ignore them, but soon the rain was pouring down hard. They found shelter beneath a tree. Adija unwrapped one of her packages and draped a *kente*-cloth over her head and Gordon's. She had a new skirt, some new shoes, and several cloths. She hadn't asked Gordon for them, but he hadn't been able to resist buying them, she'd admired them so.

A Mercedes roared into view. Gordon went out onto the road and waved his hand. The car slowed, then the driver, an elderly European, caught sight of Adija standing under the tree. The engine accelerated: the car splattered mud as it sped by. Cursing, Gordon returned to the tree. Behind them a cow munched grass noisily, stealing long curious looks at them between bites.

After more than an hour, another car appeared. This one stopped for them. Gordon wanted Adija to sit in front with him, but she feared they would be too crowded, and sat in the back with her packages.

The driver was a red-faced New Zealander who managed a coffee estate in Kijambe, near the Congo border. He had been to Bashiri on business, and was returning home for the last lap of his contract. "Home!" he laughed out of the side of his mouth, and spat out the window. "Some bloody home!"

He was obviously lonely after nine months in the bush, and talked a blue streak all the way to Musolu. His favorite subject was the Maori chaps in New Zealand, how they were a hell of a better lot than these local blokes. Gordon was glad Adija knew so little English. Now and then, he tried to change the subject and bring her into the conversation, but the New Zealander's Kisemi was of the ki-settler variety, consisting of nouns and commands, and Gordon gave up after a while.

Adija didn't mind. She didn't want to try to talk with a strange European, especially this one, who spat out the window repeatedly, catching her with the edge of his spray. She enjoyed the ride, opening and shutting the ashtray on the armrest and pushing her toes into the carpet. This was the third time in her life she had ridden in a private motorcar, and the first time in such a new one. The car smelled sweet, of leather and pipe tobacco, and it didn't bounce at all, not even when they sped over potholes. It was very

much nicer than a country bus or a taxi. Adija fell asleep
with her head swaying on the soft back of the seat.

"I hear there's trouble up in your area," the New Zealander said to Gordon. "Swila swoopin' down from the
north, terrorizing the locals with their Russian rifles and so
forth."

"There's rumors," Gordon said. "I think that's all they
are. Things are pretty peaceful where I am."

"They may be rumors, but they're upsettin' people all
over this fuckin' country. You know what I think?" The
New Zealander leaned close to Gordon. "I think the army's
usin' it—and a lot of other things—for an excuse to show
its muscle. Gettin' ready to take over, if you ask me."

"There do seem to be a lot of soldiers around."

"You ought to see it in Karela. Friend of mine's houseboy, he went out one night and came back all bloody, his
lip split open. 'Soldiers, *bwana*, soldiers!'" The driver blew
out a long stream of smoke. "They don't like the Asians or
the whites either, those blokes, but they're bidin' their
time."

The only news Gordon got from the capital was from
the newspaper, which arrived several days later and only
carried stories that were favorable to the ruling party. He
didn't trust the driver's views either, but he couldn't help
but feel depressed by them.

"The Prime Minister's mad, lettin' his boys run loose
like that. They're goin' to turn round and run his arse out
of the country. Not that that'd be such a bad thing." The
driver laughed. "Your people are gettin' worried. A bunch
of women and children got evacuated from Masakua."

"What people?"

"Americans. You're a Yank, aren't you?"

"Oh. Yeah. But I'm not leaving."

"Welcome to it, mate." the driver relit his pipe, filling
the back seat with clouds of smoke. "All I know is that
when I get one more harvest out, I'm off to South Africa.
Had enough of this Oo-hoo-roo nonsense, I have. They
know how to treat a white man in South Africa!"

Gordon kept silent. After several miles, the New Zealander gestured toward the back seat. "What's that, your
wife?" he asked out of the side of his mouth.

"Sort of," Gordon said.

The driver nodded, grinning. "Know what you mean.

Got one myself. When in Rome, I always say. They're not half bad, the women out here." He puffed luxuriously on his pipe. "That one you got, she's a beauty. What's she, a Moslem from up north?"

"No," Gordon said, "she's Japanese."

The driver made no more inquiries.

Adija, Gordon said to himself, you can help me shop for a car of our own as soon as we get back to Musolu. That bicycle of mine is no damn good for the two of us.

17

THE NEW LIFE WAS NEARLY ALWAYS EMPTY during the afternoons; anyone with time on his hands was at the *baraza*. Salome leaned on the counter, reading a week-old Azima newspaper. "MORE TERRORISTS SURRENDER," screamed the headline. She stared at the photographs on the front page: Five guerrillas in ragged shirts, their eyes huge and wild, their hair hanging to their shoulders in matted locks. Like hundreds of others, they had not believed that the war had ended five years ago, and had stayed hidden in the forests on Mount Bashiri. They were right, Salome decided—the war was not over. Bashiri had a new black government, but the Europeans still controlled the country—you had only to glance at a newspaper to see that. It was full of advertisements for motorcars, tractors, liquor, cosmetics, airline holidays, medicines, electric dishwashers, televisions, dog shows, horse shows, musical comedy shows—everything that African peasants wouldn't want or couldn't afford. There were more advertisements than news. The news was mostly about African politicians opening new foreign-owned factories, meeting foreign trade delegations, thanking foreign technicians for helping the new nation of Bashiri to catch up with foreign countries.

The newspaper was calling the guerrillas "terrorists" again—just like during the war. The five men in the photographs looked like the people she had brought bullets and food to during the war—one of them might have been Kariuki, if he hadn't been killed. During the Uhuru night celebrations, they had been called "freedom fighters" and displayed on the podium with their matted hair and rifles for the people to cheer. Now they had their old name back and the new Bashiri army was ferreting the last of them out of the forests. The Bashiri Prime Minister had declared that any guerrillas who were still at large after the Uhuru amnesty were living in defiance of the law. The brigadier of the Bashiri army, an Englishman with a white mustache, stated that by the end of the month he expected all the remaining "terrorists" would be captured or "otherwise defeated."

Too angry to read further, Salome stood in the doorway watching the street. Every day her exile presented her with the same scene. She was sick of it. With Adija here, she didn't notice the town much. But Adija was not here today.

Under an overhanging roof across the street, a man was repairing a broken bicycle; he filled the street with clang-clang noises, smacking the fender with his mallet. Women poked around inside the shops, picking up boxes and packets, prodding them, sniffing them, dropping them back onto the counters.

A barber under a nearby acacia tree ran his clippers carefully up the side of his customer's head. Some old Poken women sat down on the curb and passed a film cannister of snuff around. They leaned forward, one by one, and sneezed. Then they wiped away the strings of snot hanging from their nostrils.

Salome could smell the Poken women from across the street—the cattle dung they used to mat their hair was well seasoned. Dung, dust, and beer, she said, shaking her head. I probably smell of it too. Dung, dust, and beer. Probably will smell of it for the rest of my life . . .

Gordon and Adija were inside, talking. They must have come in the back way; Salome hadn't seen them. She went inside.

"Why are you sneaking in the back door these days?" she demanded.

"We didn't," Adija said.

"We walked right past you," Gordon said. "We said hello. You nodded back."

"Oh." Salome nodded. That was possible. "Yes, I remember."

"The hell you do." Gordon laughed.

Salome ignored him and went around to her side of the bar to get a drink. She and Gordon coexisted mostly by ignoring each other. Both wanted to yank Adija away, to have her exclusively. But Adija could not be yanked away, she could only be yanked apart. Salome remembered many years ago she had fought with another child over a radiant yellow butterfly. She had taken one wing in her fingertips; the other child had done the same. Each was left holding a powdery membrane that disintegrated between the fingers. On the ground at their feet, a black, wormlike thing writhed about, dying.

"That's my newspaper you're reading," Salome said.

"Mmm." Gordon finished reading a paragraph. He was leaning on the counter, smoking one of his foul cigarettes as he read. "You want it back?" he asked.

Salome looked at the headline: "MORE TERRORISTS SURRENDER." "No," she said.

She watched him read. His eyes were looking tired these days, tired and hollow, almost wild at times. His hair had grown shaggy; he was constantly brushing it off his forehead with angry flicks of his hand. He was drinking more than before too, Salome was pleased to note. The long Adija-less nights and days were getting to him too.

"What do you think of this?" he asked, tapping the newspaper.

"Shit."

"You don't even know what I'm pointing to."

"I don't have to." Salome leaned over to look. A photo showed two young Samoyo girls staring into a shiny petrol station window. The girls carried gigantic bundles of firewood on their backs that were held by leather bands strapped around their foreheads. The caption read: "Industrial Development at Kuria." Salome's home village. "Shit," Salome repeated. "Think how those girls will benefit. They'll get to look at more tourists and politicians stopping in their village to feed their motorcars."

"Progress," Gordon said. "Development."

Adija had been standing at the end of the counter, listening. "What's wrong with motorcars and things?" She squinted at Gordon, as if that would help her to understand him. "Everybody likes to have nice things except you and Salome. You like to pretend you're poor."

"If you show people how much money you have, they want to know where you got it. They also want to help you spend it," Salome said. "In my case, that's true. Him, his case is different." She pointed to Gordon. "He is a Christian."

"He's been buying more things lately," Adija said, grinning at him. "Next he'll have a motorcar, *eii?*"

"Maybe," Gordon said.

"I hope he drives it better than he drove Jeremiah's," Salome said, recalling the time Gordon had borrowed Jeremiah's Zephyr to take Salome and Adija shopping in Mbure.

"The brakes and steering were wrecked," he said.

"You almost killed me in it."

Gordon glanced up from his beer bottle. His half-smile said: Next time I'll be luckier.

Salome acknowledged his look with a disdainful tongue-clicking. She stared down at the newspaper. "Here's one for you, *mzungu*. It says here that some big white farmer has just died. Another white man, a reverend, has written about him. Do you want to hear?"

"No."

"Why not? It's good for you to hear about your kin. Educational." Salome cleared her throat. " 'His life was spent taming the land and bringing forth fruit from the wilderness. Today the laborers file into church on this man's farm, clothed in bright new fabrics, singing their simple hymns of praise to the greatest of all God's work: civilization.' " Salome poured more brandy into her glass. "Let's drink to 'civilization,' " she said, and glanced at Gordon. "What's the matter, you don't like brandy and Coca-Cola?"

Some men stepped into the barroom from the pavement. "Salome is making a speech," one of them said, grinning.

She ignored them, continuing to glare at Gordon. "They conquered the land—you whites did. You took our strength and used it to conquer us. You gave us Bibles in return for our land, and when you ran out of them, you gave us civilization—things. Strong medicine, the things you sell us. We get bottled beer and brandy to help us forget our sadness of not being allowed to brew our own liquor anymore. We get Aspro and Bicarb to take away the sicknesses of eating imported foods we have to buy because what little land is left to us is too worn out to produce enough food. We get plastic baby bottles to fill with expensive powdered milk so that our women won't look uncivilized with their breasts showing, even though European women get paid a lot of money to show theirs in the films you charge us to see. We get skin-lightening cream and cinemas to teach women how to look pale and sexy and to kiss and behave like white women. So that a woman can look more civilized to a man and entice him. So that a man can look more civilized to a woman and conquer her. So that men and women can use each other and mistrust each other. You poisoned us into believing that we couldn't get along without all these things, and so we have to keep swallowing up your ways of getting them—mistrusting, enticing, conquering."

The men applauded. Some were laughing. "What about your way of getting things, Salome?"

"What about it, moron?" Salome shouted back. "They made us servants in our own land. Now anyone who's not a whore is somebody's servant."

"What's that you're drinking with your brandy, Salome? Coca-Cola?"

"We survive on what they've left us. You expect me to go on a hunger strike?" Salome demanded. "Myself, I'm finished with starving."

The men laughed louder, but now many of them were grinning at Gordon as well—the man from the land of Coca-Cola. Salome was better than the politicians on the wireless. The men called their friends in from the street to listen.

"You made civilization bring forth fruit in the wilderness," she went on, glaring at Gordon, gathering steam. "Your civilization, *our* fruit, *our* wilderness. In return for our fruits and our wilderness, what do we get? We get the chaff of the grain, the gristle of the meat, and all the shit of civilization. All the shit that would clog the rivers of Europe and America if it didn't overflow onto Africa. It flows over us and through us, into our mouths and up our nostrils. We swallow it and choke on it. We spew it out and gobble it up again and climb all over each other fighting for more of it to stuff ourselves with."

Gordon was leaning back tight against the bar, sweating, trying to ignore the looks of the men in the doorway. "I don't know why you do that," he said.

"Why! Because we've nothing else now. We're nowhere. We're not tribal and self-sufficient any longer. But we're not shrewd and cold and powerful yet. We're cracked,

empty shells. We grumble at our emptiness, our incom-
pleteness, and we toil to our graves in terror of never being
able to fill ourselves up enough."

Salome took a long gulp of her drink. The men's nervous
laughter enraged her; she began shouting. "No, we haven't
filled ourselves up enough, not yet! But someday we will.
The grumbling will tremble the earth then! We'll be heavy
with your things, *your* things and *our* rage. We'll overrun
your world of things and civilization. We'll suck the life
and strength out of you, this time. We'll eat your brains
and hearts—not just *things* any longer. Then we'll shit it
all back to you in pretty packages and teach you to beg for
it." Salome slammed her fist on the counter. "If you did it,
why can't we? Aren't we human too?"

The bar was quiet. The men watched Gordon. He stared
down at the newspaper, shaking his head slowly. Finally he
raised his face and looked at Salome.

"*Eii?*" she demanded.

"What you say is true. The longer I live here, the more I
see it. I don't want to see it, but I do. I don't know . . ."

"What?"

"I don't know if I'm supposed to answer for it all personally."

"Why don't you know that? You're a teacher—you're
supposed to know things."

"Maybe," Gordon said. "But whether I'm supposed to or
not, I'm not going to answer for it. I can't. I'd wear myself
out trying, and I'd never even come close to succeeding.
Anyway, I've got better things to do."

"Like what?"

"Teaching."

"Yes, your teaching." Salome gripped the Coca-Cola
bottle tight. Her head was spinning with brandy, and her
voice had a jagged edge to it. "You say you teach history,
but you teach a lot more than that. You teach—you
teach—"

Salome's eyes blurred in rage. Her arm coiled back and
snapped forward, the bottle aimed at Gordon's head. It
flew wide of its mark and shattered against the wall.
"Aaagh!" she cried, and aimed a kick at his groin. He
turned in time to block it with his leg.

Adija wailed. Two men shoved her aside and held Salome's arms. For a moment she thrashed against them, and

probably could have succeeded in freeing herself. Then she pitched forward and came to rest with both elbows on the counter, her head thrust down. "Let go, you bastards! I'm all right!"

Four or five men stood around her in a semicircle, watching her shoulders heave as she breathed. "Be careful, Salome," one of them said.

"You protect . . . that European . . . that's right, go ahead, protect him—"

"We've enough trouble here with this *baraza*, without you assaulting a foreigner," the man said. "Do you want Elima's police sirens screeching through the street, woman?"

"Police sirens won't help him," Salome grunted. She lifted her head and looked at Adija, who was swaying dizzily back and forth in place between Salome and Gordon. "I'm sorry, Adija." Salome swallowed hard. "Are you all right?"

Adija sat down. She touched the place where her arm had struck the counter when the men had shoved her aside. "I'm all right."

"I drank too much of this shit," Salome said, gesturing toward her glass.

"Perhaps we shouldn't come here anymore," Adija said.

Salome stared at her. She knew who "we" was. "No, no, Adija, I was just—" She glanced at Gordon and managed a false, toothy smile. "Your teacher, he is not afraid to come here, is he?"

"No, he's not!" Adija stared up at Gordon. "You're not afraid, are you?"

"No." He sat down at the table beside her. "Fuck you," he said to Salome, glaring at her.

Her eyes suddenly smiled darkly and focused on Adija. Then Gordon knew: Adija needed Salome as much as she needed him. Salome knew it too. He and Salome were locked into this dusty little border town like souls shackled together in Purgatory, waiting for Adija to make a choice that she could not afford to make, ever.

18

SEVERAL WEEKS LATER, ADIJA RETURNED from a day trip to Mbure to find Salome in a foul mood again. Not, Salome said, because of Gordon, but because her Mercedes had been stolen in the Congo. Her one-fifth of a Mercedes, rather, which amounted to a loss of about seventeen thousand shillings. Salome was suddenly aware of the lightness of her strongbox. The ten- and twenty-shilling notes she had been feeding it had not fattened it appreciably. Hefting it in her hands, Salome was more aware than ever of her own unfed feeling, and she was doubly disagreeable to everyone she met.

The Mercedes' driver, a young Indian mechanic, had been on his way to Kabolo to make the sale when a squad of Congolese soldiers stopped him at a roadblock. Finding a jackknife in the glove box, they arrested him for attempting to smuggle arms to the Katangalese rebels. It was a crime punishable by death, but the soldiers agreed to drop charges in return for the vehicle. The driver also lost his wallet and several teeth during the transaction, which occurred on a back country road before a gallery of cheering villagers. Elima, who had a one-tenth interest in the Mercedes, heard of the arrest on his police radio. He immediately shook down Patel for his lost share. Patel complained of his suffering to Salome. Salome had no one to complain to but Adija.

"You come back from Mbure laden down like a donkey, with your packages of fine clothes and your belly full of European food—and meanwhile, I've been wiped out!" Salome shouted. "I'm breaking my back, doing the work of two in this stinking bar just to keep poverty from sucking us under. You know, if I starve to death in this place, you'll starve too!"

Adija bit her lip and glanced at Salome's belly. Salome

didn't look as if she were starving yet, but Adija didn't say so. "I didn't know you had a Mercedes. Do you know how to drive?" she asked.

"Oh, shut up!"

Adija had been eager to tell Salome about the beautiful Morris motorcar Gordon had bought from the butcher's brother-in-law, but she decided this was not a good time. "I'll work hard," she promised. "We can buy some goats. I'll slaughter them and cook them with spices, the way we do on the coast. Everyone in Musolu will want to come here to eat."

"You slaughter a goat, and everyone will think somebody is having a baby." Salome glared at Adija. "And it won't be me, because my insides are all rotted out. Has that *mzungu* given you a half-caste baby?"

Adija turned away. "Of course not!"

"Mind that he doesn't. You might find a family to take an African child, but not a half-white one."

"I think half-caste babies are beautiful," Adija said, pouting. "I was one. If I had one myself, I wouldn't give it away."

Salome returned to her scrubbing. "Well, don't expect me to be your midwife," she said. "Let the missionaries at the school take care of you."

So Salome was angry with her, after all. Adija took care not to wear her new clothes for several weeks. On the day she finally wore her new skirt, she gave Salome a set of Kashmiri bracelets and a silk scarf from Taiwan.

"Why should I wear such finery in this dung-heap town?" Salome said.

"Because I like to see you looking beautiful." Adija helped Salome wrap the scarf around her head, fastening it with a red glass pin over her forehead. Salome stood before her mirror. She did look impressive, she had to admit.

"You look like the Queen of Sheba," Adija said. "Stretch out those bracelets and wear them above the elbow, there . . ."

Salome bought herself a larger mirror. No, she didn't look bad at all. It had been a long time since she had bought luxuries for herself. Not, of course, that she could afford them now, having been wiped out by the Congolese army, but Adija liked so to bring her presents.

"You should get yourself a boyfriend," Adija laughed.

"You could have lots of nice things. That Jeremiah, he would take care of you, if you let him."

"I'll get what I want for myself," Salome said. "It's all right for you, though—it's about time you opened that schoolteacher's wallet, and not just his trousers."

If Salome wanted to believe Adija was just using Gordon to get gifts, she could go ahead and think so, Adija decided. Thinking of him merely as Adija's benefactor, Salome could greet him almost politely when he came in for his evening beer. Problems arose when Salome found it curious that Adija should return from visiting him without any gifts. Adija became uneasy about having nothing to show her. Once or twice, she asked Gordon for a "loan," simply to be able to display the cash to Salome. She hated to ask him for gifts.

Salome couldn't understand why Adija didn't want to go with other rich men on nights when Gordon was absent.

"Suppose he comes looking for me, and I'm with some-one else?" Adija protested. "You see, I'd get nothing from him after that."

"Probably he would just want you more," Salome said. "Anyway, tonight you'll have to risk it. Some army men are coming to observe the *baraza*. From the Ministry for Defense."

"I don't care."

"Look here, one has to take care to show the government big men hospitality. If you're nice to them, one day they might be nice to you. How do you know you might not find yourself in the city one day, without your *mzungu?*"

Adija shook her head. She was, in fact, terrified of government men, especially soldiers. But the army man Salome introduced to Adija wasn't wearing a uniform. He was small and good-natured. Really, he was no more than a clerk, Adija decided. What harm could it do—just to please Salome?

She gave Salome the twenty-shilling note the man had given her. "To feed your strongbox," she said, laughing.

Salome had not had such an easy time with her army man. He was a barrel-chested loudmouth and very rough. Salome decided she would have to import new barmaids soon if the New Life was going to cater to men like him. "He thought he was very amusing, using my anus for target practice," Salome said, grimacing. "Well, my behind isn't laughing. I think that is how they do it to each other in the army."

Thinking Adija had suffered a similar ordeal, Salome was effusive with remorse. She hugged Adija close beneath the blanket, warming her against the damp winds blowing in under the roof. "I'll never send you out whoring again," she moaned, forgetting that before Gordon, going with a man after a few beers had been as ordinary a part of Adija's life as picking her teeth after eating.

"It doesn't matter," Adija said. "Don't worry about me."

Salome took a swig from her brandy bottle. It eased the pain between her buttocks. She was very drunk. "If I ever find out you've become like me," she sniffled, "I'll die."

Adija washed Salome's inflamed skin and rubbed jelly into it. Poor Salome. If she knew that Gordon had bought this jelly for her . . . It was hopeless pretending to feel nothing for Gordon. And then, with him, pretending to feel nothing for Salome. Neither Salome nor Gordon were fooled. Why keep it up?

Don't worry about me, Adija had said—but she hadn't meant it, she realized. She worried about Salome; she wanted Salome to worry about her. It was the same with Gordon. Before, she had never had anyone to worry about, and no one had ever worried about her. Now she had two people. Worrying was painful, but it was good, sometimes.

But suppose she had a baby and Gordon wanted to marry her? That was what most girls wanted, wasn't it? It was the surest way of getting a husband. Her mother had gotten a man that way—and a beating every day for the rest of her life too. No, Adija didn't want a baby, not just yet. Not that Gordon would beat her, but . . . well, it was risky, that was all. Being his woman was risky enough. She was changing so fast that a part of her was being left behind; now and then it wailed at her like a child abandoned in the market. When she heard that child howling and beating its little demon fists against the insides of her head, she thought her head would shatter to pieces.

I am like a restless spirit, she thought, fluttering from place to place. Strange places too. She had entered the ruined shrine of ancient white priests and stood without quaking as thunder smashed the skies around her; enjoying it, she had let a white man stain her with his tube of

powerful medicine, stain her perhaps forever; within the
four dim drunken walls of her Africa, she had survived
like a darting gecko lizard among the feet of marching men
with identical faces; she had survived the hot violent bed of
a woman, absorbing her powerful medicine of darkness.
Her white man and her dark woman did not belong anywhere either—because they knew her. Like a witch, she
was prying them loose from their groundings. As they
yanked at her, they wrenched themselves from the places
they belonged. And meanwhile, she fluttered from place
to place, a spirit—a lizard with wings, a butterfly without
feet, whatever she was—daring not to find a place on
which to land.

What place was there? But she could not ask Salome—
even if she had known what it was she needed to ask. Nor
could she ask Gordon. Before she had bewitched them, she
could have asked them anything, she could have been satisfied with whatever answers they gave her. Now she saw
only herself reflected in their eyes, reflections of longing
and confusion like early flashes of lightning in the tense
empty air before a storm. She had only herself to ask
questions of, over and over and over, hoping for and
dreading the events that would bring the answers crashing
down upon her.

o   o   o

The students' reaction to Mr. Lockery's new history syllabus was to go out on strike. Gordon found them milling
about in the corridor outside his classroom. His mind was
on the day's lesson; he trudged through the mob, head
down, arms laden with stacks of notebooks. He arranged
everything on his desk, wrote the date on the blackboard,
and turned around to face his class. The room was empty.

A voice spoke up from the doorway. "Excuse me, sir.
We are on strike."

"On strike," he repeated. An alarm clock rang in the
room next door, signaling the beginning of the period.
"Well, why don't you get in here before the headmaster
sees you, and we can discuss the strike."

"We can't come in, sir. We are on strike."

"Who is that? Wanjala—listen, you can't present your
demands standing around in that corridor. Send a delegation or something, and we'll talk about it."

The students buzzed. Wanjala and five other boys were chosen as the delegation. They sat somberly in the front row. Wanjala stood up. "One, we demand the new text-books you promised. Two, we demand notes. You write the notes on the blackboard for us to copy." Wanjala sat down.

Gordon sat on the edge of his table; he wiped his fore-head. "One, the textbooks are due this week. The ministry notified us that they're being sent. They probably just had trouble finding a van."

"They are six weeks overdue," Wanjala said.

"Yeah, I know. But the order went in on time. I sent it myself."

The students leaned toward each other for a conference. Wanjala stood up again. "And demand number two?"

"I'll give you outlines on the board for you to fill in. I've already been teaching you how to make your own notes. Obviously we've got to spend more time on that. We can begin today, if you want."

Wanjala shook his head. "You are the teacher. You must write the notes."

"Listen, I'll read you the new directive from the Minis-try. It's not just my idea to have you write your own notes—it's national educational policy." Gordon rifled through his papers, frowning. Here he was, quoting gov-ernment policy to students, trying to avert a strike. And two years ago, he was demonstrating against his govern-ment and its war, arguing to shut down a school in protest. That was different. Like hell it was. It was, though. Oh, shit. "Damn it, my other class has learned to take their own notes. You were in that class last term, Wanjala. What're you complaining about?"

"I speak as a representative of my entire form," Wanjala said. "We have solidarity in our form. We are on strike!" He strode toward the door. The other delegates followed. Cheers echoed in the corridor. The boys spilled out of the building and marched toward the headmaster's office.

Mr. Griffin already had Peterson's and Braithwaite's classes to deal with. Those two masters had refused to discuss any issues. They had confronted their students in the corridor and ordered them into class. Shouting matches had ensued. The boys assembled outside the chapel, wait-ing for Mr. Lockery's class. Just as they decided to pro-

ceed on their own, Mr. Lockery's class appeared. Wild
cheering and shouts of "Form solidarity!" and "Down with
the imperialists!" rang across the compound.

Vexed as he was, the headmaster gave a tiny silent
cheer. He was glad to see that Mr. Lockery, who had
started this trouble in the first place, was not immune to
student strikes.

"You Form 3's are one of the best forms we've got
here at Musolu," the headmaster began, pacing slowly back
and forth in the shady spot in front of his office. "I'm
sure you're feeling confused, however, about some of the
rapid changes in our educational system. So was I, at first,
I'll admit. You're all bright lads, and I'm sure you'll appreciate learning how these changes came to be instituted.
Now, when I first came out to the Protectorate. . . ."

The boys shifted their weight from one foot to the other.
They stretched and yawned, scratched themselves and
gazed up at the hot blue sky. The headmaster droned on.
The leaders whispered together, and one asked him to respond to the demands.

"Yes, I'm just getting to that. Thank you for your pa-
tience," he said. "Now, the teaching of history is a terribly
important business of any school curriculum, as I'm sure
you'll all agree. . . ."

The headmaster paced slowly back and forth in the
shade. His voice was calm and slow as a water current
through a stagnant bog. The sun beat down. The boys
coughed and wiped the sweat off their foreheads and
fiddled with their shirt buttons.

"I want you all to know that while I cannot, of course,
approve of your tactics of striking, I am sympathetic with
your eagerness to learn." The headmaster paused, his
hands clasped behind his back, his face pink and benign.
"Youthful eagerness is a vital natural resource to any nation, especially to one that, uh, may be lacking in other
natural resources. Youthful leaders often forget, however,
that there are more sensible means of presenting their
complaints. This, of course, is the way of youth. I think it
was Milton who said. . . ."

The strike died of boredom. The strikers straggled back
to their dormitories, moaning.

Gordon was told to take more care in introducing new

teaching methods. "And for God's sake, get those new books," the headmaster said. "You were so keen on ordering them, you can be in charge of distributing them."

Gordon drove to the railway depot in Mbure to see if the books had arrived by train. They had, two weeks ago. The freight office was packed with book cartons up to the ceiling. Gordon loaded them all into the school's Land Rover and drove back to school, scraping his rear bumper all the way.

Gordon had six hundred and twelve textbooks to stamp, number, write student numbers in, pass out, get receipts for, and record the receipts alphabetically in triplicate.

Adija was delighted to help stamp and number books. She could never have imagined herself doing such important work.

"Important, my ass!" Gordon said, ripping open a carton. "It's a god-awful shitty job!"

Adija laughed and shook her head. He was just being humble.

After stamping and numbering her first hundred books, however, she began to see his point. Anxious to get finished, she worked faster. On three occasions, she wrote the same number in two books. That meant that all the books had to be renumbered from her first mistake on.

Gordon had never screamed at her before. Adija retreated to the bathroom and burst into tears.

Hunched over his table in the sitting room surrounded by book cartons, Gordon growled and sweated and cursed. He checked down the list of numbers. He had written the same number in two books as well, two times. He called Adija out of the bathroom, and hugged her tearfully.

Adija began stamping. That, at least, was no problem. Gordon fed her the books, she whacked them with the "GOVERNMENT OF MAREMBO ° MINISTRY OF EDUCATION" stamp. The stamp pad went dry with fifty-nine books to go. "GOVERNMENT OF MAREMBO ° MINISTRY OF EDUCATION" then had to be handwritten in each book. Gordon wrote out the words for Adija to copy.

She was very sleepy. After the first ten books, she began writing "BOVEMENT" for "GOVERNMENT" in each book. She wrote it twenty-one times before Gordon noticed. The twenty-first book flew through the sitting-room window. Glass shattered all over the floor. Adija fled to the bathroom again.

The morning sun peeped bleary-eyed into the room. Its pale light illuminated vast numbers of books that had not appeared in the circle of lantern light. Books and papers and cartons and glass were strewn everywhere. The room stank of cigarette smoke, sweat, and that exhilarating brand-new-book scent. Gordon slept with his forehead on the table. Adija left a cup of tea steaming beside him and tiptoed out of the house.

"I think being a big boss at the school doesn't make you happy," Adija said, midway through their third night of book sorting.

"I think you're right," Gordon muttered. "It's so damn confusing. I'm worse than you are. We're the blind leading the blind."

"Still, I'm glad for you—that you're so important now. You have a lot of power."

"God, yes! Master of all I survey!" He surveyed the stacked books, smudged receipt forms, empty cartons. " 'Look on my works, ye mighty, and despair!' "

Adija went to the door and opened it. "When you speak English in that tone of voice, I think you're mocking me."

"No, no. I'm sorry," he said, switching back to Kisemi. "It's just that I thought teaching was going to be different. But these kids have been taught such rubbish about what education is all about. . . . Adija?"

She had stepped outside and was flapping her opened *kente*-cloth against her body to cool off. She'd been sweating in the room, and the smoke was making her nauseous. She touched her belly cautiously. This was the third month since she'd menstruated. She began trembling, but not from the chill air. She would ruin Gordon's career, just as he started to become important. No, he wouldn't let her do that, he'd leave her, he'd refuse to know her. No, he—

"What's the matter?"

Adija opened her cloth and enveloped him in it, throwing her arms around him and holding him tight against her. "We don't have nice times anymore," she whispered in his ear, her lips startlingly cool against his skin. "You're always working."

"I know." He ran his hand down her side beneath the cloth. "This will be over soon, I promise."

"You have to do your work. I'm not angry."

"I know."

"You want to go on holiday soon?" she asked, her face brightening. "Please don't say no!"

He grinned. "I won't."

"Jeremiah wants us to come to his family's farm next Thursday. His cousin is having his circumcision ceremony. Salome is not refusing anymore."

"Can you both get away?" Gordon asked. "Why don't we let Salome go, and we'll stay here."

"No." Adija pouted. "I'm tired of tending men and scrubbing tables. Let Patel work—it's his bar."

"Do you trust Jeremiah? Salome says he's Special Branch."

"I don't know," Adija said. "But his family must be all right. They are farmers—just villagers. And there will be dancing. I like to dance very much."

Gordon smiled. "I can't go with Jeremiah on Thursday, but I could drive up and meet you on Friday after school."

Adija flung her arms around his neck. "We'll go—you and me and Salome!"

"Mmm," Gordon said, frowning within Adija's clasped arms.

"Perhaps I will have some good news for you then," Adija whispered. She held her breath.

"What?"

"Nothing." Adija hugged him again, shutting her eyes tight.

PART FOUR

19

Salome heard the faded "ENTERING BA-
SHIRI" sign fly past the car with a barely perceptible
whishing sound . . . and nothing happened. What did she
expect—armed soldiers leaping out of the scrub bushes to
ambush her and drag her off in chains? Or perhaps herds
of angels riding dust clouds, reaching out to carry her over
the hills toward her natal home?

The way Jeremiah was driving—rarely lifting his foot
from the accelerator, riding out the curves pressed hard
against his door—Salome was certain she was headed
toward angeldom. But soon the sight of Bashiri out there
made her forget the danger on the road. She cranked down
the filthy window, and the wind struck her eyes. The air
was sweet—had she ever smelled air so sweet? Had the
colors of the land ever shone so brightly? The sun leaped
out at her over the tops of hills; it sprang from tree to tree,
ricocheting through the webbing of branches like a berserk
red-orange monkey. It blinded her—yet she felt she had
never seen so clearly. She felt the countryside brushing
against her and leaving bits of memory clinging to her.

"Three years," Salome said, speaking into the wind rushing in her window.

"You've been out of Bashiri three years?" Adija asked.

"More. I was in school, in the city, and in detention—
none of them were truly Bashiri. *This* is the place I've
wanted to find again—look!" Below the ridge the countryside spread out before her in patches of red-brown and
green.

Adija squinted, but everything far away was a blur.
"What do you see?"

"I can see huts, and people—look close! Those lines,
they're paths."

"Oh, yes," Adija said, staring into the blur.

Salome sat back. Trees shot past, tall brittle ones, thick old ones with vines snaking up the trunks. Leafy gardens of cabbages went by, and maize rows heavy with green-wrapped cobs. "There are no fences here, no big estate houses with hedges round them. You can walk wherever you please, from field to field, and no watchman will stop you. No one will ask you which reserve you come from, or which white man your family works for." Salome gazed out the window. She wished the car would slow down and stop, and she could step out and disappear down the embankment into the foliage. "You can walk and feel freedom with the soles of your feet here," she said. "You can know that it's not something given to you by Europeans or politicians. It's something that's never been gone and can't be taken away."

Adija nodded. She was trying hard to keep up with Salome's thoughts. If Salome drifted away from her, she would be very much alone here.

Salome peered into the distance. "This country is like the country of my people before the Europeans built their farms. I wasn't alive then, but I feel as if I can remember those times. Why is that?"

"I—I don't know."

"And listen, why is this?—when I was a child, and I worked in the fields and chopped wood and carried stacks of it on my back, I said to myself: When I am grown, I will never grub in the earth again. I will never strain my back under a load of wood. I will never choke my lungs out over a cookfire or lie shivering in a mud hut waiting for a drunken husband to lurch through my door. I promised myself: I will never grow old and wrinkled at forty, with breasts like dangling strips of leather and a shaven head all knotty and calloused. No, no, I said—that life is not for me. I'm clever. I will slave for no man. I'll get out of this village. I'll wear nice dresses and drive in motorcars and go to cinemas and restaurants. Why did I say those things to myself?"

Adija shook her head slowly. "Every village girl thinks those things sometimes. Even myself, I did."

"You had no choice—you had to go to the city. That's the only place half-castes can survive," Salome said. "I had a choice. I still have."

Adija winced and looked away. "I had a choice too." She sighed and looked out the opposite window. The countryside was nice, but it wasn't so different from the land around Musolu. Hadn't Salome once told her that boundaries are just lines drawn on maps? For some reason, Adija was near tears. Her stomach hurt. Salome had been acting so strangely, ever since she'd agreed to come out here. "Are you angry that I wanted you to come?" Adija asked.

"Not anymore."

"You see—" Jeremiah turned around in the front seat, grinning at Salome. "You thought I was going to put you in jail."

"I can always run away from you . . . you're much too fat to catch me. Look out!" Salome pointed out the windshield.

Jeremiah yanked the wheel, and a tree seemed to swing away from the car at the last moment. "You're too nervous, Salome," he chuckled, making the engine roar with a plunge of the accelerator.

More people began to appear beside the road as the car descended into the lowlands. When they saw the car approaching, they retreated quickly into the long grass. Billowing clouds of dust drifted over them, leaving their hair speckled and their eyes running. Jeremiah picked up speed, anxious to escape the angry glances of his people; the faster he drove, the more dust he made. He tried to relax— after all, he was coming home—but every time he saw more people on the roadside, he cursed silently and his muscles tightened. Men turned their backs, women held their babies' faces away from the car and covered their breasts. Only the children smiled and waved, ignoring the dust and fumes in the excitement of seeing a motorcar.

The road widened briefly. Then they were in a town. It looked no different from Musolu—two dusty rows of shops lining the road. Jeremiah pulled up in front of a petrol pump and stepped out. He pointed toward the petrol tank of his car, then started across the street.

A man who had been leaning against a shop door dropped his cigarette stub and shuffled over to Salome's window. He was barefoot and shirtless. "Full-tonk, *Memsahib?*" he asked.

Salome's mouth fell open. "I'm not *memsahib!*" she spat. "Does my face look white?"

Adija started to giggle, but Salome silenced her with a glance. The man's face went blank. He knew no Kisemi, only Rukiva and the English question "Full-tonk?" which he repeated.

"Ask that one across the street—the big man in the black suit," she said, pointing toward Jeremiah.

"*Eii?*"

Salome pushed open the door. "*Ndio.* Yes, fill it. Full tank." She stepped past the man. "All we need is to get stuck out here without enough petrol to reach Jeremiah's farm," she said to Adija.

The petrol man gave both women a contemptuous look and picked up his cigarette end from the ground. It took him three matches to get it lit again, he was staring at the backsides of Salome and Adija so hard.

"The fool probably never saw an African woman in good clothes before," Salome said, after some distance. "The sight of us and the car upset him so much he couldn't see skin color."

"Even some African women—politicians' wives—they are called '*memsahib*' nowadays. I heard it several times in Jinjeh," Adija said.

"I've been away too long," Salome said. "Look at the wonders I've missed."

Both women felt uncomfortable in their city clothes. No one in this little town had ever seen a miniskirt like Adija's before. "We should have stayed in the car," she said. "My legs feel like they're naked." She was not doing very well in her high-heeled shoes either. They sank into the soft, uneven ground and made her ankles wobble outward as she walked.

"I'm not going to hide in any car," Salome said. "Jeremiah expects us to sit here and roast—no good! I'm going to have a look round."

A group of women approached, whispering and staring. Salome mumbled a greeting to them, but they didn't reply. One mother, whose breast had been dangling over the front of her dress into her child's mouth, suddenly scooped up her breast and dropped it down inside the dress out of sight. Salome glared at her. Just because I wear city clothes, am I not a woman too? she screamed silently, clenching her teeth.

She looked out over the distant hills. Their lush green-

ness soothed her. I fought for this, she said to herself. Then
she looked down at herself, at her breasts pointing straight
out in their brassiere, at her shiny red dress and yellow
shoes. She touched her wig; suddenly it felt like a furry
caterpillar that had attached itself to her with suction-cup
feet, sucking blood through her scalp. I fought for *this?*
She yanked the wig from her head.

A small crowd had gathered in front of the shops. She
could hear them whispering and laughing. Their faces
formed a huge banner strung along the sidewalk from one
end of town to the other. It read: LOOK! THIS WOMAN
HAS JUST PULLED HER HAIR OFF! SHE HAS
DROPPED IT INTO HER PURSE! SHE IS SCRATCH-
ING HER NOSE NOW! WATCH! SHE MAY PULL IT
OFF TOO! Not since the last planting season, when the
U.N. antimalaria film van showed pictures of giant pills
beating dog-sized mosquitoes to death with clubs, had the
people of the town seen anything as fantastic as Salome.

Walking up the incline toward the open market, Salome
glanced into the side door of a shop and saw a young girl
watching her. She wore a cheap faded dress that stretched
tight over the small bulges on her chest. Behind her were
crates of beer. The shop was a bar, the girl was its barmaid, and she was staring at Salome and Adija with un-
concealed envy. For an instant her eyes clinked together
with Salome's like raised glasses; then the girl hid a grin
behind her hand and ducked back into the doorway.

"When I hung about the little town on the edge of the
reserve, I looked like her," Salome said. "But I was harder.
I pretended to notice nothing and I saw everything. That
girl stares and smiles—she will be nothing but a fat village
whore. One night someone will play too rough with her,
and her body will be found the next morning in a dustbin."

"She was staring at our clothes," Adija said. "It's too
bad she's not pretty."

"It's too bad she's as pretty as she is. If she'd been uglier,
the townspeople would have sent her fleeing back to the
farm."

Adija glanced at her curiously. "You think it's better to
be hoeing in the fields than living in the towns, don't you?"

"Think?" Salome laughed. "What I think, say, and do
are three different things. And that's partly your fault."

"Why?"

Salome sat down in some soft grass under a tree, within sight of the market. "Before you came to Musolu, I didn't think or say very much there. I just did things," she said. "Now I still do things, but I have to think about them. You ask me questions constantly, and I have to talk about them too. Then I see that the doing and thinking and talking are different people trying to be the same person. They're like different tribes, with different languages and customs, trying to be one country. They don't trust each other and they fight."

Adija nodded slowly. "I know. I am different people too. I hate it. I'm always changing back and forth."

"'When elephants fight, it is the grass that loses.'" Salome stared ahead of her, her eyes focusing on nothing.

"What?"

"You're left empty, like a womb that's been scraped in an abortion."

Adija turned away sharply. "No!"

"No?"

"Stop it! You talk like a madwoman! I can't understand anything you say!" Adija was shivering. Why did Salome have to talk such craziness about wombs? She hated it when Salome stared off into space like that, leaving her stranded. But I've been stranded before, haven't I? she thought. All my life I've been bouncing off different towns and beds. Why should I fear being stranded? Because now I know something better.

Jeremiah appeared, walking toward the fenced-in patch of grass that was the market. People parted quickly to let him pass. He walked as if he would have bumped into them had they not backed out of his way. He gave the watchman a ten-cent piece to let him through the gate, and stepped inside.

Salome and Adija had brought no money. They sat back and waited beside the market fence.

Business was brisk in the market. Most of the sellers were hefty middle-aged women in long dresses and head cloths. They chatted with each other, tended their childrens' unbuttoned shirts and dirty faces, counted their change, rearranged their merchandise in little piles, haggled and shouted at the passers-by—all at the same time, it seemed, in one continual sequence of motions, accomplished from a sitting position on the ground. When they spotted Jeremiah in his suit, smiles spread on their wide crafty faces. Their voices grew shrill. "*Eii!* Nice clothes here! Yes, yes, less *shillingi* than Asian shop! Yes, please, big-man!" Jeremiah passed them with a distant look on his face. He wouldn't have denied that he was a big-man but to have people address him as such was an affront to his dignity.

A *mganga* strolled by. He checked his collection of herbs and dried bones on his blanket, then strolled past Salome and Adija again. Grinning, he held out a dried hawk's claw for Salome to examine through the fence.

Salome shook her head, signaling no, she didn't want it. But the old man just kept grinning, rearranging the leathery wrinkles of his face. He pushed the hawk's claw closer to Salome. His grin widened. Salome could smell the black stubs of his teeth.

She took the claw through the fence and stared at it. The man nodded vigorously. Some nearby women laughed. The claw felt like a dead insect in Salome's hand. She didn't know what to do with it and was about to hand it back when suddenly it moved. The sharp points of the claws scraped across her palm. She let out a scream and leaped to her feet.

Laughter rippled out from the crowd, high-pitched and unmuffled. The claw dropped to the ground and hopped along like a tree spider. Salome jumped back and gaped at it. It scurried to the edge of the wire, then rose in the air and flew back through the fence.

When it fell to the ground again, Salome saw what had made it move—a piece of thread the old man had been pulling. She spat at the claw, then turned away sharply.

"Those people at the market, they're just ignorant," Adija said when they were back in the car again.

Salome was breathing hard. "No, it was me. I behaved like a stranger. That is what you can expect when you behave like a stupid stranger."

Adija lit a cigarette and sat back. Being a stranger was nothing new to her. One could not help being one; it didn't mean you were stupid! She lifted the cigarette to her lips, and the red glow lit her cheeks, leaving her eyes in dark hollows. Her face looked like a hard ebony mask. It said: Now you know what it is like to be a stranger, Salome.

"That old man probably plays the same trick on every newcomer to the village." Salome tried to laugh.

"Yes, but not everyone throws a fit about it," Adija said.

"I didn't throw a fit!"

"You did! You spat!" Adija's voice was suddenly shrill. "I saw you!"

"So? What could I do?" Salome demanded. "The thing felt awful. If it had moved in your hand, you'd have fainted!"

"It was just an old bird's foot!"

"Shit—it was one of his charms!"

"I thought you didn't believe in witchcraft."

Salome turned around to glare through the windshield. "I don't," she said. "But it's not a good sign, that's all."

"T-t-t!"

"It wouldn't have bothered you—you know all about birds' claws and curses. You don't fear them because you're a witch yourself!"

Adija attempted a dry laugh. "You looked funny, jumping away from that claw," she said. "You looked like a madwoman!"

Salome whirled around in her seat; her arm lashed out. The back of her fingers struck Adija's cheek with a sharp sound. Adija pitched sideways, her eyes wide with panic.

Salome glared out the back window, breathing hard. Finally, she leaned over the seat. "Adija?"

"I'm sorry," Adija sniffled.

Salome peered at her.

"I'm sorry I mocked you."

"Why did you, Adija?"

"I don't know," Adija wiped her eyes. "I don't know."

Salome felt her heart thumping. All the rage was drained out of her. "I never thought I would ever hit you."

"You should. You should hit me. I'm very bad."

"No."

"I am. Please, hit me again."

"Don't talk nonsense, Adija."

Adija cringed. "You should beat me."

Salome leaned over and ran her fingertips down Adija's cheeks, wiping away the tear streaks. "No one should beat you," she said.

They waited in silence, staring out the car windows as the evening obscured the village in a darkening red haze.

*   *   *

Finally Jeremiah appeared, walking very rapidly beside a fat man who took long strides across the street. Jeremiah opened the door, and suddenly a light went on. "I need to get in here," he said to Salome.

She expected to be introduced, but when Jeremiah said nothing about her to the man, she got out and sat in back with Adija. He removed a thick manila envelope from the glove compartment and handed it to the man. Salome could see only the man's belly—tops of trousers and bottom of shirt—through the window. And belt—a cloth one with a small shiny buckle. It was a military buckle, stamped with the seal of the Bashiri army. She saw the man counting a large wad of shilling notes he had taken from Jeremiah's envelope.

"What's Jeremiah paying him for?" Salome whispered. "And what's an army man doing so far out here in the bush?"

"How do you know he's from the army?" Adija asked. "He hasn't a uniform on."

"Look at his belt."

Adija squinted through the glass. The man's buckle was only a blur. "I wish they'd hurry. It's dark already."

"Well, Jeremiah's business is none of mine," Salome said, but she continued to try to understand the Rukiva the two men were speaking. She peered out the window at them until the army man strode away.

*   *   *

The car sped through the countryside, its beams illuminating endless scrub bushes along the road. When it climbed a hill behind the town, Salome couldn't see the buildings, the night was so dark. Only one light was burning, a pressure lantern, probably from the town bar. The few people standing in the doorway had no faces, no arms or legs; they were flickering black sticks, memories fading in and out of sight with the pulsing of that silver lantern glare that streamed around them, between them, almost through them, as if they were spirits with no substance to them. Suddenly they were gone, swallowed up by the night that hung about the car as black and motionless as the bottom of an ocean.

Salome shut her eyes. The car rocked her and she slept, Adija's head bouncing against her shoulder. She dreamed. Adija was nursing a baby. It looked like her baby, her Wairimu. It *was* her Wairimu. The baby waved at a passing car. Salome tried to cover its head with a *kente*-cloth to protect it from the dust clouds. Goddamn cars, speeding through the countryside, spreading dust and fumes. When the dust clouds settled, Salome looked under the cloth for the baby. The baby was gone! She and Adija searched frantically. After a while, Adija got bored with searching and turned on the wireless. Adija, we haven't time to play! Wairimu's gone! We have to find her! Adija, help me look! The wireless screeched. It made a clanging sound, like cowbells. Clang-clong, it went. Clang-clong . . .

"Look!" Jeremiah braked suddenly. The headlight beams were alive with running boys. Above the sound of the engine, Salome heard cowbells clanging. Whistles squawked. Some boys were shouting, some shaking bells, others panting through tin whistles in lung-bursting rhythms. Jeremiah honked his horn, and they all veered off the road together, swooping into the bushes like a noisy flock of birds.

Jeremiah pointed to a light several hundred yards from the road. "That's where they're going. The other boys are chasing the one who is to be circumcised. When he arrives, the dancing will begin. In the morning, he will feel the knife and become a man."

"Will they dance all night?" Salome asked.

"Yes. Everywhere around the country, you can hear the noise of the dancing. Tomorrow night it will be for my cousin."

The sounds of bells and whistles faded out, but Salome kept listening for more. She recalled the excitement in her village at circumcision time: The secrecy, the fear, the proud, serious looks of the elders. This countryside no longer seemed empty; the night was rippling with invisible commotion and anticipation.

"Wait till the dancing starts, Adija," Salome whispered. "People will think we never left the villages!"

Adija sat back and looked away from the window. She wished it were Friday and Gordon was with her.

The car bumped off the road onto a footpath. Salome and Adija awoke to see tall grass falling away from them, illuminated, wave after wave. Grass scraped the underbelly of the car, a startlingly loud ripping sound.

They stopped near a dark cluster of huts. No moon or stars were out; Salome and Adija found themselves stumbling about blind. Voices whispered in Rukiva nearby. Someone brought a lantern and led them to one of the huts. As Salome stepped inside, she brushed the top of her head against the overhanging thatched roof; bits of straw and dirt rained down on her. She had the grit in her hair and down her dress. She cursed silently at herself—had she been away from the villages so long she had forgotten to stoop when walking through a door?

The woman with the lantern followed them inside and pointed to two straw mats on the floor. Women were already sleeping around the room, their dim shapes looking like sacks of charcoal. When the woman took her lantern away, the sacks became breathing, snoring things in the dark.

"Ow, it's hard!" Adija lay down gingerly on a straw mat.

Salome wrapped a blanket around her. "Don't tell me you slept on a bed when you were a girl in your village."

"No, but we had palm mats. They were softer," Adija said. "I'm used to a bed now."

"One sleeps better on the ground," Salome said. "You'll see."

Though she wouldn't have admitted it, Salome was used to a bed too. Her body ached on the hard earth. Adija went to sleep quickly, but Salome rolled about for hours, trying to find a comfortable position. I'm heavier than Adija, she told herself; it's harder for me to fit my weight to the shape of the ground. Snores of the sleeping women mocked her logic.

Salome awoke smelling the dry odor of a hot straw roof. She sat up, feeling sticky. Speckles of sunlight, filtered through worn spots in the roof, littered the floor like bits of yellow glass. All the sleeping mats were empty, including Adija's. She leaped to her feet. Already it was late into the morning.

She found the compound deserted. Huts in a dirt enclosure, some granaries, a tub in which beer was fermenting, a few chickens pecking stray maize kernels, but no people.

Everyone else had been up since sunrise—why had they let her sleep?

She found Adija sitting outside one of the huts, talking with a young Rukiva woman whose name was Odui.

"*Jambo*," the woman said, smiling. She was holding twin babies in her arms, both languorously sucking.

"*Jambo, mama*," Salome greeted her.

The woman looked up at Adija, embarrassed.

"She knows a little Kisemi, but not too much," Adija explained. "I've been talking very slowly with her, like I used to do with Gordon."

"You . . . sleep well?" Odui asked Salome.

"Well, yes. I should have awakened earlier. I want . . . to help with the woman's work."

Odui shook her head. "No, no. You are . . ." she grinned, looking hard at the sky for a moment to try to remember the word, ". . . a stranger," she said, nodding.

Of course, she hadn't meant "stranger," but merely "guest"—the words were similar, Salome knew. She smiled, though, trying to convey gratitude—these people's custom was no doubt to let guests sleep as late as they wished. "Your babies . . . are fine-looking," she said.

"Thank you." Odui glanced down into the half-asleep brown faces.

"Myself, I am sorry . . . I should have learned your language," Salome said.

Odui laughed, nodding.

Salome looked around helplessly, smiling periodically at Odui. They were both trying to think of something simple enough to say in pidgin-Kisemi. Salome's eyes fell on a mortar and stone in the doorway of Odui's hut. Nearby was a stack of maize. "While you feed your babies . . . I can help you with the maize meal," she said. Salome walked to the mortar and sat down on the ground—never mind her fine city dress. Damn Jeremiah for asking her to wear it! At least she'd left her shoes in the sleeping hut. She picked up the stone. "Is it all right . . . for me to do this?" she asked, not wanting to offend the woman's hospitality.

Odui laughed. "No custom for . . . strangers—" she glanced at Adija, then back at Salome. "Is all right. Is good. You can."

"Good." Salome picked up a maize cob and rubbed it

with the stone. She had not had a pestle in her hands for many years. Salome worked carefully, her face clenched in concentration.

Odui spoke to Adija. "You and Salome . . . you work . . . office, Jeremiah says."

Salome frowned. So Jeremiah was telling people she and Adija were secretaries. She had to be careful of what she said. "Yes, office," she said, filling Adija's confused silence.

"Azima," Odui said. "What kind . . . office in Azima?"

Adija looked at Salome in panic. What kind of offices were there?

Salome strained to remember some offices she had seen. "Caltex House," she said, remembering one. She wrinkled her nose as she said it, picturing the secretaries swishing out the door at lunch hour, giggling and gossiping with their noses up in the air.

"Husband-for-you . . . he work office too?" Odui asked Adija.

"No, he . . . teacher." Adija gazed out across the compound.

"Is good. We proud . . . have you here." Odui smiled. She rewrapped her babies' heads in their carrying cloth. They were dozing, so she buttoned the front of her dress. It was a faded print dress that reached her ankles, very clean except where her milk had stained it. "When come . . . baby-for-you?" she asked Adija, looking up again.

"For me? I—" Adija stared at the rooftops, wishing she could rise from the ground and fly off past them. "I don't know."

"You've been spinning your tales again?" Salome asked her, speaking very rapidly.

"No, she saw me vomiting this morning. She thinks I'm pregnant," Adija said, also too rapidly for Odui to understand.

Salome stared at Adija's belly. It looked as flat as ever, though in the loose white jumper, she never looked as if she had any shape. "Are you pregnant, Adija?" she asked.

Suddenly Odui leaned forward, pointing to the mortar. "*Aaa-aah!* Sorry—"

Salome had been rubbing the maize cob so hard that the kernels were spilling over onto the ground. She looked down and gasped. "Sorry, sorry," she said, and scooped up the kernels.

Odui gathered that Adija's baby was not a good topic for discussion. "I show you beer," she said, getting to her feet. "Rukiva beer . . . very good."

Salome and Adija followed her to a wooden tub of beer. Beside it were three large gourds where more beer was brewing. The beer looked like brown porridge and smelled bitter.

"Tonight . . . beer goes into the house . . . near the fire," Odui explained.

"My people, they put beer by the fire too . . . to ferment," Salome said. "We make beer . . . from honey."

Odui shook her head, indicating she didn't know Salome's last word.

"Honey," Adija repeated helpfully. "You know, bees—" She made a buzzing sound and moved her hand in an arc, like a bee flying.

Odui grinned. She moved her hand in an arc too, and made a buzzing sound.

"You'll have her thinking we make beer out of bees, Adija," Salome said. "Forget it."

"You want?" Odui pointed at the tub.

"Thank you," Salome said. Odui produced some long reed drinking straws. The women were privileged to taste the beer as it was prepared, ostensibly to see if it had enough of the right ingredients in it. "Beer tasting gives the women a headstart on the drinking when the celebrations begin," Salome explained to Adija.

"My mother's people, the women made palm wine," Adija said, annoyed. "I am not a stranger to brewing."

More people were arriving in the compound now, relatives and friends of the family from nearby farms. They carried sacks and gourds, gifts, no doubt, for the family. Salome watched them greeting each other, laughing and shaking hands. The men leaned on their walking sticks and talked in long roars that ended in laughter. The women's greetings to each other were laced with high-pitched *eiiii*'s and *aah-aah-aah*'s. Salome recalled the clan gatherings of her childhood. If she had learned Rukiva, she could have been among these people being introduced, complimenting women on their children, laughing and talking.

Odui excused herself to greet her relatives. The women all *eiiii*'d at the sight of the twins; they touched the babies faces and hugged Odui with quick lunging movements.

"Odui, I'm going . . . to finish the maize," Salome called out.

"Jeremiah . . . come back soon. He with my husband."

"Jeremiah's uncle, he is your husband?"

"Yes. Husband want Jeremiah give school fees . . . for his children. Children of first wife. Jeremiah very rich, yes?"

"Yes." Salome waved goodbye. "Now I know why Jeremiah was invited here," she said to Adija, "but I still don't know why we were."

20

GORDON DROVE TO THE VILLAGE WHERE Jeremiah, Salome, and Adija had been the day before, and found the dingy African Star Bar that Jeremiah had directed him to. Inside, the teenage barmaid frowned at the mention of Jeremiah's name. Pressing her arms across her skinny chest, she shook her head vigorously and rushed out the back door. Gordon looked around, worried. The few men drinking home-brewed beer at the tables looked away from him. Finally, a fat man in sharply creased trousers and a khaki shirt strode in through the back door.

"Are you looking for Jeremiah Kongwe?" he asked in English.

"I'm supposed to meet a friend of his here—to take me to Jeremiah's farm," Gordon said. He was surprised to find someone so neatly dressed in such a dirty bar. "The friend's name is Wafula."

The man smiled. "Right. He will be here in a few minutes. Please wait." He strode out the back door again.

Gordon preferred to wait on the step, away from the smell of urine that wafted in from the alley behind the bar. After a while, a man in dusty shorts and undershirt came outside and sat near him.

"Are you a friend of Jeremiah Kongwe?" he asked in Kisemi.

"Well, I know him." Gordon said.

"You police?"

"No."

"Army?"

"No."

"Special Branch?"

Gordon tried to laugh. "No. I'm just a schoolteacher."

The man eyed him dubiously. "Teacher," he said.

"Don't people around here like Jeremiah?" Gordon asked.

"I don't know. I don't know Jeremiah." The man stood up and went back inside.

Gordon watched him go. He was puzzled that anyone could think he was from the army or the Special Branch, until he remembered that he was in Bashiri now, a country where a great many white people still lived. Not only was the brigadier of the army a European, but the head of the Special Branch was the same white Bashirian who had once led the hunt for Kariuki and other guerrilla leaders during the revolution. No wonder the local people were suspicious of foreigners.

A man in a tattered shirt approached from the direction of the market. He was small and muscular, with a deep scar across one cheek. "I am Wafula," he said, shuffling directly up to Gordon. "We go now."

"What's going on here?" Gordon asked as casually as he could manage, as they drove out of the village.

Wafula scratched his chest and looked straight out through the windshield. "No trouble," he said.

"No?"

"Secessionists just making problems."

"What problems?"

"They saying the government is accusing them of taking help from the Swila. Taking Russian guns from the Swila." Wafula laughed, scratching his chest again. "Is all nonsense. Big joke."

"You think so?"

"Sure, sure, man. You can't listen to secessionists. They just ignorant, don't like government."

Gordon kept his eyes on the road. All this political intrigue was interesting—material for his contemporary history classes, perhaps—but it wasn't anything he wanted to be mixed up in himself. If he pumped Wafula for information, he might learn more than was good for him—if he hadn't already. The rest of the journey went by in silence, broken only by Wafula's grunts and gestures telling him when to turn right and left. Gordon kept track of the turns, fearing that he might have to make the return trip without a guide. And as soon as they reached Jeremiah's family's farm Wafula disappeared; Gordon reckoned that he would not see him again.

Jeremiah greeted him warmly, grasping Gordon's hand in both of his hands. He introduced him in Rukiva and Kisemi as a schoolteacher who had come all the way from across the seas, from America, to help the African people acquire a good education and build the new nation of Bashiri in the true spirit of Uhuru. Gordon didn't understand all that he was saying; he smiled stiffly into the respectful stares of the assembled family.

Attention soon refocused on Jeremiah. Men and women stepped up, jerked his hand up and down. Some little girls shrieked, trying to get a glimpse of him through the crowd. Small, half-naked boys ran their fingers cautiously along the body of his car. They rubbed dust from the chrome strip and pointed excitedly at the shiny metal they had uncovered. Jeremiah's uncle stood beside him. He was taller than Jeremiah and balder; he appeared proud of Jeremiah, but Gordon noted a look of apprehension on his face as he glanced at his nephew from time to time.

Jeremiah caught sight of Salome and Adija and beckoned them to come forward. He introduced them to Gordon as if they were meeting for the very first time. "Just so that everything looks quite proper," he whispered to Gordon.

Salome tried to nudge the confused look from Adija's face, and herself managed a respectful downward-gazing smile in front of Gordon. Adija had been entertaining notions of passing herself off as Gordon's wife—since she had to pretend she was something she was not, why not go all the way? This was impossible now. Her heart sank. Simultaneously, she was so happy to see Gordon she could scarcely contain herself. She squeezed his hand tighter, probably, than was proper, but she didn't care. Her face was a confusion of expressions: Her lips formed a thwarted smile, her enormous eyes burned with longing. Whispering spread quickly around the crowd: People had noticed her looking the European directly in the eyes. Was this the custom of her tribe—whatever tribe that could be? Was she half-European? Or pretending to be? Or a Swila? Or was she just brazenly rude?

At tea time, Jeremiah brought out his gifts. A crowd of boys followed him to his uncle's house and jammed the doorway to steal a look inside. Jeremiah placed two large sacks on the table in the center of the hut. The guests took their seats on chairs along the wall to watch him take out a tin and present it to each person in turn.

It was an exotic display. There were Mandarin oranges from Taiwan, applesauce from South Africa, ham from Poland, tuna from Alaska, sardines from Norway, as well as British and local products. The guests passed the tins around so that everyone could get a look at the pictures on them. Sounds of shock mixed with laughter followed the sardines around the room. On the tin was a picture of a bearded old man in a mackintosh; someone joked that the people in the country of Norway must be very primitive if they put the bodies of their dead into tins for eating, instead of giving them a proper burial as was done in Africa.

A young girl entered carrying a tray with bottles on it—Coca-Cola—which she distributed around the room. Each time she stopped before a guest, she smiled and lowered her eyes and murmured a greeting. She looked perhaps eight years old; the faded dress she wore might have fit her properly when she was six. At last, someone else in a mini, Adija thought.

After the Coca-Colas came a pot of tea. Later yet came bottles of Tusker beer for the men. The afternoon wore on. Adija was separated from Gordon by the table, and could only sneak quick glances at him. Once the initial hubbub over the gifts died down, no one left his seat—to do so, it seemed, constituted a breach of manners. Adija squirmed in her chair, her buttocks aching, her eyes darting around the room as she attempted to follow the foreign conversations.

By chance, Salome had been seated next to a middle-aged man who knew some Kisemi. The conversation was difficult to keep up, but she was gratified to see that she was blending into the crowd by joining the talking. Salome had not striven to make a good impression on people for many years, and she was rusty. Some coarse words escaped her lips that might have told more about her than she wished known; fortunately, they were not words anyone was familiar with.

After the empty beer bottles had been cleared away, another daughter came around with a bowl of hot water and a towel. She stood before each guest while he washed his hands, then left and reappeared again carrying a stack

of enamel bowls and a platter heaped with chicken and
steamed maize meal. Everyone leaned over the table with
heads nearly touching, and dipped meat and fingerballs of
maize meal into the juice.

Gordon enjoyed the meal—everyone chewing and talking and laughing and sucking juice that dribbled over lips
and chins. Voices came from close around him; he felt as
if he were joining in the conversations, even though he was
only joining in the eating and slurping. It wasn't necessary
to talk now. Even though he knew no one expected him to
know the language, he had felt lonely before, sitting so
long in silence. His isolation was over—eating was something even Europeans knew how to do. The ritual of hospitality that had dragged on all afternoon now had a focus
and a meaning, and he was part of it.

The chickens were reduced to a pile of clean bones. The
bowl of water and the towel were taken around again.
Sitting back in their chairs, the guests picked their teeth
and belched appreciatively and complimented Jeremiah's
uncle on the quality of his wife's food.

Gordon leaned his chair back against the wall. A smile
that originated in his belly seeped upward into his face. He
waited.

Then he stopped waiting. There was nothing to wait for.
This was it, there was no "next." He smoked and passed
his packet of cigarettes around. Conversations in the hut
had diminished to a murmuring sound, like that a river
makes when you are listening under water. Gordon felt he
could understand the drift of conversation; it no longer
mattered that he did not know the language. With smiles
and nods, he entered the sound, then withdrew into silences. Silences were part of the process of joining in; they
were times to absorb and be absorbed. The process did not
seem like a "first . . . then . . ." sequence: it occurred in
one unbroken motion, suspended from time by its circular
continuity.

Gordon had always envisaged time as a kind of dust
storm swirling along an upward-sloping plain. The storm
was made up of particles of the past, reflections tinged with
melancholy sunset colors of regret. Time also was a pointil-
list image of the future, blurred and blazing with longings
that ached to be satisfied. He was either fleeing the past
storm, driven on by loathing, or he was being sucked into

the future chaos, unprepared and paralyzed by dread. His progress, though painful, was always in one direction: forward. This was the only direction that offered any hope. It was also the only direction there was. Or so it seemed.

Recently, though, the plain had been leveling off. He was learning about the present.

Before Adija, the present had been a mere point on a line which, as in mathematics, had no dimensions of its own. The present had been a vantage point, an anthill on the plain from which he inevitably stepped down as soon as he had glimpsed as much behind and before him as he dared.

But now the present was becoming a real place too. It could be even vaster than the past and future combined. It came into focus as this hut. This hut, this body resting in a chair, other bodies, toes scratching ankles, hands moving toward mouths to puff cigarettes. The present was not made up of mental particles; its substance consisted in people's movements, sounds, expressions, gestures, glances. He was part of this substance, and he had some control over its destiny and his own.

He especially was sharing this present, this room, with Adija. He looked at her until she noticed him. Their eyes touched. They smiled and glanced away. But this moment of touching was preserved like the image that remains behind after lights have been switched off. The image began to fade only when he began to want a fresh one. And then he had only to look at her again.

Jeremiah stirred. He had suddenly looked at his watch and stood up. What an incongruous thing to do, Gordon thought. Way out here in the bush, among barefoot farmers, surrounded by huts and fields and sky—someone looks at his wristwatch. What for?

Jeremiah excused himself and left the hut. People kept talking until they heard the sound of his car engine. They had assumed he was merely going to the latrine. The car drove off, its sound fading quickly. The guests looked at one another quizzically, as if to say, "Who can explain the ways of the big-men?"

Gordon and Adija exchanged panicky looks that quickly became smiles. Adija had been frightened by Jeremiah's departure—he was, after all, their host and guardian, their only link between this place of strangers and the familiar world of Musolu. But of course he wasn't the only link—there was Gordon, Adija thought to herself, the strongest link of all.

"Aren't you glad I got him to buy a car?" Adija whispered to Salome.

"Why should I be?"

"So that if Jeremiah disappears, we have a way of getting back."

Salome stared at Adija, her eyes unfocused. "We are back," she said.

Adija looked away, frowning. She did not feel back anywhere, except surrounded by the sort of people among whom she had found it impossible to live. She wished she could get Gordon's attention again, but he seemed lost in reverie. She was nervous and wanted one of his cigarettes. Just as his gaze was about to reach her, however, she turned her face away, remembering that, according to these people, only disreputable women smoked cigarettes.

*   *   *

Outside in the compound, Mutali, the man who had been talking with Salome, explained the circumcision ritual. All week the boys had been running about the countryside blowing their whistles and clanging their bells to announce to the people the coming ordeal. By tonight, the circumcision boy would be so strong and trim he would be able to dance all night without stopping. He will dance around that flag, Mutali said, pointing to a scarf nailed to a high pole in the center of the compound. By morning, his muscles will be almost numb. After a short rest, he will be dragged from his hut and run down to a secret place in the stream. There he will be rolled over in the cold mud to numb him. Then, very quickly, his foreskin will be cut. Mud mixed with straw and cobwebs will be applied to the wound and his whole body will be coated with clay. When the people see the red-brown figure approaching from the river, they will rush to him and push flower petals in the sticky clay.

"Who does the circumcising?" Gordon asked.

"A very old man. He has a sharp knife, even sharper than your razor blades. He learned his skill from his father before him."

Gordon nodded. "Does he have any special powers?"

"Some people believe so, his hand moves so quickly with the knife. He is not the diviner, the *mwaguzi*, though. That is the *mwaguzi*—over there."

Everyone looked. Under an acacia tree, a gnarled scarecrow of a man was sitting with his knees drawn up close to his chest. He wore tattered flannel trousers and rubber-tire sandals. His hair stood up in a shock of white fuzz, as if it had been frozen in a moment of terror. Adija had noticed him before; she thought she had felt him staring at her. Every time she glanced at him to be sure, he seemed to recede into the distance, his gaze gone far away.

"What does he do?" Gordon asked.

"He reads the entrails of a goat." Mutali glanced about uncomfortably. He did not like explaining these things to a foreigner. "If the entrails are all right, then the ceremony can proceed."

"And if they're not all right?"

Mutali frowned. "Really, it is just a custom nowadays. Every family invites him to come to the celebrations, and gives him some beer and a few shillings. But people don't believe in entrails and those things. We are all Christians."

"My people have diviners as well," Salome said.

"Yes, it is very common," Mutali said quickly.

Mutali had been hearing a great deal about the similarities between the ways of his people and the ways of Salome's people, the Samoyo—a tribe with which his people were on increasingly bad terms these days. He was tired of talking with a woman, and invited Gordon to accompany him to see his farm. He suggested that the ladies seek out Odui, who would entertain them until the dancing began.

"We could all go with you," Gordon said, glancing at Adija. She perked up with the suggestion.

"Men can talk better when there are no women present," Mutali said. "It is the same for women, I think." He smiled firmly at Salome.

"Yes," she said. "Thank you. We will find Odui."

Romulus and Moses, the two schoolboys who were hoping to get school fee money from Jeremiah, offered to show them to Odui's hut. The boys' green uniform shorts and white shirts were dusty, but they walked along as if they were wearing new three-piece suits.

"Do you like gramophone music?" Moses asked Adija, grinning brightly.

"Oh, yes," Adija smiled. She didn't want to be thought rude by these people—they thought her strange enough already. "Do you have a gramophone?"

"Of course," Moses said. "We must go to my house and listen to some records."

"Why should I trust you in your house?"

"You can trust me." Moses grinned. "I would not harm such a beautiful lady."

"I don't think my friend Salome likes records."

"Of course, she does. She is from the city, isn't she?" Moses called out to Salome in English. "Hey, baby, how about a party at my place?"

Salome slowed her pace. "I think you've been seeing too many films. You talk like them."

"Nonsense." Moses laughed, pleased that this woman had detected that he was a cinema-goer. "Hey, I got Elvis and Jim Reeves and Soul Brother Number One James Brown. Let's go, hey?"

"If we go with you to your house, people will think ill of us," Salome said. "Among my people, it's forbidden for men and women to touch each other before the time of circumcision."

"All people have different customs," Romulus said. He lit a cigarette and held it out to Adija. No man had ever offered Adija a cigarette in that fashion—people in films must do it that way, she decided. She took the cigarette and drew hard on it until she saw Salome frowning at her. Then she handed it back.

"Your people don't have that custom of not touching?" Salome asked.

Moses puffed on his cigarette, stalling. That this half-caste girl smoked confirmed his suspicions about her. Why did her friend, who was probably no more respectable than she, insist on behaving so properly? "I was thinking merely we would dance and drink beer," he said. "There is nothing shameful in that."

"No, but the effect is the same if people think more is happening than dancing."

"It is only the ignorant old people who would talk. We don't care about them—we are modern men!"

Salome laughed. "Thank you. But we want to join the women."

"Perhaps your friend Adija would prefer to join us."

"No," Adija said quickly. "I go with her."

In fact, she was disappointed that Salome was refusing to visit the boy's hut. Not that she had any love for school-boys. No. But she would have felt more at ease listening to music and drinking beer than trying to talk with the other people here. She was more like a student now than a peasant, she realized. But Salome was cutting her off from the boys, just as that man Mutali had cut her off from Gordon. Neither Salome nor Gordon were any help to her at all out here. She was cut off from everyone out here.

*   *   *

Adija sat on the ground near Salome; Salome turned from her and entered a conversation with Odui, who trans-lated her comments to the other women present. Salome was inquiring about country matters—gardens and babies—and telling the women they were similar in her part of the country. Adija tried to look interested, but after a while she gave up. The sun was hot; its heat seemed to reflect on her jumper, making it shine even whiter than it was. The stares Adija received from time to time made her skin itch be-neath the silky material. These women reminded her of her mother's friends, who were forever sitting around on the ground in their faded dresses, gossiping about the neigh-bors and listening to her mother's stories about the cruelty of the Arabs. When Adija approached to seek something from her mother, the women's voices hushed. Pity and scorn ran together in the wrinkles around their mouths. Some would tuck their children's faces beneath their head cloths while Adija was present; they never said so, but they feared Adija's enormous Arab eyes. Her mother often ac-cused her of having the evil eye. For years, Adija went about squinting to make her eyes smaller. Her weak sight was a result of squinting, she decided, a kind of punish-ment for making people uneasy. As she sat listening to these women now, she found herself squinting again. What was worse, she found that she was unable to stop squinting even when she tried.

These women can't bother me, she thought. I'll never

have to live among people like them. Gordon will see to
that; he'll see to everything. Gordon was such an important
man at his school now that no one would dare stare at her.
He was such an important man—Adija shuddered. He was
too important to care for someone like her. He would want
an educated, important woman. Before, he had feared he
could not make a woman happy, but now he knew he
could. Adija had helped him learn that. So now he was
ready to move on. Already he had moved on—to Mutali's
house. Mutali was an important man here. Gordon was
trying to do what Salome was doing—become part of the
life here. He was becoming a man who could get along
anywhere. And she—where could she get along?

She peered out over the heads of the women, trying to
listen to the silence that was spreading with the late afternoon shadows over the sloping fields below. The women's
buzzing and staring swarmed around her face. She was
sweating. The sun glared out of the sky, a great gash in the
bright white clouds, stinging her eyes as if filling them with
blood. She wiped her eyes, half-expecting her hands to
appear ghastly red. Then wouldn't these women gasp!

Adija smiled to herself, rubbing her thumb and fingers
together and feeling their dampness. She imagined they
were wet with blood instead of sweat. Wouldn't Salome
shriek! She would quickly stop pretending to be a Rukiva
then! Adija would stagger to her feet, the blood dripping
down her cheeks, and the women would scatter like panicked crows. Your stares have stabbed me! she would shout.
Did you think I was made of metal, like a motorcar?
Now look! Do I turn your stomachs? Too bad! You
weren't shielding your eyes from me before—don't shield
them now! And the women would scramble away, screaming.

"I would like to see such places . . . as you have in
Azima," Odui was saying to Salome. Several of the women
nodded in agreement, though "Azima" was the only word
they had understood.

"It's not good to see them . . . if you can't afford to
enjoy them. And you just have to watch . . . other people
enjoying them," Salome said.

Odui didn't seem to hear. "Yes, I would like to go," she
said. "Perhaps my sons . . . they will take me someday.

They will have motorcars . . . and work in houses made of glass." She looked down into her wrapper, where the two brown faces were peering out now, awake and curious. "Will you . . . take me to the city, *eii*?" she asked them.

"I think they will," Adija said suddenly. "They will do many good things for their mother."

The women looked startled, but she didn't care—she had receded too far away with her gazing into the sky, and was anxious to come back.

Odui smiled. Her babies were getting restless. She took them out of her wrapper and passed them to the women. The women's voices grew soft and cooing. They laughed and made puckering sounds with their lips as they passed the babies around. The babies enjoyed all the touching and tickling. One was laughing as a woman passed him to Adija.

Adija reached out eagerly and pressed the child to her chest. "Oooh, *jambo!*" she said to him, her voice suddenly a whisper, as if the touch of the child had taken her breath away.

Finding himself squeezed against a strange new body, the child thrashed about and peered up into Adija's face. "*Waaaaaaaa!*" Suddenly his mouth was wide open and he was howling as if a snake had bitten him. "*Waaaaaaaa!*" His head shook violently from side to side; tears flew in all directions.

Adija looked pleadingly at the little face that had been so smooth and happy just a moment ago. Then she shut her eyes tight, as if that would make the baby's screaming stop. Her hands went limp on its sides. The child would have tumbled from her lap had not Odui reached out and scooped him up.

He hid his face against Odui's shoulder and continued weeping loudly, sucking in gulps of air between sobs. His brother watched him placidly for a moment. Then suddenly his mouth opened tragically and let out a wail.

"*Pole*, children. Sorry, sorry," Odui murmured.

"I think they've not seen one like me before." Adija turned her face away.

"They are always like that," she said, bouncing them in her lap. "What one does . . . the other must do." Both babies turned to stare at Adija with bulging wet eyes. Their

shrieks implored their mother to remove this terrifying
creature and restore their familiar world. "You are right . . .
they have seen only Africans before," Odui said.

"I was born in Africa," Adija said softly, turning her
face further away. She felt blood soaking her eyes again,
stinging them shut. "I am not an albino either."

"No, I was meaning . . ."

"Salome, albinos are good luck, aren't they? Like twins?"
Adija suddenly turned toward Salome. "Only perhaps
these people are fearing them. They think I am one and
they are fearing me for a witch."

"That's nonsense."

"I'm not an albino," Adija insisted, "I'm not an Arab.
Not a Rukiva or a Samoyo, not a Swila either. I'm not—"
She rubbed her eyes furiously with her fists. "I'm Adija.
Just Adija."

"Stop it!"

Adija opened her eyes. She saw Salome glaring at her.
She had disgraced Salome!

Adija staggered to her feet. She rushed away from the
women across a clearing. A form on the ground was in her
way; she veered around it—that old man, the *mwaguzi!* He
looked up at her with his whitish glazed eyes. He had seen
everything. The old man's eyes were still on her; she could
feel them like dogs snapping at her heels. She hurried on,
down the slope, through a maize field, the dry leaves brushing against her face. Her feet touched dampness.

Suddenly she was standing up to her thighs in a stream.
Red-brown mud was swirling up from where her feet had
disturbed the water. Feeling dizzy, she lifted her foot up
and down in the mud and watched the water darken and
flow away. Look how I can spoil this stream, she thought,
suddenly fascinated. Look at that muddy patch swimming
away from me—I made that! See how it spreads and
swells! Rubbing her eyes and laughing tearfully, Adija
waded across the stream.

21

GORDON WAS INTERESTED IN SEEING MU-
tali's farm, but once he had seen it, he began to grow
restless waiting inside the hut for tea. Mutali too looked
uncomfortable. He frequently inspected the cracked skin of
his knuckles and his bare knees, breaking off to smile up
at Gordon. He realized that everything he had shown the
teacher—his cattle pens, his huts, his granaries, his wife's
vegetable garden—were all sights that the teacher had
seen many times before. Mutali grew apologetic, having
run out of things to show him. Then he became resentful
that the presence of the foreigner should make him feel
uneasy. Conversation ran to questions and answers. What
type of maize do you grow in America? What breeds of
cattle do you raise there? The teacher was abysmally ignorant for someone with so much education. He seemed
to know nothing of crops and cattle and other basic things
of life.

Gordon took up the questioning, asking about Rukiva
customs and the way they had changed in recent years. He
inquired about customs that Mutali had never heard of—
he must have read books about different parts of Africa.
Mutali was forced to think up answers about the customs
anyway, lest he appear ignorant and displease the guest.
The teacher was curious about the diviner he had seen
earlier in the afternoon. He seemed to know a lot about
witchcraft, a subject about which Mutali had always stayed
as ignorant as possible.

"There are no witches here," he said, casting about
wildly for some answer that would conclude the subject.
"We burned them all. Now we worship only the Holy
Ghost." He pointed to the colored photograph of Jesus on
the wall for emphasis, but he could see the teacher was not
convinced. He lapsed into silence. The teacher fidgeted.

Mutali's wife appeared, a shapeless middle-aged woman in a faded cotton dress. Gordon shook her hand solemnly. She said she would bring squash directly, and that she had sent the neighbor girl for some fire to make tea. Mutali told her to hurry up, it was rude to keep the guest waiting. Chagrined, the wife backed out the door.

Presently, Gordon heard the wife dropping charcoals into the brazier outside. After what seemed like a long time, he smelled the scent of burning paraffin. That meant that the charcoals had just been lit; they would have to burn until they glowed white, then the tea would have to be brought to a boil. The ritual was no longer new to him; he had sat through it many times during his visits to Mr. Longo at school and to other local Africans. He tried to content himself again with sitting in silence, but with Adija not there to glance at, it was difficult. He found himself anticipating the smells and sounds of each step in the tea-making process.

The two men sat facing each other in their wooden chairs across the packed mud floor, staring at the walls behind each others' heads. Jesus hung behind Gordon; behind Mutali was last year's African Railroads and Harbours Ltd. calendar. It showed a zebra watching a locomotive puffing by.

"Have you ever seen a zebra?" Gordon asked, for something to say.

"No," Mutali said. "They are in game parks, where the tourists go. The cousin of my wife's aunt, he has seen one. His teacher took him to a place near Azima where there are animals in pens—what do you call those places?"

"Zoos," Gordon said in English, knowing no Kisemi word for them.

"Zoos, yes." Mutali nodded and looked up in the air, as if he could imagine nothing more foolish than putting animals into pens for people to look at.

His wife brought in a bottle of orange squash and an aluminum tin of water. The label on the bottle was peeling and yellowed—obviously the squash was saved for very special occasions. The water was murky. The wife must have walked to a nearby stream to get it just to serve him. Gordon squirmed in his hard wooden chair, trying to look enthusiastic about the drink. He had come to hate the stuff, squash being about the only thing served at school functions. Squash and milk-tea and jam slices.

"Does it rain very much in America?" Mutali tried a question.

Gordon cleared his throat. He explained that in certain areas of America it rained a lot, in other areas very little, and in other areas it rained only a moderate amount. He put the sentence together carefully. With Adija, he didn't have to consciously compose his sentences in Kisemi, but with others, speaking the language was still somewhat difficult.

Mutali nodded, smiling. "What time of year do you harvest your maize in America?"

Gordon began to explain that he didn't know—he was from the city, where no maize was grown. As he spoke, he realized that Mutali didn't really care what he answered—Mutali was not the slightest bit interested in knowing what time of year maize was harvested in America. He seemed surprised, however, that no maize was grown in New York City.

"Not even in the people's back yards?" he asked.

"No."

Mutali shook his head. "The cities are no good. Even here it is getting the same way. People move to the city, they forget their old ways. These times—t-t-t-t-t!" He glanced at Gordon, a look that said: Ever since you foreigners came and brought your customs, nothing has been right here. Both guest and host fidgeted in their chairs.

The tea finally arrived. With it was an enamel plate with slices of bread on it, triangular slices smeared with—Gordon groaned inwardly—purplish jam. He tried to drink his tea fast, the sooner to be able to leave. That was a mistake—he burned his lips. When he was finally able to get down a cupful, the wife appeared again with the pot and refilled his cup right up to the top. He sat back resigned, watching the flies buzz around the jam slices. Two, three, four cups of tea he drank. Now he was drinking slowly, hoping that Mutali would get ahead of him and finish the pot. But no, that would have been rude. Mutali sipped even more slowly.

A little girl stood in the doorway, staring at Gordon. She wore a ragged dress that reached only down to her waist.

Her eyes were running with pus: Flies buzzed around them, lighting and crawling about on her damp cheeks. She scratched idly at the brown lips of her vagina, watching Gordon's cup rise to his mouth and return to the table. She looked starved. Gordon wished he could give her all the tea and bread; she would probably wolf it down. But no, that would be rude, he had to stuff it into himself, gorged as he was already. Mutali noticed the girl and shouted at her; she disappeared quickly.

"More tea?" Mutali clapped his hands to beckon his wife again.

Gordon was seized with the desire to leap to his feet screaming: No, I don't want any more fucking tea, I'm sick of sweet milk-tea and squash and slices of sticky bread and I'm sick of sitting around your barren house. I'm sick of well-meaning people who have nothing to talk about but farming and ask me questions they don't really expect answers to. And I'm sick of feeling guilty because your overworked wife has to carry water from the stream for me, and because my visit here is nothing but a massive inconvenience for you and you're only having me because you're afraid if you don't you'll be offending a bigshot *mzungu* from America—and meanwhile your daughter or whoever she is stands here drooling, with her finger up her crotch and going blind from glaucoma.

The wife entered the hut again, wheezing. She held a large wireless set, borrowed no doubt from some affluent neighbor, and showed it proudly to Gordon. Gordon thanked her. Only one station came in clearly. The Voice of Bashiri was playing Country-Western ballads. Mutali sat back and smiled, pleased to have produced American music familiar to his guest. He did not see the stricken look on Gordon's face.

Finally, Mutali suggested that they leave, and Gordon began to relax again. He was glad there were several miles to walk before reaching Jeremiah's uncle's farm. By then, night would have fallen; there would be no more hospitality rituals to sit through and the dancing would have started. He could be with Adija at last, perhaps even alone with her for a while. Just a few hours away from her, and he missed her so.

He was ashamed how quickly his ability to live in the present had exhausted itself. He made renewed efforts to make intelligent conversation with Mutali. Other men joined them on the path, which became a motor road after a while. Swinging machetes at their sides, the men laughed and talked in Rukiva. Sometimes it was easier for Gordon to get along with people when he didn't understand their language.

A motorcar came up behind them and suddenly swerved by. Used to the everyday sound of cars, Gordon didn't move quickly, and had to be yanked up onto the embankment by one of the men. A cloud of dust enveloped everyone. Gordon covered his face as best he could and shut his eyes. He was coughing even after the dust had settled.

The men complained bitterly as they reassembled on the road.

"They are saying people in motorcars are no good," Mutali explained. "Especially those men who just passed us."

"Do you know them?"

Mutali nodded. "One is the Agricultural Extension Officer, the government man. A Samoyo." Mutali wrinkled his lips as he spat out the o's. "The other is a Samoyo chief. Now he is a local Bashiri Party chief. The government gave him an office, and now he just sits in it all day giving orders. He is chief for Samoyo, but he thinks he can give orders to Rukiva!"

"I've heard about the troubles over here," Gordon said.

"We're going to make plenty more trouble. All the Rukiva are going to vote to be separate from Bashiri and Bashiri Party."

Not if the government finds some excuse to cancel the elections, Gordon thought, recalling the newspaper articles he'd read. But he kept his mouth shut.

"These BP politicians, they ride by in their fine motorcars. One day one of them will hit someone. Then we'll come out of the bush and give him a proper driving lesson." Mutali went on. "Why do those city people do things like that? Once they were people like us. Look at that damned Jeremiah." Mutali wiped his nose hard. "They have home villages too, those big-men. Their people are poor like us. They tell us to go back to the land—why don't *they* do it? Why does everybody have to go to the cities?"

Gordon shrugged. "Not enough land to farm, no jobs in

the country. People in the country migrate to the cities—
that seems to be a kind of law of nature."

"Why we can't change these laws? When the British left,
the politicians told us they were going to change all the bad
old laws."

"It's not a law like that. People need cash. They want
bicycles and metal roofs, they want to send their children
to school . . ." Gordon left off explaining: Mutali had
begun talking in Rukiva again. He hadn't wanted to have
his question answered, he had only wanted to vent his rage.
What is going to happen to all this rage? Gordon wondered.

The road was cast in deep shadow now, but the hillsides
were still ablaze with light: Sharply defined areas of red-
brown and green, glowing with an intensity that appeared
to rise straight up out of the earth's core. Red-brown and
green Africa, Gordon reflected. He had even begun to
dream in those colors.

And after the rain, he often smelled them both, the red-
brown and the green, a startling clash of scents that made
him think of death and fertility battling one another, made
him feel an urgency in the air, a tension that was never
resolved but hung and dispersed, the resolution postponed
until the next rainfall, and the next, and the next.

The people appeared to have learned to live with the
constant postponement of resolution. At times, they
seemed quite stultified by their harsh environment. But
never for long. Their faces were alive with defiance. When
they moved, they were quick and decisive. Or so it seems
to me, the foreigner, Gordon thought—Africa, the land of
violent contrasts.

This incomprehensible alliance between the forces of
sluggishness and vitality set him on edge, as if a dissonant
chord were constantly ringing in his ears. He wanted to
flow with the slow pace of life, but instead exhausted himself fighting inertia. Then again, he wanted to vibrate with
the energy he felt around him, yet he avoided surrendering
to it, fearing that he would be shaken too violently.

Yes, he shied away from participating in the extremes he
sensed around him. He approached, peered, then retreated.
What he really wanted to do was to snatch pieces of life,
then run back to a safe place where he could analyze and
embellish and tame them to his own dimensions.

But he *did* want to do more than observe. Because of Adija. Adija was the resolution, somehow. He could not be content, though, to merely be interested and delighted by her if he were to experience her the way he needed to, and love her the way she deserved. He might well have to leave Musolu soon—he would have to *do* something about taking her with him and providing for her. Otherwise, he would find himself observing their relationship from the vantage point of memory, like a man hearing the sad arias from a production of *Madama Butterfly* he had once seen.

As he walked along, the orange squash and tea he had drunk sloshed in his belly; his bladder was swollen to what felt like the size of a pumpkin. Damn, why hadn't he used the latrine before he'd left? Every step hurt. Now and then someone noticed him walking a little stiffly and gave him a strange look. Gordon flashed smiles back and tried to straighten up.

He dug his hands deep into his pockets. His penis felt swollen. Soon it would start to dribble. Please God, let there be a latrine beside the next hut. Or a big enough tree. Maybe just a medium-sized anthill? But there were only small helpless-looking bushes along the road as far as the eye could see.

He couldn't just step over there and pee all over the bushes, just like that. A white man couldn't just stop and piss on Africa, as if it were his bathroom or something. What a barbaric thing to do. Everyone would halt and stare. And there he'd be, his white thing sticking out and gushing all over the place.

He walked beside Mutali, sweating and peering down at the ground. Sorry, sorry, sorry, but this is it. Not one more step. "Mutali, I have to—"

At just that moment, Mutali looked up at him. The same pained expression was on his face too. He opened his mouth to speak, but no words were necessary.

They dashed to the side of the road and let the bushes have it. Looking up, Gordon noticed several other men standing in a line, also draining their systems of too much racial awareness. The ground in front of the bushes splashed merrily, like a row of lawn sprinklers.

*   *   *

Salome found Adija asleep on the bank of the stream, lying with her knees pressed close to her chest, her arm hiding her face. She knelt beside her and touched her hair. It was damp and tangled with bits of cane, leaves, and burrs. Slowly, Salome combed it out with her fingers.

Adija opened her eyes. "Salome?"

"Yes, I'm here."

"I'm sorry, Salome."

Salome gently pushed Adija's shoulder down again. "Lie still, rest. Let me get these things out of your hair."

"I disgraced you."

Salome squeezed a strand of hair and tugged out a burr. "When I've finished, you can wash in this river," she said. "Are you all right now, Adija?"

"I think so."

"You're not used to places like this."

"No."

"Jeremiah shouldn't have told lies about us. It makes me nervous too—having to tell stories to these people."

Adija laid her cheek down on her arm. "I didn't think you were nervous, Salome. You seemed like one of them. I hardly knew you anymore."

"Stand up, now. Let me see how you are." Salome steadied Adija as she got to her feet and guided her toward the stream. "We'll get Odui to lend you a dress."

"Odui, she is good."

"Yes."

"But not the others. I am fearing them," Adija said. "My mother used to tell me stories of faraway tribes. She said if I wasn't good she would sell me as a slave to them. The more far away these people were, the more foreign and horrible they were. The tribe farthest away ate human flesh and the fathers raped their daughters. They were called Bunii, my mother's people said. Today I was fearing these people here as Bunii."

Salome nodded. "Myself, I also heard nonsense stories about faraway tribes. But these people are just Rukiva, like the people in Musolu."

"I know. Yet . . ." Adija's voice faded.

"You were the one who was so eager to come here." Salome sighed. "Let's just get washed. Then we'll get a dress for you. It won't fit you, but it will be clean."

"Yes." Adija nodded, her eyes focusing again slowly. "It will cover my legs."

Walking up the hill toward the compound, Adija felt giddy; she walked slowly, making sure of the firmness of the earth as she took each step. Behind them, across the stream, the grazing fields were rippling in the breeze. The sun made a fiery grate of a cattle pen leaning against the side of the hill before them. Now and again people passed, the men swinging pangas, the women carrying bundles and water-tins on their heads.

Adija wanted to rest. They stopped in a clearing beside the path, where a stack of tree limbs lay. Salome picked up an axe and hefted it on her shoulder.

"What are you doing?" Adija asked, sitting on the ground.

Salome lifted the axe and, for an answer, swung it down with a swift "chunk!" sound that echoed against the opposite hill.

"Someone will see you!"

"Let them. I'm only doing useful work," Salome said. "It feels good."

Salome went into a frenzy of wood chopping. The muscles in her back warmed; her breasts flopped hard against her belly with every stroke. She smashed the cut pieces into smaller pieces and split the smaller pieces into kindling.

"It's good." She panted as she rested. "You should try it."

"I chop a lot of wood in Musolu," Adija said. "I even chop the wood for Gordon's stove sometimes."

Gordon. Salome raised the axe and swung it down hard against a limb. Severed, the two ends jumped into the air and rolled away. Now look at your schoolmaster, she thought, but she did not say it. There were other enemies around her. As she exposed the pale insides of a log, she thought of all the white faces that had glared at her. There were black enemies too. "Here, Elima, how does it feel?" she grunted, whacking a log apart. Policemen, soldiers, politicians, big-men of all colors and sizes fell before the strokes of her axe.

"I am God in his Judgment!" she proclaimed, grinning. She raised the axe high over her head. "Sinners, you are destroyed!"

"I had better run then." Adija laughed uneasily.

Salome's eyes flashed. "Destroyed!" she shouted, making chips fly in all directions with another blow.

"God isn't like that."

"Hah!" Salome lifted her skirt to wipe the sweat from her eyes. "How do you know?"

As she chopped, she was aware that Adija was staring up at her. She could no longer lose herself in her work, though she kept up a savage pace. Adija was cringing with each blow of the axe. She looked terribly beautiful, Salome thought, sitting like that with her eyes turned up to her, the sunlight glowing gold on her face. The fear in her eyes was only of the violence in the chopping; as soon as the firewood was cut, the fear would be gone. Then how lovely she would be!

No, more fear would come to her, fear and despair, in wave after wave—fear of not having her greed satisfied. This frail small girl, full of such enormous greed, such terrible longings. Salome rested her axe, and there! The look was gone; only Adija's dazed smile remained.

Again Adija stared at her, the greed threatening to cloud over her eyes. A strange feeling entered Salome's hands, as if the axe handle had a power of its own and was about to move without her being able to stop it. Such greed, this Adija has, Salome thought. And such power in her longing eyes to suck the heart out of me! Such destruction she can bring, with her refusal to choose, the refusal swelling inside her, inside me, like burning pus. If only the greed were cut out of her!

Slowly, Salome raised the axe. She glanced about in panic; she saw only Adija's eyes, huge and calm and gleaming. Something was in the axe, pulling it higher—

"No!" Salome forced her fingers open. The axe dropped. Salome turned her face away. "Craa-aang!" The blade struck stone. Then it was gone, flipping end over end with a buzzing sound along the ground.

Adija rolled over, clutching her leg. The axe lay still in the grass just beyond her. "Oww," she whimpered.

Salome rushed to her. She pulled Adija's hand from her leg. At first she saw no wound. Then she saw it, a hair-thin line of blood along her skin. Pressing her cheek against Adija's leg, she removed the blood with a swipe of her tongue. A pale slit remained in the skin, filling with red again.

Adija stared at her leg, too shocked to speak.

"I'm sorry, Adija. I was—I was careless. I didn't mean to hurt you!" Salome's eyes swam. "Are you all right?"

Adija nodded. "We shouldn't have come here," she whispered.

Salome stood up and retrieved the axe. She turned it over in her hands, examining it, then threw it down beside the woodpile where she'd found it. "The axe felt as if something alive were in it," she said. "As if the handle had become a serpent. I was struggling—" She held her hands up, as if holding the axe, then dropping them quickly. "Now I'm the one talking nonsense," she said, laughing dryly.

Adija's face remained blank. She didn't laugh. She stared at Salome in such a way that Salome was certain she understood about the serpent that had entered the axe handle . . . knew more about what Salome had felt in her hands than Salome herself did.

A LANTERN NOW HUNG FROM THE TOP OF THE
pole in the middle of the compound where the scarf-flag
had flown during the day. Adija, wearing a long purple
dress that was several sizes too big for her, stood on the
edge of the circle of light, looking for Gordon. Blurred
shapes of dancers poured around and around the pole,
turning the grass to a shiny dark ring of earth. The rhythm
of the dance was supplied by cowbells, jingling bells tied
to ankles, and copper whistles blown at quick intervals,
one squawking note over and over that seemed to mock
Adija's search. She stepped up closer to squint into the
circling crowd, her head spinning with its motion.

"I'm going to find Gordon," she said to Salome, beside
her. "He's not here."

"No." Salome held her arm. "You're not supposed to
have met him before today. Do you want these people to
think you're a slut?"

"I don't, but—"

"You're a guest here," Salome snapped. "You have to
respect people's customs."

Odui approached them from the crowd of spectators.
Her face shone in the lantern light. Without the babies in
her arms, she moved with a bounce in her walk and
grinned like a woman who'd earned a night of drinking and
dancing. Adija wanted to slip into the crowd and hide for
shame, but she knew it would be futile. A zebra cannot
take cover among buffalo.

"I think you feeling better now," Odui said to her.

"Yes—yes, I am. Thank you." Adija tried to smile back.

"The sun . . . it was too hot this afternoon for you,
yes?"

Adija nodded vigorously. "I think so, yes."

"The beer is good now. We can go . . . taste it."

The beer had been moved indoors to ferment beside a bed of charcoals. Upon entering, Adija felt suffocated; the air was hot and thick with smoke. She made out shiny sweating foreheads in the shadows around the walls. The faces were deep, deep black, darker than any people looked in daylight. Adija covered her mouth with one hand and sat down.

Odui gave her a reed drinking straw. Cautiously, she sucked up the thick beer. It was bitter, but the liquid felt good in her throat. "Can we drink quickly and leave?" she whispered to Salome.

She didn't hear the answer. The murmuring in the hut swallowed up Salome's voice. The strange Rukiva language flapped around Adija in the clouds of smoke, swirling and spreading slowly up from the coals. Adija sucked hard on her drinking straw.

Odui was smiling at her. Adija nodded back. Odui's face faded back into the smoke. Salome and Odui were sitting in front of the tub, their legs stretched out along the mud floor. They look alike, Adija thought. Of course, Salome is bigger, but her hair's short again, without her wig, and she has a round black face like Odui's. If Salome stays by Odui, people will think she is just another village woman and Salome will be very happy.

This smoke is so thick, Adija thought, it's a solid door between us. You can't take hold of the door to open it, you can only walk through it, choking. She shuddered at the thought—only witches could walk through closed doors. Her head was spinning from the beer. Now the floor, and not just the roof overhead, looked rounded and cavelike. The bottom of the cave was the bed of charcoals. Suddenly, Adija wanted to get away from these coals—she might fall into the fire. Then the hut would fill with the stench of burning flesh. Salome would rush over and find her roasting there. Everyone would say: Is that girl who is roasting herself *your* friend? Salome would say: That is merely Adija trying to singe her hair short and darken her skin. I am sorry for the smell she is making. What she is trying to do is really very hopeless, of course. Here, I'll take her off the coals. You see, she is dead. You thought she was a witch, but she was not. A witch might have changed her form and risen anew from the fire, but Adija merely died. She died so quietly I didn't even notice. She was very brave, this Adija. I am sorry I was cruel to her sometimes. Please, Adija, please forgive me.

Adija leaned back against the wall of the hut. She felt something against her back. A calabash with a twisted neck. She set it in her lap and squinted down into it. The stench of spoiled milk rose into her nostrils.

And I would hear Salome speaking, Adija thought. I would hear her through the mouth of the calabash. I would weep to hear her, but when I tried to speak, the only sound I could make would be a hollow wailing, like wind blowing across the lips of a calabash. I would be bursting to speak. I would fly about the hut, dashing myself against the walls like a blind sausage-fly. The people would shriek to see the flying, wailing calabash.

You are the witch, Salome! they would shriek. You who make calabashes fly and wail! Salome would cry out: No! She would plead—

Adija found herself groping along the wall toward the doorway. She stumbled outside. I'm drunk, she said to herself, recognizing the spinning sensation. In Musolu, no matter how much she drank, she could always find her way back to her room. But out here there were no familiar pathways and doors. And no Salome, now, to help her to her feet if she stumbled. In Musolu, she was the person most like Salome. But here, Salome had found another who was more like her.

Would Odui and Salome like each other the way she and Salome did? Adija wondered. She couldn't imagine it. In this place, such things were unheard of, except among witches. Adija shuddered. Perhaps these people could tell that she and Salome did those things together. The old man, the *mwaguzi*, he could see it in her; she could tell by the strange way he stared at her. Only such people as diviners knew that women like her existed. But he did not stare at Salome—no, Salome was not like Adija here. Adija shut her eyes tight and promised: I will find Gordon, and he will take me from Salome, and I will never even think of such things again.

She wandered out onto the periphery of the circle of dancers. Children scampered past her; whistles blasted in her ears. Suddenly, Gordon was before her. He was sitting on the ground, playing with some children who were sneaking up behind him to touch his hair.

Adija sat on the ground a few yards from him. She felt curiously shy, almost as if she *was* meeting him for the first time, as Jeremiah had pretended earlier.

"Gordon?"

His face turned sharply. "Adija—you startled me!"

"Sorry."

"No, I just didn't see you." He laughed.

"Then you're the only one."

"What?"

Adija didn't reply. She watched the children moving back from him. They would run away now, she was sure of it. "You're gentle with the children," she said. "You don't mind them touching you?"

"No. Why should I?"

"You shouldn't. I mean, it's good that you like them to touch you. Most Europeans wouldn't like it."

"Maybe not." He moved closer. "How are you, Adija? I've missed you today. Were they showing you around?"

Adija cast her eyes down. "Yes," she said. She felt an insect brush the back of her neck, and shook her head. "The people here have been kind to me. Do you like them?"

"Yes, but I wish that Jeremiah hadn't made up stories about you—acting as if we'd never met before."

"I wish he hadn't also."

Gordon looked at her, waiting to see if she would say any more. Jeremiah's story had not been the only one he'd heard; there was another version of Adija going around. He wasn't sure this was the right time to ask Adija about it. She was shaking her head again. "What's the matter?" he asked.

She reached up and slapped the back of her neck. "Mosquitoes." Then she heard whoops of laughter mixed with fear, and turned around to see two small figures scampering around the side of a hut. "No, it was those children touching me!" she cried. "I didn't know—I didn't mean to frighten them!"

"You didn't." Gordon glanced back at the hut. "They're just playing."

"I know, but I spoiled their playing."

"They're just children, they don't know any better. Here—" He picked up a handful of Adija's hair and stroked out a long, thick wave. "*Watoto, tazame!*" he shouted at the children, beckoning them.

"They don't know Kisemi. They've run away now. Their parents are probably scolding them—they're making them wash their hands."

"Nonsense, Adija—look."

"What?"

"Shhh—just sit still."

The children were approaching again stealthily. Their padding footsteps came nearer. A little girl approached. She ran her fingers through the thick strands of Adija's hair, squeezing it as if she would like to steal some for a souvenir. Adija turned and smiled at her. "*Jambo*," she whispered.

"*Jambo*," the girl whispered back.

Adija reached around and touched the little girl's hair. Though she had felt woolly hair more times than she cared to remember, she pretended that the hair felt new and strange to her. This was the funniest thing the girl or any of the children had ever heard of—imagine, someone who did not know what human hair felt like! A crowd of children gathered. One by one, they touched Gordon's and Adija's hair, got touched in return, and ran away giggling.

"You made them come back," Adija said after they had gone. "They like you."

"And you."

Adija nodded slowly. "Yes, because I was with you."

Gordon looked closely at her again. "You haven't been having a very good time here, have you?"

"Oh, yes!" Adija nodded. "I am just a little drunk."

"You don't seem that drunk."

"I am. You see, I drank the native beer. I'm not used to it."

He touched the sleeve of her new dress. "Are you cold?"

"No." Adija looked down at herself. She was hugging her arms across her chest and shivering. "Yes," she said.

Gordon stood up. "You see that hut. My car's behind it. I'm going to walk around the hut and get in the car. You come join me in a few minutes, all right?"

Adija smiled. She did as she was told. Amazing, how steadily she could walk now. She crawled into the front seat beside Gordon. "Let's drive back to Musolu. Right now!"

"Do you really want to?"

"Yes." Adija thought hard. "No," she sighed. "It would disgrace Salome."

"Damn Salome," Gordon said, his lip curling back from his teeth.

Adija started. She'd never seen him look so fierce. "If we left now, I think it would be rude to these people."

Gordon nodded. "You're right. It would. And we'd miss the dancing."

Adija stared out the windshield. Drops of fine rain were streaking down the glass. She could hear them ticking on the metal roof. "Your car, it's not broken, is it?"

"No, of course not. Why?"

"I want to drive back with you. I don't like Jeremiah."

"Yes, we'll go back together. That's a promise," Gordon said.

"Good."

"The people here don't seem to like him either."

Adija watched the rain splattering harder against the windshield. Beyond, she could make out the shape of a car; it was resting at a strange tilt, its rear bumper almost touching the ground, as if the trunk were loaded down with heavy rocks. "Jeremiah must have come back," she said. "I think that's his car."

Gordon switched on the headlights to look. "Yes, it is. But Jeremiah's not what's bothering you, is it?" He put his arm around her.

Adija shook her head slowly. She waited for Gordon to speak again. If only he'd speak! She was conscious of holding air in her lungs and releasing it slowly, making a hollow sound in the car. Her breasts and belly ached. Now her eyes filled with tears; she was powerless to dry them.

"I'm afraid . . . of bewitching!" she blurted.

Gordon tightened his grip on her shoulder. "You think someone's bewitching you?"

"No—I don't know." She remembered the old white-haired man, and chased the picture of him from her mind. "Maybe I'm the one doing it."

"Why do you think that?" Gordon stared at her.

"You think I'm foolish, don't you?"

"No—"

"Sometimes I'm clever—about people and the way they are. But sometimes I'm very stupid. I don't understand politics, the way Salome does. And other things too." She wiped her eyes. "Do you mind that I'm stupid?"

"You're not stupid, Adija. If I thought you were, I wouldn't be here with you."

Adija nodded.

"But that's not what we were talking about, is it?" He wanted to ask her, Is it true what I heard—that you've been telling people you're my wife, and that you're pregnant? But there was this other weird business to get through first. "What is this bewitching you're scared of?" he asked.

Adija took her hands from her face and looked wide-eyed up at Gordon. "I ran away this afternoon."

"I know."

"You know?"

"Yes. You've been acting strange this evening too. I don't understand it. Please, can't you tell me?"

"Maybe . . . I'm just feeling my strangeness here." Adija was not convinced. It was a good explanation, like being drunk was a good explanation. Good, but not right, really. It explained what she'd been feeling, but not what she'd done. How could she explain her running away this afternoon, and finding that old man everywhere, and the way Salome had flung the axe at her? "When I'm with you, Gordon, I can't believe in bewitching. I think it's just primitive nonsense—because I know you don't believe in it. But I'm not always with you. And sometimes, even when I'm with you, I'm not always with you with all my mind. I'm talking craziness."

"No." Gordon touched her cheek, wiping away a tear.

"I want to believe you—to think like you do," she continued, "because you're clever and educated and good. But there is a thing you don't understand because you weren't born here. Myself, I don't understand it either, but I know of it. I know that if people think this thing is powerful, and if they think you have it . . . inside you, then it get power to hurt people, somehow . . . I can't explain."

"You're doing all right."

"It makes people strange. Or maybe strange people make it. I don't know. But out here, I am more different from others even than in Musolu. It makes me scared. Just to talk about it is bad for me. And then—" She shut her mouth hard—having almost mentioned her suspicions of being pregnant. There was just too much to think about.

She pressed her face into Gordon's chest and began to weep softly.

Holding her, Gordon wanted to cry too, but he couldn't. He never could. He couldn't make Adija feel better or make her any less of a mystery to herself—or to him either, for that matter. He'd never realized that she *was* such a mystery. She'd always radiated an aura of mysteriousness that had fanned his imagination—he had to admit that at first he had found her exotic, even though later he'd discovered that this sort of attraction was based on nothing more than his own ignorance. What she was struggling to show him now was a real mystery—a mysterious *complexity*—and damn, it was different. "I don't find you so strange," he said finally, his words catching in his throat. "I love you as you are. I don't understand everything about you yet, but that doesn't mean I won't—or you won't, either."

Adija was coughing, trying to stop crying. "Myself, I too—I love you." She wiped her nose hard with the back of her hand. "But I'm fearing—" Fearing what? She didn't know. Telling him about the baby. Fearing that he wouldn't want her then. Fearing that he would. But why should she be fearing him? All the bargirls she had ever known—except Salome, of course—spoke hopefully of having half-white babies and marrying Europeans. A girl in Mirini had actually had such a baby and married the father. Adija had envied that girl—what was her name?— for her cleverness in getting the man to marry her. But she didn't want to be clever in that way herself, not with Gordon!

"Gordon, I want to stop thinking," she whimpered, pressing herself close to him, her eyes flooding again. "Make me stop thinking! Please, make me forget, make me different!" She pressed her face against his, her tongue licking him furiously. Her body squirmed against him. "You like me, don't you? My hair is not bad for you, is it?" She swung her hair back and forth against his face. "And my breasts, you like them, *eii*? Take them, Gordon! Kiss them like you do—" She tugged open the buttons of her dress and pulled it back sharply from her shoulders. "You like them, I know you do! They're bigger now, see?"

She swung her leg over his thighs and pulled her dress up, ripping it. "Look, Gordon—touch it—" She spat into her hand and rubbed herself. "I'm open, I'm ready for you—*please!*"

He was not ready for her. When she clawed open his trousers, she found him small, smaller than ever, as if he were shrinking into himself. "*Eii*, what's the matter? You drank too much?"

"No—I'm upset about this . . . ow!"

She let go of him and tried to slide down to take him into her mouth; she bumped her head against the steering wheel. "Bastard!" she cried, hitting it with the palm of her hand. She clutched him again. "Don't you like me anymore, Gordon?"

"I'm sorry." He shut his eyes tight in misery. "I—it's too fast! Try and relax, let me relax—I have to stop thinking too." He stroked her sides, trying to slow down his breathing.

Adija sat back on her haunches, staring at him. "I've bewitched you!" she whispered, covering her face.

"Stop it, will you!"

She was sobbing now; suddenly she gasped. Gordon's hand was finding its way to her. She squeezed it tight between her thighs, rocking against him. *Eii*, what was she doing? But she couldn't stop her thrashing, even as she felt him growing hard in her hand. She never wanted to stop moving, she had all the room in the world to move now; neither the car nor her mind were crowded any longer, she had broken out, she—

"Turn over." Gordon pushed Adija around so that he could kneel behind her. But she wouldn't release his hand. "Oh, no!" he groaned. He was small again, small and spent.

Adija's body shuddered; she cried out and sank slowly back against him. She turned and stared at him wide-eyed. "Gordon?"

He pulled his hand back slowly. "Yeah—"

"Thank you," she gasped.

"Don't . . . mention it."

Adija wiped her fingers along the back of her thighs. She squinted at her fingers, then licked them. "Perhaps I didn't bewitch you completely," she said, and turned to sit beside him. Her head slumped to his shoulder. Her entire body went limp. "I want to sleep. I'm so tired. If I don't sleep, I'll start thinking again, Gordon."

"I know what you mean. One of us ought to get back, though."

"I need to sleep." Adija's eyes were already closed, her words slurred.

"All right." Gordon stroked her hair. He opened the door and stepped out of the car. "We'll talk. We'll be together later. For a long time."

"Yes." She sniffled and rubbed her nose back and forth against the seat. "I believe you," she said. Wrapping her arms around her raised knees, she rested her cheek against the back of the seat.

Gordon let go of the door; it closed with a click.

23

THE INITIATE DANCED IN PLACE IN THE CENter of the circle. The boy's eyes were half-closed with exhaustion, his mouth open and panting, his face shiny from a continuous stream of sweat. His headdress of white feathers bobbed up and down with the dazed, rolling movement of his body.

Watching him, Gordon felt dazed too. His mind tried over and over again to unsnarl the meanings of the scene with Adija. Several times he turned from the dancing, determined to go back to the car. Each time, he stopped himself, and allowed the monotonous circular movement of the dance to mesmerize him.

This is my own initiation into manhood, he thought. My second one. And maybe I am failing it. I wish it were a ritualized initiation like the boy's: Without ambiguity or agonizing decisions, with the elders telling me exactly what to expect during and after it, and with a family, a village, a tribe waiting to receive me when it's over. . . .

"Hello, sir."

Gordon looked around. He hadn't heard "sir" in days; it wasn't a welcome appellation. The schoolboys, Romulus and Moses, were standing beside him. They were still wearing their school shorts and shirts, but were looking even dustier than before. Their round brown faces were identical in the dim lantern light.

"Yeah, hello," Gordon said.

"Don't you want to join the dancing?" Moses asked.

"I don't know the steps or anything."

"No one would expect you to know them. You can dance anyhowly."

Romulus nodded. "People will be glad to see you joining them. It will show you're liking their hospitality."

"I guess I'd better dance then, hadn't I?" Gordon took

the stick Moses gave him and began moving around the pole. All the male dancers carried sticks, thrusting them up and down in rhythm to the clanks and jingles and squawks. At first, Gordon moved cautiously, trying to see how the other men were stepping. Soon, though, he relaxed and stopped worrying about what his feet were doing. He caught the rhythm and the general movement of the crowd, and that was good enough; it was very good, in fact. People stared at him for a while, but soon he ceased to be a novelty, and they returned to their talking and dancing, unperturbed.

It was true what those boys had said—no one expected him to dance like an African. No one expected him to be anything but himself. He could live in Africa without understanding everything right away. He would always be different from Adija, and from his African friends, but gradually their differences would become unimportant. Gordon grinned as he bounced and shuffled around and around the pole, his body loosening, his mind wandering peacefully as it had after the noonday meal. He could just *be*.

The song ended. The rhythm of the whistles and bells faded, but continued faintly in the background. Someone was shouting for the initiate. The circumcision boy's face grew tense. For the first time in hours, he moved away from the center of the circle. The crowd parted to let him through.

A man in long trousers and a torn white shirt stepped forward to meet him. He stood stiff and erect, the muscles in his chest straining beneath the shirt. He shouted a hoarse command, and all voices ceased. The boy stood motionless, his eyes focused on those of the man. The crowd closed around them.

"What now?" Gordon whispered to Moses, who had come to stand beside him.

"The testing," Moses whispered. "That man is the elder in charge of the ceremony. He asks the boy if he is ready for the ordeal. He has goat's entrails in his hands."

"Does he use them for divination?"

"No, for the testing. The old man, the *mwaguzi*, will use other entrails for divination afterward. You'll see."

The elder shouted at the boy. When the boy nodded stiffly, the man appeared not to believe him. He stepped

back, looking enraged. Veins stood out on his forehead. He
let out a roar of disgust, paced around in a circle, grumbled and spat on the ground.

The man suddenly showed the crowd what he was holding in his hands. People gasped theatrically. The man addressed them, pointing at the boy with a disdainful finger.
Then he whirled and flung a strip of raw flesh at him. It
splattered against his chest, but the boy did not flinch.
Thrice again the man flung bits of entrails, each time
harder. One struck the boy on the cheek and stuck; blood
dribbled down his face. His eyes dilated with fear, but he
did not turn them from his attacker.

A flicker of a smile appeared on the man's face. Someone in the crowd laughed with relief. Others joined in,
many applauding. The whistles and bells grew loud again.
The boy turned and returned to the dancing area, the
crowd following him jubilantly.

Only a few people remained behind to watch the divination. The old man squatted over the freshly killed body of
a goat. He was shaking his head slowly. Then more people
arrived to listen to him. He turned his face up toward
them, his eyes wide open, his white head shaking stubbornly.

"What's going on?" Gordon asked.

Moses looked disgusted. "The man says the entrails refuse to tell him anything."

"What are they supposed to tell him?"

"Aah, he is supposed to read the entrails and tell the
people that the ancestors are satisfied with the boy—this
means the ceremony can continue."

"But this time it can't?"

"He is very obstinate, that old man. He won't tell what
he has found."

"So what will happen?"

Moses looked away. "This is embarrassing, sir. We are
all Christians here. It is just that we do these old things out
of custom. This wasn't supposed to happen."

Gordon stared at the old man. A large crowd was form-
ing around him, a low murmuring passing through it.

"Will the ceremony be stopped now?" Gordon asked.

"I don't think so. Probably they will bring the old man
another goat if he can't make up his mind. The people say
there is something wrong with this goat."

"But you don't think anything's wrong with it?"

"Goats are all the same, inside. We learned about organs and things in biology class. Nothing's wrong with the goat, or the boy, either—only with these people who are so ignorant to worry about such nonsense." Moses wrinkled his nose. "We can return to the dancing," he said.

"You call your own people's customs ignorant?" Gordon asked, but Moses was looking away distractedly, something more than embarrassment clouding his face.

* * *

Odui excused herself to go check on her children; Salome remained behind in the beer hut. Bringing her reed drinking straw with her, she moved to a more comfortable spot against the wall, the spot that Adija had vacated. She hadn't noticed Adija leaving; there was no reason to worry, though. Adija and Odui would be back soon. Meanwhile, there was all this beer to help drink. Salome stretched her legs out and basked in the warmth of the coals.

Any anxieties she still had about being among country people dissolved in the bitter liquid sloshing into her belly. She was one with these people now, sharing their drink, their food, their work. Bashiri was no longer a place to fear—it was her place, and she was ready to come back to stay. Salome's eyes stung from the smoke, but she did not wipe the tears from her cheeks. Hadn't she spent the first half of her life in smoky huts like this one? She would grow used to it again in time. Especially if the hut were her own, built with her own hands on her own farm, high in the green hills above her village . . . a spot on the edge of the forest, with maize growing beside the path and tall gum trees rustling overhead.

She closed her eyes. A mistake. A half-asleep mood came over her, the one that came to her in Musolu in the morning as she tried to prevent herself from waking up to a new day. Dread seeped in through the cracks in the wall like a gray poisonous vapor; it hovered close to her skin. Salome struggled to escape into sleep.

Again, she and Adija were searching for the baby, Wairimu. They walked cautiously along the rows of white-washed huts, peering into every dark doorway. The day was cloudy and damp; the hard gravel paths were deserted, each family was huddling in its own hut. Adija reached the

end of the row of huts. We should try the one over there,
she said, pointing to a tin sentry hut beside the main gate.
Her voice sounded gay. She seemed to regard the search as
just another game to relieve the boredom of life in the
penned-in concentration camp. No, not in there, Salome
called, but not too loud, for she didn't want anyone to hear
her. Already people were suspicious of them for walking
about looking into the huts. Adija only smiled and kept
walking, as if she hadn't heard. Not in there—no, Adija!
Salome cried, but Adija disappeared into the hut. Villagers
gathered around Salome, whispering. She must be a spy,
they whispered. We will kill her when she comes out. We'll
burn her at the stake, the filthy traitor . . .

Airplanes roared overhead. Everyone but Salome ran for
cover. Salome dashed across the clearing, past the coils of
barbed wire, and into the tin sentry hut. It was a long,
dimly lit room, much larger than it appeared from the
outside. Tables and chairs were set up along the walls, as in
a bar. The guards were slouched at the tables. They were
all drunk and laughing. Hello, Salome, they said. We've got
that girl you sent us. Which girl? Salome demanded. The
guards laughed.

I didn't send her to you! I didn't tell her to come here!

The guards laughed louder. The European officer with
the guards was laughing the hardest of all. Where is she?
Salome screamed: What have you done to her? But no one
listened. The white officer grinned. Salome Wairimu stood
screaming in the midst of the men, buried in their laughter.
Now they were pulling at her, their hands tight around her
arm—

"No!" Salome pulled her arm back.

A man said something in Rukiva to her. He was trying
to climb past her.

"Where is she?" Salome asked him, blinking her eyes
hard against the smoke.

The man shook his head and disappeared past the beer
tub. Salome scrambled to her feet. The doorway was just
ahead. She stepped over someone's legs and plunged
through it.

The top of her head struck the edge of the roof outside.
Dirt and bits of straw rained down on her. Look at yourself, Salome raged, brushing herself off. You who've been
pretending to be a peasant woman and can't even remem-

ber how to go through a door. All you've accomplished
with your act has been to drive Adija away!

Salome wandered about in the clearing, lost. Adija was
not among the dancers, not among the spectators. Had
those two schoolboys dragged her off? No, they were here.
Gordon. Where the hell was Gordon?

No, she said to herself—I am here, I am just going to
dance. She joined the circle. Her body began to bounce, her
feet stomped with the thudding rhythm of other feet rever-
berating up from the ground. The lantern light shone down
on half the circle; streams of people entered it from the
other half-circle that was in near darkness. Each time they
came around, they looked changed, as if, having bathed
themselves in the dark half of the circle, they were somehow emerging from it with radiant faces.

Salome forgot she was dancing. She was less a creature
of flesh and bones now than a moving piece of a larger
continual motion. Going from darkness to light was as
natural as blinking, or as traveling from night to day. The
dance *was* the nights and days, the seasons of drought and
rain, the bad years and the good . . . the dance was the
people repeating the cycles, over and over, never changing,
never ending . . .

Suddenly the singing stopped. The whistles and bells
faded into a confused noise. Someone was shouting. Now
the older men were leaving the circle, following a tall man
in a torn white shirt. The air seemed shattered by the
absence of rhythm. Each falling-off squawk and bell-clank
struck Salome like a sharp knife poking all the muscles of
her body, making them plead for the rhythm to begin
again. Individual faces appeared. Mouths frowned, grinned.
Gossipy voices rasped. Men squatted in clusters to confer
secretly; women gathered to whisper in malicious tones.
The cycles were fragmented, the rhythm lost. And Salome
knew, again, why she had left her village many years ago.

She wandered among the huts, peering into the empty
doorways as she passed. Each hut looked the same, a
round knot of darkness against the dark sky. She could tell
by the sound of the darkness inside the huts that no one
was there. She wandered on.

"You!" There was Gordon coming out of a hut. She
strode up to him and clutched his arm. "Where have you
been?"

He yanked his arm back. "Drinking beer with the men. What do you want to know for?"

"I want to talk with you!"

From behind the huts, someone started shouting another song, trying to start a new dance.

"I don't want to talk with you," he shouted over the noise.

"Where is Adija?"

He glared at her for several seconds. "She's resting."

"She's resting," Salome repeated, squeezing her fists tight. "What is she resting from?"

Gordon did not speak. A fine rain began to fall again. He and Salome both felt it; neither of them made a move to wipe the moisture from their faces. The huts around them seemed to lean forward dumbly in anticipation. The clanking, squawking rhythm pulsed in Salome's head; then it broke again, a shelf of instruments tilting and crashing to the ground. She tensed, glaring, waiting.

Gordon opened his mouth slowly. "She's resting from you," he said.

Salome's foot shot out, aimed at his groin. He jerked sideways; the blow struck his thigh and knocked him off balance. Her fingernails clutched at his face, sharp, hot, groping for his eyes. He fell back away from the fingers; a great weight toppled him to the ground, fists and knees pummeling him like a hundred wild animals.

Suddenly he was fighting for his life. Heaving himself along the ground, he scrambled to his feet, and turned just in time to deflect Salome past him as she charged. She whirled and came at him again. This time he was not quick enough to dodge, and had to block her full on with his lowered shoulder. Slowly he lifted her from the ground, regained his balance, and flung her down on her back. She rolled sideways in the dirt, gasping for breath. He could have ended it then by leaping on her and pinning her arms; he hesitated, and she was on her feet again, charging.

They faced each other, arms outstretched and straining against one another, fingers locked around each other's forearms. Pushing and twisting, each tried to fling the other to the ground. The sweat dripped from their faces, their eyes bulged. They inhaled the stink of each other's hatred. Around and around they strained in a plodding, grunting dance. Salome opened her eyes wide, as if by glaring hard enough she could burn Gordon's face away. Her eyes sucked him toward them; she pulled her face back slowly, as if giving ground. Then, with a downward chop of her forehead, she butted hard against his cheek. Crying out, he pitched sideways. Together they rolled over and over in the dirt. Gordon felt teeth ripping his shoulder; his fists struck muscle, fat, air. Then he was on top of her, squeezing one of her thrashing legs between his knees, and shaking her by the neck. Again her eyes burned; again he leaned closer to her, but now the look on her face made him shake her harder and harder. Her head thudded against the earth, until finally her clawing fingers dropped away from his wrists and he felt her body go limp beneath him.

Gordon pulled his hands slowly from her neck, feeling the ache in them all the way up his arms. He gasped for breath. Salome was not moving. Her eyes were wide open and glazed; her tongue lay in the corner of her mouth in a froth of red foam.

He stared at her mouth. Suddenly he seemed to be focusing down upon her as if from a great height. "Salome!" he choked, and started to lift himself from her.

The leg between his knees moved sharply. A sickening pain shot up his body from his groin. Screaming, he toppled sideways. Salome rolled away. She saw double images that tilted and rolled above her. The sky descended and hit her like a careening load of rocks.

Opening her eyes, she found herself lying down again on something lumpy and hot. Him. The huts and sky no longer just swam before her eyes, they spun past her like meteorites. All she could do was try to balance them there, hoping they would not all crash down on her at once. She could hear Gordon's breaths rasping in unison with hers. He slipped in and out of focus; his breath roared in her ears now like the rush of an enormous pulse. She strained to move away from him, but her limbs were numb. She and Gordon, too weak to move, remained lying, entwined, sucking in what little vile air there was between them and releasing it in unison.

At last Salome was able to push herself sideways and stagger to her feet. He too stood up, tottering, dropping to all fours and pushing himself up again. She saw him as two figures, bent silhouettes wavering and blending together and splitting . . . and finally hardening into one man, secure on his feet, blocking her way, capable of moving in whichever direction he chose.

He was in pain, she knew, but not dizzy and spent, as she was. Her moment was gone, her attack finished. Nothing remained for her now but the taste of blood in her mouth and nausea in her throat. Slowly she turned and slumped away.

* * *

Salome found her way eventually to the river. There she washed herself in the cold water. Her breasts hurt from his fists. She tried to imagine how badly he must be aching now in his testicles, but she couldn't imagine it and even if she could, she would not have felt any better. Nothing could make her feel better. Adija was gone. He still had her hidden somewhere—"resting"—and would keep her there until he was through with her. But even now, Salome knew she could not afford to rest.

She climbed back up the hill slowly, her eyes instinctively continuing to search for Adija.

She came to a clearing. A group of men were sitting in a circle around a lantern, arguing in low tones. The man in charge of the initiation ceremony was there. Salome stayed in the shadows; she heard no word in any of the languages she knew.

Further on, she came upon two men talking in Kisemi. One of them was Mutali. She hid behind a granary to listen.

They were talking about the divination that had occurred after the boy's testing. Someone was endangering the boy—that was why the diviner had refused to divulge the message of the entrails. He did not want to give the witch warning. The *mwaguzi* had referred to the witch as "the one who absents herself." Who but a witch would go wandering about the countryside alone, especially with such important events as the initiation going on? The *mwaguzi* must have been referring to one of the guests.

Salome's heart beat loudly. Had her absence been noticed? But the men were not talking about her.

"The light-skinned one, I think," Mutali was saying. "She has been behaving strangely all day."

"Is she gone even now?"

"She's not been present since before the testing. It is said by some that she is the woman of the European. They were seen together in the European's car. Even now, she is in his car."

"Perhaps they just didn't know about the prohibition against intercourse during this night. They would not have been the first to break it, in any case."

"It's not just that. They were seen doing it in a strange way, a way not known to our people," Mutali said. "It is not good to discuss such things tonight, however."

"True. I've seen the European dancing, and he is looking strange now. His clothes are torn and dirty, and he walks with a limp. He will say nothing about it. He tries to smile, but there is a look of pain in his face. Not ordinary pain. The sort of pain that gives a man strength to do things he could not do before. It is hard to explain."

Mutali shook his head. He lit a charred cigarette butt, inhaled, and let the smoke out of his mouth slowly. "That Jeremiah should never have invited any of them," he said.

The other man nodded. "Jeremiah should never have been invited himself."

Salome crept away. Her mind began to work again. She had to get Adija out of Gordon's car and have her seen among the dancers. Adija must not learn of the danger she was in. She would panic if she knew; then there would be no limit to the damage she could do.

24

AFTER HER SECOND MEETING WITH GORDON—
after washing his wounds in the river and making love and
talking of marriage—Adija wandered through the rest of
the night, happy and relieved, and confused and terrified.
She did not know where she was going, but it didn't matter—there were always paths leading off somewhere. She
followed them wherever they wished to take her.

What have I done? she asked herself.

I have left someone behind. Not just Salome. I've left
Adija behind. I am mad. If only Salome were here, I could
ask her: Where is Adija now? And Salome would say:
Adija is neither place—where she was, or where she will
be. And Adija would then ask: Is that what it is like to be
mad?

Eventually she found herself in a clearing near the sleeping hut. The sky was paling. The ground beneath her feet
was damp with dew. She walked into the middle of the
clearing, trying to work up the courage to walk into the
hut. Did she have the courage to tell Salome? Not tonight
—tomorrow, when they were all back in the New Life:
she, Salome, and Gordon.

In motion, her thoughts came clearer. Miriamu, she
thought suddenly. Miriamu was the name of the girl in
Mirini who had married the European. He was a rich old
Englishman, a gun merchant with a bald head and no eyebrows. How we envied Miriamu. But we mocked her too as
she rode down the street in her motorcar with her European. Miriamu thinks she is European now, we would say.
Her bullet-headed-man's skin grows darker in the sun and
hers grows lighter. Perhaps he will start to grow hair and
she will get bald! The girls chattered around the bar, within
earshot of her. Miriamu had nothing to do in the daytime,
so she came back to the bar; she missed talking with the

girls and drinking her beer. What is it like? Adija asked Miriamu once. I mean, with a whiteman? Oh, it is no trouble, it is a soft thing, like a skinned banana, and it is finished quickly. Then he is happy and gentle and likes to take me to the shops to buy me new dresses. Miriamu had many new dresses, but she didn't look comfortable in them—

Adija screamed and stumbled backward. She clapped her hands over her mouth. She had nearly tripped over someone. The man's legs protruded past a bush; they were as brown and brittle as the branches. The man appeared to be sleeping, sitting with his arms folded on his drawn-up knees and his face resting on his arms. Slowly he raised his head.

Adija stifled another scream. The man's hair was fuzzy white, his eyes were whiter still and staring directly at her.

"Please, I'm sorry," Adija whimpered. "Leave me alone, *mwaguzi*—please!"

The old man said nothing. Slowly he opened his mouth, his pink gums glistening out of his dried face. He rose slowly to his feet. Then he leaned over and picked up a carved black walking stick. Adija could hear his bones creak as he straightened his body again. He turned and walked away. He was not planting his stick in the ground beside him as he moved; no, he was waving it out before him in the strangest way. When the stick struck a stump, he stopped short, then walked around the stump in a wide arc, as if he could not see it. He *couldn't* see it! He couldn't see anything in front of him!

Those whitish eyes that had stared at her so knowingly —they had been blind eyes! How could he have seen so much of her? He couldn't be blind! But look at him, shuffling cautiously along, tapping every little knoll and bump in the ground. Blind!

Adija watched him go around the side of a thorn hedge and disappear. Then, running through the brush with no thought of the noise she made, she raced back in the direction of the compound.

*   *   *

Gordon slept silently, his mind finally at rest. Salome's power over Adija was finished; he understood that now.

Suddenly, everything seemed clear. No wonder Adija had been frightened of being bewitched. Salome must have seduced her that first day in Musolu when Adija had arrived lost and helpless. Salome had kept her under her evil spell thereafter, exploiting Adija's beauty to attract men into the bar, forcing Adija to satisfy her desires, threatening to turn her loose into the world if she complained. And when he had arrived in Adija's life, Salome's hold on her had begun to weaken. Salome's desperation had driven her to violence. Gordon had never touched a woman in anger in his life; the recollection of his fight with Salome still made him shudder.

But there was no need to think of it any longer. It was over. And as Adija had washed him in the stream, he had allowed himself to feel that as awful as the fight had been, it had been worth it.

Afterward, he had not found it difficult to ask Adija the question he had been holding in so long. He was finally in control of himself and his situation; it was the inevitable thing to ask now: Are you pregnant?

Her answer had been arrived at by the same process as his willingness to ask it: She had simply exhausted all possibility for further procrastination.

Yes, I'm going to have a baby.

Her calmness had been alarming. Her face was drained of expression. She didn't squirm in place or tug at her hair or go through any of her usual mannerisms, but merely answered another question without his having to ask it:

I think the baby is yours, but I'm not sure. There were some soldiers one night. I was fearing them—

She turned her face away, as if expecting a slap. Her confession had come as no shock to Gordon. What was shocking was that she was being so straightforward with him when she had so much to lose.

You're not angry? she'd asked.

No, Adija.

Because you are good.

Because I love you.

Yes. That is why I told you.

And if I have to leave Musolu, Adija, will you come with me?

Yes.

Do you want to marry me?

I want to be with you. If you just move into a house with me on some school compound, people will say that I'm your whore.

I won't let that happen. But if we can, we'll wait to marry until after the baby comes. That's the custom here, anyway—right?

Yes. Adija laughed. You're learning.

If it isn't my baby, it'll be easy to tell, I should think. I don't want people to think you've tricked me into marrying you. But after the baby's born, and we still marry, no one can think that.

Adija nodded. There can be no talk of trickery then, she said. She had seemed very pleased with that idea.

And if the baby's mine, there'll be no problem.

No problem. Here she'd appeared to be thinking hard about what she was saying. The dreamlike expression left her face. She stared off toward the hills solemnly. No problem, she repeated.

I mean, of course there'll be problems. But we can deal with them. We love each other. We know each other. We have control over our lives.

Then her gaze had returned to him. She watched him attentively, like a student waiting for clues about the contents of a forthcoming test. Gordon laughed and kissed her.

Adija had made love without desperation now. Her happy trance returned; her cool body was like a gentle stream flowing over him. Slowly they caressed each other, stopping momentarily to smile into each other's faces and break out into inexplicable fits of laughter. Exhausted, they lay together in a bed of coarse grass. An ant crawled onto Gordon's forehead. He looked at it cross-eyed. Adija rolled her head back and laughed almost hysterically. As her eyes filled with tears, she kissed him on the forehead, ant and all. She spat sideways, then grinned into his face. Goodbye, ant, she said. Tell your brothers and sisters that Adija has spared your life in honor of her love for Gordon.

She lay on her back beside him, staring up at the sky. He thought surely she was asleep, she was lying so quietly. When he leaned over to look at her, he discovered her eyes still open and still damp. They had that same lost expression in them that he had noticed on that first day when she had come to his house in the rain. What is it? he asked.

Nothing. The look turned quickly to an uneasy smile. I must go now.

Why?

I must join the other women, or they will think bad things about me. These people are not advanced, they do not understand the way people like us behave.

All right. I'll walk back with you.

But tomorrow—tomorrow is already here . . . Adija looked up at the streaks of gray light in the sky. Tomorrow we will drive back to Musolu.

Yes.

She'd said nothing more. He had left her still looking a little dazed outside the women's hut.

Waking up now, he saw that the men had all left their sleeping mats. The dawn was glowing in the open doorway. He got dressed sleepily.

Outside, the new divination was about to begin. Gordon wanted to see it. Afterward, the boy and the elders would go down to the stream for the circumcision. He probably would not be invited to witness the actual circumcision, but that was all right. He'd been asked to join in the dancing and beer drinking. These people had been more than hospitable to him. He stepped back to get a good view of the divination.

Suddenly he grew anxious. Was that Adija, across the open space in the crowd, being held policeman-fashion by some old man? He pressed forward, standing on tiptoe to look. She was there all right, and looking very pale, but no one was holding her arm now. Salome was there, arguing with a man who stood beside Adija. Gordon tried to make his way over to Adija, but the crowd had become too thick: a wall of elbows and backs and thighs kept him from moving more than a few paces in any direction.

Arguments were breaking out all through the crowd. Jeremiah was trying to explain something to the two schoolboys; they stared down at their feet, mournful and silent. The older people around them were shouting at Jeremiah.

A goat bleated pitifully. The crowd grew grumblingly silent. A young man in ragged khaki shorts tugged the goat into the center of the crowd and laid it down on a mat of green banana leaves. He knelt over it, pinning the forelegs beneath his knee, and wiped the blade of his machete with a leaf. The blade shone silver in the pale hot sunlight. The goat's squealing grew louder, like the noises of a pleading child. Then with one quick stroke, the man slit the goat's neck. The goat jerked against the man's restraining hands, shuddered, and collapsed back onto the leaves. Blood spouted from its neck into an earthenware bowl that one of the men thrust forward. As soon as the goat's sides stopped bellowing in and out, the vein was tied in a knot.

The man with the machete rolled the goat over and slit its stomach from one end to the other. After a few seconds of cutting, he pulled the animal cleanly out of its skin. The goat glistened damp and pale on the grass.

The crowd parted, and the old white-haired man shuffled forward. As he knelt beside the goat, the people crowded close. Adija opened her eyes—she had slaughtered goats before, but something about the way these people had done it made her sick with fear. She saw the crowd as a blur thickening around her, heat and weight drawing close against her.

The diviner gave the signal to the man with the machete, and the man sliced into the carcass. Plip-plip-plip, the intestines rippled out as the silvery underskin parted behind the moving blade. A pool of intestines, pinkish lungs, and a black liver lay ready for the diviner.

Gripping the machete, the diviner sliced off a piece of liver, put it in his mouth and worked it around the inside of his cheeks. Then suddenly he spat it out.

Adija held her breath. The hush of the crowd fell over her like a frost. For a while all whispering and shuffling of feet ceased. Then someone gasped, and the voices rose around her. She clutched Salome's arm and shut her eyes tight.

Everyone was murmuring at once. The crowd swelled with voices—angry, shocked, questioning. Salome felt the pressure of bodies give way behind her. She stumbled backward into the sudden vacuum, pulling Adija with her. A hole in the crowd opened around them. Eyes bored into them. Behind the scuffling figures, the diviner's voice rose, a high, cracking sound of rage, prophecy, and doom.

Someone toppled back against a granary, knocking it

over. An old woman tripped over the granary with a shriek, and stepped on the goat. She fell, umf, rolled away. The goat's silky coat was covered with mud and blood. The old man sat down hard on the ground, his toothless mouth hanging open. The circumcision boy knelt before him, pleading, but the old man stared sightlessly ahead, panting and shaking his head.

Men pointed their fingers at Jeremiah and then at Adija. Machete blades flashed. Voices spun around Adija. Eyes narrowed at her, lips curled back, words struck her face like spit.

Odui stepped forward, standing between the men and Adija. She spoke tearfully. Grumbling, the men stepped back, lowering their machetes.

Jeremiah's uncle approached him. The older man tried to speak, but no words would come out. Finally he made a slow sweeping motion with his arm: Go! Jeremiah turned and hurried away, no longer trying to keep his head high.

Hands grabbed Adija and flung her after him. She would have fallen, had not the hands yanked her along. For a moment she struggled to free herself, then she went limp, allowing herself to be shoved and carried along.

Gordon ran around the crowd toward his car. "Adija!" he screamed, but his voice was swallowed up in the noise of the people. Already they had shoved Adija into Jeremiah's car. Salome plunged through the crowd and threw herself through the open back door after Adija, just as Jeremiah started the engine. Exhaust fumes belched out of the tailpipe. People scattered. The tires whirled, spraying dirt over everyone. The car shot forward. Trailing a cloud of dust, it bumped away across the fields toward the road.

Gordon slid into the front seat of his car and turned the key hard in the ignition. A faint humming sound. Then nothing.

He jammed the key in and out and tried again. Humm. Nothing.

He stared around him. The dashboard light was off, even though the door was open. He opened and shut the door. No light, not even a flicker. He had turned the lights on last night to identify Jeremiah's car and had forgotten to switch them off again. The battery was dead.

Trembling, he stepped outside. The compound was deserted. He walked among the huts, glancing into their dark doorways. All was quiet. He remembered the scenes of the day before—the peaceful meal, the walk through the countryside, the exuberant dancing and drinking. He felt those people around him again, felt their activity as if their spirits were inhabiting the compound now. But the space they had occupied was empty. What had happened? God, what had happened?

He arrived at the open space where the divination had taken place. Vacant doors stared mournful mouths at him. There was a blood-stained trail on the grass where the goat had been dragged hurriedly into the bushes. Beyond the trail of blood, the dancing area was a circle of cracked, dry mud, blackened by the glare of the sun.

A figure emerged from one of the huts. Mutali. He walked stiffly up to Gordon. "You need help?" he asked.

"My battery is dead. I need a push." Gordon wiped his forehead, breathing hard. "What happened this morning?"

"The diviner said your friend, the half-caste girl, was a witch."

"Witch?" Gordon gaped at Mutali. "No, wait—"

"He says so because she was wandering about alone last night. Until morning, in fact," Mutali said, his voice even and weary. "The elders saw her and the diviner saw her."

"That old man's blind! How could he see her?"

"He says he heard her speak and felt her presence. Her presence here made the circumcision of the boy too uncertain, too dangerous."

"Jesus!" Gordon shook his head. "Do you believe that?"

Mutali looked away. "It doesn't matter what I believe. The elders believe it. I am a Christian, but I do not argue with the elders. This is my home and I must remain here." Mutali stared down at the ground, looking simultaneously embarrassed and angry. "The circumcision is called off. Later this month, the boy will go to the government hospital in Kepuria for the operation."

"Perhaps that's safer, anyway," Gordon sighed. "But it's not the same, is it?"

"It's not the same." Mutali stood motionless, waiting, hoping that the European's questions would cease before he was forced to become rude.

"Adija was with me last night. That's why she wasn't with the others."

"She was seen alone as well," Mutali said. "The people

are blaming Jeremiah for bringing her. They are not blaming you. But since you were with Jeremiah, and since it is rumored that the—the girl is your friend . . ." Mutali shifted his weight from one foot to the other. "It is best that you leave. We do not need any more quarreling."

Gordon hurried to his car. Almost as soon as he was in the seat, the car began to roll forward. Dozens of men had suddenly appeared. Brown hands gripped the windowframe beside his face; there were so many bodies clustered around the car that he could barely see out. The car rolled backward and turned around. The steering wheel spun in his hands—he had no control at all over the car! It moved forward again, startlingly fast. Men grunted in his car. The dark arms in his window gleamed with moisture. The car was thick with the smell of sweat. Gordon hunched over the steering wheel, peering between the straining backs before him.

Faster and faster the car rolled forward, in eerie silence. Gordon turned the key and stepped hard on the accelerator, letting out the clutch. The engine caught. The men all grunted and gave him one last heave forward, and the car shot out over the field.

After a few dozen yards, Gordon braked and revved the motor. He looked back, about to wave his thanks to the men and ask directions to Musolu. But the men had not stayed to watch him. All he saw of them was their backs.

Then they were gone. Without looking behind them, they had walked together into the compound and melted in among the huts and granaries.

25

SALOME AND ADIJA SAT GRIPPING THE ARM-
rests and each other. The car lurched from side to side as
it careened around curves, skidded, and hurtled forward
again. Blurred bushes and trees flew by. The rear bumper
scraped the road. Heavy pieces of metal clanked back and
forth in the trunk.

"Slow down!" Salome screamed. Her voice was lost in
the roar of the engine. She watched Jeremiah's face swing
off the rear-view mirror as he leaned into a turn, tugging
the wheel sideways. After a second's delay, the car swerved
sideways, scraping a row of bushes. Shredded leaves
snowed into the back seat.

Adija kept her eyes fixed on the road ahead of her. It at
least stayed in one place. People appeared on the road;
they leaped away, backstepping in mute terror. A boy on a
bicycle—wsh!—gone. Two women with babies—gone. A
red flowering bush—gone, like a sucked-away breath of
flame. A car, swerving sideways, hitting the rim of the
road—gone, leaving the wail of its horn behind it.

Jeremiah slowed down momentarily. He lit a cigarette
and flicked the match out of the window.

"Fool—are you trying to kill us?" Salome shouted at
him, out of breath.

"Shut up, woman." Jeremiah gripped the steering wheel
tighter. "You and your friend have caused me enough
trouble already."

"Shit, if you hadn't been arrogant to your people, if
you'd given those schoolboys their fees—" Salome shut her
eyes, as the car swerved to miss a cow. "If your people had
respected you, you could have talked the elders out of all
that witchcraft nonsense."

"It's no nonsense. You're a pair of witches!"

"Why did you bring us, then?"

Suddenly Jeremiah laughed, a low chuckle that erupted into a guffaw. His bald brown head bobbed up and down with the bouncing of the car. "I wanted to leave an impression no one could forget," he said, gasping amid his laughter. "I succeeded, didn't I?"

Salome turned away from the grimacing face in the mirror. The car turned onto a wider murram road that vanished faster and faster under the front of the car like an endless red-brown waterfall. The contents of the trunk began their sliding, scraping noise. More people were on the road now. Another car skidded out of the way, blasting its horn. Jeremiah turned around in his seat to scowl after it, jamming the accelerator to the floor.

Adija squinted out the windshield. No one saw the man but her—the one with the worst eyesight of anyone! The man was trying frantically to pedal his bicycle out of the road, but the load of cane on the back was so heavy the bicycle appeared only to be wobbling in place. Adija opened her mouth, but no sound came out. She raised her hands before her face as if to push the man away.

Jeremiah slammed the brake pedal down and yanked the steering wheel. The car neither slowed nor swerved. Then the brakes caught and squealed; the car lurched sideways. The man's face expanded in Adija's window, wide-eyed and pleading; suddenly it burst against the glass in the center of a jagged star of cracks.

Adija slapped her hands over her eyes. She tilted sideways, rose, and slammed into Salome. The car balanced on two tires, then crashed down on all four again.

Adija slid across the seat, Salome tumbling after. They sat squashed together against the door, desperately sucking in air. Jeremiah's head appeared above the top of the front seat. The road was gone. Green bushes settled into place around the car.

Something was different. The motion of the car was gone! The roar of the engine had faded. Everything was very, very still.

They could see so many bushes around the car because nothing blocked their view—two of the car's doors were open, one was gone altogether, and the glass in the remaining door window had vanished.

Jeremiah stepped out and walked slowly away on unsteady legs. He was muttering "Jesus! Jesus!" over and over

again. Beyond him two things lay in the short brown grass.
One was the car door. The other was not recognizable at
first.

"*Eii!*" Groaning, Jeremiah turned away. The second
thing in the grass was the man that the car had struck. He
was crumpled in a ball, knees crushed up against his
shoulders; his head, connected by damp threads, was torn
backward, so that his face was hanging upside down in the
middle of his back. The hot bright air hummed a terrible
silence.

A man walked out of the bushes toward the car. He was
carrying a stick. Another man appeared on the other side
of the car. Voices sounded from all sides. Jeremiah tried to
run on his rubbery legs. Salome watched calmly, as if the
events outside the car were occurring in a film whose colors were too bright. Jeremiah looked comical—his knees
rose and his feet flopped as the top part of his body tried to
jerk forward ahead of his legs. He fell into the driver's seat
and groped at the dashboard for the key. His breath burst
from him in loud whines. Desperately he jabbed the key
against the switch.

The car darkened. A wall of bodies blocked out the
bushes and the air. Then the wall was gone; the car was
flooded with sunlight again.

The mob crowded around Jeremiah like safari ants on a
beetle. Arms and sticks thrashed in the air. Jeremiah's high-
pitched screams rose above the shouts of the men. Salome
caught a glimpse of him as he went down on his back, his
legs kicking in the air. His mouth gaped open in a shriek;
the sound was cut off by a heavy stick smashing his jaw
away. He disappeared behind a blur of kicking legs. The
only sound now was the thunk, thunk, thunk of feet and
sticks falling.

When the men finally backed away from Jeremiah, he
barely looked human. A weeping boy kicked the shiny
place where Jeremiah's face had been. The men dragged
the boy away. He broke from them and ran wailing to the
body of the cyclist and collapsed beside it, burying his face
in his hands.

Adija made a choking sound. Her mouth fell open. A
stream of vomit poured down the front of her dress into
her lap.

The men walked around the car, peering in. A few of

them laughed with unsmiling eyes when they saw Adija covered with vomit. Then they left; they took the body of the cyclist with them and disappeared into the bush as quickly as they had come. The stillness hung humming in the air again.

Eventually, Salome and Adija had to get out of the car; the air was too hot and stinking to breathe. Outside, Adija turned to steady herself against the door, then jumped back. The wheelless bicycle was embedded in the metal like a squashed black wasp, fender-wings and handle-bar antennae flattened out akimbo. Adija stumbled away, gripping her stomach.

Salome took her arm. Together they walked dizzily to a tree and sat beneath it. They stared into space, their eyes avoiding the sight of Jeremiah.

Finally Salome stood up and walked to the car. She touched its burning blue side, as if to see if it, and the rest of the last few minutes, were indeed real. Then she leaned against the trunk, wiping her face.

The trunk clicked open. The top of it was bent, and it stayed up in the air. Salome stared into the dark space for some time. "Look," she said finally.

Adija stepped up beside her. In the trunk lay several dozen rifles. "Guns," Adija said, blinking. "But why?"

Salome shook her head. She inspected the rifles more closely. "I've never seen rifles like these before."

"Oh." Adija gazed about her. Her eyes skipped over Jeremiah and searched the road.

"They have strange writing on them."

"What?"

"These guns. It looks like Arabic."

Adija looked. "It's not Arabic. I don't know what it is."

"We have to leave here right now!" Salome clutched Adija's arm.

"We're just going to leave him?" Adija twisted her face in the direction of Jeremiah's body. "How can we?"

"What do you want to do, dig a grave for him?"

"No—I don't know—but—"

"The Poken leave their dead out for the jackals to eat. We can too."

"But he's not Poken, he's Samoyo like you."

"He is not like me!" Salome snatched a handful of leaves from a bush and thrust them out toward Adija. "Wipe yourself off and go fetch your pullover. Don't leave anything behind. We'll go along that pasture and stop the first car that comes along."

"Gordon will come. He left just behind us."

"He's lost his way if he hasn't come by now," Salome said. "Anyway, you can forget about Gordon, after this."

Two cows ran snorting across the pasture. When a brown shirtless herdboy came chasing them, Salome ducked behind a bush and pulled Adija down with her. Adija didn't know why they were hiding. She began to glance around her as she walked, suddenly fearing that someone might appear among the trees. The sound of the cattle's hooves faded, and again the landscape was quiet. The sky was cloudless blue and serene. Adija sweated in her pullover. She wished she had remembered to fetch her purse from under the seat of the car—there was a handkerchief in it she would like to have tied over her head. She couldn't go back now. Salome was in a hurry. Salome would be angry with her for forgetting her purse, though she didn't know why. She also didn't know why Salome had said to forget Gordon. She wished Salome hadn't said it.

Adija stopped short. She felt her belly carefully. It felt little different from before. It was moving. Rather, something was moving inside it.

"What's the matter, Adija?" Salome paused.

Adija was smiling. "My baby—he's not hurt! It's alive in my belly! It's kicking!" she said, and burst into tears.

PART FIVE

26

THE STUDENTS ENTERED THE CLASSROOM AND
went straight to their seats. They did not remain standing
at their desks, waiting to be given permission to sit down.
That colonial ritual had been dispensed with, and no one
minded any longer. Seeing Mr. Lockery writing on the
blackboard, they quickly took out their notebooks for a last-
minute review. They had made this week's set of notes entirely on their own, and though they were proud of them,
they had not used the notes for a test before and were
nervous. Gordon gave them some extra time to review,
writing slowly on the board.

"O-okay!" Gordon said, and the boys mouthed the o's
along with him. "Close your notebooks, and take out some
paper. You have . . ." Gordon looked at his watch. Several
boys looked at their wrists, grinning; they were used to his
ways.

This time, though, he didn't say ". . . ten minutes—go!"
as anticipated. The classroom door opened and Clive
Wickham-Marshall stepped inside. "Mr. Lockery, may I
speak to you?"

Gordon walked to the door, hoping Clive's business
wouldn't take long; he had a lot to cover today in addition
to the test.

"The Head wants to see you in his office," Clive whispered, smiling apologetically. "Says it's important."

"Okay, thanks. I'll see him after class."

"He says he wants to see you now, I'm afraid."

"What about my class?"

"I'm supposed to take it."

"Oh." Gordon glanced at the expectant student faces
watching him. "Go ahead. Get started," he said to them.

The boys fidgeted. "How much time, sir?" one asked.

"Uh, the usual. I'll be back in a few minutes."

Still fidgeting, the boys set to work. "The usual" was an uncomfortably vague time limit.

"They're having a test," Gordon told Clive, glancing inside. "When they finish, you can just go over it—if I'm not back."

"Fine." Clive nodded.

"Hey, congratulations on your engagement. Pamela told me," Gordon said. He was paying more attention to being friendly to the other masters since the headmaster's report on him. "Will you be going to England for your honeymoon?"

"No, we'll be in Iowa for the wedding. Then I'd like to see some of the States." Clive smiled, still nodding. "After that, I've accepted a job at Rugby. In England."

"You're not coming back here?"

"No, my contract's up next month, and I'm packing it in, I'm afraid. I wanted to stay on—we both did—but . . ." Clive's smile faded. "Pam and I'll tell you about it. I think you ought to go now, though. The Head was looking rather impatient."

"Right. See you later."

Gordon walked across the compound, taking puffs on a cigarette he hid cupped in his hand. He had been smoking, illegally, between every period these days. The trouble at the circumcision ceremony was still bothering him. Adija had been moody all week too. She wouldn't talk about anything that had happened. He worried about her silences; she looked about to explode at times. Once she had started crying in the middle of the night for no apparent reason. All she would say was that she had been thinking about a woman called Odui, and how kind she'd been; Odui had given her a dress to wear, and then she hadn't had a chance to give it back to her.

You can give it to Jeremiah the next time he comes, and he can take it back there for you, Gordon suggested. Adija grimaced horribly and turned away, burrowing her face in her pillow. What was so awful about that suggestion? She'd refused to lift her face from the pillow to answer him. All night long he had lain on his back listening to her muffled whimpering.

And now more trouble—from the headmaster, this time. Gordon stomped out his cigarette and knocked on Mr. Griffin's door.

"Come in, come in. Take a seat, please." The head-master, in a more cheerful mood than usual, looked up from the form he had been reading. Two months ago he'd requested a transfer for Mr. Lockery, and nothing had happened as a result—until suddenly the request came back approved, and by government courier, no less. Mr. Griffin smiled, recalling the urgent look on the driver's face as he thrust the papers out to him. There was no rhyme or reason to the way these people did things. He gave his signature to the transfer orders an extra flourish.

Then he forced the smile to leave his face. His eyebrows dipped at the outer corners; his mustache drooped. "Mr. Lockery, I have some, well, unpleasant news for you." He picked up the papers and handed them across his desk.

Frowning, Gordon read the top sheet. It was on thin, grayish government stationery, with the paragraphs numbered 1., 2., 3., for fast reading. Gordon read the letter a second time very slowly. He looked up, dazed. "I'm supposed to report to some school in Jamhuri—*today!* What the hell's going on here?"

"I really don't know, Mr. Lockery."

"They can't do this—just send me off to another country!"

"I'm afraid they can." Mr. Griffin sighed. "As a civil servant, you're required to go where you're posted, on a moment's notice."

"But to another country?"

"Right. You can be posted to any of the countries that subscribe to the Common Services Agreement. I looked it up in the regulations for you." Mr. Griffin smiled and stroked his mustache.

"Thank you." Gordon lit a cigarette, his hands trembling, and stared at the gray letter.

"Awful nuisance, these orders can be. I remember when I first came out here, I got transferred to a school so far upcountry I had to hire a canoe to get there. They gave me a day to report. Canoe capsized twice, I remember. I got there wringing wet."

Gordon stood up. "Where is this place—Ngombwe, Jamhuri—anyway?"

"In the west somewhere." Mr. Griffin went to his wall map. "Yes, here it is—Ngombwe."

Gordon looked. The town was a tiny dot on the map,

about fifty miles from the Burundi border. The road that led to it was represented by a thin black line: "Unimproved murram, passable in dry season only." The road ended at Ngombwe; no other roads went there. Ngombwe was the dead end of East Africa.

Going back across the compound, Gordon felt like a visitor. This wasn't his school anymore. He had no function here. Suddenly he was very aware of the familiar sounds coming from the classroom windows: The scraping chairs, the drone of a teacher's voice, the eager shouting to answer a question.

He'd only just begun to get to know the students and now he'd never see them again. He'd never know what would happen to them! He watched Wickham-Marshall pacing around the room as the boys read aloud. As each boy was called on, he stood up to read—a colonial custom from the pre-Lockery days. The custom will endure long after I've gone, Gordon thought. He turned and walked away across the playing fields toward his house.

Packing slowly, he took only an hour to gather his possessions into two suitcases and two straw baskets. As he folded the *kente*-cloths from his walls, he imagined them on the walls of a similar house he and Adija would share in Jamhuri. Jamhuri would be a better place to start his life with her than Musolu, he began to tell himself. Salome would be out of the picture. Gordon began to feel better. For a while there, unseen forces had seemed to be taking over his life. Now that the initial shock of being transferred was over, though, his orders began to seem like a stroke of good luck. He couldn't wait to tell Adija. She'd forget about the circumcision ceremony disaster in no time now.

He took another hour collecting his personal books from the library. Some had been borrowed; he made arrangements with Mr. Longo to have them sent on to him in Jamhuri. Mr. Longo was one of the few masters he was genuinely sorry to say goodbye to.

"This is terrible, they should transfer you like that." Longo was frowning so intensely that Gordon felt uneasy again. "I've never heard of the government requiring a teacher to report on the same day he receives his orders."

"Yeah, it's strange," Gordon said. "But I'm not going to rush."

"This thing smells of politics." Mr. Longo scratched his head. "What did Griffin say?"

"Nothing. He just said goodbye. I didn't notice any tears in his eyes."

"He didn't offer to try to block the transfer?"

"No, I didn't ask him to, either. I didn't know it could be done."

Mr. Longo nodded, seeing the futility of the suggestion. "At any rate, you will see more of Africa."

"True."

"Will you take your woman with you?"

Gordon looked up. "You know about that?"

"Of course. This is a small community."

Gordon smiled. "Yes, I'm taking her with me."

"Well, good luck to you." Mr. Longo extended his hand. "Between you and me, you were one of the best teachers this school has ever had. When I am headmaster, I will try to encourage teachers like you, not get rid of them."

"Thanks." Gordon shook Mr. Longo's hand. "Have you been named head?"

"Two months. Griffin's contract is up then. He is going to 'train' me in the meanwhile." Mr. Longo laughed. "I will have to grow a mustache and learn to say 'Carry on, chaps!'"

"Right." Gordon smiled. "I'll write you from Jamhuri. Don't let the bloody British get you down."

On his way out of the library, he passed the school messenger, who dropped two newspapers on the periodicals table. One newspaper was from Karela, one from Azima. Gordon was in a hurry to leave, and didn't look at them.

He drove into Musolu and parked outside Adija's room. No one responded to his knocking. He knocked again, harder. Silence. Her room was empty. But this was the time of the afternoon she always took off! Her door wasn't locked. Neither was Salome's. That was very strange. He walked quickly around to the door of the New Life. Neither Adija nor Salome was there, either! What the hell was going on here?

He stepped up to the bar to talk with Patel. When he lit a cigarette, he noticed his hands were trembling again. That feeling of being buffeted about by unseen forces was creeping up on him again. "Where's Adija today?" he asked Patel, trying to make his voice sound calm.

"Don't know, Mister Lock'y. They just—" Patel waved his hand toward the door, "—just go. I am angry for those two. How old man like me to work bar alone?"

Gordon poured the beer Patel had brought. He fixed his eyes on the foam bubbling up toward the top of the glass. "Why did they go?"

Patel shook his head. "Police come in, they talk, then police go out. Later, they go. Maybe go shopping, get lift from police van."

"Yeah, maybe they went shopping."

"They must come back, those two. No one is cook supper, wash glass, nothing."

"Thanks, Patel. I'll wait here for them."

Adija and Salome did not return that afternoon. They did not return after the supper Patel grumblingly cooked. Gordon sat numbly at a table in the corner, drinking beer and staring at the door. The street outside grew dark. Patel lit the lantern for the evening crowd.

Toward nine o'clock, Simon Waga came in. Gordon told him what had happened at the school. "Bad business," Waga said. "Some kind of politics."

"Mmm."

"Where's Adija tonight?"

"I don't know." Gordon stared at the table full of empty bottles. Beyond, the orange "MAREMBO UHURU" mural flickered in the lantern light, as if the paraders and musicians were doing a jittery dance as they marched toward him. Gordon was in no mood to talk. "Tell Adija, if you see her tomorrow, that I've had to drive to Jamhuri on school business tonight," he told Waga. "I'll be back to see her Friday night." He gulped down his beer and left, stopping by Adija's room again before going to his car. The room was still empty, her door ajar, as before. Gordon paced the room, touching her dresses and sarees hanging on nails in the wall. He picked up her hairbrush and put it down again. The bottle on her bedside box smelled of her—hair oil. The breeze from the window made her empty dresses whisper as they swung gently from their nails. *Where was she?* Gordon sat on the edge of her bed, his face buried in his hands. Soon he left and went to his car.

The town was pitch black. In his headlight beams, the letters of the New Life sign on the wall of the building were just streaks of thick dirt decomposing under a layer of dust. Musolu was just another dusty little town now—two rows of shops and a potholed fruit-rinded dog-turded main street. His first home in Africa, but he was glad to be leaving it. It was time to get Adija out of here.

At dawn he stopped in a small town on the Jamhuri border for petrol and breakfast. Only one eating place was open, the Mzuri Mama Hotel, a vacant lot where someone had set up a signboard against a tree. Gordon sat on a bench drinking sweet milk-tea and eating bread, shielding his eyes from the bright morning sun with his hand as he ate. Some newspapers lay on a nearby bench, but he didn't feel like reading.

The headmaster of the Ngombwe Secondary School was not annoyed with him for arriving late. He thanked him for coming as quickly as he had. Mr. Isimu was the head-master's name, a bright young African recently graduated from the University of Budapest. He wore no khaki shorts and bush jacket, but the sort of worn-out clothes Gordon wore, including rubber-tire sandals. He leaned back in his chair and rested his feet on his cluttered desk as he spoke. "You may find our place uncomfortable, after Marembo," he told Gordon. "But I think you will like the school. We are very progressive here in Jamhuri—going our own way, instead of trying to imitate the West."

"I like it already," Gordon said, thinking: if only Musolu could have been in this country—how different my life might have been.

"We've been having a teacher shortage for one year now. The boys will be glad to see you." Mr. Isimu took a packet of cigarettes and a chipped saucer ashtray from his desk drawer and offered Gordon a smoke. "We've only five teachers, three Africans, an Asian, and a South African—a white. He's married to a Cape Coloured girl. They're political refugees enjoying their first breath of African Socialism."

"That's a coincidence." Gordon grinned. "I'm about to marry a Coloured girl too. A Bashirian."

"You're all so eager to lose your freedom to our girls!"

Mr. Isimu laughed. "We'll get the local people to build another room onto your house. It's too small for two of you."

The teachers' houses were of mud and wattle, with corrugated iron roofs and wooden windows. Bathrooms were latrines in the back yard; running water came from a pump shared with the rest of the school. He'd have to work to make his house comfortable, but he and Adija could do it together. It would be fun. He preferred mud and wattle to cinderblock any day. Adija would have the walls covered with pictures in no time.

Gordon was too busy meeting students and teachers to read a newspaper on Wednesday or Thursday. During his free period on Friday, he glanced at Wednesday's *Jamhuri Liberation*. An item on the front page caught his attention:

RUSSIAN GUNS IN BASHIRI?

Two dozen rifles said to be of Russian make were found in Bashiri near the Marembo border, four miles from the town of Musolu, Marembo. They were discovered Monday in an abandoned motorcar by a Ministry of Works maintenance lorry driver. The car has been found to be the property of a Bashirian, Mr. Jeremiah Kongwe.

People on both sides of the border have been speculating that the rifles may have been intended for delivery to Swila rebels, rumored to be active in the border area. Chief of Police for Musolu, M. Elima, states that there is no cause for alarm. He plans an investigation. Local units of the Marembo Army have been alerted in case any trouble results. Bashiri troops may be called in to patrol the Bashiri side of the border area. Bashirians in this region are to go to the polls soon, and disturbances are feared, especially as a result of this recent incident. A police spokesman in nearby Kepuria, Bashiri, had no comment, except to state that his office also planned an intensive investigation of the matter.

Gordon gripped the edge of the newspaper tight. He read the article through a second time, and a third time. Jeremiah. Salome said he was some kind of spy. He'd told her himself that he was a Special Branch man, with a phony job cover of some kind. Monday the car was found. Tuesday Gordon had received his transfer orders, and by special government courier. Tuesday had also been the day that Adija and Salome had disappeared. Disappeared. He hadn't thought of Adija's absence from Musolu as a disappearance, but the word had just come to him, suddenly sounding very sinister. Gordon set out immediately for Musolu, driving as fast as he could over the rutted dirt roads.

27

THE BABY WAS QUIET NOW, ASLEEP IN ADIJA'S belly beneath the palm of her hand. Adija shivered again. Every time the baby grew still, she was seized with fear. She told Salome about it: "I want him to live," she said through the bars of her cell. "If they beat me and kill him, I will go mad."

Salome rolled over on her bench and fixed Adija with an exhausted stare. "You say that a hundred times a day. You will go mad just from saying it. Why don't you sleep?"

"I can't. He kicks too much!" Her voice was suddenly, incongruously gay. "He loves to kick me!"

That was not the reason she couldn't sleep, though. She feared that if she slept, she would wake to find him gone. And then—she did not know what she would feel then. She might be happy.

That was her second fear. "Do you think that if a woman loses her baby, and she is glad, that it means she is mad?" Adija asked.

"It means nothing." Salome rolled over again and ran her eyes along the cracks in the cinderblock wall. "It means nothing," she repeated.

"Oh." Adija was not satisfied. It was possible that the movements within her might be made not by a human child, but by a spell. And if she lost the movements, the spell would be gone, and she would be free of witchcraft.

When had she first thought seriously about being a witch? When she had first known about the—whatever it was—inside her? When she had spoken about it to Odui? No, long, long before that. But ever since she had spoken aloud of being pregnant, everything had been going wrong. The old man had started following her everywhere with his blind eyes. Salome had fought Gordon. Adija had prevented the boy from being initiated. The man on the bicycle had appeared in the window, when no one else had seen him, and then shattered before her eyes. And then Jeremiah—even his death could have been caused by her. He would never have been driving like that if his people had not been angry with him for bringing her to his home. Of course, those men had killed him—but who had called them out of the bushes? How was it that the men had all been right there, seconds after the cyclist had been killed? And why had Jeremiah hit that particular man in that particular place—just at a time when a group of the man's friends were nearby? Why? Adija touched her belly again, as if by feeling herself she could tell what manner of creature was living within her.

But surely it was a baby. Her worries meant nothing—just as Salome said about everything nowadays. It was a little half-caste baby. Like herself.

Like herself: That was the trouble. It would be even more like herself than herself—it would be even more mixed: African, Arab, and probably European. Its presence was evidence of even more boundaries crossed, more laws transgressed, more peoples betrayed. Her mother had betrayed her people by producing an offspring of an Arab, and then by giving up her religion. Adija had gone one step further by turning her back on her sex by touching Salome, and on her Africanness by agreeing to be Gordon's woman. She could not reverse what she had done. The evidence was in her belly, whether human or spirit. Everything would come out, just as the policeman had said. They would force her to tell everything.

Adija clamped her eyes shut, trying to sort out her fears. Thoughts scrambled and rescrambled themselves in her mind; like snakes wriggling about in their sleep, they squeezed each other tight and hissed menacingly at each other; they bit each other's tails and crawled over each other to stretch toward the sunlight, but there was no sun in the tight damp pit of Adija's mind.

Sometimes she gazed past the bars of her cage at the locked steel office door. Through the window in the door, she could see figures moving about in the office, and she could see whether or not it was raining outside. She did not need to see the rain to know it was raining, however. She heard it clacking on the tin roof above her. And the walls sweated. She watched a drop of moisture make its way down from the ceiling along the mortar strips between the cinderblocks. It rolled sluggishly toward her bench, leaving a trail of shiny wetness behind it.

She stared at the window of the door. The window told her about Gordon. The window was her enemy. But she could not keep her eyes off it. The window had told her: he is not coming.

If he had come to see her, she would have seen him through the window. He would have walked in and leaned across the policeman's desk. He would be out of breath, his face shiny with sweat and smudged with dust where he had brushed the damp hair off his forehead. Where is she? I have to see her!

She would have seen him pleading, gesturing with his hands, perhaps offering the policeman money. Then, dejected, he would have turned and walked out. He would have tried again and again. He would have found a way.

And she would have known he was trying to see her. She would know that he did not think she was to blame for all the terrible things that had happened.

"Do you know, I was going to marry him?" Adija exclaimed out loud.

Salome lifted her head. No, she hadn't known that. If she had had a pot in her cell, she would have flung it through the bars at Adija's head. "It doesn't surprise me, you'd do a thing like that," she said. "It doesn't surprise me that he hasn't come to claim you either."

"You hate him," Adija said.

Salome turned to face Adija again, groaning as her ribs pricked the inside of her chest like daggers. She counted four of them broken, but there must have been more. "No. I don't hate him. I did, for a long time. Not just because he was a European, or because he was your lover."

Adija squinted at Salome, at her lips, at the creases below her broad nose, into her bruised eyes. "Why then?"

"Because he was like me. He had everything, but he was still like me. That's why I hated him."

Adija shook her head, not understanding.

"He was clever—he was the only person in that stinking town clever enough for me to waste my time talking with.

Also, he was different from the rest, like me—he wasn't like the Africans or the other Europeans. No one else could have . . ." Salome winced from the pain in her chest. She decided not to finish the sentence, which would have gone: No one else could have taken you from me but him. "Myself, I was like him," she continued, "but what did I have? Nothing. Half a filthy fly-buzzing bar. Nothing. Him, he had everything. A good job, respect, power, book learning. He had Africa, and he could go home to his own country whenever he wanted to, as well. And he had you."

"You envied him."

Salome made a face. "He is made of flesh and blood, and jelly in his heart. What's to envy? He fears things. And when he fears, he runs, just like other people. That's why I'm not surprised he hasn't come here."

"He's fearing me." Adija sat up straight, staring at the window. "Yes, he must be."

"No, just fearing trouble. No one wants to get involved in trouble."

Adija didn't hear her reply. The thought of Gordon fearing her had lodged in her mind like a machete stroke. Of course, he feared her. Look how she attracted disasters. "He has stayed away because he fears, not because he doesn't love me." Adija tried the thought out loud. When she glanced at Salome, she saw that Salome was asleep again.

Poor Salome. Her face was contorted into an expression of pain. One leg was stretched out beside her, the one that would not bend. The other was bent tight beneath her. Her hands were clenched in fists and she groaned with every breath.

All Salome had done was to ask the policeman a favor—to deliver some message to Patel in Musolu. She'd offered the policeman her last thirty shillings too. He snatched the note from her, then refused her request. First, you sign this confession, he said. Salome read it, spat on it, and threw it in the man's face. Then he beat her. Adija screamed at first, then closed her eyes tight, trying to shut out the picture of the man smashing his truncheon down on Salome again and again.

"I won't sign the paper either," Adija had shouted, when the policeman had finally finished with Salome. It wasn't fair that Salome should be beaten and not her—when she had caused all the trouble in the first place. "Go ahead, beat me!" she screamed.

Then the army officer had pushed open the door and grabbed the policeman. He took one look at Salome and slammed the policeman against the wall. The suspects are not to be harmed! he'd shouted. They must be alive to stand trial! Now get out!

Adija had thought perhaps the army officer wanted her for himself, but he merely turned and walked out the door, shoving the policeman ahead of him.

Another policeman had been on guard the night afterwards. His friend must have been sacked, Adija thought. The new man approached Salome's cell, threatening revenge on her. Salome was asleep. The policeman thought Adija was sleeping too, but she watched him as he loosened his belt and opened his trousers in front of her door.

"No!" Adija whispered loudly. "She has had enough!"

The man glanced at her, undecided. Adija rose from her bench and pressed herself against the bars. She caught his eye in the glare of the light bulb. She opened her eyes very wide, as she rarely dared do when looking at anyone, much less a man. As she stared, she began to press her thighs against the bars, as if her body were yearning for him. All the while, her eyes kept drawing him toward her. If I have the evil eye, I will make the most of it, she thought, grinding her hips against the cold metal.

So he had opened her door instead of Salome's. As he pried her knees apart and entered her, she looked at Salome, thinking: Please, don't wake up, Salome! Salome's eyes were swollen shut. The thought struck her: If I can do this with a man, then I am like any other woman—I can't be a witch. She rested her head against the wall and tried to concentrate on the feeling he was giving her, to convince herself that it was really happening. Shivering, she felt the man withdraw. She lay down against the wall, clutching her belly. No, he hadn't penetrated far enough to stab her baby. Was she glad? She didn't know. Since that night, her hand never left her belly for an instant.

Adija stared around her. The door had opened. The army officer and a policeman had come in.

Salome groaned and rubbed her eyes.

"Not that one," the army officer said, as the policeman stepped up to Salome's doors. "We've got hers from Azima. We need the other one's."

The policeman went to Adija's cell and unlocked it with his big clanking key.

"When are you going to tell us why you're keeping us here?" Salome demanded.

The policeman ignored her. "Come on, you!" he said to Adija.

"No!" Adija whimpered.

"She doesn't know anything. Leave her alone!" Salome shouted.

"Shut up, both of you." The policeman yanked his key from Adija's door with a loud, scraping noise. Adija pressed herself back against the wall, turning her face sharply sideways. As the policeman approached, she shut her eyes tight.

"Stand up, woman. We just want you in the office for a moment."

Salome pushed against the bars, trying to shake them. "She doesn't know anything!" she screamed.

Again the policeman ignored her. He grabbed Adija by the wrists and lifted her to her feet.

The lights in the office were bright; long tubes of glowing white glass buzzed and vibrated and stung her eyes. She stared at the wall inches from her face, not moving until the policeman yanked her arm.

"Give me your thumb," he muttered, prying open her fist.

"Why?"

"Just hold still, damn it!" He jammed her thumb down hard onto a soft, cold pad. Then he picked it up again and pressed it onto a piece of paper with English words on it. Adija stared at the paper. When her thumb came back, it was purple. There was a mark on the paper that looked just like the skin of her thumb.

"No!" Shrieking, she wrenched her hand away. She dove directly for the eyes of the policeman, her fingers extended.

She twisted and thrashed. She shook her head back and forth wildly, tears flying off in all directions. The army officer pinned her arm high behind her back. The pain froze her. Gasping, she let the guard take her hand and press it, finger by finger, onto the pad and then the paper. He did the same to her other hand, his grip making her wrist burn. Then, muttering, he pushed Adija toward the door.

She walked limply back into her cell and collapsed on her bench.

"What did they do to you?" Salome pressed her face against the bars.

Adija raised her hands, showing Salome her purple fingers.

"Oh. I thought they were beating you, the way you were screaming." Salome lay down again. "Wash your hands."

Adija did as she was told. The tap was near the floor. As she squatted to hold her hands under the water, urine rushed out of her, splashing hot against her ankles. Adija watched it splatter against the cold cement, as if she did not know what was making it do that. "It stings," she whimpered.

"What's the matter, Adija?"

Adija shook her head.

"Use the paper there. What's the matter with you?"

"They took my fingers. They squeezed them down, and when they took them off, they had—they had the skin of my fingers, just there on their paper."

"So?"

"They can harm me. They just have to do things to my fingers on the paper, and I—they can poison me, they can make me do anything, say anything."

"You believe that?"

"They could kill my baby!"

"Nonsense, Adija."

"I know. But I fear it. I can't help it."

Salome lay back, resting her head against the hard wood of her bench. "You're hopeless, Adija. In one breath, you say you want to marry a European, and in the next, you are fearing people will use your fingerprints to make magic against you."

Adija sat on her bench, shivering. Her teeth were chattering so hard she thought they would break. "I won't let them hurt me," she said, pressing her arms over her belly. "My magic is stronger than theirs." She stared through the window of the door, her eyes wide.

Salome rolled over. She wanted desperately to sleep. But there was never any darkness in this cage. All day and all night the light burned. No matter how hard she shut her eyes, the light singed through her eyelids and turned everything to a quivering pinkish gray, as if she were being forced to stare at the inside of her guts.

Adija was speaking. "Why do you think they took pictures of my fingers, and not yours?"

Silence.

"I think I know. I think I know why they wanted me," Adija said.

Salome groaned and lay still. Then she spoke in her mind: I don't know why, Adija—but go ahead and imagine that you do. Imagine that they want to control your magic powers. But don't ask me about it. I don't know anything. I have no answers. Do what you have to do to look for answers, but don't expect me to do it for you. Perhaps I will do it *with* you, but not *for* you. Perhaps. Perhaps. That is the best answer to any question. Try out anything. If you want to try madness, try it. If you want to think you are a witch, try that. It doesn't matter what you try. It is all the same in the end anyway.

Be a witch. There are witches too. Like madness, they are not so difficult to find. You find them in a dark slimy corner of your heart, if you are truly willing to look there. Being a witch is not a bad way to be, considering the alternatives. All you have to do is say: All right, I am indeed what you always suspected—look! But beware, now. No more jokes, no sly allusions—I am just what I seem! So treat me with caution.

Say to them: You want to taste my powers—come! Dip your softest part into my softest part for a moment. Stir it around in my cauldron. You know you've always wanted to experience a whore's forbidden darkness, a little smoldering pungent heat, a little mystery. There's your mystery, look—your softest part is even softer, even smaller. You're lucky I didn't dissolve it in my juices and make it disappear altogether. Now pay for your visit, and pay well. I have left a spell on you: guilt. It will eat away your heart if you do not pay. There, thank you, the spell is lifted—until the next time. And the next time. Those next times will come, those urges to seek the slime, to pit your strength against my juices. That much of a spell remains with you.

Say to them: You can never pay enough to remove it. But don't let that stop you from trying!

Salome's grin faded. She turned slowly and stared at Adija.

I have learned a lot about witchcraft from you, Adija. Never had I touched a woman's body the way you taught me to touch yours. When I had done it, I felt the spell. I thought: Now I must be good to this girl. I was thinking as a man thinks—I owe her something: How can I rid myself of this uneasiness? This debt.

I thought I had to pay, like a man. But I have to pay for nothing. Your spell over me is broken. You broke it with your European. I watched his face, suffering from what he thought was love for you. Love! I knew that feeling: Love Adija, protect Adija! Soft, fragile, scurrying Adija. If you don't, your brain and your heart will be eaten away and something soft and fragile within you will die. Let Adija be hurt, you hurt yourself; love Adija, and learn how to love yourself.

Ha! It was so plain on that white man's face. He hated himself so! The white man's guilt is such a fertile field for harvesting! Centuries of cruelty, enslaving, trickery, exploitation—each new white man must pay for it all by himself.

But I am no European, and no man. I may have European knowledge in my brain. I may be nearly as strong as a man—I learned this behind those huts with your European. But my brains and my strength meant nothing that night, and that was something I had to learn.

I am a woman in a cage, like you, Adija—nothing more, nothing less. If they release me from this cage, other cages will lie in wait to snap around me—the sky, the horizon, city streets, barrooms and bedrooms. Eyes and windows and mirrors will reflect reflecting my hollowness. I will fall into a cage each time I peer into the pit of my soul; I will never live without a cage to struggle against.

So I will just keep fleeing from my cages. But I will not pay for having been caged. I have nothing to pay for, I have nothing to pay with. Here I am: Salome fleeing, Salome.

Keys clanked against metal. Another beating, or another bowl of maize-meal porridge, Salome thought, pretending to sleep. Just let it be over with quickly.

The policeman leaned against the bars of Adija's cell. "Your friend is asleep again, Adija. She is missing the fun."

Adija turned her face away.

"Have you missed me, Adija?"

"No!"

"What's that you say?"

Adija pressed herself back against the wall, drawing her knees close to her belly. "No," she said.

The policeman laughed. He took a bottle of home-brewed gin out of his tunic, drank from it, and then wiped his mouth. The whites of his eyes shone with red veins. "Then I will go next door, as I was going to do last time." His lips twitched into a smile. "I prefer a woman with some meat on her, anyway."

"No. She can't. She is injured." Adija glared at him.

Laughing, the policeman replaced the bottle in his pocket. He unlocked Adija's door. As she watched him, she numbly rearranged her legs on the bench. When he pushed between her knees, she held the shaft of his penis in her hand to make sure he did not push in too far. Whatever I have in my belly, she thought, I am going to keep it.

Salome turned over groggily. Then she leaped to her feet and clutched the bars. She pressed her forehead against the cold metal, staring. Adija's head bobbed back and forth with the man's thrusting movements. Her eyes were half-closed. When she saw Salome, she stared back. Adija's lips were tight, but a weary smile entered her eyes.

"Adija!" Salome tried to shake the bars. "You don't have to—not for me—"

The policeman stopped moving. Adija sat back, resting, her gaze still on Salome.

"Go away, woman!" The policeman shouted at Salome, panting.

"Bastard! Where do you think I can go?"

"Turn your face away!"

"Why—is what you're doing so personal?"

Adija laughed. She looked up into the man's face, her eyes growing enormous.

"You, what do you think you are doing?" The guard slapped her with the back of his hand. Her face turned back toward him, smiling strangely. His heavy breathing was suddenly loud in the cell. Moisture dripped from the ceiling and hissed against the hot light bulb.

"All right, if you keep playing games, you'll get no supper tonight." The man took out his bottle again, waiting.

Adija moved sideways on the bench toward Salome. She reached out her hand and gripped Salome's around the bars.

"Stare all you want, you pair of witches!" He tipped his bottle up to his lips, then stepped closer to Adija again. "Stop moving around!"

Adija spread her knees for him, and he stepped between them, grinning.

Salome's arm shot out. She caught his wrist and pulled. Off balance, the man fell. Salome's other arm went around his neck and yanked him tight against the bars.

No matter how he struggled, the man could not free himself. He tried to cry out, but only a gasp escaped, as if his windpipe were collapsing.

"Now, policeman, where is your great power? Shriveled!"

Adija laughed. Then her face grew frightened again. "Are you going to kill him, Salome?"

"Perhaps." She tightened her grip on his neck, showing that she could do it if she decided to.

"We can take his key," Adija said.

"No, that army man is in the office."

Adija's face fell. "Oh."

"This man can do a good deed for us, though. Because—" Salome spoke into the policeman's ear. "You know what happened to your friend, *bwana*, the one who beat me. You know he got sacked, don't you?"

The man gurgled. His eyes had begun to bulge.

"Now, here you are with your cock dangling out. If we start to scream, and that officer comes in and finds you, you are finished."

The man tried to struggle free again, but Salome froze him with a tightening of her arm on his neck. "Listen, think about losing your job. All we have to do is complain to that officer, show him your cock and your gin bottle, and you're through. Think of that."

"We should complain about him," Adija agreed.

"Wait. I want him to think about losing his job. No more happy life, no more bribes coming in, no more pension accumulating. You'll have to wander about looking for work. But a sacked policeman—who would trust a man like that? And your wife—what will she say?"

The man tried to shake his head. "Stop!" he gasped.

"Ha! 'Stop' is what she'll say. You'll tiptoe into your bedroom, and there she'll be—curled up on her side, her back to you. 'Stop. Don't come in here begging for my thighs to open for you. You have no job, no respectability. Don't you try to disgrace me with your filthy cock. Go dip it into some prisoner!' That's what she'll say!"

"Everyone will know about it," Adija added. "Your friends will laugh at you."

"You'll wander about the roadsides, drinking your cheap gin and muttering to yourself. You'll go back to the land and scrape the earth for a few vegetables—that's all that will be left for you. Your back will ache and your children's bellies will puff out with hunger. People will say, 'He was a policeman once, but he disgraced himself with a woman prisoner, and now no female will have him but the sow in his neighbor's sty!' "

The man's lips grew paler and paler. His legs gave out beneath him, but Salome's arm held him up by the chin.

"Look at Adija!" Salome continued, hissing into his ear. "See how she stares at you. Look at those enormous eyes. You will never forget them. You will see them even as you fall into the gutter and gasp your last stinking breath."

Adija's eyes glowed. The man tried to turn his face away, but Salome locked his head in place.

"Perhaps, though, you'd help us, in return for us letting you keep your job." Salome relaxed her grip on his neck long enough for him to nod in bug-eyed agreement.

The man slid to his knees, gasping and holding his neck. Salome took some sheets of folded toilet paper from her bodice. "Take this note to Patel, the shopkeeper in Musolu. Tell him to write his name on a paper. Bring it back to me, so I will recognize his handwriting and know you've done as I told you." Salome tossed the papers down. "Don't bother trying to read it, though—it's in English. At last I've found a use for my education." She laughed.

"Why are you writing to Patel?" Adija asked, when the man had gone. "What can he do for us?"

"He can give my message to your schoolteacher friend," Salome said, smiling. "Gordon is going to make himself useful, finally."

28

ELIMA WAS FURIOUS. HADN'T HE BEEN THE one to apprehend the two criminals? Hadn't his statement been the first to appear in the newspapers? What right did the Bashiri police—and army too!—have to move the two to Kepuria? He was the one who should have jurisdiction over them.

He ran his handkerchief around the back of his thick neck; then he polished the brass buttons of his uniform with it. The handkerchief came back filthy. Dust. Always he was covered with dust. The police station at Kepuria had an electric fan, and an electric water machine with a big bulb of cool water gurgling on top of it. What did he have to keep him cool? A handkerchief!

He read over his report to the Bashiri police that stated the behavior of the two defendants at the time of their arrest. Without that report, they would have no case. Adija had plainly admitted their guilt! "I knew we couldn't run away. I knew they would come for us," she had stated.

Elima had much more information about the two, valuable information. But was he included in the briefing session for the prosecuting attorney and the Bashiri police? No. He was merely told to go back to the Marembo side of the border and say nothing to the press. Who did those Bashirians think they were, ordering him about? They were not going to silence him.

"You may enter now!" he called through the open door of his office.

A young man rose from the bench in the corridor. He walked rapidly into the office of the Police Chief, his notebook and pencil ready. Elima greeted him, tugging his tunic down over his protruding belly before offering his hand. "Be seated," he said, pointing at a wooden chair in the corner.

"I have a statement ready." Elima glanced over the notes on his desk, reports two of his constables had given him concerning what they had overheard at the briefing session in Kepuria. "This is a case of murder," he began. "If people in Bashiri want to believe political intrigue is involved, that is their concern."

"Intrigue?" The reporter looked up.

"Let me go on. A murder case, I say. Both women had excellent motives to kill Mr. Jeremiah Kongwe. Fact: The defendant Salome Wairimu was connected with Mr. Kongwe during the struggle for Independence in Bashiri. She had betrayed her people by giving information about guerrilla activities to the British, to a Captain Ennis. Mr. Kongwe told me this himself. Salome Wairimu was fearing that Mr. Kongwe might make this information known here in Marembo and have her repatriated.

"Fact: The defendant Adija had been accused of witchcraft at the initiation ceremony of the son of Bartholemu Ojika—this was reported to me by Mr. Ojika himself, following the identification of Mr. Kongwe. Adija blamed Mr. Kongwe for not defending her against the accusation. She also feared that her story would be made public—her reputation in this town was suspect anyway. These are the facts in this tragic case."

The young man scribbled frantically in his notebook. "And how was the murder accomplished, in your opinion?" he asked.

"The two women found themselves alone with Mr. Kongwe in a deserted place," Elima said. "They did him in with a tire iron—this weapon was found near the scene of the crime. Then they attempted to destroy his body beyond recognition by beating it with sticks. They made a crude attempt to smash the car, to make the death look like the result of an accident. The two women then fled."

"How did you come to suspect them?"

"One of them—Adija—left her purse in the car, under the seat."

"I see." The reporter chewed the eraser of his pencil and looked cautiously at Elima. "And the rifles? Can you say what they were doing in the boot of the car?"

"The rifles, they were doing nothing. They were merely lying there." Elima chuckled. He narrowed his eyes at the reporter, to show that his joke was a subtle way of saying that he had been entrusted with secret information about the rifles that he was not at liberty to discuss. In fact, he had no idea how the rifles had come to be in the car.

"Would you say that it is possible that the two women were in collusion with the Swila rebels, and planned to deliver the rifles to them?"

"It is possible." Elima thought for a moment. "No, not possible. That would have meant Mr. Kongwe would have known about the rifles. You must print nothing like that. Scratch it out."

The reporter drew heavy lines through his notes. "Did you see the rifles yourself?"

"Oh, yes, I saw them," Elima smiled. "I was the first police officer on the scene, and I saw them very well. The Bashiri police did not arrive for hours afterward."

"I see." The reporter sat up eagerly. "Would you describe the rifles, please?"

Elima frowned. The Bashiri police had warned him not to say anything about the rifles. But so what? He was not a member of the Bashiri police force. "They were clearly not British or American rifles. The letters on them were not English letters—they were not even the kind used in any other language I have seen."

"Had you ever seen rifles like them before, in your experience?"

Elima shook his head slowly. "Never, in all my experience."

The reporter smiled. His writing hand was trembling with excitement, and his notes dashed all over the page of his notebook. "And the two women, the suspects—who are they?"

"They were barmaids, in Musolu. Both Bashirians, however. One is from Azima—she was the one who was a terrorist and a betrayer at one time, according to Mr. Kongwe. The other one, Adija, she was probably a Moslem from the Northern Frontier Province."

"MOSLEM (?)" the reporter wrote in capital letters across the top of a new page. "And how long had they lived in Musolu?"

Elima frowned. Salome had been there two years without papers—an embarrassment for him. "I'm not at liberty to give any more information," he said. "My statement is finished."

"Do you have any photographs of the suspects?"

"No." Elima said. "But you can take a picture of me."

* * *

Approaching the Marembo border, Gordon saw a green army van and slowed down. When he had entered Jamhuri from Marembo two days ago, he hadn't seen any border guards, only a single mud hut with a woman grinding maize in the front yard. Today, though, a border guard stood in the middle of the road. He wore a khaki tunic, with a white wrapper that flapped in the breeze around the tops of his black boots. Seeing the man raise his rifle, Gordon rolled to a stop.

"Passport," the man said, craning his neck to look into the car.

Gordon handed him his passport through the open window. The man removed a cracked pair of spectacles from his tunic pocket and opened the little book. "America?" he said, glancing up.

Gordon nodded, drumming his fingers against the window frame. Dammit, was this guy going to read the entire book?

The man turned the pages slowly. "No stamp Jamhuri. When you enter?"

"Two days ago—Wednesday. Very early in the morning. No one was here."

The man nodded and took the passport into his hut. When he finally came back with it, it was stamped with an entry pass to Jamhuri dated Wednesday and a Marembo entry permit dated Friday.

A few miles past the border post, within sight of the village where he had stopped for breakfast Wednesday morning, Gordon's car began bouncing noisily. He drove on slowly, hearing a scraping noise from the rear wheels. It grew louder as he drove into the town.

"Shocks, finish," the mechanic at the garage told him.

"Can the car be driven anyway?"

"Without shocks—no. Springs go quick. Then axle. Then car, finished."

Gordon clenched and unclenched his fists. The late afternoon sun glinted on the tin roof of the garage and ricocheted directly into his eyes. "Can you replace the shocks?"

"No, not today."

"It has to be done today. It has to be!"

"Take one hour, two maybe. I go home, fifteen minutes."

"How much do you want for the job, dammit?"

The man frowned. "No dammit."

"All right, all right." Gordon shuffled his feet in the dirt. "Sorry, *bwana*. It's an emergency. How much, please?"

"Two hundred fifty shilling."

Gordon swallowed hard, and nodded.

The Mzuri Mama Hotel was serving supper: rice and charcoaled meat of some kind. Gordon wolfed it down with a beer. He asked the proprietor if he had a newspaper. No, he had none. The merchants along the one street of the town had no newspapers either. One old Indian told him to check at the garage; an African lorry driver named Mohammed always came through on Fridays and he might have a newspaper from Karela. Mohammed had already gone, but he had left some newspapers and magazines in the office. The office was a patch of earth covered with a tarpaulin stretched over four poles. All of Friday's paper except the want ads was missing. It had been used to soak up an oil spill. Gordon cursed so loudly he had to apologize to the mechanic. An old copy of *Life* and a British football magazine remained. Gordon sat on the ground against a tree stump and smoked cigarettes. He leafed through the magazines without really seeing any of the pictures. The sun set before him, sinking slowly in the coral-like branches of an acacia tree. The plains glowed a deep purple. Tropical birds sang passionately. Some monkeys scampered down a tree and chased each other to and fro, screeching and snorting. It was the sort of scene that magazine photographers waited a lifetime to capture. African sunset, Gordon thought, closing the *Life*. His eyes ached.

*   *   *

He decided to drive through Mbure, to check with Elima. Just in case. Mbure was on the way to Musolu anyway—it would take only a few minutes. He turned into town, then skidded to a halt.

An army van faced him, its lights glaring against his bug-spattered windshield. The van stood directly in the center

of the road. On both sides of it loops of barbed wire coiled
into the bushes. A uniformed soldier approached Gordon's
car, his rifle lowered.

"What's the matter?" Gordon asked, leaning out the
window.

The soldier shone a torch in his face, then swept it over
the interior of the car. "This is a restricted area," he said.
"No entry without special permit."

Gordon dropped his forehead against the steering wheel.
"Since when is this a restricted area?" he asked, lifting his
head.

"Since this morning." This soldier eyed him carefully.
"If you have no special permit, you will have to go away.
The road to Azima is still open—you can get into Bashiri
that way."

"I don't want to go to Bashiri. I want to go to Mbure."

The soldier shook his head.

"Why is this a restricted area, all of a sudden?"

"Trouble."

"What's going on?"

"Trouble." The soldier's face remained immobile. "You
can go to Bashiri on the Azima road. This road is closed."

"I don't want to go to—" Gordon wiped his forehead.
His heart was pounding wildly. "How can I get a special
permit? Can I get it from you?"

"No. In Karela. You can go to the Ministry of Home
Affairs."

"Karela!" Karela was five hours away. Then five hours
back. Just to get a lousy piece of paper! "Can't you issue
me a temporary pass or something? I just want to visit for
a few minutes, for Christ' sake!"

The man shook his head. "The Ministry of Home Affairs
is open on Saturday mornings from eight-thirty until noon.
They can give you a permit."

Gordon stared at the headlights of the van on the road
before him. They stared back with a gaze of bureaucratic
obstinacy. He turned his car around.

The road to Musolu was open. But just beyond the
entrance to the school, the road was blocked again: another
van, more coils of barbed wire, four soldiers standing outside a tent. Gordon turned off the road and drove to the
school. No point in being told again to go to Karela. He
parked in front of his old house. No one had replaced him

in it yet; the windows were shut tight. Fuck it—when I find Adija, I'm going to come back up here and build a fire in the stove and take a long, hot bath, he thought. Walking across the compound, he remembered the first time Adija had taken a bath in his tub. Gordon ran down the path toward the town.

The government office was ablaze with light. The noise of shouting rose up the hill. Gordon stood behind a tree, watching. Several glaring pressure lamps swung from the porch roof of the building. The porch and all the open space of the *baraza* were jammed with people. They were pacing about, shouting at one another and the building. Around the periphery of the crowd were blankets tended by old men, *waganga*; these men were doing a brisk trade in roots and herbs.

Walking in a wide arc around the *baraza*, he entered Musolu from a path that came out behind the New Life. He stopped outside Adija's and Salome's rooms. They were locked with heavy padlocks. Bigger and newer padlocks than Adija's and Salome's. Gordon caught his breath, and raced around the building into the bar.

No Adija. No Salome. He leaned against the doorframe, sweat trickling down his sides.

The bar was crowded. Bottles stood three and four deep on the tables. The wireless was blaring Kisemi pop music. Gordon searched the room again. Several men in uniform, many men whose haircuts and shoes revealed that they had recently changed out of uniforms. But no Adija.

Patel and his son Rajni were behind the bar, rushing back and forth with trays and glasses and bottles. Patel's face gleamed with sweat; its mottled skin looked pock-marked with worry.

"Patel—where is she?" Gordon demanded.

Patel rushed past him, glancing away.

"Where is she, goddammit—please!"

Patel snatched up a bottle and put it down before him. "Three shilling fifty cent," he said loudly, then lowered his head. "I don't know. I don't know anything. Not to ask me!" he whispered.

Gordon watched him rush away. He took a long gulp of beer from the bottle. Wiping his eyes, he looked around the room. Simon Waga was sitting alone at a table in a corner, mercifully out of the main glare of light.

"I thought you were in Jamhuri," Waga said, extending his hand uneasily.

"I came back," Gordon said. "I want to find Adija."

"Aah . . ."

"Where is she?" He sat down, clanking his bottle against the table top. "What's going on?"

Waga looked at him over the top of his glass. "You've not heard, have you? *Eii!*" He shook his head.

"*Eii* what, man? What's happened?"

"She's in jail. She and Salome. They took her to Mbure on Tuesday, the day you were looking for her. Elima took them that morning."

"She's in Mbure now?"

"No, they transferred her to Kepuria, across the border."

"But why have they got her in jail?"

Waga glanced around the room, then lowered his head to speak. "They're saying Adija and Salome murdered Jeremiah Kongwe. He was killed on the road near here. It was in the newspapers."

"I saw that story. But why the hell do they think—" Gordon lowered his voice and leaned forward. "Why do they say she and Salome *murdered* the bastard?"

"Is nonsense, I think. Politics. Very bad business."

Gordon took a long gulp of beer and swallowed hard. "Are they serious? Murder?"

"That's what the newspapers say. Elima gave a statement to the Marembo *Journal.* As soon as the paper came out, the area was sealed off—no more journalists allowed in. Elima is in big trouble."

"Good." Gordon looked around dizzily. "This is crazy. This is—Waga, listen, can I borrow your motorbike to go to Kepuria?"

"You don't want to go there. The place is seethe with police and soldiers."

"What?"

"Seethe. Seething with police. Is that not right?"

Gordon peeled the label off his bottle, his fingernails digging hard into the damp paper. "Yes, yes. It's very good. But I have to get to Kepuria."

Waga leaned forward again. "How did you get here? Didn't you get stopped by the soldiers outside the town?"

"I left my car at the school and walked."

"You have no special permit?"

Gordon shook his head.

"Better you don't stay here. At the school, you are out-side the permit area, but here—" Waga glanced around, "—these men, they can arrest you."

"But I have to get to Kepuria. I have to see her."

Waga shook his head slowly.

"Tell me what this is all about, Waga! Why has she really been arrested?"

Waga reached onto a chair and picked up two news-papers. He dropped them in front of Gordon and stood up. "Read there—then go back to the school, and get into your car. Go back to Jamhuri tonight."

"Why?"

"I don't know. But I know that if the government wanted you here, they wouldn't have sent you to Jamhuri."

"What do you mean?"

"I just say: Go back to Jamhuri."

Gordon shut his eyes. "I can't. I can't just *leave!*"

"Listen, people in here know you knew Adija. They can make trouble." Waga gulped down the last of his beer. "Myself, I have to leave now. Come to the dispensary—but don't follow too close behind me."

Gordon shrank back in his seat as he watched Waga walk away. For the first time in months, he was aware of being the only European in the room. He had no special permit. Without a dark skin and a special permit, he felt stark naked; he was an open sore no one could help notic-ing. He held the Karela *Journal* up in front of his face. But his white knuckles were protruding around the edge of the paper. There was no way of hiding. His eyes skipped all over the page, incapable of taking in anything but head-lines. Elima's face, fat and shiny in the photograph, smiled at him.

MBURE POLICE CHIEF'S STATEMENT LINKS
BARMAIDS TO KILLING OF BASHIRI MAN
Ex-terrorist and Moslem Woman Held

Gordon felt sick. More headlines:

TROOPS CALLED TO BOTH SIDES OF BORDER
Swila Activity Rumored

WEAPONS IN ABANDONED CAR
NOT BRITISH OR AMERICAN
Musolu Police Chief States

He rose slowly, and taking a deep breath, strode across
the room toward the door. He tried to look casual; when
he felt eyes on him, he covered the lower part of his face,
pretending to cough. Once out the door, he broke into a
run toward the dispensary.

Waga was eating dinner with a United Nations nurse, a
plump Trinidadian with a high squeaky voice and hair
braided into ringlets, West African style. She brought Gordon a bowl of steaming gumbo.

"You look terrible," Waga said. "I think you are suffering from hypertension."

Gordon sat back in his chair, blinking at the lantern.
"Yeah," he said.

Waga poured him a glass of brandy. He watched Gordon drink it down and refilled his glass. "Why are you
back? You know you can do nothing here, except get en-
snarled in the long arms of the law."

"I'm going to Kepuria," Gordon said. "I'm going to get a
lift with a lorry or something. If they catch me, they can
throw me out, and I'll just come back in again. At least I
can see her."

Waga sipped his brandy. "A man so much in love—it is
a sad sight sometimes."

Gordon lowered his head over his bowl of gumbo and
ate several spoonfuls. It was burning the roof of his mouth,
but he didn't care. "Mmm?" he asked. "Yeah, I'm a mess.
Maybe I could sleep here tonight, do you think?"

"Of course." Waga stood up and paced around the table.
"There are troops everywhere now. You can't get through
to Kepuria."

"Perhaps he can get a permit," the nurse suggested.

Gordon shook his head. He felt sick.

"Don't you like the gumbo?" the nurse asked, looking
concerned. "I always make it for Simon when I visit."

"I like it very much, ma'am."

"My name is Cindy," she said, giggling.

"Right." Gordon rubbed his eyes. Waga had introduced
Cindy before. "Sorry."

"Not to worry." She looked at him closely. "Simon, your friend needs some more brandy."

Waga continued to pace. Suddenly he slammed the table with his fist. "You should not go to Kepuria!" he shouted. "There's too much trouble there—don't you hear me!"

"I'm going!" Gordon shouted back, glaring up red-eyed at Waga. He sat back, breathing hard. "Man, if I think about it, I come up with a thousand reasons to run back to Jamhuri and forget the whole thing," he said. "But I still keep struggling to get to her. This thing's gone out of control now. I have to get her back!"

"All right." Waga nodded, sighing. He took some folded tissue paper out of his desk. "A man came from Kepuria today. He brought these from Salome, and gave them to Patel. Patel gave them to me, since I can read English. He didn't want any part of them, and neither did I."

The first part of the letter deeded Salome's share in the New Life Hotel to Patel, instructing him to keep that money for her. It then gave directions to a box of money Salome had hidden in a rafter above her room. Instructions followed to take the box to a certain attorney in Azima and offer him its contents in return for his services. Then the letter went on to tell the attorney what to say at Salome's and Adija's trial. This was the part of the letter that alarmed Waga.

"You see, it is political," he said, when Gordon put down the papers.

"I understand," Gordon said. "I'm finally beginning to understand."

"That attorney would never say those things that Salome writes."

"I could say them, though. Anyway, I'm a witness—I drove Jeremiah's car. I know how dangerous it was."

"Maybe they'll believe you about that, but not about the other things."

"When they hear about Jeremiah, they'll listen," Gordon said.

"They don't want to hear that," Waga said. "They don't want to know."

"There's been too much I haven't wanted to know too . . ." Gordon folded the papers and put them into his pocket.

"I'll have to borrow an axe or something from you, Waga. I'm going to break down Salome's door and get that box."

"And take it to that lawyer?"

Gordon nodded.

"All right. I can't stop you." Waga shook his head. He glanced at Cindy, and she went to the stove to fill Gordon's bowl again.

29

B EFORE ENTERING POLITICS, MANFRED OGOT had gained fame by defending African leaders accused by the British of aiding the guerrilla fighters. He had enhanced his notoriety by marrying a British actress and keeping a number of African mistresses, one of whom had been Salome. Following Independence, he shocked his former comrades again by resigning from the Bashiri Party and helping to organize the new Bashiri African Nationalist Union. In the recent election—held in Azima though canceled in the Western Province—he had lost by a close count to a BP candidate. People were surprised that he had agreed to serve as defense counsel for two barmaids accused of murder in a remote western border region. It was agreed that his presence there could clarify the political significance of the trial that the newspapers had been hinting about. His appearance in Kepuria made good copy for the papers, and caused a flurry of embarrassment among local government officials.

Ogot arrived in Kepuria driving a yellow MG convertible. This in itself made a stir among the local people, who had never seen such a vehicle before. Tall, prematurely balding, he looked very smart in his three-piece English suit and pointed Italian shoes. Flashbulbs popped as he stood beside his little car signing the forms that permitted him and his witness to enter the courtroom. Evading the press, he wandered through the market, then cut back into the town and entered the Uhuru Bar.

Gordon was waiting for him, sitting at a corner table with a bottle of beer. He had bought a suit in Azima, and had his hair cut, but his shoes were caked with red-brown dust.

"You look as if you walked here from Azima," Ogot said, joining him at the table.

Gordon took a gulp of beer and stared down into his glass. "That's the way I feel too."

"How did you get here, by the way?"

"I left my car outside of town and walked in."

"No special permit?"

Gordon shook his head. "I couldn't get one. I'm not a resident here."

Ogot frowned. He ordered a brandy.

"They can't keep me out of the courtroom, can they?"

"I've got your form for the courtroom," Ogot said. "Once you're inside, you're perfectly safe, I should think."

Gordon shrugged. "As long as I get to testify."

"Right." Ogot looked at him closely, almost sadly. "I thought you might want to back out. I see I needn't have worried."

"I thought about backing out. I think about it every day." He lit a cigarette. His face was blank and weary; his fingers trembled as he held the match. "But somehow, I'm here."

"Well, cheers." Ogot lifted his glass, smiling professionally. "To Adija."

Gordon glanced at him, unsmiling, and drank down the last of his beer. "Adija," he murmured.

Ogot adjusted his face. "You know what to say?"

Gordon nodded.

"Whenever you're ready, then." Ogot rose, tossing down his brandy.

"Any chance of seeing Adija before it starts?"

"No, no. That would ruin everything."

Gordon sighed. "All right. Let's get it over with."

The Police Court was a gray rectangular building; like the jail and the police station, it was constructed out of cinderblocks and wood and resembled a grain warehouse. Its red tile roof was the only spot of color in the dusty little town. The light in the courtroom came from a row of dim naked bulbs in the ceiling. It bounced off the gray walls and dust-caked windows, giving the room the atmosphere of a heavily overcast day, even though the sun was blazing outside. A large fan revolved slowly above the magistrate's desk, flickering the light but cooling no one. Wooden folding chairs had been set up before the bench. The first row was reserved for the press, but was occupied by only two men, reporters for the Karela *Journal* and the Azima

Nation-Builder. Photographers and foreign journalists had been barred from the proceedings.

The spectators were a curious mixture of people. Some men wore light tan suits with BP pins in their lapels. The rest of the crowd was dressed in ragged short trousers and shirts, and long dusty dresses. Angered by the postponement of the elections, these people had entered the courtroom with an air of suspicion. They had received their court passes in the market from the men in the tan suits, who had asked them in English if they would like to attend. When someone responded that he did not speak English, he was given a pass and pointed in the direction of the courthouse. The trial was to be conducted in English.

Gordon made his way along a row of spectators to find a vacant seat. Conversations momentarily ceased while he edged in front of people, as if he were the end of a beam of silence passing through the crowd. Once he sat down, the babble around him resumed. Men called to their friends, women scolded their children for playing beneath the chairs. Gordon lit a cigarette. *"Sigara,"* the man on his left demanded. Gordon handed him a cigarette and lit it for him. The man poked his wife, and she offered Gordon a hard-boiled egg, which he accepted. She smiled and resumed suckling the baby in her arms.

Soon Adija will have one like that, Gordon thought. The baby stared at him. How soon would he be with Adija, though? How soon? He tried to concentrate on a picture of his little house in Jamhuri, with Adija and the baby sitting before it. Even thinking in Kisemi, it was somehow hard to imagine himself as part of that scene.

The first *bwana mkubwa*—"big man"—to enter the court was the "yellow-car-man"—the attorney for the defense. People craned their necks to get a look at Ogot, and there was much giggling from the younger women. A policeman walked to the front of the courtroom and spoke to the spectators in a stern voice. Everyone rose on signal as the magistrate walked up the center aisle, his black robe trailing behind him.

Adija and Salome, under police guard, entered from a side door. Adija did not look around at all. Gordon sat forward on the edge of his chair. Her eyes were dark-rimmed, as if from crying. Except for the bulge in her belly, she looked very thin; her wrinkled blue prison dress hung limp from her shoulders. Gordon followed her face until she turned to sit at the desk with Ogot. Then suddenly, after whispering with him, she twisted around and stared. Gordon caught one anguished look from her before Ogot gripped her arm and forced her to turn around.

Salome was the first defendant called. Heavy and ominous, she limped to the chair beside the magistrate's bench. The prosecuting attorney at first leaned over her to ask questions, an intimidating posture that failed. Salome's face looked capable of butting down steel doors; when she turned it up toward the prosecutor, he blinked and stumbled over his words. Soon he was strutting about at a safer distance as he questioned her.

Ogot rose to question her. After she had recounted Jeremiah's road accident, he asked, "Are you aware that Corporal Ennis, whom you were accused of robbing during the Emergency, retired to the United Kingdom in February of this year?"

"Yes," Salome said. "Jeremiah told me, many months ago."

"And you knew that if you returned to Bashiri, Corporal Ennis would not be there to press charges against you?"

"Yes."

"You were not afraid of anything that Jeremiah Kongwe might say about you, if you returned to Bashiri?"

"He could say nothing about me that had not been said already. People say many things about me. I can't care what they say. I am ashamed of nothing. I helped Bashiri in its struggle for independence." Salome sat back in her chair, glaring out over the heads of the spectators. "I was not fearing Jeremiah Kongwe. He was only a little man. He was nothing to me."

Salome stepped down.

The prosecuting attorney conferred at length with his assistant, another young man in a tan suit. Finally the prosecutor rose and faced the bench. "Your Honor, the prosecution is sure that there are other charges against Salome Wairimu pending in Azima, charges that she feared the late Mr. Kongwe would bring to the surface. We ask for a recess, to obtain them."

The magistrate frowned. He was a small dark man, looking hot and uncomfortable in his black robe. He removed it, and gestured to his assistant to do likewise. Without his vestments, he looked somehow even more uncomfortable. "Many of us have driven some distances at very short notice to attend this trial, Mr. Prosecuting Attorney. I would like to hear more business before we have a recess. At the end of the day, you can return to Azima to check police records."

The prosecutor sat down hard. Around the room, men in tan suits were whispering angrily, their shiny faces creased in frowns. Gordon glanced around and smiled. Already the prosecution had a weak case—perhaps there was some hope, after all. Then he caught sight of Elima, dressed today in civilian clothes. His buck teeth flashed as he whispered to the men in the tan suits. Gordon's smile faded.

Jeremiah's uncle was called to the stand. Through a Rukiva interpreter, he told the court that Adija's strange behavior at the initiation ceremony had caused many people to believe she was a witch.

Adija was then called. She did not stand up until one of her guards pulled her to her feet. She sat down in the witness stand and immediately hung her head, hiding her face from view.

"The defendant will face the court, please," the magistrate said.

"Sit up, woman! Face the court!" the Kisemi interpreter translated.

Adija raised her head and looked straight out over the heads of the spectators. Her gaze dipped down toward Gordon, then flew about the walls like a trapped moth.

"Please inform the defendant," the magistrate said wearily, "that when I say face the court, I mean that she should face me and whoever is asking her questions."

The interpreter did so. Adija stared at the prosecuting attorney's shiny black shoes.

"State your full name, please."

"Adija."

"Just Adija?"

"Khadija bint Omar Mohammed El Ahmed."

Gordon thought: I never even knew her full name.

"Thank you. That is a Moslem name, is it not?"

Adija hung her head. "Yes."

"All right. Now, did you understand the testimony given by the previous witness?"

Adija wiped her eyes. "I understand."

"Is it true, that you were thought a witch by those people?"

The defense counsel leaped to his feet. "Your Honor, we are not in sixteenth-century Britain! This is not a witchcraft trial!"

Adija looked up, startled. People in the gallery were whispering; they liked the way the Yellow-Car-Man jumped and shouted. Things were livening up.

"Order!" The magistrate rapped his desk. "Counsel, the prosecuting attorney is attempting to establish a possible motive for a killing. That is his job. I will let him continue his questioning."

Ogot sat down, his lips wrinkled in disgust.

"Were you afraid," the prosecutor continued, "of what people in Musolu might think if they heard about what happened at the ceremony?"

Adija listened to the translation, comprehending little. Her eyes darted about the room again. "I was fearing," she whispered.

"How afraid were you?"

"I was fearing very much, this witchcraft." Adija wiped her eyes.

"If you could have done anything to get rid of this fear, would you have done it?"

"Oh, yes. I would do anything."

The prosecuting attorney rested his elbow on the corner of the magistrate's desk, leaning close to her. "The people of Musolu, what did they think of you before Jeremiah Kongwe's death?"

"I don't know. I think—some of the men, they liked me."

Gordon heard Elima laughing, along with the men in the tan suits. The spectators, watching their faces, watched Adija with disapproving looks.

"Were you not known as Swila Number 101, or some such number?"

Adija glanced away. "Some people called me that. It was for a joke, I think. They were thinking I was a Northerner, but I am not."

"Whether or not you are actually a Northerner is not so important, in this context. What is important is what people thought you were."

Adija looked even more confused, as she listened to the translation.

"You are aware, no doubt, that many people in Musolu feared the northern rebels—the Swila—in the same way they feared witches. Now, do you think these people believed you were a Swila, or in sympathy with the Swila cause?"

Ogot was on his feet again. "The prosecution is attempting to confuse and intimidate the defendant, Your Honor," he shouted, waving his fist in the air. "The defendant is plainly not comprehending anything that is going on!"

The magistrate wrinkled his brow. "Objection overruled."

"They called me Swila sometimes," Adija said wearily, "it's possible. I could be anything, I think."

"All right. That is settled. You feared that the people might think you a Swila. To them, you were not an ordinary African barmaid. Is that correct?"

Adija nodded.

"Now, do you think that this is possible: That the people of Musolu, finding you somewhat strange already, might have heard the news of your effect on the initiation ceremony from Jeremiah Kongwe, and decided that you were a witch, and should be punished?"

"Your Honor, this is clearly nonsense!" Ogot strode toward the magistrate's desk. "Not only is the prosecutor asking the defendant to make pointless conjectures, he is playing on her fears and superstitions in a most disgraceful way."

The magistrate shook his head firmly. "Sit down, Mr. Ogot. Whether you or I believe in witchcraft is not the point, and the prosecuting attorney has demonstrated that he knows this. That many people believe in witches, I think you must agree, is unquestionably true. Mr. Kamau is attempting to discover what the witness believed, not what she is. One can fear that people will think something, even if that something has no basis in reality."

"True, Your Honor. But I am not at all sure, from listening to the defendant, that she is clear as to the nature of either her own beliefs or of reality."

"Are you saying that you wish to have the defendant examined by a psychiatrist, Mr. Ogot? You did not enter a plea of insanity."

Mr. Ogot stroked his jaw, thinking. "No, I am not saying that."

"Then you will please sit down," the magistrate said. "Mr. Kamau, will you repeat your question?"

"Yes. Adija, do you think it is possible that some people in Musolu might have thought you a witch and might have wanted to punish you?"

Adija nodded.

"And this is partially because you believe people have been suspicious of you in the past."

"I think so."

"Why—do you think so?"

Adija stared in panic at Salome, but Salome's gaze remained as hard as stone, focused on the far wall of the room. Adija looked for Gordon among the spectators; her eyes watered and blurred. "I am not like others, it's true," she said slowly, squinting hard at the floor. "I don't know what I am. Some days I am an African, some days I am an Indian in a pretty saree, some days I am a European, stamping school books. I can change myself, like that. My eyes make people fear me, but they make some people want me too. I think witches and *jinnis* are like this. Also . . . also I do things no other woman would do. I made Salome do them too. She'd never done them before, and they made her fear very much. But she couldn't stop doing them because I didn't want her to stop." Adija was weeping now, but her voice was stronger than before. The words rushed out of her like a spray of warm ocean water, cleansing her as they stung in her mouth. "I touched Salome as a man touches a woman. Sometimes I even liked doing it, and I made her like it. No, I am not an ordinary African barmaid. I can touch a man's body and like it, and make him like it also. I can change myself like that too. It is a mystery to me, but I can do it. So I think I can cause things to happen, somehow. I spoiled that boy's circumcision. And when Jeremiah's car hit that man on the bicycle, I saw him before anyone else. His eyes came closer and closer to mine. The eyes were pleading with me just behind the glass. Then they broke, right into my face. I think that is not an ordinary way for one to die."

Adija raised her head, breathing hard. Her vision unblurred somewhat. She saw a light-colored patch among the dark faces: Gordon. She shivered. "Now that people know about me, they'll be afraid of me. They'll know what I am, and they'll leave me to be whatever I am. Just now, I'm not fearing people so much. My fearing is less than before. I'm not afraid of what it is in me that makes me strange. I think I will just wait and learn to see what it is." She wiped her nose hard with the back of her wrist. "If you listen to me and then you decide I caused Jeremiah to die, then I will know that much. I will not be angry if you decide to punish me."

The prosecuting attorney returned to his table, frowning. The courtroom was alive with whispering. The few people who understood Kisemi were translating for the others. Several women made soft quavering sounds of anxiety. Children were snatched from their seats, dragged along the rows and up the aisles toward the exit. A woman could be heard gasping and vomiting outside the door. "Kill her!" someone shouted, and several voices echoed loud agreement.

A uniformed policeman stepped to the front of the gallery. The noise died down. Those who were about to leave ran down the aisle and disappeared. The rest took their seats, murmuring and staring at Adija. She had slumped back in her chair, and appeared to be either laughing or crying, it was impossible to tell which.

The defense attorney stood up and glared at the magistrate until the room was silent.

"Mr. Ogot, I think your previous point has been made," the magistrate said finally. "You may have a recess to reconsider a plea of insanity if you wish."

Ogot looked satisfied. "No, your honor. Not at present."

More whispering broke out, this time among the tan-suited men in the gallery. Evidently they had been hoping for a plea of insanity, which would have been seen as an admission that some crime had been committed. The magistrate slammed his gavel down in frustration.

"I think the defendant is under stress," Mr. Ogot continued, "and is perhaps deluded in her thinking, but at present I do not doubt her fitness to stand trial. I wish to question her and another witness, before I should decide to ask for a recess. With your honor's permission."

The magistrate nodded.

"I wish to steer the questioning away from the subject of witches, *jinnis*, and elves, if my distinguished colleague,

Mr. Kamau, does not object." Ogot stepped up to Adija. "Would you tell us your full name again, please, Adija?"

"Khadija bint Omar Mohammed El Ahmed," Adija whispered.

"You have stated that this is a Moslem name. Are you a Moslem?"

Adija shook her head. "No. I'm a Christian."

"Why did you become a Christian, Adija?"

"Because—well, my mother did. The Moslems in our village were abusing her. She didn't like them."

"And you—did you like the Moslems in your village?"

"No. They were cruel to me as well."

"So you are a Christian girl, by conscious choice, who does not have any sympathy for Moslems." Mr. Ogot paused and stepped back. "Thank you, Adija. Now, just for a moment, we will return to the subject of witchcraft. I want to keep the prosecuting attorney from falling asleep, you see. You just have to answer what you know, there is no cause to worry."

"All right." Adija nodded. She had Ogot in focus now, her eyes clinging to him.

"A witch wishes to harm people who have hurt her. I think that is correct. Is that your understanding?"

"I think so."

"All right. Now, is there anyone you can think of who has hurt you, whom you might be angry with."

Adija frowned. "The guard," she said softly.

"The man who brought you in here?"

Adija glanced at the guard. He squirmed in his seat beside the table. "That one too. I was thinking of the other one. The other one beat Salome."

"Did you wish to punish him for beating Salome?"

"Yes."

"What did you do to him, then?"

"Nothing."

"Why nothing?"

Adija shook her head. "I couldn't! What could I do?"

"All right." Ogot raised his hand like an orchestra conductor, calming her. "Now the guard who is sitting over there. You are angry with him too. Why?"

"He made me fuck with him."

The magistrate scowled. Some laughter and whispers disturbed the court momentarily.

"I see. What did you do to him afterward?"

"Nothing."

"Why don't you do something now?"

Adija's brow wrinkled in puzzlement.

"Can you make his wife barren? Can you cause his hut to catch fire? Perhaps make his teeth all fall out?"

"No!" Adija covered her face. "I can't do any of those things."

This time, the prosecuting attorney jumped to his feet. "Your Honor, the defense counsel is attempting to ridicule the previous testimony of the defendant! He is attempting to make a travesty of this trial!"

"That takes no effort on my part at all, Mr. Prosecuting Attorney," Ogot said.

"What is it that you are attempting to prove, Mr. Ogot?" the magistrate asked.

"If you will allow me a few more questions, I think my point will be made."

"Proceed." The magistrate sat back and wiped his forehead with a handkerchief.

"All right, Adija, you can't do any of those things. Can you cause the guard to die?"

"I don't know." She stared at the guard. He looked strong and mean, with his truncheon at his belt. "I don't think I could kill him."

"Would you like to, if you could?"

"Oh, no."

"Why not?"

"I'd be too frightened."

Ogot nodded. "This man who raped you, and the other who beat your friend Salome—you are very angry with them. And yet you say you don't want to kill them. Tell me this: Did Jeremiah Kongwe ever beat your friend Salome or rape you?"

Adija shook her head. "No, he didn't."

"Thank you, Adija. No more questions."

The magistrate looked at his watch. "If there are no more witnesses . . ."

"I wish to call one more witness, Your Honor." Ogot stepped forward.

The magistrate sighed. "I will call a recess at five o'clock. You have twenty minutes."

The attorney for the defense faced the gallery. "I call Mr. Gordon Lockery to the stand."

People turned their heads as Gordon rose and edged his way toward the aisle. So that was why the whiteman was present.

Gordon walked slowly and wearily, keeping his eyes to the floor. He took the oath and sat down on the edge of the chair. It was still warm from Adija. He ran his fingers along the armrest, feeling the dampness her tears had left. His own eyes blurred momentarily.

"Mr. Lockery, will you tell us what you know about the motorcar that belonged to Mr. Jeremiah Kongwe?"

"It was a Ford Zephyr," Gordon said, looking straight ahead. "Its brakes were shot."

"Pardon—shot?"

"They didn't work properly. They didn't stop the car or even slow it down until the pedal was pushed clear to the floor. Also, the steering was extremely loose. You could turn the wheel and nothing would happen—the car didn't turn right away, then it turned sharply and erratically."

"How do you know this—just from what Salome Wairimu stated earlier?"

"No, I drove the car myself once. I damn near got into an accident with it."

"Was anyone with you when you drove the car? Did anyone see you driving it?"

"Yes. The nurse at the dispensary. Simon Waga."

"Thank you, Mr. Lockery." Ogot turned away and waited until the men in the tan suits had stopped whispering. "Mr. Lockery, as you have heard, this court is interested in motives this afternoon. Do you know anything about Mr. Kongwe that explains why he made his trip north with the two defendants?"

Gordon took a deep breath. "I know that he was a member of the Special Branch—"

The objections of the men in the tan suits burst forth only a fraction of a second before those of the prosecutor. "Your Honor, this is irrelevant conjecture!" he shouted. "I demand this line of questioning be stopped at once!"

The magistrate pounded his desk with his gavel. The newspaper reporters ceased their frantic scribbling to stare at Gordon, pencils poised.

"Mr. Lockery, what makes you think Mr. Kongwe was Special Branch?" the magistrate asked.

"I heard him tell Salome, and so did other people. People heard him tell Elima, the Police Chief, too. Elima's here." Gordon looked to the side of the courtroom. "You can ask him."

Elima glared at a spot over Gordon's head, his buck teeth biting hard into his lower lip.

The magistrate frowned. "Mr. Ogot, will you tell the court what relevance this line of questioning has to this case?"

"With your permission, I would like to put that question to the witness."

"Permission denied. I would like you to answer it. You are conducting the inquiry."

Ogot nodded slowly, thoughtfully. He looked confused. A thin professional smile spread across his lips. "You are correct, Your Honor. I am momentarily at a loss as to what to say. I was not aware that the witness would answer as he did. I have no knowledge of Mr. Kongwe's belonging to the Special Branch—if that is true at all. May I ask the witness himself why he has stated this about Mr. Kongwe? Perhaps then the witness will clarify his statement for us."

"Yes, all right." The magistrate glared at Gordon.

"You asked me why Mr. Kongwe made that trip north," Gordon said, and paused. His hands were trembling. He had only a few minutes to speak; there was no way to say what he knew without being silenced. He had asked to be trapped on the witness stand; he no longer had the option of backing out. He stared at Adija and cleared his throat. "Mr. Kongwe went north, I believe, to collect the rifles that were found in his car. He disappeared several times from his uncle's farm, giving no explanation. One of those times, he loaded his car up with something heavy enough to weight down the tail end. I saw the way his car looked. I think his plan was to bring the rifles back and leave them around to be found in the border area. He knew their discovery would make everyone panic. People would think they were Russian-made Swila rifles. When people panicked, the government would have the excuse it needed to bring in troops and postpone the elections. Had they voted, the people would have voted against the government—"

"This man is making inflammatory conjectures!" the prosecuting attorney shouted. "Your Honor, he is a foreigner meddling in the affairs of our nation—"

"And so—" Gordon continued, his voice rising, "when the government was embarrassed by a Special Branch man's car being found stocked with rifles, it turned what was an accident into a murder trial, to distract attention from how the rifles got into the area. This whole trial is nothing but a distraction! There's no case against Adija—"

"That's enough, Mr. Lockery!" The magistrate pounded his gavel. "No one asked you for a speech. You are in contempt of court. Will you step down, before I have you removed?"

Gordon rose to his feet. He saw Elima's buck teeth flashing, saw him reach out to grab the arm of a court policeman, alerting him to move toward the witness stand. Another policeman strode past Elima in Gordon's direction. "You know she's done nothing!" Gordon shouted, turning one last time toward Adija. "You let your men rape her and drive her half-crazy. You've already punished her—and for what?"

One policeman grabbed him around the neck, cutting off his breath. The other twisted his arm high behind his back. Together they dragged him from the witness stand. He heard Adija make a small cry as he was dragged in front of her, and tried to call out to her, but his voice was buried amid the shouting and gavel banging. The noises swelled, a hurricane in his ears. Wrenching sideways, he felt a ripping in his shoulder that dropped him to his knees in pain. He saw a truncheon swing above him; beyond was Adija: mute, wide-eyed, and suddenly blasted into darkness.

30

THE LATE AFTERNOON SUN GLINTED IN THE
side-view mirror and reflected red off a policeman's rifle
that lay across the car dashboard. The shiny spot on the
rifle barrel looked like a patch of blood; it throbbed in
Gordon's eyes no matter which way he turned. Gordon felt
his eyes. An enormous lump protruded above the left one.
It stung. When he pressed it, a dull ache spread far back
into his head. Also, each time he moved, a paralyzing pain
shot through him from his shoulder. Worst of all, his bladder felt ready to explode. All these sensations were a new
experience for him. Their intensity blurred his mind in terrible new ways.

Coming down from the mountains, the car grew oven-
hot. Half-conscious and soaked with sweat, Gordon stared
out the window. Beside the road—a vertical mile from the
edge of the escarpment—was the Great Valley of Bashiri.
The valley's floor spread out to the horizon, along which
mountains surrounded by clouds rose into the sky, each
looking like a volcanic island floating in a purple sea.
Gazelles and zebras lifted their heads as the car approached the valley floor. Several gazelles leaped along
beside the car, then were lost in the red dust of the plains,
silhouettes rising and falling in graceful arcs along the
grass.

When this is over, I'll take Adija to the game reserves in
Jamhuri to see the wildlife, Gordon thought suddenly.
She's been in jail, she'll appreciate those open spaces. We'll
go on our honeymoon . . . He gritted his teeth, feeling as if
someone were mocking him.

Later, he awoke to find the sun gone, the car careening
through darkness. Occasionally a headlight beam illuminated figures beside the road: a man swinging a lantern, a
girl with an immense load of firewood on her back. Gor-

don turned to watch them out the back window. Each time he turned, his shoulder ached and he had to gasp for breath, but he wanted badly to see these people before the darkness swallowed them.

He sat forward again, exhausted. "Where are you taking me?" he asked suddenly.

Silence. The man beside him shook his head, indicating that he was not to ask questions.

"What are you holding me for? What are the charges?"

The policeman in the passenger seat mumbled something to the policeman in the back seat. The policeman in the back seat scowled at Gordon.

"No talking," he said.

No talking. How many times had he said that to his students? Wanjala, put that pencil down, the test hasn't started. Otieno, have you got your paper ready? Good. You have . . . ten minutes. Go! No talking.

How long will my test last? Gordon thought. It would not be so bad if the time were not so indefinite. And if I knew why . . .

But he did know the answers to his questions. He was charged with contempt of court, entering the country—and a restricted area—without a permit. All punishable by fines, no doubt. But what was the punishment for Saying What No One Wanted To Hear? Headlight beams swept past, stirring up the darkness, making it settle back around him like an avalanche of black snow. He shuddered.

No one else would have said what I said, he thought. Not the lawyer, certainly not Salome. Salome didn't have to say anything—she just wrote it all out on her tissue-paper note and I said it for her. God, how she must be cackling now! And Adija—what is she doing now? At least she is free.

Gordon woke next to the crackle of the police radio. The driver was speaking into the microphone attached to the dashboard. "Don't bring him here. Repeat: Don't bring him here," a voice from the metal grill said. "Wait for instructions."

The car turned off the highway into the industrial section of Azima. Dark warehouses, high wire fences, abandoned tea kiosks with tarpaulin roofs drooping and streaming rainwater. A smell of damp soot. No sounds anywhere except for the hum of the car motor. The driver parked beside a grime-covered wall. A dog slunk into the headlight beams, its eyes turning to glowing disks. The three policemen in the car grunted and stretched.

No one else would have said what I said, Gordon thought. What does that make me? Never mind. Adija is free. At least, Adija is free.

Is she? How do you know?

She has to be! Gordon shut his eyes, picturing her running free across the grass of the school compound, her purple *kente*-cloth flapping at her ankles, her eyes laughing and bright. He tried to seal the picture tight within his mind, but his mind was too porous to hold it.

The car radio crackled again. The driver spoke into the microphone, then started the engine. They rolled out of the industrial section, past the floodlit gate of a police barracks without stopping. So they weren't going to put him in jail here. Where were they going to put him? He stared out the window, waiting. The car sped through the commercial district, past tall glass offices and tourist hotels, white figures drinking wine in a sidewalk cafe, a black beggar hobbling on homemade crutches, a neon sign flashing pink and silver-pink EQUATOR CLUB - EQUATOR CLUB, pink and silver women with dark faces under the sign watching the cars, a uniformed man with a truncheon guarding a huge bank door, traffic jams at the intersections, horns blasting, car radios screaming Kisemi song lyrics. Out of the city now, a traffic circle swirling with headlights like an overloaded carousel, a highway splotchy with fogged lights. Where did it lead? Past tall housing projects like granite icebergs, tile-roofed residences with neat flowering hedges and clipped lawns and "BEWARE OF THE DOG" signs, a flock of small planes crouched motionless on the runway of a private airport, a golf course, "JAMES BOND · THUNDERBALL" at the Drive-In Cinema . . . Gordon shut his eyes tight. Where was he? Had they deported him already?

The car slowed along a stretch of wire fence. Gordon focused his eyes again. Sentries. A torch shining in his face, white acid in his eyes. Someone was nudging him forward. He was walking into a building.

"Wait here," someone said.

He waited, blinking.

Two policemen disappeared into an office. Fluorescent

lights flickered on. Another policeman stood across from him in the corridor, his rifle at a slant, aimed at Gordon's feet. If I make a move, he'll shoot my feet off, Gordon thought. He tried to lean against the wall, fearing he would collapse, but he could not do it without moving his feet. He swayed in place, his legs growing numb.

"I have to . . . urinate," he said, suddenly feeling his trousers. They were damp.

A soldier appeared, also with a rifle. He conferred with the policeman.

"You are now in military custody," the soldier told Gordon.

"I have to piss," Gordon said.

The soldier pointed his rifle down the corridor. Gordon walked ahead of him into the toilet. He stood at the urinal, staring at his distorted reflection in the chrome flush handle.

"Hurry up!"

Gordon shut his eyes and tried to concentrate. He tried to think of other scenes. He pictured his classroom . . . he was standing by the blackboard, discussing the history of the Independence movement. And right now he didn't have the freedom to piss without asking permission!

"You hurry up," the soldier shouted, "or I'll open up a hole in you for it to pour out of!"

Gordon strained, trembling, but only a few drops dribbled into the urinal. A hand reached over his shoulder and yanked the flush handle down.

"I can flush it myself, dammit!"

The hand gripped his sore shoulder and flung him sideways. Gordon shrieked in pain and fell. Urine streamed down his pants leg. He lay gasping and leaking until the soldier pulled him to his feet and shoved him out the door. Fumbling with his zipper, Gordon lurched down the corridor.

He sat down in a wooden chair in an office and shut his eyes, waiting for the spasms of pain to subside. A soldier in a gray uniform sat across from him in a swivel chair. The soldier sat with one leg crossed over the other, motionless, his eyes fixed on the middle of Gordon's chest.

Gray dawn crept through the windows. Gordon smoked the last of his cigarettes. He stared at it as it burned down in his shaking fingers. What if they didn't allow him to buy cigarettes? A stupid thought, but it brought his mind into focus. He read all the notices on the bulletin board beside him until, mercifully, his eyelids dropped again.

At midmorning, Gordon was pointed down the corridor again. A soldier opened the door of a car for him and waited until he had crawled in to shut and lock it. Later, another soldier appeared with a cup of sweet milk-tea, and a bowl of beans, rice, and potatoes all mixed together. It was tasteless, but Gordon wolfed it down. His head cleared again.

"Can I buy some cigarettes?" he asked the soldier.

The soldier appeared not to hear.

Gordon lay down on the seat. The air hung hot and stale. He inhaled his own stink. No matter how he lay, he could not avoid the stink or hide his face from the sharp rays of the sun.

The car was taking him back over the same road he had traveled yesterday. This time, he did not watch out the window; he was too weak to sit up for long. His head was beginning to throb. He felt stupid with exhaustion. His eyelids jiggled up and down with the bumping of the car. Each time they began to close into sleep, the car hit another pothole, and the sun dug its fingernails into his eyes.

"When is this going to be over?" he mumbled.

The three soldiers in the car all looked at him at once. Then they continued talking among themselves. Something about football pools. It doesn't pay to bet on those things, man. Maybe, but my wife's cousin won fifty quid in the pools two years ago. Wasted it on some no-good woman . . .

The soldier in the back seat, noticing Gordon was awake, offered him a cigarette. Gordon took it and held it bobbing between his lips as the car bounced along. The soldier lit it for him with some difficulty. Gordon's head cleared again.

"What are you going to do with me?" Gordon asked.

The soldier looked at him sadly. "You? I don't know. No one knows what to do with you. It seems that you're some kind of a problem." The soldier glanced away. "We just have orders to take you back to the border."

"Then what?"

"Then you go some place else, I suppose."

The fever spread like lava from his shoulder along his back, up his neck and into his head. The pain was less acute now, swaddled behind a dull ache. He turned his head slowly and looked out the window. Coils of barbed wire and a makeshift shack beside the road.

It was the border. Again. The car stopped beside the shack. Gordon started to get out, but a hand yanked him back against the seat. Seeing the glint of a rifle, he shut his eyes and sat very still.

I must have passed through Kepuria if I'm at the border, he thought. I might have caught a glimpse of Adija. She might have been coming out of the courtroom as the car passed by. I've missed my chance to see Adija! His eyes flooded. At least she's free, he repeated to himself until he could see again.

The door opened. Gordon was pulled outside. He saw a Marembo flag beside the shack. He had crossed the border. The sun made his eyes swim. Adija was in Bashiri and he was across the border in Marembo. He was moving further and further from her. That is what I—we—are being punished for, he thought. We have crossed too many borders.

He was in a different sort of car now. The soldiers wore brown uniforms instead of gray. This car was a Morris. He had owned a Morris—months ago, it seemed. Perhaps it was still sitting in the underbrush back in Bashiri. No, people had probably found it and stripped it by now. First the tires, then the chrome, the seats, eventually the engine. They would pull the body apart and bang it flat with mallets and use it to repair the roofs of their huts. They would make sandals out of the tires and the kids would use the steering wheel for a hoop. There is a use for everything. Except me. No one knows what to do about me.

He wanted a cigarette. As long as he felt that craving, he was not entirely defeated by fever and pain. None of the soldiers smoked. When he asked for a cigarette, the soldier in the front seat turned around. He had a high brown forehead and small eyes. The shiny visor of his cap pointed beaklike at Gordon, and he laughed.

The car stopped in a larger town. Two soldiers got out, and returned with some bowls of steaming banana. One gave Gordon a bowl and poured some brownish groundnut sauce over it from a glass. These days I am really eating African, Gordon thought. I am really into Africa now. He scooped up the paste with his fingers. It had no taste. A soldier handed him a bottle of warm Coca-Cola. It made

him feel nauseous but he drank it all down. Afterward, he
was even thirstier than before.

"Can I have some water?" he asked. "And some cigarettes," he added stubbornly.

"You give me money," the soldier said.

Gordon reached for his wallet. It was gone! He searched
through all his pockets. No wallet, no passport, nothing!
How could he have lost them? He began to tremble. One of
the soldiers must have lifted them from him somewhere
while he slept. A thousand shillings—gone! No passport.
He had nothing. He did not exist. He could be found
along some roadside, stripped down like a car, and no one
would know who he was.

Wait, he had some change. Two shilling pieces. He
handed them numbly to the soldiers, his eyes blurring with
tears. The soldier went away and returned with a glass of
water and a pack of Crane Birds. Gordon clutched the
packet with both hands. The Cranes were the last thing
that he had that was African. He turned the orange packet
over and over in his hand. The cigarettes would all burn
down, disappear into smoke. And then he really would
have nothing left.

Another wire fence. More sentries. Gordon was transferred to another car. A soldier drove along a row of
military Quonset huts. Then around the corner of a cinderblock and tin garage. He parked with one side of the car
flush against the wall, and got out. A soldier set a folding
chair under a frayed banana tree and sat with a Sten gun
over his knee.

Sounds of hammering blasted out of the garage. A drill
whined. Metal ground against a whetstone. Engines roared,
over and over again, like elephants hawking up phlegm.
Gordon, drenched in sweat, wiped his eyes. The car was
broiling in the sun. He had to get out!

He pushed the door open. The soldier stood up.

Gordon put one foot out. A clacking noise sounded,
even louder than the noises inside the garage. Dust was
jumping just ahead of his foot, like hailstones bouncing.
Not hailstones—bullets! Gordon slammed the door shut.

Night. The car stank. The air was too hot to breathe.
Gordon managed to remove his shirt and lie down on it.
The seat was damp and small. Familiar. A Morris back
seat again. They had let him go, they had brought him

back to Kepuria and dumped him back into his own car. He smelled motor oil and flowering bushes.

No, he was in Karela—those bushes, he remembered the smell from the university. His eyes opened. A spotlight was focused on the car. Sometimes there were two of them. The white light streaked apart and flashed back together again, like phosphorescent birds crashing in midflight. Even when he shut his eyes, the birds continued streaking in the darkness.

The only relief came at dawn, between the time when the lights were extinguished and the time when the sun grew hot. The pounding and clanging and roaring beside him meant that it was day. He tried to cover his ears, but his shoulder was encased in an iron grip of pain that would not let him move his arm.

The soldier outside had a transistor radio now. It rested on his lap beside the Sten gun. Electric guitar notes shot out of it, spraying the air, filling in the gaps between the garage noises. Gordon recognized some of the songs he had heard in the Karela dance halls. He remembered Karela . . . the university . . . all those clean bright American students, so long ago, trailing their golden threads of continuity in neat patterns across the lawns of the campus, out into the hills and plains of Africa and back in graceful loops to Iowa and Connecticut and California. But hadn't he found a thread of continuity to his life too? He seemed to remember that he had, but he didn't know where it was now.

Karela . . . soon he would awaken and everything would be settled. He would walk down to the Speke Hotel and drink a cold beer. God! a cold beer. He'd sit there on the verandah under the flowering trees, listening to the sounds of crickets in the warm evening air.

He heard the dance hall music. Yes, and later he'd pedal down the hill, along the red-brown roads, past the huts with children playing outside. He passed the house where the girl was pumping her sewing machine in the doorway, the folds of blue cloth billowing at her knees. Her knees were raised, but she was not moving now—she was in a frozen tableau. Suddenly she blended into another girl with her knees raised, this one lying on her back on a mat in a dark mud hut. The two tableaus separated and melted together again like the spotlight-birds, blindingly bright. The picture was of Adija now, not running across the grass in her *kente*-cloth, but spotlit on a stage, kneeling. She was wearing a phosphorescent Japanese robe and holding a dagger pointed at her chest. Her lips were open, and she was singing plaintively, a confusion of melodies and lyrics.

He understood nothing of what she was singing, only that she was singing to him, and that he could not stop hearing it.

Pressing his face into the seat, he tried to obliterate the sound, but only succeeded in driving it deeper into his head. No more Karela. He had to get out of Karela. To Musolu. She must be back in Musolu now. He had to get there. Or to get a message to her so that she would stop crying out to him, so that she would know that he hadn't run out on her. . . .

Musolu. Musolu was changed. Was he in the right town? The New Life Hotel had been replaced by a gray cinder-block courtroom building. Inside, a group of people were sitting on the floor, waving machetes and shouting. Pressure lanterns swung wildly from the rafters, their glare hissing back and forth over people's shining faces like waves of surf. The judge in black robes was sitting beside him behind the bar, pounding the counter with a brandy bottle. The judge was Salome. Adija stood on the other side of her, mute, wide-eyed, her face frozen in panic as if a machete were about to slash down on her. "Guilty!" Salome screamed, and smashed the bottle to pieces against the bar. Someone picked Gordon up and flung him head-first into the middle of the crowd. Women shrieked, men scrambled out of the way. People's feet trod on him, caused spasms of pain in his shoulder and forehead. The wireless blared and crackled. Dancing feet trampled his fingers, scuffed against his face. "Why don't you leave, man?" Simon Waga asked him, leaning over. Gordon shook his head. "I'm staying," he mumbled into the floor, and tried to stand up.

Eyes and glasses and bottles revolved and tilted over him. Light beams flashed down between the figures of the dancers, impaling him like strokes of lightning. A purple gauze passed in front of the light. A fragrance of sweet hair oil, enormous eyes that narrowed to squint at him— Adija? He cried out her name: Adija? The purple was gone; Salome's black robe swirled around and around, blotting

out the light like a storm. She was cackling and laughing at
the top of her lungs. Beer foam bubbled from the corners
of her mouth. It dribbled onto him, soaking his face, his
shirt, his groin. Her laughter rose with the screech of the
wireless as he struggled again to stand up . . .

Gordon opened his eyes. Pain. Racket of machinery.
Garage yard. Rust-colored roofs. Banana tree. Guard with
his Sten gun across his knees. Heat.

His face was soaked. He wiped it on his wrist. His wrist
came back shiny red. He choked. Pushing himself up in the
seat, he stared at himself in the rear-view mirror. His forehead was purple and lumpy, his left eye full of blood and
almost closed. He didn't recognize himself.

Adija wouldn't recognize him. He had to get a message
to her.

The effort of pushing himself up on the seat made him
dizzy. He didn't know if he had the strength to get out of
the car and stand up, but somehow he managed to push
the door handle down and swing his legs outside. The
banana tree melted and solidified and melted in the orange
glare of the sun. He blinked hard, forcing his eyes open.

Someone was shouting at him. He heard a loud clacking
sound, and felt dirt flying up against his ankles.

Screaming, he pitched forward out of the car.

❋   ❋   ❋

The car was passing the university. Up a winding road
toward a modern white building. Green foliage beside the
road, trees shaped like flowering coral, lush shaggy green
bushes. Traffic circles glowing red-brown in the sunlight.
Paths winding into the underbrush, a man pushing a bicycle through the red-brown and green . . .

"Eat."

Gordon shook his head.

"Eat."

Steamed banana with a thin brown sauce. A mug of tea.
He sipped the tea. Sweet and milky and a strange medicinal
taste. He drank greedily. A pressure around his head, but
no pain. He touched his forehead. A bandage. His arm in
bandages too. His shoulder hard, in a cast.

He was surrounded by white. White walls, white table
top, a white dress with a dark face. Not black. Goldish. He
looked up and managed to smile.

"Is it over now?"

The woman nodded. "Drink your tea. You'll feel better."

Only the skirt of her uniform was white, the top was a gauzy yellow. A saree. An Indian nurse. Gordon squinted hard. "You look a little like her," he said.

"Pardon?"

Gordon drained his tea mug. The bottom of the mug smelled very strongly of medicine. A dizzying smell. "You look a little like Adija," he said.

"Oh . . ." The nurse glanced around nervously. Three soldiers stood around her, watching him. They held rifles at a slant.

"Is he ready?" one of the soldiers asked the nurse. His voice was hard.

"You said it was all over," Gordon protested to her.

"Yes," she said distractedly. Her hands were shaking. "Yes . . ."

The ache in his shoulder was going away. His body felt limp. "I'm not ready," he said to the nurse. "I've been sleeping, I don't want to sleep anymore. I want to go to Musolu . . ."

"Please," she said, biting her lip. "Please go to sleep."

"No—I have to see Adija. I have to tell her . . ." He tried to push himself up from the table, but the sleepiness had soaked into his arm, and he had no strength in it. He wasn't even strong enough to keep his eyelids from drooping. "Listen," he murmured. "Will you give Adija a message. . . ?"

* * *

". . . a message," he said, opening his eyes.

"Yes?" A woman leaned over him. "Feeling better, are you?"

Gordon shook his head slowly, trying to focus. His ears were clogged with a constant roaring noise. The woman was different. Her saree was gone. She was pale, pale as his own skin. She wore a light blue blazer with a crest on the pocket. She did not carry a rifle, she carried a tray. On the tray was a picture of an airplane. The roaring noise hung in the air. It was not going to go away.

He sat up and stared out the window. Clouds. Through the clouds, he could make out bleached brown countryside far below, flat and pockmarked in the reddening dusk. A gold-colored ribbon wound across the land.

"That's the Nile." The woman pointed out the window.
Gordon gazed down. Sunlight glinted on the wing of the
plane. The river and the land were floating backward beneath it. He tried to keep the continent from fading, but
his vision blurred, leaving him only that shiny thread to
focus on. The thread wound through his head, hot as a
thin stream of molten gold. He felt it slipping away. Suddenly he was without a mooring—the thread was gone,
played out. And he knew, as Africa receded fast beneath
him, that he would not find that thread again.

PART SIX

31

ADIJA WAS FRIGHTENED OF GOING TO PRISON
because of the stories Salome had told her about prison
camps in the days of the war. But she found that this
prison wasn't like those. This one had a toilet and a tap in
each cell, and electric lights, and doctors to take care of
you. She didn't like working in the garden but after a week
they let her stop. She was put to work making sheets and
pillowcases. She liked that. A woman taught her how to
use a sewing machine. She was so skilled at the machine
after a few weeks that the woman sent her to a school in
the prison, where a group of women were learning how to
make dresses. Adija made many beautiful dresses for herself and Salome, and also some tiny shirts for the child in
her belly. The teacher let her set aside her wages for a
sewing machine. After five months she owned one. It was
old and rusty, and did not look as if it could be useful, but
Adija could make it do magical things to a piece of cloth.

The doctors were kind to her. One was a Christian
Indian woman who invited her to her office each week just
to talk. The woman made sweet tea with spices in it on her
electric hot plate. All week, Adija looked forward to the
taste of that tea. At first, she told the woman that she was
an Indian. Later, she confessed that she was not. The
woman was not angry with her. Adija began to confess
many things, and the woman did not seem shocked at all.
The woman explained that there were even people in India
who thought themselves to be witches. This woman said
she herself had once believed in things like witches—spirits
and charms and gods who took the shape of cows and
elephants. Now she believed only in the Blessed Savior. He
alone could drive out the demons that burrowed deep into
people's minds. Sipping her tea, Adija agreed.

One day the Indian woman told her that there was a new government. This was the first news Adija had received about the world outside the prison since she and Salome had been snatched from the courtroom in Kepuria. Now all charges against her and Salome were dropped. They were free. The Indian woman said she would keep Adija's sewing machine and clothes until Adija found a place to live. Or better yet, she could stay another week, until her baby was born. But Salome wanted to leave.

"I'm going back to Musolu for a few days, to get my money back from Patel," Salome said. "You stay here and have your baby."

Adija shook her head. "I want to go to Musolu," she insisted.

Standing by the road outside the prison, Adija began to fear again. She thought of Musolu, and began again to ask the questions she had put out of her mind months ago. "What do you think he'll say when he sees me?" She pressed her hands over her belly. "I wonder if he'll think me ugly."

"He'll probably look the other way, but not because you're ugly."

"Yes, he'll be ashamed. Because he never came to visit me. I will be very angry with him. I'll make him weep and beg me to forgive him."

"Then of course you'll forgive him."

"I think so." Adija sighed. "Of course, I'll have to."

"And you'll be married," Salome said in a singsong voice. "And you'll live in a big house with motorcars and televisions."

Adija frowned. "I don't care about motorcars and televisions."

"That's just as well," Salome laughed.

They walked into Azima and caught the bus that went through Musolu. It felt strange to be riding a bus again, surrounded by ordinary men and women. Nobody can tell that I just got out of prison! Adija thought, surprised that no one was taking any notice of her at all. Women and babies slept, their heads bobbing with the bumping of the bus; men stared out the window at the Great Valley, smoked, read newspapers. One man looked up from his paper and gave Adija an inviting smile. Then, catching sight of her swollen belly, he laughed apologetically, just as he would do to any other woman on the bus. I don't look much different from any other passenger now, Adija thought. She gave the man an outraged look, as she imagined a pregnant peasant woman would do in response to an improper invitation. The man retreated behind his newspaper.

Adija smiled to herself, immensely pleased. At the prison, they had cut her hair off. It had grown back a few inches, but she had not oiled it, so it lay flat on her head in the brushed-back style of many Samoyo women. At first, she had felt ugly without her long, thick waves. She kept remembering how Gordon had loved to stroke them and bury his face in their softness. She was used to short hair now, though, and was beginning to like it. Perhaps she had only liked long hair because it made her different. People stared at me with my hair and sarees and miniskirts, she thought, and I always complained about my strangeness. But if I hadn't had that to complain about, I would have had to compare myself with women who were not strange. I would have found myself lacking—no family, no home, no husband, no money or education or respectable appearance. And no children to show that I was a woman like other women. Adija looked down at her belly and smiled. She did not mind that the dress that covered it was faded and frayed at her ankles, or that her feet were bare—it all went with her short hair and bulging belly. There was no incongruity or mystery about her at all. I don't know how long I can survive looking like any ordinary African woman, she thought, but I'm going to try to enjoy my new appearance as long as I can.

When the Marembo border post came into view, Adija thought of Gordon and grew afraid again. The post was new, a concrete building surrounded by a high wire fence. On the Bashiri side, there was only a hut and one soldier, who waved the bus on. But on the Marembo side, five soldiers with rifles and Sten guns were stopping every vehicle. Why was this? Adija asked.

Salome explained that in Bashiri, the government was going to hold elections finally. The secessionists, realizing that the Western Province could not survive as a country against the Bashiri army, had agreed not to vote or hold any more political rallies. In return, their people were being let out of prison—as Salome and Adija had been. The government was also promising to bring some of its foreign money to the area—here, Salome laughed—and was keeping all but a few soldiers away from the province as long as people remained peaceful. So, in Bashiri, the government was no worse than it had been.

But in Marembo, it was worse. The new president was a general who had told the people that the Bashiri army had come to the border to attack Marembo. He had thrown out the old president and killed his supporters.

"What about the king?" Adija asked, remembering the picture on her wall.

"He was thrown out long ago," Salome said. "He went to England and ran out of money and died in a cheap hotel."

Adija shook her head. "That's sad."

Salome told her it was not so sad compared to what was happening now. The country was being run by soldiers who could rob or kill anybody they pleased. If any soldiers asked Adija for papers on the bus, she was to say nothing; Salome had papers that she'd bought for both of them in the back streets of Azima.

Two very large soldiers did come on the bus, frowned at everybody, but did not ask for any papers. They made the bus wait for a long time. Through the window of the concrete building, Adija saw more soldiers watching an Indian woman and her son who were leaving Marembo. The men stood in a circle grinning while the mother and the little boy had to take off all their clothes to be searched. Both of them were crying. They were made to stand naked in the sun while the soldiers jacked up the car and poked under it with their bayonets. When the woman and her son were finally given back their clothes and told they could leave, their car had four flat tires from the bayonets. But the woman, holding her saree against her chest, drove into Bashiri anyway—on the rims—the car bumping wildly over the potholes. Some of the people on the bus were laughing, but Salome's face stayed tight, and Adija wanted to cry.

"It's good that I don't look like an Indian anymore," Adija whispered. "They might have searched me."

"They might have done more than that," Salome said.

The rust-colored roofs of Musolu looked warm and familiar. Adija wanted to feel better, but she didn't. She was thinking of Gordon again, and now her brain hurt worse than her stomach. Her mind was being stretched apart—that terrible old feeling that she had almost lost in prison. She felt like a person standing on two chairs—one foot on each—and watching the chairs slipping out from under her in opposite directions.

She had to talk. "What will you do after you've seen Patel?" she asked Salome.

Salome looked at her in silence. Adija felt as if Salome's eyes were reflecting the question back to her: What will *you* do? "Do you think Patel will give you back all your money?" Adija asked, glancing away.

"He'll have to. I know too much about him." Salome glared out over the heads of the passengers, removing the pressure from Adija. "I won't get it all at once, but I'll get enough to start."

"To start what?"

"Some kind of business. A bar, perhaps. I can brew beer. Anything that grows, I can turn it into liquor. I was thinking of a bar with a garage in the back."

"For customers to leave their motorcars?"

Salome laughed. "For stolen car parts. The husband of one of the women on our cell block, he takes parts off wrecked cars, to sell. As soon as there's a smash, he's there with his tools, even before the bodies inside are cool."

"This place—will it be in Azima?" Adija asked. "You're not fearing going back to Azima?"

"No. You heard what I said at that trial."

"Myself too," Adija nodded. "That was when I stopped fearing."

"Azima," Salome said. "I was thinking of it while I was lying about in that prison, wondering if I could live there again." She stared past Adija, far away. "I was thinking of the shacks of tarpaulin and scrap metal, and also the cinemas and nightclubs and the banks that are guarded by police with savage dogs. I remembered the beggars and hawkers and whores and the armies of people drifting from factory to factory in search of jobs that didn't exist, and everywhere the blasting of motorcar horns and police whistles, and the stench of lorry engines like smoke farting up from the street, and the stink of the foul little river that flows through the shack town like an open sore. I was wondering, could I live in a tiny room, surrounded by old newspaper to hide the smoke stains on the wall, surrounded by other rooms squashed full of babies screaming and women fighting with their men and ragged children stealing and starving, and with no space around me—no fields of maize, no mountains, no trees, no sky but the gray diarrhea of factory chimneys. No friends to trust, no family to care for, no ancestors to watch over me." Salome lit a cigarette and screwed up her face. She could afford only cheap cigarettes now. "Then I thought—but where else can women like us live? We who have no customs, no families, we who have abandoned our ancestors—we are the people of the future. Well, you and I have lived in the future already. We can thrive in the city like weeds in a shit pile."

Adija stared out the window. Suddenly the wide plain of lush green bush looked inviting. She shook her head, pushing away the question of where she would go. The pressure in her belly was growing worse. It reminded her that she could not push away the necessity of making plans. There was just one hope left, one chance that she would not have to plan her own future: Gordon. Thinking of him made her as uneasy as thinking about the city—neither choice seemed satisfying now. "There are many people in the city," she said finally.

Salome nodded. "So many people with money to be taken."

"And many people trying to scheme up ways of taking it," Adija said.

"But if you're clever, you can get money even from those who are scheming to take others' money."

"And what then—what if you get the money?"

Salome sighed. "Then perhaps buy a little farm. That is what all the city people dream of—going back to the land."

"You're not a man—how can you buy land?"

"I don't know. But why not?" Salome laughed. "I used to think that way—how can I do anything? I let men do the scheming and use me in their schemes. Then I stopped doing that and tried to scheme like a man. But I think it's better I'm not a man. If I were, I might become a big politician and wreck everything in the nation with my scheming—if I wasn't arrested first, for talking too much against the other politicians." Salome laughed.

Adija stared at her uneasily.

"No, I don't want to talk politics anymore. I've nothing to prove. I'm free of having to show anyone anything. For now, there are better things to do."

"Yes," Adija said, thinking vaguely of Gordon.

"I'm a woman with a beautiful big body and a powerful brain and I can get anything I want." Salome glanced at Adija's belly. "Almost anything," she said, and looked away.

Adija was trembling when the bus stopped in Musolu. Salome had to help her out the door. Adija glanced up at the top of the bus, where the man was handing down boxes and bunches of bananas and straw baskets. She had no straw basket today. She had nothing but the stub of a used-up bus ticket and a child inside her who would soon be wailing for food.

While Salome went in search of Patel, Adija lingered outside the shops. The town seemed not to have changed at all. The man on the curb was still hammering away at a broken bicycle. Dusty paper flags still hung limp along the shop roofs. Women haggled and chattered and spat. The barber under the tree clipped hair. Dogs slept in patches of shade along the pavement.

Some of the shops, though, were closed, Adija noticed —the ones that had belonged to Indians. In each of the open shops, a framed photograph of the country's new president was displayed over the door. He was a soldier with many ribbons on his chest; his lips were smiling, but his eyes looked like the lead tips of two bullets. They seemed to be watching her. Fortunately no one else took any notice of her. And if people had seen her standing there in the shadows, who would have come to greet her?

Salome returned with some news of the town. Elima, the Police Chief, had been killed; the soldiers had "made him disappear" when he'd refused to share his bribes with them. Simon Waga had finally gotten a scholarship to study medicine; he was leaving for Europe next week. Patel too was leaving soon. He was selling his business and all his possessions as fast as he could. Salome had made no inquiries about Gordon.

"Patel wants me to take his money out of the country for him," Salome said. "That's what his son told me."

"Will you?"

"And risk getting stripped at the border? Don't make jokes."

"Did he give you your share of the money?"

"He's going to Mbure today, selling things. He'll be back with it tomorrow."

Salome and Adija went across the street to their old rooms. Salome's door was smashed in, but nothing except the money box had been taken. Adija's door was locked with a big padlock; the rusty hinges broke loose with two blows of a stick of firewood. Her belongings inside had been rifled and left lying all over the floor, but nothing had been taken.

"Strange, how they left it all these months," Salome said. She blew the dust out of one of Adija's combs. "Perhaps people were afraid our things would bring them bad luck."

Adija stared at the pictures on the wall. All the smiling faces. They were barely recognizable through the coating of termite sawdust that had fallen from the rafters. She thought of wiping them with a handkerchief, but she felt too tired. She was so very tired. The pictures, clean or dirty, could not take away that awful tiredness.

"Can we sleep here until tomorrow?" she asked, turning her eyes away from the pictures.

"Why not? Who's to stop us?"

"What will we do?" Adija watched Salome's face carefully.

Salome met her gaze. She sat down hard on the bed. The air in the room was hot and stale. "Do what you have to do, Adija," she said.

"Will you come with me?" Adija asked.

Salome lay back on the bed and stared at the ceiling.

"Will you?" Adija's voice sank to a whisper. "Salome?"

"No," Salome said.

Adija climbed slowly toward the school. At the government office, she stopped to rest beside a bush. The ground around it was empty, though the grass still had a trodden-down look about it, as if the crowds of people who had assembled every day for the *baraza* had just left and would soon be coming back. Adija was surprised to see the place so deserted, even though she knew that the army was not letting anyone have *barazas* any longer. It was hard to remember what those troubles, or any of those politics, had been about. She wished she didn't have to try to understand politics. She had never cared about them until Gordon had gotten involved in them.

She wished she understood why he had talked about politics at the trial. She knew Gordon would not have spoken like that if he hadn't read the note that Salome had written in jail. Perhaps Salome had wanted him to read it—because she wanted him to get into trouble. Adija tried to feel angry with Salome about that. But she was too tired and nervous to be angry. At any rate, Gordon would never have seen that note if she herself hadn't helped Salome frighten the guard into delivering it.

Gordon would explain everything. Once she heard what he had to say, she would know. She would know, one way or the other. Adija continued slowly up the hill toward the school.

The compound was greener than she remembered it. The classroom buildings shone white in the slanting rays of sunlight. There was Gordon's classroom, where he had written her name on the blackboard. It was empty now; classes were over for the day. Schoolboys shouted on the games fields, and smoke was rising from the cookstove outside the dining hall.

She started to walk around the edge of the compound. Then, for no reason she could have explained, she cut straight across it toward Gordon's house. Passing schoolboys stared at her and whispered, but she hardly saw them. Holding her belly, she padded up the slippery mud oval that connected the teachers' houses. By the time she reached the hedge outside Gordon's door, her feet and ankles were spattered with mud. Squatting, she wiped them with her petticoat, then stared straight ahead over the hedge. No bicycle leaned beside the door. He must have sold it, for he had that motorcar. But no car stood under the carport beside the house. Tire prints were faintly visible in the earth beneath the thatched roof. They were

very old tire tracks. Her mind refused to register their
meaning. She walked up to the door and rapped on it with
her fist.

She struck the door again, harder.

Silence.

The door opened. A face appeared. A white face, but
not *his* face. This person wore thick spectacles and had
very little hair. The eyes were small and impatient-looking.
Adija's vision blurred. "*Ninataka* Gordon?" she asked.

"Gordon?" An older man's voice was speaking something in English that she couldn't understand.

"*Ninataka* Gordon," she repeated, shutting her eyes.
"Gordon *uko wapi?*"

The voice receded. Adija squinted into the house. Suitcases and tied-up stacks of books lined the sitting room.
No bright cloths hung on the walls. The walls were gray
and blank, all but one stripped bare. There a gilded
wooden cross hung at a slant, like a one-legged man trying
to dance. The interior of the house melted.

A black face appeared before her. "What you want?" it
asked in bad Kisemi.

"I want Gordon," Adija repeated. "Where is Gordon?"

The lips curled scornfully. "There is no Gor-deen here."

"But who are you?"

"I am Jefferson Sadaki. I am houseboy for *Bwana* Hen-
derson." The man glanced down at Adija's protruding
belly. "You must go away and not to bother *Bwana* Hen-
derson."

"*Bwana* Hennassah," Adija mumbled.

"He will think I made that bastard you carrying. Go
away!"

Adija blinked her eyes into focus. "I am looking for
Bwana Gordon Lock'y. He is a teacher in this school. He
knows me."

The houseboy shook his head.

"Did he leave a message, then?" Adija screamed.

"There is no *Bwana* Lock'y for this school!" The door
slammed shut.

Adija wandered away from the house. She felt faint
and sat down beneath a tree. Schoolboys in green uniforms
blurred in and out of her vision. She watched European
masters walking slowly across the games fields, their heads

lowered in conversation. Now and then the breeze brought snatches of their talk to her, foreign words in strange-sounding intonations. Once she had dreamed she could live among these people. It must have been a dream. It must have been a dream that she had ever stayed in one of those square white houses. "There is no *Bwana* Lock'y . . . there is no *Bwana* Lock'y." Her mind repeated it over and over again until she began to hear it.

A twinge of pain shot through her. The pressure was sinking lower and lower in her belly. No, there truly had been a *Bwana* Lock'y. Now she could not even pronounce his name—if she had ever been able to. But she did know that house across the compound. From long ago. Now it was a house of strangers. She had stayed in a house of strangers.

Adija rested her head against the tree trunk and wept silently.

She recalled the cross on the wall of the house, and she remembered some words that the Christian woman in the prison had read to her: "Thou shalt dwell in the House of the Lord Forever."

I have stayed in the House of the Lord, she thought, and I have found it a house of strangers. Now part of me is condemned to stay in houses of strangers forever. The city is the future of Africa, Salome says. You are the future, Adija said to the baby in her belly, and wiped her eyes. You will thrive in the House of the Lord like a weed in a shit-pile.

The rains caught her outside the government office, but she did not stop under its porch to rest. She walked on down the hill, her head bent, her feet slopping through puddles. Rain soaked her hair and her dress and streamed down her face. A motorcar honked her out of the center of the road. Then it slowed. A voice asked her something in English that must have been an offer of a lift to town. She walked on without a reply.

*   *   *

Salome brought her a bowl of rice with sauce and chunks of meat. She spoke to her, but Adija could not hear over the clatter of rain on the roof, and did not want to ask her to speak louder. After Salome had gone, she stared at the bowl of food. By now it was cold and soggy, the sauce flecked with congealed white fat. Adija squinted at the dreams on her wall.

In the night, Salome heard her wailing in her room. She found her the next morning lying stiff with her eyes wide open. "Drink this—you don't want your baby to starve, do you?" Salome put down a pot of milk-tea and a mug.

Adija drank the entire pot. She pulled the blanket up over her head and remained motionless on the bed for the rest of the day and night.

The next day, Salome yanked the blanket from her. "I have five hundred shillings!" she said, and threw an envelope down onto the mattress."

Adija blinked in the sudden light.

"Tomorrow, six thousand shillings. Then we can leave!"

Adija started to touch the envelope, then clutched her belly.

"Are you all right?"

Adija squeezed her eyes shut. "I'm all right."

Salome slept beside Adija. They lay quietly in the darkness. Dogs barked far away; the hum of insects faded and swelled in the night outside the room. Adija's belly was round and hot. Salome curled herself around it, being careful not to lie heavily against it. Once she felt a movement in the belly, waking her from half-sleep like a gentle nudge. Her own child had kicked like that. Salome felt a fullness inside her own belly. She got up. As she paced about the room, she found herself guiding her protruding middle like someone pushing a wheelbarrow. She slid back beneath the blanket and lay with her cheek against Adija's belly.

As the night grew longer, Adija seemed to grow bigger and bigger. You are expanding and I am shrinking, Salome thought. But Salome was not shrinking, her belly still felt heavy and full. There was no room on the mattress to lay it down any longer. Salome fetched her own mattress and put it down on the floor beside Adija's bed. Now I can catch you if you roll off, she thought. Even from the floor, she could feel Adija's movements. She knew when Adija was lying awake, staring at the wall, and when she sighed off into a fitful sleep.

A loud groan. Salome sat up. She heard a high piercing sound that became a whimper and a prolonged grunt and then all the sounds of pain in the world, uttered together in one piercing note. Salome leaped to her feet.

"It hurts!" Adija screamed. "I want to go to the dispensary!"

"I didn't think it would be so soon. Stop screaming!" Salome sat down hard on the bed.

"The dispensary!" Adija gasped.

"Sure?"

Adija shrieked. Salome snatched up her machete and dashed out of the room, across the street, and up to Patel's door behind the shop. She pounded on the door with the handle of the machete. Finally Patel stood before her in his floppy trousers and undershirt, rubbing his eyes.

"Hurry up!" Salome screamed. "Get your car. The baby —Adija's baby's come!"

Patel blinked hard. "Car no good now. Radiator is finish."

"Don't say that—repair it! Adija's baby's come—you want her to die?"

"No—"

"You want money? Here's your money back!" Salome yanked a handful of shilling notes out of her bodice. When Patel didn't move, she pounded on his chest with a fistful of money, screaming. He stumbled backward. Salome waved her machete over his head. His wife appeared, jibbering and whining and clutching at Salome fearfully, like someone trying to stop the blades of a fan. Patel's son Rajni tried to wrestle the machete from her. She hit him in the mouth with her fistful of shilling notes. He sprawled back against a table and fell amid a shower of money. Salome sat down in a heap beside him. "I'm sorry," she cried. "You must help us! Help Adija!"

Salome, Patel, and Rajni raced outdoors. The only vehicle on the street besides Patel's disabled Mercedes was a handcart leaning at an angle by the curb. They wheeled it at top speed to Adija's room.

She had crawled outside and was lying on the ground in a puddle of liquid. Seeing Salome, she shrieked rhythmically with every breath. Salome picked her up by the shoulders and slid her onto the cart. Patel and Rajni lifted the shafts and began to pull, with Salome walking beside, holding Adija with one hand and pushing at the wheel spokes with the other.

At the base of the hill, Patel slipped and fell under the front of the cart, Rajni, trying to stop it, made it pitch sideways. Salome was knocked to her knees. A long, high scream blasted in her ears.

The slats in the cart's side had broken, and Adija lay tilted half out of it, her legs thrashing at the ground. Something dark and shiny rolled onto the grass, and suddenly a new voice was yowling.

Salome held the baby, staring at it. It was so slippery she nearly dropped it. Laying it down on the grass again, she groped about in the ditch for her machete. With one stroke she chopped the cord in two. She tied the ends with long grass stalks, her fingers trembling.

Patel carried the baby wrapped in Salome's pullover; Salome and Rajni carried Adija by her feet and shoulders. The dispensary was dark, but the door was unlocked. Salome kicked it open and pulled Adija through into the dark room. All but one bed was empty. She lay Adija down and rushed outdoors to find Patel sitting on the ground, panting, the baby screeching in his lap. She snatched it up and raced to wake up Waga.

* * *

"Where is he?" Adija opened her eyes and squinted up at Salome and Waga.

"Just here," Waga said. He was sitting on the bed beside Adija's bed, washing the baby while Salome held it. "It's a she, a girl."

Adija lifted her head. "Where is he?" she cried.

"She means the father, I think," Salome said.

"If she means the schoolteacher, he's gone." Waga shook his head.

Adija lay back, her eyes closing again.

"Where is he gone?" Salome asked.

"He's gone back to America."

Salome nodded. "I thought that's what he'd do."

The baby began to yowl. Adija sat up, blinking into the lantern light. She saw the baby in Salome's lap, and her mouth opened wide. "Ohhh. I want it," she gasped.

Waga took the baby and placed it in her arms.

"What—what color is it? I can't see?" Adija asked.

"It was dark and slimy with its mother's blood, like any

other baby born in this world," Salome said. "You ought to be glad it's alive."

"I am." Adija squinted down at the baby. "I can't see."

Waga moved the lantern closer. "It's brown, a healthy brown baby. It's the same color as you, exactly."

"As me?"

"The father might have been African, or he might have been European. I'm sorry, that's all I can tell."

Adija held the child's face gently against her breast. "That's all right."

"You won't be able to tell whose it is for some time."

Adija shook her head. "I know whose it is," she said, touching the baby's cheek. "It is mine."

*   *   *

Salome waited in Waga's office, drinking glass after glass of his brandy. After a while she was drinking straight out of the bottle. Patel appeared with her pullover. He held it out to her and averted his eyes as she pulled it on over her petticoat. It was sticky with blood, but Salome didn't care by this time.

"Have a drink, uncle," she said.

Patel wiped his mottled forehead. "No. Hindus, they not for drinking."

Salome pushed a half-full glass across the desk toward him. "Tonight, you can."

Patel looked hard at the glass, then picked it up and drained it. "You should come back to my house. Get money you throw everywhere."

"I will." Salome belched. Then she looked at him. "I'll take your money for you too."

"Yes? You'll take it to my brother, in Azima?"

Salome nodded.

"How you can get it out? The soldiers, they search people."

"They won't search Adija's baby."

"So . . . I can trust you?"

"You can do as you please, *Bwana* Patel."

The old man's cracked brown teeth showed when he smiled. "You come tomorrow, we can fix it."

Salome raised her glass. "Good night, uncle."

Later, Waga brought the baby into the office wrapped in

a blanket. The baby was asleep now, just a tiny dark spot in the bundle of cloth. "Your friend must stay here tonight. The doctor will come in the morning and check her."

"All right." Salome sighed. "Have a drink."

Waga looked forlornly at his nearly empty bottle. "You're generous," he said, and poured himself a glass.

"What of the baby?" Salome asked.

"You'd better keep it until tomorrow. There's a man here with hepatitis." Waga said. "I'll give you some tinned milk and a bottle."

"After tomorrow, Adija can leave?"

"If she feels all right. She should rest a while, before traveling."

"She'll feel all right." Salome stood up unsteadily. "She won't want to stay here."

Waga looked up. "One more thing. She's saying that she doesn't want to give the child a European name."

"No?"

"Nor a Moslem name."

"Oh." Salome took a fast slug out of the brandy bottle. Her hands would not stop shaking. She gripped the bottle tight, squinting at the lantern flame through the curved dark glass. "What name?"

"An African name—of the Samoyo people."

"Wairimu."

Waga smiled. "That's it."

Salome relaxed her grip on the bottle. "Wairimu," she whispered.

✺   ✺   ✺

In Adija's room, Salome laid the baby on the mattress and refolded the blanket around it. The child's eyes bulged under their thin eyelids. Salome stared back. Your mother's reckless, she thought, naming you before you're even a day old. If you die now, we've lost a human being. Naming you before you've proven you can survive is like spitting in the eye of death.

The child cried softly. "What the hell are we going to do with you, Wairimu?" she asked it. She placed the rubber nipple of the bottle in its mouth. Sucking hard, the child was quiet.

After a time, a motorcar drove by, rattling the street

outside. Its headlight beams swept through the room, igniting for an instant the pictures on the wall like a life flashing before one's eyes, then vanishing down the dark street. Salome lay down and held the child close against her. She listened to its breathing until she was sure it was sleeping well. Then she began to pack Adija's things for the journey to the city.

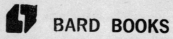 **BARD BOOKS**

the classics, poetry, drama and
distinguished modern fiction

FICTION

ANAIS NIN READER Ed., Philip K. Jason	49890	2.95
ANYA Susan Fromberg-Schaffer	48645	2.95
THE AWAKENING Kate Chopin	50948	2.50
BETRAYED BY RITA HAYWORTH Manuel Puig	36020	2.25
BEYOND THE BEDROOM WALL Larry Woiwode	47670	2.95
BILLIARDS AT HALF-PAST NINE Heinrich Böll	51383	2.95
BLANCO & THINGS ABOUT TO DISAPPEAR Allen Wier	49114	3.50
CALL IT SLEEP Henry Roth	49304	2.50
A SINGLE MAN Christopher Isherwood	37689	1.95
CATALOGUE George Milburn	33084	1.95
THE CLOWN Heinrich Böll	37523	2.25
DOM CASMURRO Machado De Assis	49668	2.95
EDWIN MULLHOUSE Steven Millhauser	37952	2.50
THE EIGHTH DAY Thornton Wilder	44149	2.95
THE EYE OF THE HEART Barbara Howes, Ed.	47787	2.95
GABRIELA, CLOVE AND CINNAMON Jorge Amado	51839	3.95
THE GREEN HOUSE Mario Vargas Llosa	42747	2.75
GROUP PORTRAIT WITH LADY Heinrich Böll	48637	2.50
HUNGER Knut Hamsun	42028	2.25
HOUSE OF ALL NATIONS Christina Stead	18895	2.45
IN EVIL HOUR Gabriel Garcia Marquez	52167	2.75

THE LAST DAYS OF LOUISIANA RED		
Ishmael Reed	35451	2.25
LESBIAN BODY Monique Wittig	31062	1.75
THE LIFE TO COME AND OTHER STORIES		
E. M. Forster	48611	2.95
THE LITTLE HOTEL Christina Stead	48389	2.50
A LONG AND HAPPY LIFE Reynolds Price	48132	2.25
THE LOST STEPS Alejo Carpentier	46177	2.50
LOVE STORIES BY NEW WOMEN		
Charleen Swansea and		
Barbara Campbell, Eds.	48058	2.75
THE MAN WHO LOVED CHILDREN		
Christina Stead	40618	2.50
A MEETING BY THE RIVER		
Christopher Isherwood	37945	1.95
MYSTERIES Knut Hamsun	25221	1.95
NABOKOV'S DOZEN Vladimir Nabokov	15354	1.65
THE NEW LIFE HOTEL Edward Hower	76372	2.95
NIGHT Elie Wiesel	46797	2.25
NIGHT BOOK William Kotzwinkle	49106	2.50
ONE HUNDRED YEARS OF SOLITUDE		
Gabriel García Márquez	45278	2.95
PNIN Vladimir Nabokov	50906	2.50
PRATER VIOLET Christopher Isherwood	51912	2.25
THE RECOGNITIONS William Gaddis	49544	3.95
A ROSE IN THE HEART Edna O'Brien	50021	2.75
THE SEVENTH BABE Jerome Charyn	51540	2.95
THE STORY OF HAROLD Terry Andrews	49965	2.95
STUDS LONIGAN TRILOGY		
James T. Farrell	31955	2.75
SUN CITY Tove Jansson	32318	1.95
SWEET ADVERSITY Donald Newlove	38364	2.95
THE TARTAR STEPPE Dino Buzzati	50252	2.75
TENT OF MIRACLES Jorge Amado	41020	2.75
THREE BY HANDKE Peter Handke	32458	2.25
THE TWO DEATHS OF QUINCAS		
WATERYELL Jorge Amado	50047	2.50
THE VIOLENT LAND Jorge Amado	47696	2.75
YIDDISH STORIES OLD AND NEW Edited		
by Irving Howe and Eliezer Greenberg	47803	2.50

Where better paperbacks are sold, or directly from the publisher. Include 50¢ per copy for postage and handling, allow 4-6 weeks for delivery.

Avon Books, Mail Order Dept.

224 West 57th Street New York, N.Y. 10019

BD (2) 10-80